Tertiary

Tertiary

A tale of two civilizations and a third way

First published 2005 by Lulu.com

Front Cover design by Jeannette Absenger

To contact Jeanney for information
on her design or artwork email her:
designajeanney@aol.com

Publication and Back Cover design by Nicole Klein

Drawings by John Coppinger

ISBN   1 – 4116 – 6160 – 5

Copyright © John F. Coppinger 2005

The right of John F. Coppinger to be identified as the author of this work has been asserted by him in accordance with the Copyright, Designs and Patents Act 1988.

All rights reserved. No part of this publication may be reproduced, stored in or introduced into a retrieval system, or transmitted, in any form, or by any means (electronic, mechanical, photocopying, recording or otherwise) without the prior written permission of the author.

_____ Exceptions

Personal use: For a small fee the book may be downloaded from Lulu.com.

Dedication

This book is for Nicole; the person who really made it possible in the end. We live and work together and I don't think this would have happened without her love and encouragement. And I guess she liked the story!

Thanks

Lots of people have helped and encouraged me, at different times and in different places, as this story developed. It was originally a film script, then lay about for ten years or so before I decided it should become a novel. As a film script, first written long before computer generated imagery was possible, I was amazed that people didn't just laugh. It would then have cost a fortune to make, being set in both the near future and the far past.

So, in no particular order, thanks to:

Vincent Winter. Graham High. Malcolm Stone. Tony Masters.
Colin Vaines. Steve Colgan. Jon Sorenson. Gary Pollard.
Richard Noble Steven Langfield. Jeannette Absenger.

My mother, Betty, and her husband John, will naturally be the first people to get a copy of this book. Their's to read and enjoy or prop open the door with. My thanks and love go to them for being both family and friends.

IV   Tertiary

Tertiary

Part One

Discovery and mystery

Part Two

Diversion and revelation

Part Three

Escape and growth

Part Four

Return to the source

Part Five

Ancient memory

Part Six

The Spheres rise

Part Seven

The World confers

Epilogue

1   Tertiary

Part One

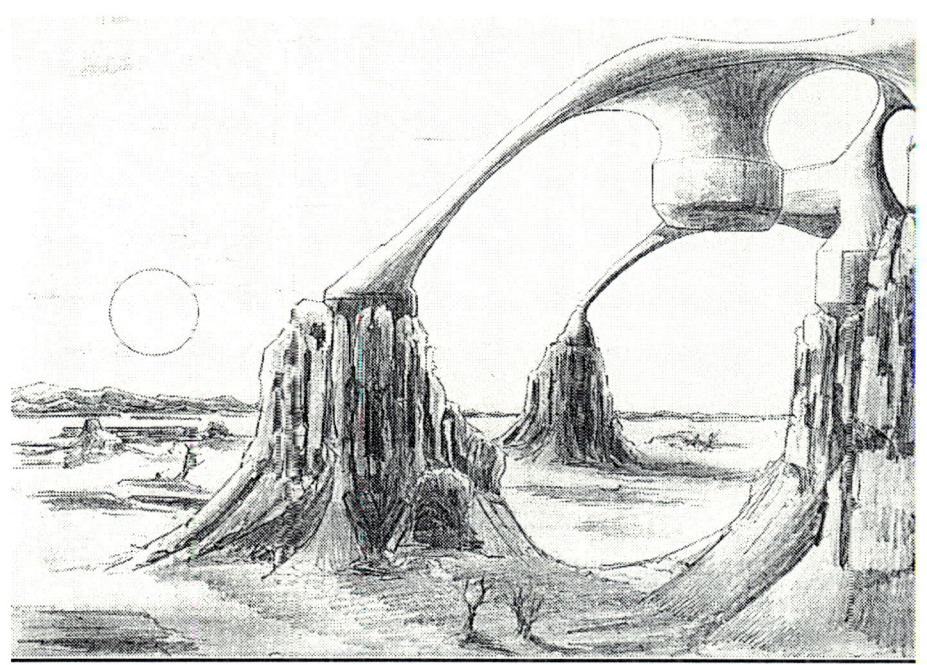

Discovery and mystery

< From 1st Transcript of the 'Tum' Archive: Worcs in the darkness. One said 'rise now' but the others said 'be still'. The new people had arrived, and the youngest of them were already close. When the mothers and fathers walked again, then they would rise to life. One agreed.>

A vast bowl of sky arched blue over the view to distant mountain ranges. The dusty Badlands of America. An agoraphobics' nightmare of space, distance and desolation.
Until you looked into the details. Down into the split of a canyon, across the boulder-full bed of its' river, and up from a rough trail on the far bank.

2   Tertiary

Shattered levels of rock and debris. Small, scrawny plants gripped into the splits and crevices. A recently trodden path to a terrace. And a shallow cave wedged into the overhanging canyon wall; an enigmatic expression impressed into the rocks' face.

Three dust-streaked, hot and willingly busy figures were hauling boxes and packages out onto the open terrace. Re-building a camp around scorched and blackened fire stones. The afternoons' shadows lengthening across their growing fatigue.

Two women and one man. Their battered Deilec Humvee was turned off the trail below them; its' overheated engine still audibly cooling down. The tings ringing in the enclosed stillness of the canyon, above the permanent presence of flowing water.

The older woman was checking date labels and seals, as each pack and box was pulled from under a camouflaged tarpaulin covered in dirt and debris. "Everything looks the same. I don't think anyone's been up here."

Steven Anders didn't look up from an open crate. "Who would have been - We hid the stuff well enough didn't we?"

Barbara Borman balanced on stocky legs, sweeping away a curl of grey hair, as she stared levelly at his bent back. "Well let's hope the second guy comes out as easy as the first – And we won't have to hang around here too long."

The junior member of the team was looking on uncertainly, anxious to defuse the tension, but unwilling to get involved. "It would be good to get back to the lab – You know, work on them properly."

Steven looked up sharply at his colleague. Laura Lovell was too much the peacemaker in his opinion. He would prefer an argument. "All I want is a good look at another specimen. If this one's as weird as the first - - -."

Barbara gave an impatient sniff, and brusquely turned her back to both of them. Laura unbraided her long hair, letting it swing around her face, as she turned to unpack cans and packets of food from a nearby crate.

Steven was still irritated. "Well how do you explain those marks on the femur?" knowingly pushing Barbara. "If they're not rivet holes, what do you say they are?"

3 Tertiary

Barbara rounded on him; her face flushed and powdered with dust. "Look Steven – We've got to work together, and I know you want to make your mark, but let's not make up shit for the Enquirer Pages. "She stiffened in an effort to calm down; shoulders still raised as she faced him. "Isn't it enough that we've got a whole new dinosaur family, without crazy ideas about them practising surgery."

Steven turned, defeated and angry, releasing his grip on the crate with a shove of disgust, and walked across the terrace to a stack of wooden specimen boxes just inside the cave. Unlatched the top one and looked down at a long, fossilised bone, still embedded in a slab of rock. Shook his head in wonder at the perfection of its' preservation. And touched lightly at the curiously regular line of holes near its' centre. Young and enthusiastic he might be, in Barbara's eyes, but he had never seen, nor heard of, such an incredibly detailed and complete dinosaur specimen of any species. And it was his team that had found it; and his team that was going to describe it.

Steven replaced the specimen box lid and moved into the deepest part of the cave, his shadow wavering ahead of him as the setting sun lit inwards from the opposite canyon rim. He crouched sideways, fingers reaching to dig at the inner rock face, and felt the curiously granular matrix crumble easily under his nails. He frowned, not for the first time, as it trickled, sparkling with a slight iridescence, to the cave floor. Then, as he stretched stiffly upwards to move back out to the terrace, his turning boot caught under an unexplored corner of the rock wall. He limped and twisted, testing his ankle for a sprain, before stooping down. His boot had exposed a small, strangely regular, crystalline sliver. It winked a tiny point of light through his flowing and shortened shadow as he bent to look closer.

Steven walked slowly back, lost in his thoughts; unaware of the last of the sunset laying a red bar along the black slab of canyon wall opposite the campsite. The others lay in their sleeping bags, facing sleepily into the flames of a brushwood fire, and watched the swing of a coffee can hanging in a hot updraft of sparks. Steven pushed down into his own bag, leaned forward to hook the can and fill his cup and held it up as he looked across at

Barbara. But she only shook her head, apparently mesmerised by the spark column, twisting upwards into thin helices of smoke.

He turned to Laura, thinking that her smile still looked wary in the flickering light. She shook her head as well. "No thank you Steven." Eyes glittering with flames. "You really think there's something strange here don't you – I mean apart from the species never having been found before?" She pushed up onto one elbow, brushing hair away from her face and the fire, and shivered as she peered into the dark wedge of the cave. The tarpaulin creaked and settled.

"I guess I have to, yes – It's not just the bones looking so damned fresh, and those weird marks on them, it's the matrix they're bedded in." He stared through the flames, not improving Laura's nerves.

"We'll have to get Arnie S. to have a closer look at that when we get back to the lab."

Laura slid down into her sleeping bag, curling up on her side, her eyes wide open; seeing Steven hypnotised by swirling sparks, as the Little Snake River rushed through boulders, and the night, below them. And almost immediately she was dreaming; her eyelids fluttering and her breathing deepening as she twisted in the hot confinement of the bag.

[A distant, rushing beat, above the river sounds. A machine. A helicopter; with an alien, flapping quality to its' thudding rotor, and a hissing overtone in the whine of turbines. The noise was changing pitch, but always increasing, as the unseen machine snaked low over the winding river towards their camp.

Then sight in the darkness, as her eyes snapped open, hair swept clear of her face, by the hot, fume-laden blast of downwash.

And the helicopter hovered like some weird, unfamiliar dragon, level with the campsite terrace.

Something wrong about its' shape; not Russian or European. The details, and some subtlety of design making the machine slide away from Laura's dream perception. Something other-worldly. Something she has never seen before - -.]

5 Tertiary

And her eyes fell open to a shock of silence. Not even hearing the river water for long seconds, as she lay paralysed by a nightmare of relaxation; not yet connected to conscious control of her body.

She dipped back down, and in and out of the dream state, trying to replay and define the strangeness.

Only a helicopter, not even a very complicated nightmare, what the hell was it? Why did it look so sci-fi, and yet feel so out of place? Somehow ancient. Just dinosaurs, she thought, shrugging inwardly. Just digging about for old bones in an old country. Disturbing the gods that wiser people once respected.

Laura turned onto her back, stretching into a comfortable warmth, and pushed the hovering image into a corner of memory that allowed her to sleep again. The night moved on, to the sounds of the desert and a thin wind. A pair of coyotes trotted forward, as close as they dared, to check out the camp and its' boxes and its' unburied rubbish.

Steven woke first when it was just light enough to see; one open eye surveying the miniature landscape between his chilled head and a thread of smoke from the fires' ash. Trying, but failing, to remember his dreams. Only a sense of subdued, anticipatory anxiety that itched like an unseen, future pleasure. He rolled over and sat up, to haul out, sliding, from the warm sheath of sleep. Observing himself as he went into an automatic routine of rousing the fire for the essential first task of brewing coffee. Passively flooding his eyes with light from the far rock wall, and jostling, sparkling reflections from the river below. Something was going to happen. A certainty in that prescience that clenched like happiness in his belly.

Barbara was watching him through slitted eyelids. Seeing a thin framed, prematurely balding man, who probably wouldn't look much different at eighty years old. And would still have most of the nervous enthusiasm of an eighteen year old. So why did she find him such an asshole at thirty seven? Or at any time of the day or night. She was tired of the exasperation that his ageless boyhood inflicted on her. She wanted to be cool and professional rather than an irritable old woman. And to get on with the job of staking a joint claim to their new discovery. Barbara shivered; decided to acknowledge that she was awake and definitely going to get up. Making a resolution, probably futile, to be calm today in the face of Steven's runaway theorising, and Laura's irritatingly anxious attempts to defuse the tension between them. She pulled herself around to sit, knees under her chin, still wrapped in her sleeping bag, and watched steam rise from the heating water. As Steven spooned coffee into the can, she pushed forcefully to her feet, kicked away the bag, and strode to the edge of their campsite terrace. Feeling that she had already failed.

Laura woke to the sound of stones. Saw Barbara's feet stamp past. Kept her eyes half closed. She disliked her nervousness of Barbara, liking Barbara herself, and the sensation of dislocation on these field trips. The scenery and the excitement de-focused her; left her feeling like a half-useful tourist. So she wanted to be back in the lab. However beautiful or awesome the landscape, however exciting their finds, she knew she would be happier immersed in her expertise; weaving her skills into some sort of achievement. 'Ah, the poet awakes,' she thought. 'Get up girl, and make yourself useful.' She grinned secretly at the sight of Steven in his 'Big Game Hunter on Safari' field trip clothing; as he willed the morning coffee to brew by staring it to the boil. She shrugged her sleeping bag away, swinging her legs round and under, to squat in front of the flames. Returned Steven's automatic smile. And saw the burn of his ambitious hopes behind the pale, steady eyes.

"Specimen number two," he said. "How much better do you think it can be?" Laura rocked forward. "Better than number one you mean? I don't see how it could be." She tapped a finger to the hanging coffee can. Whipped it away from the heat. "If it's even half as good we'll have enough comparisons to do a full reconstruction first time out."

She looked across at Steven, eyes open to his question; and opening one back to him. He stared through the steaming, swinging can. "What you said last night – Something strange here. I'm supposed to be a scientist. I'm not used to trusting feelings and intuition – But I can't shift the impression that something here is watching. Watching and waiting."

7   Tertiary

He jerked one hand out. Slopped coffee to a sharp hiss of steam in the fire. "Damn! Body and brain not yet connected." Shook himself to wake up. "Probably just my overweening ambition. Telling me there's a headline page in 'Nature' for this one – For all of us."

But Laura was staring at him. Something watching. She looked sharply out from the terrace; remembering her dream in vivid detail. Almost seeing the thunderous, fume breathing dragon hover level with the rock platform again. Barbara's voice made her jump. "How long is a pot of coffee in the morning?" She peered at Laura. "The ghosts of old Indians troubling your path - - ?"

Laura smiled upward. Barbara framed against sunlit rocks and the bright morning sky. "Just dreams. Old demons flying around."

"Jesus – Flying demons for breakfast! What do you do for nightmares in the dark Laura?" But she was smiling; her earlier irritations seemingly smoothed away.

Steven hooked up the coffee can and pushed hot stones inwards, setting the can on the flattest and lifting aside the tripod. He reached backwards for a large skillet and started hauling tins and packets from the open side of the stores crate, then looked up, grinning. "What would Mesdames require for petit dejeuner this morning?"

His eagerness to please drew a sharp look from Barbara, and Laura sighed inside. But Barbara relented. "Let me Steven – It's my turn to cook, remember. If you can stand the excitement of the menu."

Forty minutes later all three were sitting cross-legged, noisily scraping their retro tin plates, and gulping down the last warm mouthfuls of coffee. A light breeze was whirling dust along the river bank, and cloud shadows climbed the canyon wall above them.

Steven lifted his mug to a toast. "Another good day in Colorado, if we're lucky." He tilted back to drink. Then hurled the last grounds to hiss and spit in the fire.

"Actually, I'll risk the wrath of Gods, and say I don't see how we can lose. Two or three more days and we should be calling in a Disc to haul us out of here."

8   Tertiary

Barbara responded with unusual indulgence. "They'll think we've had it too easy back at base. We'll get it in the neck for going too quick on ground time - -." She looked over to the stack of specimen boxes. "Our esteemed Deputy Dog will be 'revising his data' on time allowances."

Steven smiled wryly. "Don't worry. I think we're far enough out on the fringe to escape too much notice - - - . As long as we play down what we have here."

He looked to them for agreement, and they both nodded silently. But Barbara was frowning. "That has to be you talking to you – Right Steven?" She saw his expression. "Don't get your hat on backwards, you know I can't agree with what you seem to be suggesting. But I'm in no doubt at all that this species is a major find. I mean major, capital M." She looked steadily at the younger man, then in enquiry at Laura.

Laura switched her attention back to Steven. "I agree. You know I do - -. However we see it out here, we have to play the whole thing down back home." She sat up onto her heels, balancing on folded toes. "I'll just rough out some preliminary restorations – Keep the scale small and minimise the details. Then we all act like we don't give too much of a shit anyway - - Right?"

The other two nodded, both surprised by Laura's forcefulness. Then Steven was on his feet, suddenly galvanised by the new day and a new feeling of unity within the team of three. Barbara rolled her eyes at Laura, who stifled a snort of laughter. "Come on Laura, let's get some light on the subject. Before Captain Elation here burns down the evidence all on his own!"

They walked into the shallow cave, where a small generator was set up to power portable work lights. Barbara checked the gas cylinder and set it running. The lights powered up to illuminate the rear wall. It rose vertically to waist height, then sloped back out, above their heads, towards the daylight.

Steven peered into the shadowed corners. "Apart from the diamond backs, the scorpions, and the black widows, I just love this place – Landscape to break your heart and bones."

9 Tertiary

Barbara's voice was resonant in the closed space. "Don't forget the brown recluse Steven – One bite, and you'll wish you'd slept with the widow."

"Thank you kindly Ma'am – If I'm bit and frothing, please to put me to sleep with a rock."

As Barbara and Laura set to work on their own sections of the excavation neither noticed that Steven had frozen to silence. He reached down, perceiving himself in slow motion, towards the sliver of crystal that his boot had dislodged the night before. He traced a finger along one thin, bevelled edge; clearing dust from a row of minute golden tabs that lay inset to the dense, dark crystalline material.

His staring eyes seemed to him to be zooming in; to what his astonished mind could only register as a flawless artefact – Freed from its' recess in a seam of rock proven to be at least sixty five million years old.

Three weeks later the team had settled back into a semblance of routine at Dinosaur National Monument, Utah. Their lab was situated away from the old Carnegie Quarry rock face, which was the museums' main focus of public interest, in a low white building that faced out from a side canyon. Windows overlooked the Green River, and its' emergence from the gorge of Split Mountain a few miles to the North.

Although Barbara considered that the team worked in a rats' nest of untidiness and mess, a first impression of the lab was one of very ordered, if complex, activity. A large, well lit room with cabinets and benches and machine equipment, all focused around fossil bones and skeletons in various stages of retrieval and reconstruction. At the far end, by the northern windows, was the area where Laura was sculpting. Her restoration of their new dinosaur species, armatured in mid-stride, stood on a central work stand. Several other sculpts waited on a side bench, wrapped in clear plastic for preservation of the clay. A wall board was covered in her drawings and comparative measurements.

Barbara, in the centre, was surrounded by solution tanks and benches set up with dental drills, air extraction units and a series of sand-blasting cabinets. She was engrossed in her work on one of the new skulls; carefully preparing it for a cast of its' brain cavity.

Steven was out of sight in a side office, behind a half-glass wall, hidden by untidily stacked cartons from electronic equipment suppliers. The only evidence that he was working was an occassional muffled cursing and the flicker of monitor screens reflecting onto the ceiling. He was far away in thought, unaware that Arnold Shintowsky, a member of the geological research group, was stepping carefully up to the outside door. Arnold groped for its' handle as he peered into a Paege in his other hand; spectacles balanced precariously on his balding forehead. He pushed them higher; his wry expression a mixture of puzzlement and barely concealed excitement.

As Arnold rattled the handle, too preoccupied to operate it properly, Steven came out of his work trance, hurried over to open the door and pulled their guest inside; almost knocking him down as he dragged him forwards. "Hi Arnie – What have you got for us, after all these days and weeks?"

"A smack in the molars, young sir, if you call me 'Arnie' one more time – You've been warned before!"

Steven laughed; but his respect for Arnold's opinion, and his anxiety to hear it, made his hands shake.

"Sorry Arnold. But please to share your most immense wisdom with us – Before we all forget how to breathe."

Arnold raised an eyebrow, enjoying keeping Steven waiting but finding the suspense extremely hard to maintain. As Barbara and Laura joined them he bowed from the waist, his spectacles falling forward onto the tip of his nose. He left them there for effect. "Well, my children, there is something very odd up in them there dusty hills." He held up his screen. "You have got Uncle Electron, and me, very, very confused – If I didn't know better I'd say that your new old bones were bedded down in some sort of synthetic rock."

Barbara had been glaring at Arnolds' spectacles. She considered them an affectation. Now she looked between the two men in furious amazement. Laura stepped back a pace, knowing what was likely to come next. "Did I just miss the calendar, it's not April 1st is it - - ? What in hell does 'some sort

11 Tertiary

of synthetic rock' mean Arnie? Like, does it have 'Utah Candy Company' through its' middle or what?"

Arnold held his screen out as a defence from Barbara's angry and suspicious attack. His deprecatory gesture only made her tone less strident and more bitter.

"Oh just fine, so it's take no notice of the menopausal female then. You boys should be writing scripts for Hollywood as was!"

She glared at Steven and Laura, defying them to pacify her. But Arnold was looking at her very levelly, all trace of his usual flippancy gone. "I'm not joking Barbara. Almost wish I was. Is this the 'Cool Hand Arnold' you've known so long? That new matrix is just extraordinary. Like nothing we've ever seen before – Or even thought of - - -."

Steven was looking at him very strangely. His face was pale, but the hand he put on Arnold's shoulder moved slowly and steadily. "Come and look at this Arnold. Something I didn't show you before." He took him by the arm and guided him towards the side office. Arnold looked back at the two women, shrugging resignedly; Laura's laughter immediately subdued by Barbara's expression of seething anger. "He's going to show Mr. Shintowsky his best boys' collection of flaky flakes – I think our esteemed Stevie Anders is cracking up!"

"Flakes - - - ?" said Laura.

"Didn't he show you? When we were digging out the second specimen he found some flakes of crystal near one of the hands. He tried the magic on me, then he kept it quiet – Going on about how they looked like microchips. Crazy. Like a little kid!"

Laura was stunned. She muttered an excuse and walked slowly back to the sculpting area, stopping in front of her work stand and staring intently at the figures' head. She wanted to immerse herself in the details of the restoration – To be no more than eyes and hands and mind. And hear no more about conflicting personalities, paranoia's or grievances. Barbara had frightened her; had obviously known Steven had found something but hadn't wanted to think about it, be involved or even dream about it. So there had been more than the eerie sensation of watchfulness and waiting in the excavation cave after all. Laura shivered, and snatched up a sculpting tool.

Barbara looked across at Laura's rigid back, nodding to herself, then took a phone from inside her lab coat. She stared at it in her outstretched hand, then slowly replaced it; pushing both hands deep into her side pockets. Then shook her head in self-exasperation and went back to her bench, methodically applying herself to the preparation of one of the dinosaur skulls. She very carefully ignored the muted conversation, and flickering half-light, from Steven's office.

By late afternoon the passing of the hours and the light had subtly changed the silent atmosphere in the lab. Barbara was surrounded by the faint chemical odours of her replicator tank and the slowly emerging cast. She was monitoring a final scan of the skull; the relaxed set of her shoulders marked her immersion in the complex process. Her internal critic had also moved her mood to an unusual state of regret. An assessment that she had been too outwardly critical of Steven, and for the wrong reasons. She watched the final weaving of lasers around the brain cast, and the skull rotating, and silently quoted from Shakespeare: 'That scull had a tongue in it, and could sing once – It might be the pate of a politician, or of a courtier – Why does he suffer this rude knave now to knock him about the sconce with a dirty shovel?' Suddenly surprised to find herself fearful she gritted her teeth, refusing to be distracted into making a mistake and forced herself to concentrate on the delicate process she was watching and controlling.

At the other end of the lab Laura had forgotten her own fears; absorbed in the creation of a form in clay. As always, with her best work, she felt no more than the agent of whatever process brought the cool mud to life. And a curious sense of privilege, as if she was only a spectator. Whenever possible she chose the mess and muddle of real clay rather than the convincing illusions of the labs' TrueSpace unit.

That seemed especially appropriate now, her mind floating through a brief speculation on the strangeness experience of consciousness. She was snapped out of this meditation when Steven and Arnold appeared from the

13 Tertiary

office. She'd forgotten the time, that they'd been in there so long, and realised she hadn't even thought to stop for lunch.

Laura stood back from her work, unwilling to stop the flow of visual analysis. Whether to pause or continue? She rotated the sculpt slowly. It could only ever be an educated guess at the living appearance of the long dead animal species. If she'd only ever seen the skull of an elephant, how would she know to sculpt the long trunk and huge ears; would she dare to? And the answer was almost certainly no; without evidence of the flesh from the bones how could she? Yet, when she looked at her sculpt of the new dinosaur, she realised it went far further than she'd ever dared before in the clothing of a naked skeleton. And she knew she was very close to the truth of this particular creature. What the hell does that mean? she thought, shivering. That I've sculpted this guys' portrait?

[And the switch into a waking nightmare was almost instantaneous - - - The assault of hot air. The screaming, alien machine-whine. Smell of fuel. Smell of water? Hovering in front of her. Ready to dart inwards.
And through the skin, where it cleared to eyes, the helmeted heads. The eyes within eyes. The face of someone she'd known - - someone she'd been. Eyes out of body - - watching herself brace into the air storm on a desert rock terrace; her feathers swept tightly back - - - Feathers?]

Laura rocked, moaning softly; balanced precariously back onto her tall work stool. Barbara moving swiftly towards her. "Laura - - Laura, what is it?"
Steven and Arnold looking up in alarm from their huddle in the office doorway. As Barbara sprinted forwards to catch Laura's swaying body.
Steven called out. "What's wrong with her Barbara? Should I call 911?"
"Don't know. She's coming out of it, I think she's alright."
Barbara swung her down onto a battered and clay-dusted couch; Laura's concession to the artist's studio within the lab.
The voice was low, and quietly surprised. "I'm alright Barbara - - really. Just a bit lagged out from the dig." Laura smiled up to persuade her. "What have they been doing in there all day?"

14   Tertiary

"God knows. How long does it take to read a rock analysis?"

Barbara waved at the two men. Called out, "Nothing that some coffee won't fix." Spoke low to Laura. "They're frightened of catching some woman's thing."

Laura snorted. Sat up and stretched. "I could do without these mad dreams though." Stood up, waving Barbara away gently. "I'm alright - - honestly. Let's go find out what the boys have been doing with their toys."

They walked over just as Arnold was rising to leave, and hesitated outside the office. Arnold had refused coffee, his usual flippancy noticeably absent for the moment, as he insisted on his escape from the lab. He clutched a small specimen bag in one tight fist. "Steven, I've got to take a break from this now. That set up should be what you need to carry on. That's assuming you do have both oars in the water. Let me scan these new samples, and I'll get right back to you." He paused, making a clear effort to regain his normal image. "You can be sure I'm telling no-one about this. Who needs a room with bouncy walls and no windows!"

He nodded to Barbara and Laura as he walked towards the door. "Goodnight Ladies. Your boss is a raving lunatic, who thinks he's been given a finger painting set from the KT Boundary."

Steven flinched at his last remark, only too aware of Barbara's probable reaction. And Barbara's mouth had fallen wide open. "What - - - ?"

As the lab door clicked shut, Steven's reply was quiet and resigned. "A graphics code. From the fossil memory chips. I've, er - - I've not accessed it yet."

Barbara was almost speechless, her calm resolve forgotten. Laura caught at her arm. But she snatched it away, rising up around her own in-drawn breath. "I don't believe you got any code Steven. I'm no expert at computers, but don't ask me to buy a message in a rock flake from the Cretaceous Tertiary layer. A sixty five million year old video show!"

She swung her hands apart, in a silent appeal for support from Laura. The younger woman's face was pale and drawn. "This stuff is starting to freak me out Steven. Are you sure you're not just getting feedback or something?"

15 Tertiary

"I don't know what it means either - - - ."

"It means you're hunting for ghosts in a machine," Barbara was almost shouting. "You're not a computer expert here Steven. You're supposed to be a professional palaeontologist. Why don't you just admit you've got an unusual bit of crystalline rock and get it down the Geo. Lab for a standard analysis – Instead of setting yourself up for one of Arnie's best practical jokes ever. Or better yet, get a standard analysis for yourself!"

Steven couldn't construct a reply. He just turned and walked back into the office, his shoulders tensed with anger and defeat. Laura recoiled from the volume of Barbara's complaint, and her fury, as Steven retreated. "There might well be something unusual about that crystal structure, but our guy's going crazy for real if he thinks it's some artefact. He just wants to kick up a storm - - To set up a budget extension? I don't know - - - . Can't he see that this species is a really important find ? Even if we are doing all the goddamned work!"

Laura felt some agreement with the last point, but her loyalties were still divided. She frowned at the newly formed brain cast as she spoke; her voice shaking with an old strain. "I'm tired of this atmosphere, is true. This work is the best I've ever been given. And I'm having real trouble getting any good time to really concentrate on it."

Barbara was aware of the implied criticism. She picked up the brain cast, holding it out at arms' length, as she considered sympathy, or even an apology. But then she just shrugged, glanced at Laura, and put the convoluted cast back onto the centre of her bench. She moved to put on her overcoat; it was almost the end of a working day. "Well, Mr. Angry's still at it. If he wants to play with his toys all night, I vote we leave him to it. I've had enough for one day."

Laura stared across the lab in exasperation. The outline of her sculpt was framed by early evening light, and a view of mountain ranges fading into hazy distance. A huge cargo disc was floating towards them, its' shadow sliding down the mountainsides. Her angry gesture was witness to her own disaffection. "He's the boss. If he doesn't want to be involved we can't make him. I don't care too much about who gets the recognition, but I don't want to see this project shelved."

She frowned again, uncertain about her own motivations. She didn't trust Barbara, and was becoming more than a little frightened by Steven's suggestions.

Barbara was well aware of Laura's dilemma, but was still too angry herself to be deflected, or to try to gain the younger woman's trust. "Agreed. But if Steven doesn't get his act together pretty soon I've got to think about publishing pages on my own account. Ah well – Let's call it a day Laura."

Laura nodded and reached across to the rack for her own coat. Both women moved quickly to collect up their personal things, and shut down the labs' equipment. They left the room together, without either speaking again, or saying 'goodnight' to Steven.

Laura's apartment was in the crossroads town of Vernal, Utah, about twenty miles west of Dinosaur National Monument. It was adequate to the needs of her working life, but she'd never quite found the courage to search out a mountain cabin. That would have been closer to her preference and her character. Even so she was normally happy enough with her choice.

Today she had driven home, along the Green River trail and then Route 40, in a daze of frustration. Blind to the raw grandeur of the Uinta Mountains ahead of her, cutting jagged outlines in the sunset, she thought back to the days and weeks behind her; wondering yet again why she couldn't resolve the tensions between Barbara and Steven.

Now she was letting herself into the simple three room apartment, above a convenience store, and realising that her work problems were invading her private space. Peggy, the store cat, was winding around her legs; demanding Laura's customary evening greeting. Laura ruffled the cats' neck; Peggy staring up, wide-eyed and point-eared, when she wasn't picked up as usual. Laura tugged gently at the cats' fluffed out tail, then shooed her away down the wooden steps. "Sorry Peggy - - - ."

Laura was suddenly close to tears. She went in, threw her things down on the couch, and stood staring, hands on hips, back out of the open door.

17 Tertiary

Then kicked it shut, hearing Peggy scoot down the last steps in fright. 'Damn!' Why couldn't she tell them both to go to hell, and enjoy her progress on the sculpting, why did it all have to be such a pain in the ass?

She'd wandered around, and into the kitchen corner to fix herself an allowable drink, when a rap on the door made her jump. 'Damn again! She'd forgotten that Michael was driving out from Salt Lake City this evening. Why was everyone so dependent on her staying level, and being available with her time and patience?

She hesitated, severely tempted to pretend she wasn't home. Except he would have seen her car outside. Even with Michael she wasn't sure if she was defying the conventions of family and friends, both groups having warned her off him, or just falling in with someone else's agenda as usual.

Laura glared at the door, when Michael rapped again, and looked all around the room. To hell with it. If the apartment was a refuse tip he would just have to think what he would. His own fault for turning up early. And she wasn't about to start preening herself now, with the dust of the desert dig still fogging her brain and clouding her days. She brushed her hands down the hips of her work jeans. Then pushed her hair back and tied it with the band from her wrist. Stepped to the door and tugged it open; Michael almost falling over the threshold, past his own, upraised fist.

"Hiya Laurie Lee! How's the scaly monster trace? And what'd that poor old cat do – Went past my legs like a little furry rocket."

Laura felt the insincerity of her own smile. Michael was slightly drunk, and far too happy; seeming very much the spoilt boy that people had tried to persuade her away from. Michael ignored, or was oblivious to, her silence. He walked straight to the corner of the room that was her own, home work area and picked up a small model of the new dinosaur she'd been working on in her spare time. It was even more upright and humanoid than her full size drawings at Dinosaur National Monument. He turned the model over, handling it clumsily to her irritable view. "Hey this is great Laura – Action Man Dinosaur!"

"Put it down Mike, I spent hours on that."

18 Tertiary

Michael looked at her quizzically; placing the model back with deliberate care. She glanced away from him. "It's just a fun idea – We've got this new species from the Snake River dig. I wondered how it would look if it'd had a few more years to develop."

Michael smiled, looking at her in mock disbelief. "He looks like an alien pilot from 'Star Wars' to me. Where's his laser gun?"

"Oh don't be damn crazy Mike – Dinosaurs with guns is just ridiculous. Come out of there!"

Pilot, the back of her mind whispered. Why did he have to say Pilot?

Michael was sobered by the violence of Laura's reaction. He moved back towards the door, as if he felt he should leave. "Joke Laura, just a joke. Hell, what's been happening with you – Taking that seriously?"

"You just come marching in, and pick anything up - - Oh, I'm just tired of mad ideas. Barbara and Steven are at each other all day long, and all I want is to get on with the work." She looked over to the model. "Well I guess Barbara is working, but I wish Steven would act a bit tougher. I think he's going to crack up. Barbara's trying to do a take-over on him, and I can't much blame her this time."

Laura's long hair was a fan of colour in the early evening light, as she emphasised the force of her feelings. Michael was bemused by the cliché; he'd not seen her angry before, and she was beautiful. He foolishly persisted with humour in his attempt to pacify her. "Well he must be cracking up a bit, if he's got you modelling talking dinosaurs."

But Laura lost her temper with him completely now, eyes wild as she whirled towards him. "So now I'm crazy! And who said 'talking'? I'm doing this for fun. No one asked me to."

"It doesn't look much like fun if it's making you this angry. Calm down Laury."

"Don't tell me to - - - Oh, hell!" She spun away. Turned back. "Look Mike, I'm sorry. I told you, I'm getting so tired of arguments at work. And the project is going to get cancelled if we don't all stay on the case and work together."

19 Tertiary

She stared at the model dinosaur; aware of how irrational her anxiety had become, as the figure took shape. An expression of confused pain clouded her eyes.

Michael gently grasped her shoulders. Laura froze, but didn't shake him off, as he pulled her towards him. "It's okay Laura – Let's go eat and forget all about work. And Wookiees. Maybe keep things that go bump in the night?"

Laura snorted, throwing a false punch at him, and twisted away to reach for her coat from behind the screen door. She took a deep breath; forced herself to act sociable. "It's a deal. Let's see what delights the truck stop has to offer this evening. You know, I can never work out why I love this place so much – But I do."

Michael grinned as he formally ushered her out of the door and on to the old wooden stairway. They stepped down into the dusty warmth of dusk, and made their way out onto Main Street, under wires and cables and the first flickering signs of a Western American evening. By the time they hit the street Laura felt her face relax into a genuine smile. Peggy the cat watched from her favourite looking place on top of an old oil tank; tail flicking once as she stretched down onto curling paws.

Back at DNM the team's lab was in near darkness. Just shadows and a low level illumination from bench lights in the side office. Machines and walls clicked and echoed in cooling air; the surrounding rim of mountains finally blending with the night outside.

Steven was still working. Several flatscreens and an old surgical manipulator were set up on his bench, all linked to a semi-sealed microlab and modified immersion gloves. He was cursing gently, as he removed one glove to adjust a view on the central screen. He snatched up a stereo visor and clamped it roughly back onto his head, twisting impatiently to find a fit and a view. Pushed an old mousepad aside and returned to the glovebox. The whole assembly was a lashed together mix of old and new equipment that was obviously irritating Steven immensely. His shoulders tensed once more, then relaxed as everything decided to work together.

Tertiary

His view was focused on a thin wafer of dark, crystalline material, with an array of circuitry and connectors set to one side of it. The manipulator hovered over a row of gold contacts inset into the bevelled edge, a minute wire ready in its' jaws. Steven took a deep breath, and floated the wire into place. The left hand flatscreen lit up, and a strange pattern began to form and re-form. Then suddenly jumped and changed radically. Icons appeared in rolling columns, like numbers counting down, and joined and floated apart to make new designs that rose to the top of the screen.

Steven was in a state of heightened attention, something he hadn't felt so strongly for a long time. A weird mixture of excitement, anxiety and guilt. Barbara was speaking to the guilt. Her critical attitude was a constant presence, but overridden by the unscientific intuition that in front of him was a key. The key to some amazing discovery. The bones might be important, but the real message had been wrapped around them in the rocks. He felt the electric tremor of exhaustion and suppressed elation in his hands; looked down to see them twitch and realised that the images were holding steady.

Laura's wall clock showed 1am. She woke, stretching in a languorous re-play of her last climax before sleep, with an insistent buzzing in her mind. She lay in a warm, dry pool of relaxation, unwilling to wake any further, and ignored the need to pee, and the tinnitus in her ears.

The TV – She'd left the TV on in their urgent, clothes-shedding rush from the couch to the bedroom. With a low groan, Laura pushed up and swung her legs out of the bed. Sat hunched, and then pushed up again, to weave sleepily out into her living room. The TV hissed a blizzard of white noise at her, as she stared vacantly, clutching the couch for support; expecting to see an image form from the rolling, elusive shapes in the screen. What was wrong with the damn thing, the show never stopped for the night?

A sudden chill shivered her, a movement in the side of her eye that hollowed her belly like a cold hand and had her awake and staring. Through the electric, fizzing snow-light to the small dinosauran model on her work table; gesturing like a miniature devil, exposed in the shell of a human figure.

21 Tertiary

Laura's eyes widened in fear before she could reason with herself; connect the rolling flow of TV light with the tiny dancing demon. She wrapped her arms around her shoulders. Shook herself in angry denial. And ducked down to turn off the screen; seeing the aerial lead that had been pulled out in the scramble towards bed. She glared at the model figure, as the luminous glow faded, and felt her way back through the door to sleep.

In the quiet back room of Barbara's house the wall screen showed 1.10am. Barbara was sprawled asleep with the sound turned down. On the control unit below were casts of the new dinosaurs' skull and brain. Barbara shifted restlessly between dozing and dreaming, her eyelids flickering as she mumbled some instruction to herself. Her eyes were dark slits reflecting the glimmers of a film, silently running to a climax of gunfire and smoke.

[Neither awake nor asleep, she saw cowboys turning into nightmare figures that pinned her, paralysed, with familiarity. Drawings on a wall come to life, but subtly different - She couldn't know how close Laura had come with her work at home.
The dinosauran characters stood in a vaguely alien rock gully. There was a cliff behind them, over-hanging a cave. They were arguing; standing back from each other with their large toe claws raised in threat. Barbara was frozen between fear and amusement. Why was she trying so hard to see if they were wearing clothes or not, they were still cowboys weren't they?
They had guns, certainly some sort of weapons, in their hands. The argument was getting worse, and the two figures began to fight in a furry of inhuman movements. One of them was savagely injured and fell to the ground; apparently kicking towards death.]

As Barbara's eyes blinked wide open the scene reverted to the familiar climax of a Wild West film. One of the characters was resolving the plot before death, and Barbara could suddenly move again. She lunged forward with a gesture to the controls, and the screen dimmed. Then laid back into her sofa, breathing deeply to calm herself, and wrapped herself tight into her hooded, woollen robe. She was almost immediately asleep again.

The next morning the lab was bright with sunlight. Barbara and Steven were discussing details of the restoration sculpt and Laura's drawings of the second skeleton. An uneasy truce stood between them, as Steven traced one hand up along the line of the spine. Laura had altered the set of the skull on the creatures neck the previous afternoon, and wasn't yet in the lab to explain her reasoning. But Steven was cautiously in agreement with her work. "Well, that's how it looks to me too. Head and eye lines at ninety degrees with an atlas and axis right under the skull. Same as the Apes. And us."

He was aware of the slur of sleeplessness in his voice and drank deep from his coffee mug, wondering with a dulled anxiety what sort of mood Barbara was in that morning. 'Not that I really give a damn,' he thought. 'Let her sort it out for herself, all the evidence is in clear view.'

But Barbara was peering at the drawings, comparing them to the new set of bones, and nodding her head in reluctant concession. "I guess she's right. I can't see the skull rotation working at any other angle. But that makes the spine even more upright than our first reconstruction?"

She shivered, remembering her dream, or hallucination, of the night before. Steven just nodded; frowning as he considered the new, more human pose. He wanted to move on to discuss the creatures' brain cast, which Barbara seemed unwilling to analyse. But before he could move the mornings' meeting to Barbara's work area Laura came rushing in. She was looking nervous about being late, but also tired and apprehensive about something other than Stevens' disapproval.

Steven was still frowning, lost on a new trail of thought, and staring past Laura; who assumed he was really annoyed. "I'm sorry Steven – Hi Barbara. I couldn't sleep for weird dreams. I think these guys are really getting to me." She gestured at the sculpt and drawings, struggling out of her coat and stumbling slightly as she turned.

Tertiary

Barbara caught her arm, and helped her pull her arms free. Laura touched her hand. "You know what I dreamt last night?" She threw her bag and coat onto the nearby couch. "I was a female Dino in a tribal group, and we all went out on a hunting party – Complete with spears, and bows and arrows, and then a nice little fire for a barbecue – I used a fire drill to start it!" She paused to catch her breath. Reached up to unbraid her hair, and shook it free. "But you know the weirdest bit? We, they, talked in some strange language, and I know that I understood it. I was down on my haunches, chatting away to one of the other females about her love life, and - - - It was really freaky."

She looked down, steadying herself against a work bench. "You ever had a dream where you know that you're dreaming? It was like that, only real as being here now." Her voice had dropped, and she looked up into their eyes. Barbara was glaring at her, pale with shock, but saying nothing. Laura was trying to appear casual about her dream, but was obviously disturbed as well. Steven had only half heard what Laura was saying. He only re-focused when Arnold Shintowsky appeared through the far door of the lab.

Arnold was looking even wilder around the eyes than usual, his hair flying out in an untidy tonsure above his glasses, and his oversized lab coat flapping around him as he hurried forwards. "Good morning gentlefolk. Are we all ready for what the day might bring, be it madness or mayhem?"

"Get on with it Arnold," Barbara muttered to herself.

Arnold opened his mouth to speak again, then just shook his head, and handed a folder to Steven. Laura and Barbara looked at each other; an unspoken 'what now?'

"Printed these out for you," Arnold said. "Best not left in the system right now. You'll see what I mean."

Steven looked down at folder, as if deliberately prolonging the tension, then tore its' flap open and pulled out a sheaf of electron micrographs. They showed the detailed structure of one of the crystalline rock samples. It was unmistakably highly organised despite the alien quality of its' architecture. It was very difficult to explain, except as being the product of some advanced technology.

Arnold rubbed his forehead. "I see it, but I don't believe it," he said. "There's no way I know of to explain that as natural."

Steven was unable to conceal the effects of working all night. He waved vaguely towards the office and led the way, weaving unsteadily between benches and equipment stands. His voice was low and slow. "Have a look Arnie, Arnold, something is in there, but I can't work out what it is."

Arnold guided Steven by the shoulders, through the doorway of his office. Barbara and Laura followed reluctantly, both fascinated and afraid of what they might see. But there was only the same set-up as the day before. Steven turned on the central monitor and carefully manipulated the mousepad.

The pattern on the screen was more complex; blocks of icons in a side frame moving down, then re-setting and starting again. Steven watched for a moment before speaking. "I think it's a countdown, but it gets to one or zero and then re-sets each time. Am I missing some simple entry code?"

Arnold peered at the screen, then consulted one of the micrographs. He caught Steven's arm and pointed to one side of the print. "Can we connect there? That could be a ROM segment. Still got to find a way into it though." He leaned onto both hands, head low, then straightened up. "Hellfire – And sign me up for the rubber room. I don't believe I'm buying this. But I just can't see any way that that is a naturally formed crystal."

Steven looked at him blankly, in acceptance of his own fatigue, as Arnold wagged one finger for him to stay where he was and slid into another chair. Laura looked round for Barbara, but she had moved back into the main lab. Appeared to be getting back to work on cleaning and exposing one of the skeletons.

Laura's feelings of suspicion and anxiety were worsening. She wanted to trust Barbara, but couldn't, and now both Steven and Arnold seemed to accept as fact that the strange rock flakes really were artefacts; designed and manufactured tens of millions of years earlier as components for a dinosauran computer system. Her happy little world of steady and patient study and reasoned speculation was turning into a personal and professional nightmare. She reeled as her imagination turned traitor;

25 Tertiary

hooding her around with a future of doubts and uncertainty that mocked her hopes, ambition and courage.

She found herself grasping at Steven's shoulders; heard her own voice half-strangled by fear. "Steven, you look terrible. Have you been here all night?" He looked up, distracted from Arnold's wrestling with the manipulator and low muttering at the computer. "Well, yes, I was at it most of the night. I slept a couple of hours on your couch, but my mind was on overtime you know?"

Laura nodded vaguely, looking out of the office again. Barbara was talking on her mobile, keeping her voice low but failing to conceal a furtive quality in her posture. Laura's sudden surge of anger and determination took her by surprise. Whatever it was going to be, she had to do something to make sense of this crazy situation.

Barbara was talking quickly, unwilling to be overheard, as she stepped outside the lab. "No, not at all Jim. I appreciate your input on this. I thought things might improve this morning, but now we've got Shintowsky up here again – Hard to believe, even for him, but I think our Arnie's caught the same bug. The two of them are still playing around with their 'artefacts' or whatever the hell they think they are."

She listened, nodding as the other party spoke. "Well I agree Jim, but if we're going to make a page on this new species we'd better get started right now. I can't extend my loyalties to seeing the whole project abandoned or re-assigned."

As Laura walked back into the main lab Barbara came in from outside. She stared at her younger colleague with a defiantly level expression, then turned to her reconstruction of the first skeleton without speaking. Laura felt a chill of paranoid anxiety as she shrugged on her work coat, tied up her hair and moved slowly, head down in thought, to the sculpting area. She looked out over the mountains, knowing that Barbara was watching her, and chewed over the determination to take a stand if her new suspicions proved to be true.

When she turned back Arnold was on his way out. He waved briefly, looking bemused, and she caught Barbara's curt nod to him, and her fierce glance towards the office when Steven failed to appear. Laura's new resolve was directed towards her sculpt for now; connecting earplugs for the Diamond Player on her lapel, she began to assess the clay form. 'Too damn cautious as usual,' she thought. 'This guy's going to look the way I know he should. If Steven's right, that'll be the least of our worries.'

In his office Steven was laid back, deep in his chair, as the flatscreen flickered and brightened. The original pattern was speeding up and changing; forming a scrolling column of icons that counted down, and stopped at what he now recognised as zero.

Fifteen hours later Steven was still working at his bench, totally absorbed in the self-imposed mission to make sense of whatever mystery had singled him out. Of all the fossil sites ever explored, this one, in his own backyard, was likely to be the most important in the whole history of palaeontology.

He was a long way beyond caring how the team might function, or how he might persuade the people above him to take notice. All he had to do was crack this code, and the rest would be self evident. He felt he was close, the echoes of his exhaustion fading, as he focused down into the alien landscape of a language that was becoming familiar. Always arriving at the same locked door, but seeing more and more details on the way. Knowing now that sooner or later the door would open.

At the same time, deep in the night, Laura was lying curled on the couch in her apartment, twisting restlessly into the deep cushions. Out on Main Street a heavy truck was shifting its' gears; accelerating away from the town and on into the desert night. The muffled howl of its' engine faded into the deserted silences between the mountains. A coyote called, away on the threshold of hearing, from the canyons to the North. Laura stiffened, her eyes opening wide, but she was not awake. As the dream caught her, she began breathing again.

27 Tertiary

[She was back with the tribal dinosaurans. A campfire smouldered in front of a cave under an overhanging cliff of layered rocks. Trees and creepers were filtering light from the skyline.

Several dinosaurans were talking and laughing swift, bird-like gestures and warbling speech as they cooked food at the fire. Roots, nuts and berries were gathered in woven baskets and packages of leaves. There had obviously been a successful hunt; several small dinosaurs, like elongated chickens, were taking their turn on simple spits above the flames. A watertight basket of bark held simmering liquid, and another heated stone was lifted into it with damp leaves.

Dinosauran children were playing in the back of the cave, their short tails lashing stiffly as they tumbled and twisted in the dusty sand, and their delighted cries echoed around the rocks.

Then a roar of sound, falling from above. Children huddling fearfully in the cave. Adult dinosaurans leaping up, balancing on slender, sprung legs. Staring, heads swivelling anxiously, at the sky above the rock face.]

Laura's dream was shearing and floating to the familiar thudding beat of feet or wings, or rotors, as she rolled and fell to a new focus.

[A similar place? – The same place, much later in time. The eroded outlines of cliffs and rocks just recognisable from a new ground level above the cave. Figures blurring back into view – Bright and startling in vivid colour, but familiar in their form and movement.

Dinosaurans in protective blue and yellow suits, wearing helmets, and carrying scientific equipment and tools. They were Archaeologists. An excavation of the ancient campfire site was proceeding from this new perspective in the landscape – A modern time in the far past of Earth's history.

The muted whine of turbines. A helicopter, its' rotors meshing almost silently, floated into view above the research area. Vaguely familiar blisters and turrets and metal beams projecting from its' flattened nose and back along a broad, finned belly to an open ramp under the tail. The machine hovered on cones of down-washed and heat-swirled air, as its' sensors probed and recorded.]

Laura's point of view seemed to settle within the dream. She was looking at her own hands; seeing the fine details of a delicate feather layer on their backs, and nails that were almond shaped, almost claws. A slow-motion rush of conclusions – Proof of convergent evolution in reverse. 'Perfectly designed for the job in hand.' She smiled to herself; humour that was far older than these rocky hills.

[Then alarm – The other dinosauran archaeologists had stopped working and were straightening up. They looked across at Laura; their expressions intense and puzzled as they started towards her.
Idly observing her own fear, she smiled and gestured a movement of reassurance. Even as she floated upwards, waving down apologetically to the upturned faces, and lifted rapidly into the sky.
Way below her the helicopter was landing in a haze of dust, and some sort of six-wheeled ATV skid-circled to a stop outside the arc of its' rotors.]

This is more like it – This is how a dream should be.

[Laura was buzzing with calm ecstasy as the landscape softened to a spectacular, rounded dome all around the horizon below her. Colours and patterns blending in and out of view. She felt herself at high altitude, but had no way to judge whether she was skimming rocks at eye-height or dreaming down to mountains out of orbit.
Then the scale and distance settled into a clear view. She recognised the campsite again, glittering below her in early afternoon sunlight. The hours and aeons were running together in her accelerated vision. Now the whole forested area was straddled by an enormous, enigmatic structure – Three huge pillars, each rooted into a rocky plateau, supporting slender, out-curved arches. The arches meeting at a central spindle; from which hung a gigantic sphere, at least two hundred feet in diameter. Secondary struts,

Tertiary

maybe walkways, linked straight across from the arches to points on the sphere's upper curve. A ridge circled the upper section under these points but it was impossible to tell if a thin-walled dome capped the sphere, or was just part of its' structure

The sphere itself, like its' supporting architecture, was a uniform, dusty white in colour. Very faint lines and markings delineated unreadable patterns around and across its' whole surface. There was no sign of movement or habitation, and no sounds disturbed the cool, calm air.]

Laura felt a rushing horror rise from her belly; as she fell, tumbling back to the world outside her dream. Waking, terrified, just as she knew she was plummeting into the surface of the strange, hanging sphere.

She was staring, shivering and confused, into the central light fitting in her apartment. She didn't remember leaving the light on, couldn't even recall falling asleep on the couch. She reached out for her phone, speaking the number twice before it would recognise her voice.

Back at the lab Steven was still working at his bench. He jumped when his phone rang, but didn't attempt to answer it; leaning forward and peering intently into the screen, where hints of imagery floated elusively into view. But nothing on the screen was fully focused or clearly identifiable. He lay back into his chair, and was almost instantly asleep. As if climbing up through a trapdoor, he woke into dreaming.

[He was in an aircraft cockpit. A very strange and advanced machine, with a central spine between him and the pilot, and huge transparencies that wrapped completely around both couch-like ejection seats. They both lay prone; the seats were like body-moulded and cut-down vaulting horses, with padded rests for forearms and chin.

Steven pushed up to look across at the pilot. Even masked by a complex flying suit and full helmet there was something very odd about his, or her, body form and movements.

30 Tertiary

The aircraft was moving at extremely high speed and altitude. The Earth curved away on either side, and the sky above was almost black, with bright stars shining through. Even with the early morning sun rising behind them their movement across the planets' surface was clearly visible.

A faint sheen of sunlight on waves far below, and the artificial lights of a continent arcing across the horizon, gave an eerie clarity to Steven's lucid dreaming. And the smell. The smell of a machine certainly, but disturbingly unfamiliar; smooth, sophisticated and alien.

Then the dream state was re-affirmed, with Steven's viewpoint changed to a high angle, above and behind the destroyer. He idly wondered how he knew that word translated into 'destroyer' – How did he hear any word at all? So he was dreaming for sure.

His view across the dorsal surface of the machine showed independent main wings flexing subtly in hypersonic airflow. An 'anti-sound' system on the engines filtered their roar to a low hissing, as the machine streaked across an icy sky. There was a wing like duct across the top of its' body. The sweeping fuselage chines, thin as blades, were semi-translucent; changing patterns of colour and light flickered over the destroyers' skin as it mimicked and merged with layers of cloud below.

Steven felt a sudden surge of fear and phobia. The tail cone, bulbous as a wasps' abdomen, was twitching like a machined chrysalis. Laser light stabbed backwards to a focus, and an explosion. Chilled by a phantom sweat, Steven realised an attacking missile had been detected and destroyed.

The dream flew him beside and below the destroyer and he could see the pilot, above and to his left, operating controls. The machine reared up, slowing on vectored thrust, its' main wings sweeping forward like a raptor, and a sudden blast of engine noise stunned him with a heavy blow.

Stealth colours washed away to a uniform, dull blue-grey. He knew the destroyer was diverting power to weapon systems as it prepared for an attack.

31 Tertiary

'What?' Steven screamed in soundless impotence. 'What's the target?' Twisting desperately to see. The destroyer splitting along its' underside above him to show a rail gun emerging from the bay.

An alien city on the horizon. A web of reflections flaring to brilliant clarity in first light of morning.

'No - - - - !' Steven was rolling and fighting in the screaming air, mouth and belly filling with ice.

A red lance thinned a line from predator to prey; missiles engaged and exploding in the sky ahead.

The city was doomed. The rail gun launched. Three quick shots. A harsh, rising howl of sound from thermonuclear slugs moving at thirty miles a second. And a glaring blue flash of ionised gas from upper fuselage vents.

Steven was back in the cockpit, crouched on his padded ejection seat, staring out ahead, wild-eyed, to the minutely glittering verticals of the distant city.

The cockpit whited-out, an immense flash of light. And the transparencies crashed to black. Steven was blind, thought he'd been shocked awake, until he saw the glow of instruments and screens. The blackness began to bleed open, mottling to liquid circles of light around and ahead of him.

And a view of the shattered city. Three vast, boiling, fire-swollen clouds rising; columnar tubes of ash and smoke with flattening roots stamped into the far shoreline.

Now Steven hung spread-eagled, flung backwards, with the blackness of space above him; crucified on his unremitting dream. The diminished destroyer seemed no bigger than a deadly bird as it turned and rolled; main wings twisting in opposition and the gimballed cockpit slewing towards escape. A scramjet lit in the upper fuselage duct, and the machine accelerated towards him. Away from the ruination of its' target.

The destroyer speared forwards on a shaft of flame. An intense crescendo of noise when it passed close beneath; fading as the machine outran its' own sound and away to whatever was sanctuary.

Three columns continued to rise, woven together by cross lashes of lightning; a ghastly crown of dust, blood and electrical storms. Hovering in silence above the cities' skull, while a circular cape of shock waves raced outwards across the sea. Steven stared helplessly down as the shock front passed beneath. An expanding shell of concussed air slammed upwards and past with a hideous triple-echoed roar of sound, tearing away all possibility of ever breathing again. Surely he could wake up now, gulp some cool air into his searing lungs – No one ever died in a dream did they? Spun through a half turn, forced forwards on a deeply indrawn groan, Steven found himself in the destroyers' cockpit for a third time. Terrified now of never waking he looked in horror at the pilot, who turned towards him with a lizard-like movement. Gave a form of clenched-fist salute. And emitted a chilling, high pitched roar of victory.

The pilot was a dinosauran.

Steven flinched away as it gestured to a screen set into the console between them. And spoke into his helmet intercom. He struggled in waves of nausea, realising that he understood what the creature was saying.]

Steven slowly roused himself, staring fixedly at the central monitor, as he tried to remember how to move his own body. The screen was showing the same elusive pattern as the dinosauran console display from his dream. He clawed himself upright, pulled his chair forward, and spanned his fingers above the mousepads. Took a deep breath, that gulped into an anguished sob, and blinked his watering eyes clear of tears. Then shook his shoulders, twisting in a back-pack of fatigue and tension, and followed the intuition, when it came, without question. His fingers were flying in a new fever of anticipation, his eyes locked intently on the re-constructing pattern of icons.

Suddenly he froze, one finger poised rigidly above the keys, and his expression expanded to a manic grin; a whoop of triumph echoing around the dark and silent building. "Yes - - - Of course!" Babbling to himself. "When you put it like that it's obvious. This really was written for simple minds Arnie my man. We were going far too complicated. Very clever - - Very clever indeed!"

33 Tertiary

His waiting finger punched down, and slowly lifted back, to hold, waiting for the computer to react. A picture was forming, scrolling hazily down the screen; first in monochrome, then clearing to fuzzy and distorted colour. The image of a city, seen from a great height and distance, situated on the jagged shoreline of an ocean. Sunlight flashing from waves and windows.

The city was visibly alien, in the subtleties of its' architecture, yet also immediately familiar to Steven; It was similar to the doomed city of his dream, could even have been the same. But as he peered in, trying to fix on details of memory, the screen flashed to white. Blinding light, burning from the centre, before the scene funnelled back into view – A single, huge mushroom cloud boiling up, from a column ten miles wide, out of the cities centre.

Steven punched at the keys, cancelling the image, and shoved back hunched into his chair. He was shaking violently, both hands clawed into the arm rests, and his head wagged side to side in feverish, jerking denial.

The next morning. Steven was preparing to show Barbara and Laura a download of his nights' work. They'd hardly had time to take off their coats; despite his slurred speech, and lurching movements, he was a potential explosion of suppressed excitement.

"I finally got that entry code about three o'clock this morning." He laughed with weariness. "They'd made it so simple, I just went right past it at first."

He inserted the cartridge, and waited for the first images to come up on screen. Icons flashed up and cleared to a frame.

Laura gasped, so shocked that she stepped back against a side bench, and gripped its' edge for support.

Barbara tried to maintain her critical attitude; the assumption that the whole thing was a hoax. But her fists clenched tight into her coat, throttling it, as the images flowed into a simple story.

Arnold Shintowsky had appeared at the office doorway. When he moved around, to get a clearer view, his mouth gaped open in astonishment.

On the screen:

[Elegantly clothed dinosauran figures were walking in the streets of a city. They looked into shop windows, stopped to greet one another, busily hurried to appointments, or sat relaxed at the tables of pavement cafes. Small pterodactyls flitted around the street furniture, like leathery-winged sparrows or pigeons.

There were no vehicles visible in the streets, until a single figure floated past on a powered, gyro-stabilised monocycle; moving slowly and easily through the crowd. The whole city, its' architecture and infrastructure, appeared to be very technically advanced.

A poorer area of single storey buildings, each side of a wide marketplace, was equally relaxed; the market displayed a confusing wealth of beautifully crafted and manufactured goods, all for sale from street stalls and small shops. Here people rode sophisticated, lightweight bicycles and pedicabs, and more of the powered monocycles carried their riders gently along with the other shoppers.

Then a sequence showing dinosauran transport in all its' forms. Giant flying wings cruised over wild and desolate landscapes; interior shots showing passengers gazing out from huge forward facing widows, set into the wings' leading edges.

Two thousand foot long tourist airships hovered over volcanoes, coral atolls and great expanses of rock and ice.

Mag-Lev supertrains were shown lancing silently across farmland, past villages and woods, and disappearing into tunnels, or the horizon, as fast as they'd appeared.

A 'Wing in Ground-effect' ship skimmed an ocean, like an enormous artificial stingray.

And finally a flyaround of a slender, clipper-hulled ship; cutting through sheets of spray and led by 'dolphins' as its' triple, hundred foot tall, cylindrical Flettner rotors spun it through the sparkling waves.]

"Great special effects Steven. Where did you find it?" Barbara's voice was a harsh, coughing whisper. She stared wildly down at him as he hunched in his chair.

35 Tertiary

Laura spoke slowly, not looking up from the screen. "How could he have found it Barbara? Look at the figures!" She pulled the small restoration model out of her shoulder bag. It was subtly different from her full size sculpt, a more extreme interpretation, but, apart from a slight difference in colour tones, almost identical to the dinosaurans on the screen. Then a thin folder of drawings, that were swiftly executed fashion designs; only differing within a season or two from the styles seen in the dinosauran city. "I did the sketches last night. After a dream. I couldn't sleep. And this - - -."

A full-size crayon drawing of a dinosauran hand in two views. The form, colour and texture were an exact match, particularly the pattern of scales on the palm and fine feathers on the back.

Arnold whistled through his teeth. "Jesus H. Christ - Now I know for sure I'm in sleep therapy! You dreamed all this - - - And it matches what's on the chip?"

Laura just nodded unhappily, unwilling to discuss any possible explanation. She forced herself to look at the screen again, her hands shaking, and screwed up her eyes against whatever she might see when Steven loaded another cassette. The quality of the recordings had degraded sharply, but the new set of images gave no-one any relief from anxiety:

[Scenes of civil unrest, diplomatic envoys arriving in foreign capitals, and skirmishes along national boundaries, led to stark recordings of the dinosaurans' final, fatal, planet-wide war. Compared to the previous, idealised scenes this was sheer horror.

Cities were incinerated under thermonuclear fireballs. A view from space showed an entire continent spattered with the flashes, sparks and dull glows of a massive nuclear strike. Raging electrical storms criss-crossed the atmosphere with a surreal and terminal net of iridescent discharges.]

Barbara was croaking. "That can't be true - - Can't be!" She stared at Laura's small model. "But that dream. Almost the same - - - ."

Steven turned to Arnold. His voice was flat. "Should we try to get image enhancement from NASA? Or the Hollyhouse film rooms?"

Arnold's eyes were wide with fear. And sparkling with tears. "God only knows Steve – I think they'll therapy the lot of us if we show any of this."

"Maybe. But this can only be a lead in to some other message. There's more information in that tunnel, I'm sure of it." He looked back to the monitor screen. "If the Director gave us a priority budget, we could get further in before anyone else needed to know."

"Tunnel - - - !" Barbara's voice rose to a shrill note. She walked slowly back into the main lab, confused weariness and the stiffness of furious anger in her movement, and slumped in front of her bench. Cradled one of the specimen skulls in both hands, her shoulders shaking slightly; whether with laughter or sobs was impossible to see.

Arnold nodded towards her. "Alas poor Yorick – A fellow of infinite jest!"

Laura swung to grab his arm. "Please Arnie! I don't think I can handle this – Where did my dreams come from?"

Steven twitched violently around. "You had dreams too? Oh, yes - - You told us. I'm sorry Laura - - I wasn't paying much attention to anything yesterday." He pushed wearily up to stand. "What do we do Arnie? I've got to get some sleep - - - Can't think straight about this anymore."

Arnold pressed his thinning hair back with both hands. An up-welling surge of sick panic was threatening to drown his awareness. He was struggling to control it; feeling an angry regret that he was afraid more than he was excited. He looked at Steven again over his glasses.

"I guess we do what you said – We go to the Director and see what he makes of it." He shook his head, trying to think of any other course of action. "That doesn't feel right for lots of reasons, but where else can we go?" His smile was grim. "Be interesting to watch someone else's reaction if nothing else – I can't imagine how those carpet racers will take it - - -."

He grinned at Laura then, trying to lighten the mood, but she only stared at him in hopeless confusion. Shook her head in apology.

Steven touched her arm. "Laura - Those dreams, I had them too. I don't know. I'm sorry - -."

His eyes were drawn back to the screen as it brightened. The recording had re-cycled, but this time a new, more focused image had appeared. One of

37 Tertiary

the dinosaurans was framed in close-up - It moved even closer to camera and began to speak. But the sound was distorted to an unintelligible, hissing babble.

Michael was back in his apartment in Salt Lake City. Several paege prints on dinosaurs were laying on his work deck besde the ComStack; his link to the news agencies that were his primary customers.

After his last meeting with Laura he'd found his fascination with dinosaurs had been renewed. More than once he'd reviewed Laura's reaction to his overconfidence with a shiver of shame. But there was also an excited foreboding of where her groups' discoveries might lead. The implications of her hesitant and fearful first speculations were both stunning and humbling.

In fact she'd hardly told him anything, so he was guessing between the lines, but his reporters' mind was filling in gaps that led to an immense speculation - That it might have all happened before!

He shook his head in wonder. He hardly dared believe it was possibe; the whole idea was really insane. But he couldn't shift the concept now that it was born and alive in his mind.

Then he was startled back to the present by the warbling of his HeadSet. He tapped the override beside his ear and spcke aloud. "Hi Laura. I was just thinking about you – And dinosaurs."

Laura's voice signalled her agitation; a reluctant need for help and reassurance. Michael had the sense to just listen; forced from alarm to concentration on how much he wanted to keep her close. He could fail her now, and lose her to the immensity of the problems she might be about to face. And he realised she was running through pleasantries, saying nothing, so he braced himself and dived in.

"So what was the 'Star Wars' Dinosaur story? – I'm sorry Laura, I'm serious now. I've been thinking a lot about that model of yours. Dinosaurs getting intelligent! Could they really have got as far as our ancestors? Or even us?"

He listened, tensed forward. Laura trying to sound off-hand; hints of regret in her voice for telling him anything at all. "It's like I said Mike – It was just an idea from the new species we're working on. The model is closer to the skeletons than I said - - And Barbara's got some evidence that they had large brains. And stereo vision - - They were fairly smart."

"And they walked upright, without a long tail?"

"Yes - - I guess so. But, listen Mike, it's such a great restoration project – The best sculpting job I've ever been given."

She'd paused, obviously desperate to confide in Michael, and he sensed her uncertainty about how much more she should tell him. She, in turn, knew she had to trust someone, get an outside opinion, or she would be going mad; without having resolved the new world view that she sensed. "They're so different that I've got much more to work out for myself - - - It's harder. I'm sculpting a species no-one's seen before - - Or anything like it."

"Excepting us - - - ?"

"Well, I - - Sort of. They certainly seem to have walked like us. We might be pushing it a bit there though - - Hey, Mike?"

"Okay, I'm off the subject – How can I help you my Lady? Need a lift out of your tower on a white charger?"

To his relief, she laughed. "You can come and have lunch with me in the restaurant here, is how you can help me Sir Knight – Can you make it?"

Numbers floated in front of him, and Michael frowned at his own time anxiety; regretting the new implant. He thought the thing to 'off', with an inward laugh at himself, and the numbers faded from view. "Today? Well yes, I think I can make it. If twelve fifty for one is alright I'll see you then Laury. I'd better get on the road right now - -."

There was a long pause. Then just. "Bye."

A delay before the tone of disconnection. Just as Michael would have spoken again. He sighed; what could he have said? Better to get there and take it as it came. Wild speculations and no data! Now he needed to find a hand-hold for himself. How in hell was he going to summarise this – Where did you start with shaking the foundations so hard? The only way to tell the impossible was to tell it calmly, in the right order, with no embroidery. And wait for a reaction – Right? 'Right enough,' he thought, and called out a new set of figures. 'Let truth become the best disguise.'

39 Tertiary

The administration block at Dinosaur National Monument was as light and airy, and as bland, as any other ageing institutional building. The first decade of the 21st Century had seen a slow-up in new building, after the rush to celebrate the Millennium in the late nineties. Maintenance and minor improvements consumed most scientific archive budgets in all the low expansion economies.

The long top corridor could have been almost anywhere on the planet. People in Institutes still did the deciding from the top down in most situations, and D.N.M. was no exception.

One door, in the centre of the corridor, was held open by a small boulder covered in the fossilised shells of ammonites. Words flowed in the wood grain of the doors' centre panel; announcing that 'Mr. Larson is in – Jim A Larson, Deputy Director.'

The man himself was speaking to a remote, his back to a large window and his feet up on an exercise deck. He was keeping an eye on both the open door and a monitor surveying the area outside, watchful rather than nervous, speaking with the calm assurance that his stock of power had just increased significantly. "Yes that is correct, I did say Department MJ12 – Code UDM, for Mr. John Smith."

His thin frame, thinning hair, and well worn suit betrayed a style statement tall and thin didn't need a sharp suit and hair therapy to maintain an administrators' authority. He tapped one long finger at his forehead, waiting for a connection.

"Mr. Smith? Yes, I agree your code – Larson here. The matter we spoke of the other day appears to be developing." He paused, checking the monitor while the other party spoke. Then leaned around and stared out across the mountains, far into the distant, purple haze. "Yes I remember being doubtful myself at the time – As you said yourself it sounded like a story from a film paege. Who could believe it for real? My judgement now is to check new results my contact has reported. If they look positive we then move swiftly to contain the situation " After a long pause he frowned, and then nodded "Agreed – Good day Mr. Smith."

He swivelled towards his ComStack, reviewed the conversation, and then erased it from the decks' work screen. Jim Larson's idea of successful management was an open door, and the active discouragement of anyone using it. So, for a long time, he did nothing. Internally he was reviewing a growing sense of mild amazement. 'Anything unusual in the rocks' had been the line. After a brief, bemused amusement he had thought very little about it for nearly five years. Well, now it seemed to be happening; and promised to be every bit as weird as the original request, following his promotion five years earlier. He unfolded from his chair, and stood up close to the window; staring out towards the hazed horizon again.

Forty minutes later, and forty feet further down the corridor, the Director of D.N.M. was facing Steven Anders across the level plain of his monumental desk. Steven was leaning onto the far edge as he talked, almost incoherent from lack of sleep and the desperate need to be taken seriously. He was gabbling out an extraordinary series of statements and requests.

The Director was appalled by Steven's appearance, but continued to listen patiently. He had previously assessed the man as a loner, even an eccentric, but now he was suspecting genuine insanity; he could not believe he was being asked to sanction a tunnel through fossil bearing strata. So he was silent, reviewing various responses, allowing Steven to run his course. When he eventually raised one hand, to demand his turn, Ander's first, astonishing response was to wave him down to silence. Only the famous glare, applied full strength, reminded the younger man that it might be politic to draw breath, and listen.

"What I still don't understand from your description, Steven, is what we will gain from driving a single tunnel inwards. Surely another dig along the face of the cave, assuming it can be funded, would be far more effective. Traditional methods, if you will - - ."

"But can't you see what we're looking at here! The dinosaurs didn't just get hit by a natural disaster. They wiped themselves out by developing a civilisation - - - - . And they left messages. The whole story is somewhere in that mountain!"

41 Tertiary

"Exactly what are we looking at Steven?"

The Director had fixed him with his best steely stare, and was slightly alarmed to find it ineffective. Anders was breathing heavily, looking down, deep into the depths of the desks' polished surface. His shoulders were hunched, and for one, mad moment the older man seriously considered the handgun he kept tucked beside his work deck. Steven sucked in a rasping breath. Looked up with glittering eyes. "Lock, let me run the cartridge. Show you what I got from the fossil chip last night. The images need enhancing, mostly, but you'll see enough to get the idea. They had cities, and aircraft - - - And nuclear weapons."

He moved to the ComDeck and called up a wallscreen, ignoring the fact that his boss had neither approved nor disapproved, and cursed as his fingers fumbled at the media socket. The Director moved back, sitting rigidly in his chair. Icons appeared, and the images began. "You see. They were at least as far on as us, a comparative technology, and it looks like a similar national and social structure. They made weapons - - - And used them - - - . The same madness and atrocity. It's all happened before. You see - - - Can you see - - - ?"

Steven fell silent, almost comatose from lack of sleep. The Director had been watching with a wary embarrassment; which was now expressed as anger. "Steven – All I can see are a few hazy images on a wall screen! Do you really expect me to authorise a tunnel, through a primary fossil bed, on the strength of that evidence? If you do, one of us is crazy, and I feel just fine!"

The aggressive tone, and refusal to look at, or listen to, the evidence roused Steven to a desperate response. "Okay - - Okay. You think I got the cartridge from a sci-fi takeaway. I can see how you would think that – I don't believe any of this myself. But come down to the lab. At least look at the chips – The artefacts that we found."

He was leaning across the desk again. "It's a small tunnel we're talking about, not a mine – A tunnel they made for us to find. We've got to open it up. We've got to - - - For everyone!"

The Director was shocked by the urgency of Steven's passion. Sufficiently shocked to take a more benign path. "Steven, Steven – Take it easy. Look, I can see that whatever this thing is, it's important to you. And important to your team." He looked down at his knees, then got up. "Alright, I'll come down to your lab. Give me a minute to call Jim, and I'll follow you down - - - Agreed?"

"Agreed. I'll go tell the others - - Get things set up."

The Director ejected the cartridge from his deck, handing it across with the concerned but dismissive gesture of a doctor concluding a consultation. The wallscreen scrolled a status report and then shut itself down. Steven accepted the cartridge, and the dismissal, with a mumble and a nod; stumbling against the guest chair when he turned to leave. The Director watched closely as he made his way to the door and out into the corridor. Then touched behind one ear. "Close and display – Steven Anders." The door clicked shut and the wallscreen flicked back on. "Call Jim Larson." The Log manager already comparing and summarising behaviour traits with references to earlier files.

"Jim? Look, Anders has just been in here with some wild tale about smart dinosaurs. He's walked the wall a few times before, but I think he's in real trouble with this one." He pulled out his handgun and smiled wryly, shaking his head. "I've agreed to go down to his lab, and I'd like your opinion on his state of mind. And the condition of his team. He's a good man when it comes to reckoning, and I want to know what's making him crazy."

He listened, twirling the gun on one finger, with a slight frown, and a fainter smile. "Yes – Intelligent dinosaurs it was - - I know, amazing isn't it. I can't wait to hear this one."

'Just a little heavy on the surprise Jimmy,' he thought. 'You maybe know something I don't my man.'

He put away his gun, gave the room a quick, satisfied survey as he stood up and walked out into the corridor, leaving the door open. "Lock out," he murmured.

43 Tertiary

Within half an hour the strange conference was under way in the lab. Steven had taken a full dose of synthetic herbals and was feeling slightly less awful, despite a gnawing sense of unease about the developing situation. He was aware of the foolish haste of his actions, and his paranoia, but sensed some threat beyond either: The shadow of an immense cascade of consequences if he continued.

The Director and his Deputy were both adopting politely attentive postures as they listened to him. He'd plugged up a larger wallscreen, and was running the masterstore through it. Laura had come into the office and was doing her best to back him up. She'd found courage in her determination, and realised, with a shock of empathy, how close the tide of anxiety was to swamping him. So far he was still functioning. Steven pointed at the screen. "You see, this section. Even if the film rooms had faked all this, what would be the point. Who'd put up the budget?"

The dinosaurans strolled through their cities, urbane and sociable as any confident human society. Their gestures and reactions were hauntingly familiar; their clothes and possessions creating a cornucopia of images as surreal as any costume fantasy.

Steven had calmed himself a little. 'Let them work out the cost if they can,' he thought, and continued on. "The chips are paralleled into a new graphics engine that reconstructs from common object and spatial codes. Cracking the code was fairly easy. I think it was meant to be."

The two visitors were silent, showing very little reaction. Deputy Director Larson was looking at Steven impatiently.

Laura spoke up hurriedly. "We saw it, Barbara and Arnold and I that is, when it was just a lot of weird icons. We didn't believe it then either." She hurried on from the implied criticism. "I don't know enough about computers, I'm a sculptor, but I don't see how Steven could have put all this together. Sorry Steven – But it's just too inventive. Too authentic."

He glanced at Laura gratefully, just as Barbara came into the room and distracted him with her sly nod to the Deputy Director. But Barbara had lost most of her confidence, and was ignored; Jim Larson's expression became hard and impenetrable. She masked a petulant grimace as Steven turned back to the screen. "The images so far are structured like a documentary. This sequence looks like reference and research data from atomic tests."

Landscapes, forests and buildings were seen being shattered by blast waves; both objects and frames marked with graphic size references. In one gruesome scene a small herd of quadruped dinosaurs was tethered in a compound, apparently for research; the blast and heat flaying and burning them.

"I think they knew a strategic war was close, and began compiling these records in case they didn't make it."

Barbara broke in. "But not a record for us surely?"

Steven glared at her with weary anger. Despite the tacit admission of its' authenticity she was still challenging the evidence she'd helped to uncover. Her unrepentant stare dared him to start an argument within the team.

The Director was puzzled; his uncertainty mixed with alarm. He'd put on a visor to look closely at one of the fossil chips, and was almost convinced by the whole scenario; why would most of a team set up such an elaborate hoax? But he wasn't able to trust his own judgement; the story was too fantastic to be supported so quickly. The politician and sceptical scientist within warred with the evidence in front of his eyes. He carefully took off the helmet. "These flakes are certainly very strange – Have you had a computer tech look at them yet?"

Steven was flustered, aware of both the Deputy and Barbara's hostility, if not the hidden agenda behind it. "No. I tried - - - ."

Jim Larson leaned forwards to interrupt. "If they had, we wouldn't be standing here – Am I right Steven? I don't know what these images are, but this sure is a novel way to set up a budget extension - - - Your best effort yet Mr. Anders."

Laura was amazed by the sudden attack, strongly suspecting some other motive behind this ridicule.

"That's not fair. I watched him - - - ."

"I'm not trying to be fair Ms. Lovell. I just fail to see how this 'evidence' can justify driving a tunnel through fossil strata – Your own argument proves this species is an important find. And - - ."

45 Tertiary

Steven had turned and revived angrily, but was waved down. "- - how do you propose we fund this effort? Your recent dig came out of the contingency fund, purely because of the new species potential."

Steven now shouted him down before he could continue. "You're going round in circles – This 'species potential' is unprecedented. And we won't go through fossil strata – That's what I'm trying to tell you!" He turned to the Director; lowering his voice in the hope that he might be more receptive "That tunnel was already there – Before the other fossils were laid down!"

He knew he'd not taken enough time to prepare his argument. Barbara's opposition should have warned him, she should have warned him, and that was infuriating him. He fought to speak calmly. "They left their own bones in it to lure us in – The main beds here are a distraction that they couldn't have foreseen." He looked straight at the Deputy Director, challenging him Jim Larson stared coldly back; his eyes unreadable.

"An interesting idea Steven – Very interesting in fact, or should I say in theory? But it doesn't convince me there's any more than a new dinosaur."

Laura's suspicions were fully installed now, but Larson punched in again before she could speak. "To be honest I think you've faked the whole thing up as an attention getter."

"The hell you do! You couldn't tell a genuine find from a Kentucky Chicken!" Steven had lurched to his feet. "I'm wasting my time here." He opened his mouth to say more, but waved his hand in a gesture of disgust, and stumbled out of the office.

Laura was appalled. "He hasn't slept in two days."

The Director lifted one hand. "I'm not excusing that Jim. But you were hitting pretty hard there."

The Deputy spread his hands and shrugged; backing away from any personal responsibility for Steven's reaction. Pulled a PaD from his pocket. "I'll talk to him later, when he's thought it through. Tomorrow – When he's slept."

Laura heard no contrition in his tone, only an undercurrent of purpose that she didn't understand. She suddenly realised that this man was an enemy – All the more dangerous for being hidden behind apparent loyalty. His voice was cold. "I think we should all be aware that anything seen or discussed here must remain confidential."

At one thirty Laura was in the DNM cafeteria, lunching with Michael. He'd cancelled appointments, and flown out from Salt Lake City to meet her. As they carried their trays to a quiet seat, beside a large, sunlit window, he was aware of her tension. Michael's instinct was to keep quiet and listen again. He'd guessed that Laura was struggling to trust him, and was surprised to find he wasn't offended. Whatever was happening here could be much bigger than the making or breaking of their new relationship.

Laura was eating in silence, too preoccupied to feel embarrassed. Her uncertainty about Michael only fuelled the anxiety; she badly needed to confide in someone. And she was convinced now that Steven was right, at least in his conviction that there was more to be found at the Little Snake River excavation site. She looked across at Michael, so intently that his eyebrows rose in quizzical alarm.

"Laura babe – Ya want some guys rubbed out? Just gimme they'se names honey."

Laura breathed out, and smiled thinly. "Deputy Dog Lawson would do for a start – That man is giving me the crawl. The Director's almost as bad. Both of them are patronising rug dancers. Asskissers!"

She laughed at herself, fear whistling in the high notes. "I know we didn't believe Steven at first, but that was before we'd seen - - - - ."

"Before you'd seen what?"

"Oh - - Just the brain casts and the pose. It's so obvious this species was highly intelligent, but the hierarchy men don't want to take any risks. Or see beyond their preconceptions. It's such a cliché – Till you come up against it yourself." She waved the hierarchy away. "Steven wants to go deeper, and I think he's right now. But I'm just a clay pusher."

"Ha! May I be putty in your hands - - -."

"Oh, be serious Mike! What makes me so pissed is their concern with budget and image. If something new comes up all they're worried about or interested in is their reputations, and their own projects." She was pushing a spoon round and round her coffee cup.

Michael watched her distracted, frowning face; framed by curtains of long hair. He felt a shock of desire, that was both love and concern. "Well, if you want me serious, I think you should cool it a bit Laury. No-one's going to take on a new idea overnight, specially if there's something weird attached to it." He stared into her coffee, focusing on the turning spoon. "Look, I know there's something you're not telling me. I'm happy to wait till you're ready, but I think the hierarchy men are bound to be over-cautious and suspicious if it's so big."

"Suspicious! What the hell have they got to be suspicious of, with the evidence staring them in the face? It's hard enough to take, without people playing the same old career games. That's probably what happened last time!"

Michael looked and felt puzzled, but also thought, 'Last time? Jesus, it could be true!'

"Laura, won't you please tell me what all this is about – I don't see how I can help if I've got no idea what's worrying you."

Laura turned to the window – Stared sightlessly out over sunlit lawns and neat buildings; as she struggled with the dilemma of trust in Michael, and loyalty to Steven. Finally she turned back. "Okay Mike, there is something I'm not telling you. You wouldn't believe it if I did - - - Oh, Hell! I don't care any more. I've got to show someone or go crazy. It's not as if you'd load straight to 'Time Paeges' with it."

He sat back, startled. "If it's that spectacular, I'm not surprised it's driving you crazy! Listen, I don't have to get gone for an hour. Can you show me right now?"

"I guess so – I think it would be a relief." She had spotted Barbara, on the far side of the cafeteria, apparently unaware of them in their secluded corner. She glanced at her watch. "Everyone's still at lunch - - Anyway, there's no formal security on the project, yet. It'll take about fifteen minutes to show you the playback. And the fossil stuff. Come on, let's go."

"Playback - - - ?"

Laura took his hand, touched a finger to his lips, and towed him to the nearest exit before they could be noticed. The door flashed sunlight across empty tables. Barbara watched them go, without lifting her head; staring at the door till it settled slowly back into it's frame.

By the middle of that afternoon it had been decided and everyone had moved on to a point of no return. Reality had to be faced, and allies assembled for whatever battles were about to be fought. Laura looked around her apartment, nervous of being there like a child dodging school, and indulged a moment of nostalgic regret for a pleasantly studious future. It was almost certainly cancelled. Steven was falling asleep on the couch, exhausted and curiously oppressed, now that Michael had seen the evidence and suggested a way in which he could help. Michael himself was dialling out on Iridium, confident that this would be the most secure link, standing at the top of the old wooden stairs.

Steven didn't hear him speak. He was sliding down; re-living his dream of flying in the dinosauran destroyer. Laura watched him, apparently drifting into sleep, happy that he was safe and finally able to rest.

Michael grinned from the doorway and waved one thumb; he'd got a connection to his fathers' office at the World Science Court. "Hi Dan - - - Yes, I was right, there is something forming up at DNM. Laura finally agreed to show me. It's unbelievable - - - Yes it's a new species, but it's what they found with it – What? - - - Oh yes, Steven came in while I was there. He seemed pleased to talk to someone outside the circle - - - Yes, he's with us now. He asked me to talk to you – What? - - Yes, sure! This link is terrible Dan. Can I bring him to see you? - - - Great, Yes, see you then." He folded the aerial, looking inside, and his smile froze.

Steven was back in the destroyer cockpit:

[The pilot was still pointing at the console screen. Steven stared; something was becoming clear, but he couldn't fix on it. He was shaking his head in frustration. The pilot stared at him, and pointed fiercely - - - - .

49 Tertiary

Then he was on the ground, looking around wildly; cycads and tree ferns in the distance, under a bright blue sky. Wide open space, something in the haze. Noise rising, and a black shape rushing at him — The dinosauran destroyer coming in to land. It flared into a hover on vectored thrust, the main wings sweeping forwards like a raptor hooding it's prey. Landing struts swung out and locked, and it settled gently to the ground; rolling forward on small wheels to nod to a stop in front of him. A huge elongated, insect head, glittering with reflections; strange surface iridescence and internal lights.

Steven was aware of movement around him — The ground crew? But his attention locked; focusing on the visored helmet of the pilot above him. Nothing else moved - - - - .]

Michael was shouting. "Steven! Steven, wake up! — It's okay - - - ."
Steven flailed arms and legs, thrashing on the couch. "Not the city - - Don't do it - - - - Oh, Shit!"
He was fighting his way to the floor. As Laura and Michael moved in to catch him he snapped awake, lurching back to the cushions with elbows and forearms. Then kicked back up to sit, breathing heavily.
"I don't want to watch him nuke a city again." He looked around. "What! - - - Oh fuck - - - I went out again?"
Laura nodded. "You said something about a city Steven."
"City? — Oh Christ, yes - - - I saw the city again. And he showed me a map. Or a formula — What was it?"
"Map?" Michael reached to a side table for a pen and pad. Steven took them, shaking his trembling hands, and drew feverishly. "Something like this — Maybe."
The others looked at the spidery design, then at each other. Michael tilted his head. "Sorry Steven, that doesn't say anything to me. What does it mean?"
Laura shook her head. Steven lifted the pen again, then threw it down. "I don't know. I don't think I want to know. This is all getting too much - - ."

He pushed the pad away in defeat, and flinched when Michael gripped his shoulder.

"Don't worry Steven – You just had to carry most of it alone till now. Look, if you can take a bit more, we'll show the visual to my father tomorrow. He'll cut past your hierarchy if he's convinced it's necessary. He's the original All American Senator, even if he does pretend he's retired. Does a lot of talking before reaching for his gun, but then watch out!"

Steven smiled. "He'll need more than a fast draw this time. Dinosaurs letting off H-bombs is enough to get anyone laughing therapy."

Laura grinned, grabbing Steven's wrists to pull him to his feet. "Sleep Steven. This time you're going to sleep – Okay." She ran to her bedroom cupboard for sheets and a blanket, rapidly turning the couch into a single bed.

Michael looked up as he helped her. "You'll like my Dad, he didn't fight the World Science Court through Congress for nothing, pure science and primary research is his life. So he'll see what you've got. And he'll believe you – Trust me."

Two days later Steven was back in the lab. He'd slept twenty hours on Laura's couch, and woken to find she'd covered for him; had gone into DNM, leaving him in Michael's care, and told the office that he would be off sick. While Michael arranged a late afternoon meeting with his Father, in Salt Lake City, Laura had collected all the evidence she could find, with Arnold's help, and then left early, claiming a headache. To their great relief Barbara was also absent, so they'd been able to hunt through the office without any interruption or subterfuge.

Now all four of them were discussing the previous afternoons' encounter with Michael's father, Senator Alvin. Barbara had phoned in sick for a second day so they were talking freely, over coffee, in Laura's section of the lab.

Laura was smiling at Arnold, who hadn't been at the meeting. "He is an amazing man – He watched the visual once, said nothing, then got us to run it again, and fired off questions in every direction. But he'd made up his mind after the first run.'

Arnold's worried frown remained. "So he's coming in today?"

Steven smiled in turn. "He wants to meet you Arnie. Said he's never met a mad professor for real.' He slapped Arnold on the knee. "Lunchtime, in the cafeteria. Without the hierarchy. For what it's worth, I trust him. I can't see where this is going, except I think it's the most important find ever. We need a powerful ally, fast, and he could be the one."

Laura nodded in agreement. "It's true he wants to meet you Arnie – I think he needs allies too. If anything he's more worried than we are; he saw right to what it could mean to everyone. And he's seen too many secret projects go bad."

Arnold was silent; staring down at his own hands. Then he looked up, and out across the lab. "This is all going to change isn't it – No more happy days in our little rocky holes."

Senator Alvin was early for his afternoon meeting with the Director and his Deputy. Deliberately so; he believed in checking out the ground ahead whenever possible. He was in the general communications office, at one end of the long upper corridor, chatting with the Directors' first assistant. A shrewd and confident young woman, who immediately saw through his early arrival ploy. But she saw no reason not to indulge him; responding to his stately charisma with a natural ease and candour of her own. "Oh, Steve Anders is famous round here Senator – Quiet and angry by turns. So, potentially one of our best researchers - If he can stay on the track without levitating."

Senator Alvin grinned but his attention was directed to the corridor – An anonymous looking man, in a smart grey suit, had emerged from the Directors' office. Anonymous, but also familiar from somewhere. The Senator hid his recognition behind a casual nod of greeting; receiving only a brief frown in response, as the man walked past and out of the room.

The first assistant caught his arm. "Senator. If you wouldn't mind waiting a moment longer? I'm sure the Director will be free directly. I believe you've both met before – So he'll want to give you as much time as possible."

"For sure. Jack Danovich and I know each other of old. I'll tell you no stories, none of us were men in suits when we were young. Though some might have been born to it - - - ."

He'd caught sight of the Deputy Director leaving the far office, and this time name and face had connected. The Senator had dropped in unannounced on a 'vacation course' five years previously; and he was certain Jim Larson had been there, deep inside the mountains, but not as a palaeontologist. Now he made another swift decision – Nodded to Deputy Larson with just enough familiarity to make the man uncertain. 'Dangerous games – Stupid games,' he thought.

Then he was being greeted by the Director, and they both moved up the corridor. Once inside the office the formalities were over. "I'm forcing myself on you at short notice Jack, but I'll try not to add to your load." He leaned forward and spoke quietly. "My son, Michael, called me up yesterday with a crazy tale about a dinosaur archive that your Mr. Anders has found? I watched the visual yesterday afternoon. Jack, I want you to tell me your people are nuts. Or give me your thoughts on what on earth or elsewhere those images mean." He paused, and nodded meaningfully towards the corridor. "I believe I can see why 'Other Agencies' are interested, if that recording is genuine."

The Director was furious. He didn't have a grasp on the situation, and it was already escalating. His anger, with Steven in particular, was ill-concealed. "My people', as you call them, have chosen to go outside this office with confidential material so I'll say this first - - -. Mr. Anders has shown me his 'evidence' twice now, and walked out on myself and my deputy once. On the strength of this argument he expects me to authorise a tunnel into primary fossil beds. And to do it right now!"

Beneath his mask of anger he was obviously very nervous. "As for 'Other Agencies' - - -."

53 Tertiary

Senator Alvin cut in to calm him. "Relax Jack, I'm not naming names, yet – Those boys are mostly bluster, at least at the start. And they're not known for moving with too much speed, except in the wrong direction mostly." He consulted one hand. "What I'm offering is to keep those jockeys off your back as much as I can – You know they're as likely to blast their way into your fossil beds as ask you time of day. If they get a serious feeling about what's in there."

The Director just nodded wearily and spread his own hands, admitting he was out of his depth.

"Jack, I understand you being angry at Steven's attitude. But if the boy's right, he's found something he can hardly handle on his own. He's asking for help – And if what he's got is for real, I'm going to be doing the same pretty damn quick myself."

The Director relaxed slightly, but was still frowning. "Okay Dan, off the record then, at this stage – In my opinion the new species was almost certainly our equal, at least in intelligence and language ability. The fossil evidence is fairly conclusive there. Up front of five years research, I suspect they could have been conscious, and able to organise socially." Despite his careful choice of words, he was getting agitated. "Hell – I don't know what that archive means. Those rock flakes are far too organised to be just crystals. The matrix around the skeletons is like no mineral we've ever seen before, and I've just read a crazy data report from a geophysical overflight – You tell me!"

The Senator made to reply, but was silenced by a sharp look. "Dan – I've just discovered, without being told openly, that my deputies' first allegiance is to 'another agency' as you put it."

"Yes, I suspected so."

"You knew that! - - That Larson is the link?"

"Not until I saw him here just now, and the other fellow walking out of this office. Nothing sinister Jack, just past contacts in Washington. And elsewhere." He tapped a finger to the side of one eye, then to his ear, and pointed around the room; indicating that the office was probably bugged, both for sound and vision.

The Directors' eyes widened in outrage. "Jesus – Even here? I thought the study of fossils at least could survive as pure science."

Senator Alvin nodded in sympathy and regret as he stood up. "Apparently not – I'll be keeping in touch Jack."

They moved to the doorway, shook hands, and parted without more being said. The Director turned, and stood for a long time with his back to the corridor.

Part Two

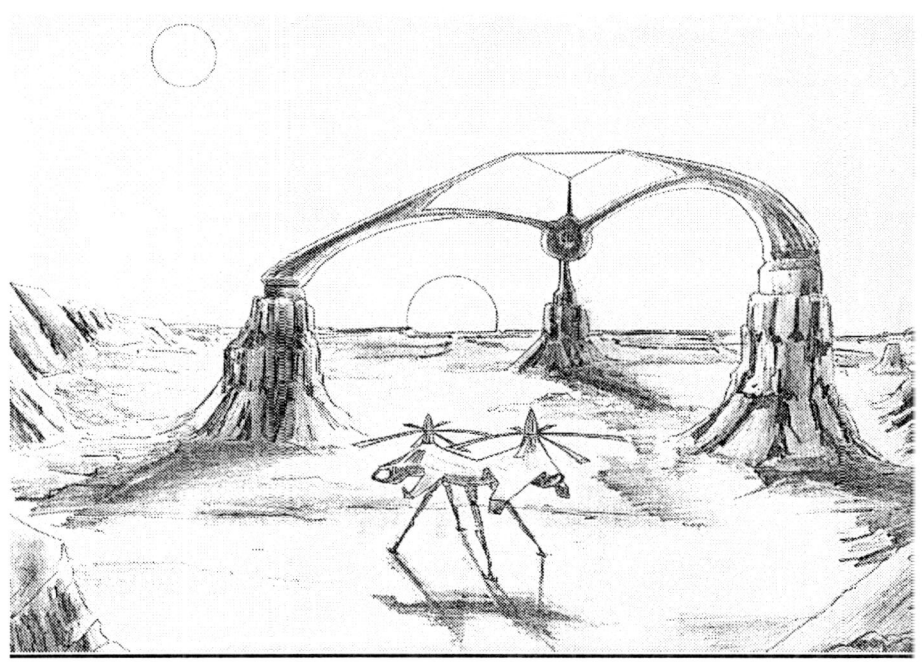

Diversion and revelation

< From 1st Transcript of the 'Tum' Archive: Time now to shape and re-shape from the formless stock of possibilities. All the ways to present what was known, and what had been saved, to the new people. But the decisions had long been made; only internal details needed adjustment as the processes began. A strange joy in such obvious activity. And the sharp sting of anticipation.>

Six weeks later the Little Snake River canyon in Colorado was a focus of intense activity. The local coyotes and owls moved off to a safe distance, eyes still gleaming at the edges of cool and silent nights. Closer in, around the cave, the murmur of generators, people and machines became a new and constant background to the sounds of water and air. During the days the people and machines had converged on the gully and cave where the enigmatic new dinosaurs had been found. The rock terrace was now cleared, flattened and fenced off, with two semi-rigid aircabins installed end-on to the cave entry and to each other.

Lower down the slope, just above the river, more cabins, food and fuel stores and a carbon-lattice helipad stood beside a new vehicle park. Pallets of crated equipment were being lifted onto a Humvee by a kevlar suited and helmeted figure wearing an exolifter. A Boeing tilter swung into the hover above the river, waiting for a Sikorsky Blackhawk to lift away from the pad. Sensor pods swelled from the modified Blackhawk's cabin. Both machines wore camouflage of dull and dusty colours, displayed 'ARPA' in small white letters on their cockpit doors, and carried no other markings. The tilter turned on its' axis inside a corona of mist and rainbows and moved in to land; dust devils whirling up from the riverside trail. The high whine of turbines changed pitch, rising and falling, as one machine climbed and the other powered down to silence.

Inside the Blackhawk the systems operator checked his console and the pilot confirmed their position above the site, locking the autopilot into its' emergency flightplan. She was pulling up into a high hover above the rocky plateau to fix the machine at a pre-set height and position. Large screens on the systems console played readouts from the geo-physics sensors. A hazy image, composed of overlaid spectra, formed from the main processors' rapid resolutions.

A huge structure became visible within the landscape – A flattened cross spanning at least a mile and centred behind the dinosaurans' cave. One arm went straight through the cave and out into thin air, its' circular base end set into the strata of the opposite canyon wall. From the air a faint shadow of debris marked its' position, where the river had cut through and undermined the structure.

Telemetry from the Blackhawk was transmitting in real time to the aircabins. In the outer cabin more powerful processors enhanced the data; pictures from inside the rocks. Steven, Laura and Arnold sat in an arc around the

57 Tertiary

screens, engrossed in the detailed images that were assembling there. The mystery they'd discovered was getting weirder by the day and no-one knew how or where to start explaining it.

Barbara was absent. She'd been promoted out of harms way by Jim Larson; a benign variant of 'shoot the messenger'. Deputy Larson also kept away from the spotlight of operations in the field, preferring his office at DNM. Barbara still hadn't admitted to having strange dreams around the dinosauran material but she was content to carry on with reconstruction of the fossil skeletons at the lab. Effectively she'd taken over Steven's post; preparing papers both for the scientific community and for public consumption. Any speculation was being damped down by her earnest and detailed descriptions of just another saurornithoidid dinosaur; Laura's sculpt had been carefully modified to appear no more humanoid than many other small dinosaur species. And the controversial brain casts were carefully lost behind a calculated debate over limb positions and the length of the tail.

Barbara occasionally pondered her own cast of the brain, alone at home but could never step into that zone she regarded as a twilight of fantasy. The dreams were slowly fading from her memory, and she slept undisturbed.

Laura floated in the opposite direction; her perception was overlaid by dream memories that conflicted with what she saw on the screen. Something was missing, but she'd no idea what that something was. Then the computer called <current enhancement maximum. Task ended>.

Steven murmured "Rotate", and the view changed radically.

Laura was launched into vertigo, thinking for a second she was somehow inside the helicopter, as the massive architectural form came into perspective. Her gasp went unnoticed by the others as they both gaped in astonishment; seeing the delicacy and scale of arches that flew over half a mile each to a union high over the ancient landscape. This was heroic engineering by any measure of technology although its' function remained a complete mystery.

Only Laura suspected that the dinosauran achievement had been even more impressive – Her dream overlay showed a suspended sphere that was missing from the sensor scan. But it had only been a dream. Maybe she'd dreamed up the sphere herself? She leaned in closer to the screen. The spindle-like detail at the conjunction of the arches and an inverted saucer shape or flattened dome, flaring from its' downward projection, both matched exactly to her 'memory'. As did the faint outlines of secondary arches or walkways connecting across to it. And something odd about the down-curved saucer; a suggestion of a shimmer around its' edge, a bluish fuzziness. Was she imagining that as well? She knew that the ARPA research team were much more interested in the teams' dreams than they would openly acknowledge. Steven had seen through the attempts at subtle questioning as well. They wondered whether Barbara had also suffered 'medicals' and subsequent surveillance.

Now Laura was tempted to open up to Steven and Arnold. Some instinct she'd never fully understood had kept her quiet about this particular vision. Not even Michael knew about it. She'd almost decided to speak when her dilemma was suddenly resolved. The aircabin's outer door was opening, letting in a rising whistle of turbines as the tilter powered up for take-off.

"Another magical mystery tour," muttered Arnold. He turned. "Hey, it's the Senator – Hi Dan."

Senator Alvin held the door open to let a stooped and elderly man enter the cabin ahead of him. "Hope we're not interrupting you folks – Bill here and I thought we'd pay you a flying visit. See how our friends in the rock and bone business were getting on!" He stretched himself and shook his head. "Boy, that tilter's some machine! We arm-twisted our seats on the executive cargo-lifter. Took more pass waving than I've used for many a year - - -."

This last was for the benefit of any hidden audience. The Senator made a questioning hand gesture, 'is the place bugged?'. Steven spread his hands in reply; he didn't know. In the meantime Dan's companion had taken a palm sized device from his pocket and was already sweeping the area; he was obviously an expert and Arnold watched him closely. Bill looked up from his seeker and nodded briefly as he was introduced more formally.

"People this is Bill Mc.Candless, congressman from the State of Utah and a good man with any kind of electronics. I was kinda interested in his opinion on these prehistoric bugs or chips, or whatever you call them - - - ." He grinned at the others, and Bill held up one finger in mock warning.

His sweep had led him to two points in the cabin in quick succession. And two tiny black discs, which he held up for inspection. He placed them onto his own device and tapped at its' touch screen, grinning broadly as he spoke for the first time. "We have a clean room to talk in Gentlemen and Lady. Any joker tuning in should now have a severe headache!" He pocketed the seeker and shook hands warmly with each of the team. "Dan's told me all about you guys – If even part of what he's told me is true it's a realisation of dreams."

Steven smiled, waving around the cabins' interior, "Welcome to Camp Silence Mr. McCandless. Arnold was fairly sure we'd caught all the cameras, but we'd just about got used to scribbling notes at each other."

Bill smiled broadly. "Sorry to tell you folks, but both those units were video as well as audio. Top of the range – I should know, one of my companies supplied them. God help us when nanotech really gets going."

Arnold looked at him sharply, as if the congressman already knew, or suspected, more than was comfortable. Steven saw his expression, and shrugged – They would have to rely on trusting to instinct as before. Dan Alvin had shown no sign of being a false friend. And who else was there to turn to? He led their guests to the inner half of the cabin. "Come into the real Clean Room. We think it's clean in your sense, but perhaps you'd better check it out."

He sized up the two men by eye, and handed them both a paper oversuit shoes and an air-filter helmet. "We found a new cache of chips two days ago. We're hoping for confirmation that the tunnel is close to some sort of central chamber. And we got a good match to the sensor readouts just now."

A radio call was coming in from the Blackhawk pilot above. "Anyone home on the farm – How'd our data come down? We got some pretty wild reconstructs off that last scan."

Steven shuffled to the console, suit around his knees. "Your data copied clear and good – We're processing now. Come see after the briefing – Thanks for all help HighScan – Out."

"Copied – Jack and Jill coming down the hill – See you after the party – HighScan out."

Arnold short-stepped over, clutching his suit around his waist, and touched instructions to the screen. The cabin flexed gently in the descending helicopters' downwash. Arnold muttered, "Always have to make their presence felt, those jockeys. Can't do without them though, look at this - - - ." The reverse time-lapse view of the structure that he'd selected was filling in the missing span; showing exactly how their tunnel entrance related to the river canyons' erosion. "This is the systems' best guess at how the structure looked when it was first built. See, if I run it up through time."

The two visitors watched open-mouthed as Arnold ran the sequence back again with an overlay of the local geology. "Lots of folding and shattering in sixty five million years or so. Could have been worse. This area would have been a syncline – Filled with sediments and sinking, then lifted up, and eroded down again. This is what we have now."

He reversed back through time again. "And this is likely how it looked on opening day. Or rather on closing day, for a time vault." Then he selected a higher view, and a more detailed simulation of the surrounding landscape. "They weren't perfect though – I don't think they allowed for the river cutting through just here - - - ."

"Allowed for? You think this whole thing was planned - - ?" Bill McCandless stared at the simulation in disbelief. "You're telling me this tunnel system, whatever, was planted here for us to find?"

"Well, when it was built it was arches, not tunnels." Arnold zoomed into the centre of the giant cross. "But it was going to become tunnels. Be buried - - ." He peered closer, rubbing the back of his neck. "Something very odd about that central chamber – Almost looks as if it's moved. Sheared sideways in the rocks - -."

"Moved – How moved - - ?" Dan Alvin looked alarmed.

"Not moved now. But it's not really where it should be. Not the way the rocks have folded. That last scan shows the whole thing much clearer. Or not." Arnold was rubbing his forehead now in puzzlement. "We'll have to cut sideways from the tunnel. The arch. I don't understand this at all." He switched back to the enhanced restoration of the structure. "X marks the spot," he muttered. "Ah, well – We'll find what we find. Sorry Gentlemen, the Clean Room awaits." He pulled his suit up his arms and shrugged it into place, zipped up the front, and led the two guests towards the inner door. The connection between the two cabins was a short corridor with a filter system. It blasted clean air onto their heads and extracted any dust downwards through grills in the floor.

<You have not secured Helmets – Please Secure Helmets before Entry>, said the far door. And flashed the same message in illuminated letters.

Laura idly wondered how the damn thing knew; then reeled back into the turmoil of her thoughts. She was missing Michael, but that was just an excuse – What she was missing was the future. She was cut adrift from her world line; unable to see its' flailing end, let alone catch it and re-connect. The whole project was becoming a fascinating nightmare. More excitement than she could deal with. And on top of all that was the ache of guilty self criticism. Why couldn't she be a person who revelled in all this strangeness? Fearlessly exploring the frontier of discovery, just as she'd always imagined herself in vaguely formed fantasies.

Then sanity settled back over her. She looked at the other suited figures, as they shuffled through the corridor, and knew they moved in the same fog of uncertainty and barely controlled fear. 'This is how it really is,' she thought, 'how it's always been probably.' Just people trying to get a handle on the unknown. Sometimes driven from within. Sometimes from without. 'To hell with it! Get yourself together girl, and get on with it.' She still wasn't sure how an artist was needed here, but she was damned well going to stay with it and be there when it all came together.

The Clean Room contained an organised clutter of sophisticated electronics, centred around a row of fossil chips. These were interconnected and interfaced to a bank of work stations — Each station equipped with two micro-manipulators.

Arnold accessed the current files and screened up the work in progress. "No-one else has seen these yet. We've managed to restrict access to them — Got everyone concentrated on the tunnel. And the Geophysics scans." He pointed vaguely upwards, indicating the sky above. "They just love to play with those big, noisy toys." He stopped suddenly, realising that he'd spoken before Bill McCandless could check the cabin.

But it was okay. Bill struggled to free his black box from within the paper suit, waved it around the space, first high and then low, and gave an 'all clear'.

Arnold shook his head. "Hell, I'm sorry. I can't get used to all this secrecy. Conspiracy bullshit. We're living in hope that the Dinos were one jump ahead of our military masters. Brothers in arms for a peaceful world." He shrugged wryly, and eased himself into one of the work stations. Called up another file onto the screen.

Laura hesitated before speaking. "We think the central chamber is a diversion."

Both the Senator and Bill looked startled. She glanced at Steven. "I dreamt about this structure. I'm sure there's something missing on the scans. And on the reconstructs."

Now Steven was surprised. "You never said that before, about dreaming I mean." He was watching her from deep within his helmet. A strong expression of doubt. "The diversion idea was only a theory. Wishful thinking really - - -."

Laura felt suddenly furious. Was even more annoyed by the feeling she was being irrational. "Well, you don't talk so much about your own dreams. I thought we'd agreed to play that whole area down. Keep the hounds off - - - ."

"Yeah, okay - Okay, you're right. We agreed to keep the psychos out. But if you think you've got a line on how this structure works - - ?"

"I don't know Steven. I had a dream, and the structure was different. That's all!"

Laura was both shamed and relieved by her lie. Steven let it go, still looking at her oddly, and sat at the work station next to Arnold. "Okay Arnie, let's see what we've got"

"Be good to have some decent VR, this military kit is hardly state of the art," Arnold said.

"Not so good for guests, we'd be sure to have three sets for six people. The TrueSpace units are on the way. What's with you?"

Arnold ignored him. He'd found a link between the first information store and the new chips. Fresh images were coming up on the main wallscreen.

[An overhead view of the tunnel architecture zoomed down onto the centre of the structure, where all three arches joined to the central spindle. Then down through the spindle itself and into the structure that hung below it, the huge inverted saucer that could be a cap or a support for Laura's missing sphere. The space was hemispherical, about forty feet across and twenty feet high at its' centre. An organic web of struts held a strangely detailed cube, just above the floor at its' centre. The struts radiated down into the floors' surface, suggesting that the cube was hung at the centre of a sphere; that the floor itself was less substantial than it appeared.]

"Very clever," muttered Arnold. "The sphere floats in the rocks. The floor forms an access level wherever it ends up."

"So where's the door, at the end of the walkway, through that saucer, dome or whatever it is?" Steven asked.

"No idea Steve. I'm sure all will be revealed." Arnold glanced over his shoulder. "Any ideas folks?"

Laura pointed back at the screen. "There's a door opening now - -."

[Dinosauran figures were entering the central chamber. The doorway was obscured as they, and the viewpoint, moved in towards the enigmatic cube. A close-up of bevelled edges, recessed panels on the flat faces, and struts fanning out from its' corners.

The cube was very small within its' supporting space, about three feet along the edges, giving it an appearance of dark, slightly iridescent, density. As if an enormous weight was concentrated at the centre of a complex web of forces.]

"What the hell are they doing?" Dan Alvin was leaning forward to peer through his diamond face shield.
"They're opening the safe Dan," Bill McCandless said, his voice flat with astonishment. "See – A minimum of three faces, whatever angle the cube winds up at."

[The dinosaurans were carefully demonstrating an opening sequence – Their fingertips pressing at slightly raised studs on each of three of the cubes' recessed panels.]

Laura was frowning. "That whole space – It doesn't fit. Go back to the architecture Steven."
Arnold looked doubtful. But Steven switched back to their own computer simulation of the dinosauran construction.
"See, there - -," Laura pointed. "Where all the arches join. The tunnels, whatever – It's like a tower, not a sphere."
"I don't get it Laura - -." Steven twisted round.
"I don't get it either. Hell, I don't know what I mean. There's just something wrong. Something missing."
"It's just a sphere that's in a tower then. And whatever that saucer shape is. Who knows, a docking port?"
Arnold was worried and twitchy. "Let's go back to the story shall we, 'case we're missing something new? This is all stuff we've not seen yet – Analysing it can wait, can't it?"
"Yeah, sure – Go ahead Arnie. I'm sorry." She squeezed through, to sit in the third chair at the console. "Sorry we're leaving you to stand." She looked up at the two visitors.

Tertiary

"No sweat Laura." Senator Alvin smiled. "We'd stand on nails to see this movie - - !"

The dinosauran visual had recycled, to repeat the cube opening sequence. Emphasising the point with a schematic, obviously designed as a memory aid. A simple pattern, with an audio rhythm, for three operators to follow. Then what seemed to be a catalogue of contents came up – An index of the cubes' contents that included designs and formulae and 3D renderings of various technologies and processes; cascading past at a faster and faster rate. Until the information was a blur of flickering and whirling images that forced the watchers to narrow their eyes, and lean back from the pulsing screen.

Just as Steven thought he'd been saturated to the point of overload the vortex of imagery and sound slowed, and focused to a new starting point. He gulped air, realised he'd been holding his breath. His heart was hammering, he'd broken out in a sweat. When he glanced at the others he saw that they weren't feeling much better. "Something subliminal there. That was hurting."

Laura and Arnold both nodded. Arnold's voice was shaky. "I stand corrected, more than enough to analyse. Take someone about five years at a guess - - - - What now?"

The screen was showing some sort of travelogue – Sweeping aerial views of spectacular landscapes, empty of any movement, or signs of technology and habitation, blended and flowed together in a succession of vast and tranquil panoramas. The audio track played haunting and ethereally alien music - Sounds at a level they'd not heard before.

Arnold snorted. "New Age therapy from the KT revival even!" Then looked embarrassed. "Sorry folks, bad nerves I guess." The screen view point was zooming down – Towards a low cliff, a system of caves, and tiny moving figures. "Here we go again, think I know what's coming next - - -."

"Shut up Arnie." Steven's voice was harsh. "They weren't to know they'd have a sophisticated audience."

Arnold turned fiercely. Then shut his mouth – Eyes drawn to the spectacle of primitive dinosaurans fighting their way through a bloody little skirmish:

[Fire hardened spear tips and stone axe heads skewed and smashed flesh and bones - Writhing and dancing figures screaming in bird-like warbles of agony and exultation. Entrails tangled in the undergrowth. The crawling wounded were gloated over, and then sordidly slaughtered. Spines arching and curling. Limbs flailing and shaking; clawing at the last moments of life.]

"Holy Jesus! – How in Gods' name was that filmed?" Senator Alvin's eyes were locked in a hard stare of shock and disgust. Bill McCandless looked away.
Steven muttered, "That has to be SynThespian, they're a few years ahead of us." He didn't sound convinced.
Laura gasped. The view had dissolved to another landscape. Another scene of conflict – This time a siege:

[The earth embankments, ramps and stone walls of an enormous and ancient castle. The stronghold spanning the neck of a broad headland, and protecting a town, built inside a ring of cliff-top walls, that lay behind it.
Roadways snaking up the cliff were choked with debris and wreathed in smoke from the burning docks and jetties below; the gutted hulks of fire ships smouldering and steaming in the choked and oily water. Waves heaved onto shingle beaches; full of rolling bodies.
Huge siege engines assaulted the landward side of the castle; the citadel walls embraced by armoured towers and gnawed by massive sheds, that shuddered with each impact of the battering rams slung from their eaves. Hairy, yard-thick ropes were stretched far back to side-harnessed sauropods in endless loops; the ram crews scurrying to clamp on as fast as the animals backed up for their next pull.
From the circling, aerial viewpoint the organised chaos of tents, fires, roadways and steadily moving or running figures made a surreal pattern of constructive violence – Destruction slowly woven from a flame-front of activity.

67 Tertiary

Then everything dissolved from a fixed view – Time speeding up as the castle fell, and writhed, flickering, to ruin. Plant tendrils swarming upwards as the walls crumbled down, and the cliffs were grated into the sea.

Then another transformation; as town and castle were rebuilt. Another siege – Vast, flattened domes floating on catamaran hulls; their angled sides lined with open gun ports and bellowing carronades. Steam and smoke venting from between the hulls; shielded paddle wheels thrashing a slow forward motion from the waves.

One took a direct hit from a rocket sledge; fire dribbling from its' roof into sizzling water. Smoke columns twisting and rolling from the burning sea where others had missed.

Inland of the new stronghold long-barrelled canon were serviced by steam crawlers and turtle ploughs, nosing up raw earth embankments. A section of castle wall sheared and fell, a crumbling sheet of stone, into the eruption of a detonating under-mine.

A snap cut into the long-past future – The cliff top town, with its' romantic castle ruins, become a tourist paradise under a summer sky. The horizon hazy in early evening heat.

Helicopters lifting and hurrying forwards from the deck of a new, sea-borne, citadel; banners streaming out behind them. The Carrier erupting in explosive coloured light. Sheets and starbursts of flame, and concussions of sound thudding across the water, mixed with the music of a mid-summer sea festival.

Then a blossom and outflash of searing white – Distance underlining a seething brain-storm of fire.

Supersonic shock slicing under the Carriers' decks and hurling it bodily, welded and melting, into the cliff face. The town above smeared away in an instant. The headland stripped to steam-sheeted bedrock.

A silence shattered beyond any sound.

A bubbling hole in the knifed-flat sea where the Carrier, hull cauterised to the water line, had floated in an innocent halo of lights and celebration only seconds before.]

"Oh, God," whispered Laura. "Why are they showing us this?" Silence in the room held on a long pause – The screen view slowly lifting up and back:

[Up into thin clouds, to sunlight, and higher – A farewell to the coast, the country, the continent. Holding a peaceful orbit above the planet. Unfamiliar but 'known to science' land masses in blue and white oceans – Tiny crosses marking, as the world turned, the focus of seven circles.]

"What - - -?" Steven's question was lost in a sudden distraction from the outer cabin. The viewscreen showed Jim Larson and two members of the ARPA management team stepping up through the outside door into the first cabin.

Arnold whispered "Store", and switched the display to the latest Geophysical scan results. The new visitors gathered briefly around the test console, then moved towards the dust extraction corridor.

"Gentlemen! Please observe clean room precautions. We have delicate materials and equipment in here." Arnold's voice, amplified by intercom, was politely correct and even.

Dan Alvin raised an amused and approving eyebrow; turning to Bill McCandless. "Bill, I think you and I have given these good people enough disturbance for one day – Seems like it's time to be leaving."

Bill didn't move. He glanced at the corridor, then back to the main screen; looking both intent and puzzled. "Do you get the feeling that this is a set-up Dan - That goody box of plans or whatever?" He glanced at the viewscreen. The Deputy Director and his colleagues had conferred, and retreated to wait impatiently by the middle door. "I can't see the military master-minds resisting a free techno jump. But it all seems a bit too easy?"

Senator Alvin nodded. Looked hard at Steven and Laura. "A diversion you said Laura. Do you think they'll fall for it? What then - - - ?"

Laura looked alarmed, caught between new strangeness and an obscure menace from the unwelcome visitors outside. Steven was equally trapped, balancing precariously on the point of some new revelation from the fossil record. He was unsure how he could reconcile what he knew with what he expected. He spread his hands. "They're showing us some sort of warning? After giving away all the formulae – If they *are* giving anything away?" He shook his head. "Why put all this in the rocks anyway? This is some time capsule. Makes the Cold War budget look quite thrifty I'd say."

Senator Alvin nodded in puzzled agreement. "Better go to it young Steven – Keep me updated." He gestured behind him at the screens.

No-one noticed a faint ghost forming within the new scan of the massive dinosauran architecture:

[A sequence through time was running – The wide-spanned cross of arches bent and flattened by inpouring sediments and the aeon-slow folding of strata. The central chamber following a curious path, as if floated in the rocks; leaving a faint trail, a dark, frozen vortex, behind it.

The ghost hung below – Visible only as a shadow of folds and sworls, stained into view in the ages old minerals. Then, like a bright light turned away from a mark on glass, it was gone.]

Without looking at the screens again all five people moved to the extraction corridor, ponderous in their suits, and processed themselves through towards the outer cabin. Strangely comical figures, seen through glass and whistling air, as they turned and bent and tugged to be free from helmets and suits.

Two weeks after the Deputy Director's impromptu visit the team was discussing progress over an outdoor breakfast. Jim Larson had arrived with an authorisation for extended tunnelling, and an apparently unlimited budget, that no-one had yet formulated let alone applied for. Initial wariness of the gift-bearer had given way to cautious optimism – 'Riding the tiger rather than being eaten', as Steven put it. But they were all tired of riding a beast they neither understood nor trusted. They'd been at the site for seven weeks and actively tunnelling for six; overseeing the work of a larger group that rotated in two teams to follow the matrix inwards. The matrix itself had twisted and sheared several times; reflecting the surrounding strata's geological history.

Ten days earlier the tunnel had reached the level where geo-physics showed the central chamber, the inverted saucer or dome, 'floating' in the rocks – Corresponding to a period of active mountain building when the rocks were crushed and lifted, and the ancient arch became a narrow, twisting seam of matrix; appearing on updated aerial scans like frozen turbulence in the strata. Yet the dome itself appeared to be impossibly perfect, apparently undamaged by time or geological pressures.

Puzzled but undeterred, the tunnelling teams had struggled to clear a way through as the trace jinked sideways and levelled out. Now they were close to the central chamber itself, apparently following the remains of the walkway that had spanned out from under the arch and linked to its' dome. Steven looked out between Arnold and Laura, across the river canyon, picking up the faint trail of matrix on the far wall; a broken shadow and slight shimmer in rocks lit by sunrise. "Nothing like coffee in the out of doors." He lifted his mug to toast the thought. "Even if we are in doubt and disarray – You think we're still ahead Arnie? No dog bites on our heels?"

"Courage mon ami. Don't get off your tiger now – Not when it's heading straight for its' own cage."

They were sitting on the far south corner of the long terrace, where it jutted out at a bend in the canyon; allowing early sunlight to strike down a side gully behind them. Their breakfast campfire burned on a tiny, pointed headland, above scree slopes that fanned down to the river.

Laura pushed a handful of underbrush into the flames. "I know you think we can't be heard here, but it still makes me nervous talking out in the open."

"Frankly I don't give a shit any more," said Arnold. "Sorry Laura, don't take offence. But I wish we could cheer you up. Think of us in years to come – People who made history." He pulled a flat, oblong panel from his shirt pocket. "And there is always this. Those surveillance boys always think they're one circuit ahead. Probably wondering why we're talking Tibetan – Scrambled egos anyone?" He laughed gently at Laura's puzzled look. "A little present from Uncle Bill. Supposed to be a voice organiser. Which I guess it is." He tucked the device back into his top pocket. "Don't worry Steven. Easy to say I know, but we're nearly there. And I honestly think they're going to go for the decoy. Amazing but true!"

Steven smiled. "We'd have better nerves if we knew what the decoy was covering. How do we know we're with the good guys – Or even if there's good guys in the game?"

"We don't," said Arnold flatly. "We're thrown back on unscientific intuition – Even faith. Voodoo? Crossed fingers?" He took off his glasses, and carefully polished them. "I know I play the fool as a blind, but I'll admit to you now I'm frightened - - - . I just can't believe the Dinos went to all this trouble – Just to be time travelling arms sellers."

Laura looked up, lacing her fingers tight together. "You're right, I know. There has to be another message, or something – But how do we find it? How do they - - - How would they have known we'd be here?"

Steven sighed and shuffled forward to sit cross-legged, closer to the fire. He held out his palms to warm them. "We don't know do we. And neither did they. But we found them, not the military. And it was set up for us people like us, to find." He tucked his hands into his armpits, and rocked "What you both said – All we have is guesses - - - and faith. All we do is go on doing what we do."

Arnold bowed to him. "Most profound. John Lennon would have been proud. Well, save me a place on the Yellow Submarine, I've got a feeling we set sail today shipmates." He pushed up to his feet, walked to the edge and stared down at the river below.

Laura stood up and went to his side. "I've been frightened too Arnie. Too much, and too often." She looked back down at Steven rocking towards the fire. "We should be excited as well – And I'm going to be."

Steven nodded up at her. Agreed with her with his eyes. But inside he knew he was afraid to tell them he was terrified. Somewhere, very deep down, it made him angry. But for now he would just have to wear it, stay functional, and hope he didn't let them down. He brushed sandy earth onto the fire. Carefully smothered it, so not even any smoke could escape.

By the middle of that morning the Right-Hand team were coming to the end of their twelve hour shift. The team leader, Tim McHawne, sat comfortably on his heels in a smoothed hollow of rock, about fifty feet behind the work face. A mini-conveyor rattled gently on the opposite wall of the drift, cables looping through its' telescopic supports. Tim marked a connector in his memory, to be checked before he moved out. Then looked back to his WorkPaege, confirming the position of a way-point marker above his head. He aimed the reader at it again to double check.

A call from the work face chimed in his ear. "Go ahead Eddie, how close are we?" He replied.

"Real close Tim. Want to go for it this shift?"

"Surely do. The Lefties lose their bet. Give it ten, and I'll call the pale-faces to the front."

"In ten agreed – Out."

Within twenty minutes the paleo team were suited and hard-hatted, and making their way into the first section of tunnel. Luminant panels tacked to the roof and walls provided a fairly even lighting. Behind them an auto-loader was re-stacking spoil bins beside the main conveyor, as a balloon-tyred tip truck moved away. The hum of its' wheel motors echoed briefly, then faded as it rolled over the terrace rim.

Steven was savouring a reflective mood. Against all expectation he felt a calm certainty, as if this day was already known; his memory moving ahead of time. The familiar tension pains in his shoulder and neck were mercifully absent. 'Don't push your luck,' he thought. From bitter experience he knew relaxing could trigger an obsessive search for any familiar source of anxiety.

But his mood persisted. He followed Laura and Arnold up to the first shear point, reviewing all the gates of change they'd gone through at the exploration site. The place they'd first known, in company with Barbara and the new species, was gone forever, except in memory. It seemed as if they'd been here for months, years, rather than just six weeks.

They edged to the left, through the shears' narrow, flattened space; the conveyor humming high above them. On a whim, he switched on his torch.

73 Tertiary

Aimed the beam up into the gloom above the conveyor; a narrow, jagged blade of space A giant crack in the bulk of the land. 'Very poetic,' Steven thought. 'I don't believe we're doing this.' Images of the central chamber produced a surreal mix of anticipatory fantasises. He imagined the space as they'd seen it on the dinosauran visual. They were guests at a party – Exotic delicacies offered from a tray. Their hostess raising a cup – Scaly little finger held decorously outwards.

Steven crashed into Arnold's back.

"Easy there Mr Anders. Don't want my head rolled down to the spoil tip."

Laura was ducking under a scoop belt, that lifted debris to the upper conveyor. A curved catch-guard angled up and over the point where the walkway jinked right and then left; to continue up a shallow incline. The tunnel was wider here; the conveyor to her left mounted on the relatively smooth floor.

She felt the trembling fizz of nervous excitement in her finger tips. Touching the wall every few paces. Feeling her way into the unknown hours ahead.

Arnold straightened up behind her. He was beaming an internal monologue to his distant sister, Pamela; the one person in the world he felt really understood and approved of him. 'See, that's where we picked up the matrix again – At the top there's another shear. Then we're near the start of the floating trail, like the wake of a boat.' The careful description gave him a sense of seeing the place for the first time, through Pamela's absent eyes. He looked back to check Steven's emergence from behind the scoop belt. 'Yes, that lifts the spoil up to the top conveyor in the first shear. Oh, yeah, we just came that way - - -.'

Arnold shook his head; gave himself a mental reprimand for day-dreaming. His previous work experience didn't give him the ground rules for tomb raiding – A Pharaoh's tomb that was sixty five million years old. Roughly.

Tim McHawne spoke into his throat mike. "Channel three, Steven Anders – Mr. Anders? Ah, good. Yes, we'll see you in about five minutes." He looked round at the three men behind him. Two working the face with minijacks; the hammer links clipped to their forearms giving and taking the blows as they punched at the rock. The third, wearing an exolifter, was scooping debris into a two-legged tipwalker.

'Archaic bloody methods,' Tim thought. 'But doing the best we can I suppose. In the circumstances.'

Now that they'd hit the wall of their goal he wondered, not for the first time that day, what their circumstances were exactly. He'd long ago decided that imagination was best kept as a useful tool. A way of thinking into other tools, and materials, or an apparently intractable mine problem.

But this job was something else. He'd worked on re-building silos and command complexes, a variety of secret military projects over the years, but never anything like this. He remembered one of his professors at the Mine School, years ago, had had a crazy theory about dinosaurs. What was his name? – Mike Magee, that was it. Professor Mike Magee. He'd reckoned the dinosaurs got intelligent and built a civilisation – Got laughed out of the college bar every time he mentioned it. Must be long retired now, but perhaps he'd give him a call anyway. See what he thought.

There was a shout from the work face. Eddie James, and his partner, Indy Joe, were shrugging off their minijack harnesses. Clipping the folding hammer links back into the pump packs. No panic there then. Tim walked up to the face.

Eddie was clawing a powdery, inch-thick layer of jet black matrix away from a smooth surface. Crumbling pieces of the material between the fingers of his ArmaSense gloves. He thumb-rolled the setting down to 'normal'. "Feels weird. Like meringue or something - - - ." A bloom of condensation on his face plate; shrinking and gone almost instantly in the helmets' air curtain. "Looked like it flowed. Just for a second. When we first hit it. I don't know - - -."

Tim pulled on a glove and laid it, palm flat, onto the surface. Seen close to, it resembled very even, finely-pitted coral. Almost pure white under the jet black layer of matrix. He picked up a handful of the dust and rubbed it in. The dust flowed away, leaving the surface perfectly clean. Tim stood, staring silently, for a long moment.

He was interrupted by the paleo teams' arrival. "Ah, Steven, Laura, Arnold – Perfect timing. We only just hit this. Have a look."

Eddie and Indy Joe stood aside, deferential and interested. Indy handed a chunk of matrix to both Laura and Arnold. Steven turned to pull Arnold forward. "I haven't the faintest idea Arnie. I didn't exactly expect a door with a nameplate and a knocker, but - - - ."

Eddie exchanged places with Laura, squeezing against the tunnel wall to let her through, as she got into her gloves. She thumbed them down to maximum sensitivity, then spanned her finger tips and pushed with both hands. "It feels as hard as it looks, but - - - ." She looked down at the minijack sets. 'Do we have to cut into it, or what?'

Arnold looked round sharply. "Take it easy Laurie. We might be tomb raiders, but we're not burglars - - - We'll need to get quite a package of equipment up here Tim."

"Knew that Arnie. I guess we can strike the conveyors now?"

"Yes - - - Yes, I think so. How long will that take?"

"Second shift should do it. Let the Left Handers burn off their breakfasts. We'll set up the details before we go."

Steven was standing perfectly still, frozen in place. "Something happening - - - ."

Arnold whipped back; bending to stare. "You're dreaming again Steve. 'Open Sesame' only works in the movies - - - . Just a minute - - -."

Indy Joe spoke for the first time that day. "Holy Shit - - - !"

Everyone was stepping backwards, waving arms to catch and steady each other. A tiny tendril of smoke or dust fluttered away from the white wall. A circular spot, like the centre of a laser burn, was spreading into view. Small flakes lifted, curled, and were caught before they fell; somehow re-absorbed by the surface. A smooth, rounded rim around a pin-prick, black hole. Then, nothing.

"It's hissing," whispered Laura. "Positive pressure - - - Or it's sampling our air."

Arnold was amazed by himself; how fast he seemed to be thinking. For a man who was impersonating a rock. Slowly, carefully, he sent signals to his hands – To release their claw-like grips on Steven and Tim's suits.

Two days later Arnold was still amazed. He sat in front of a monitor in the teams' outer aircabin. Amazed more than anything else by his own patience. While Steven fretted and Laura checked sieve cascades at the spoil processing station, he sat and waited. Perfectly happy to reflect that two days wasn't so long after sixty five thousand millennia.
He peered at the monitor for the thousandth time. Still nothing. He looked away deliberately. "Nanotech," he muttered. "Has to be. Probably doing a house clean - - - Getting things nice for the visitors."
"Say what Arnie?" Laura was stepping up through the open door. "Anything good on TV?"
"Not unless you're into Steve Warhol. Not even as exciting as that – At least he had lights going on and off." He looked up at Laura's puzzled face and grinned. "How was it for you? Watching rocks jiggle?"
"About what you'd expect." She smiled, a little tired. "Got to be done though. Waiting to find out what we're waiting for is getting kind of weird for me. How about you?"
"I guess I've pretty much lost it with weird stuff. Too many questions per pound of mystery. Just give me something to test. Sniff it, snap it in half, set fire to it – See what happens. That's me." He sneaked a glance at the monitor screen.
Laura laughed. "I came in to see if you'd seen Steven. He's turned off his set again."
"Oh, I'd leave him to it if I were you. You know. Wait for him to relax, and it'll probably all start up again." Another glance over his shoulder. "Laura. Look at that - - -."
"Steven! What the hell is he doing - - - ?"
Seen on the monitor, Steven was walking slowly up the tunnel. He stopped just outside the range of a battery of sampling sensors, and hunkered down against the wall.

Arnold peered and frowned. "God knows. We've run every passive test I know of, and all the stuff we've got up there is working. I'm surprised at me, but I seem to be happy to wait. Now that *is* weird."

"No active sampling." Laura was frowning too." Not without all the passives completed. That was the decision wasn't it? I agreed with that. And so did Steven."

"He's not actually doing anything Laura. Just sitting there as far as I can see. Zoom in if you want."

"Why don't I trust him? Even now I don't trust him not to be crazy."

"He doesn't trust himself. Cliché, but true." Arnold touched the zoom-in himself. "Oh shit, I think he's crying. Doesn't he know there's no privacy on this planet any more?" He pulled the camera view back and switched to another link.

Laura stepped away. "We don't mention it – Right?"

"Right enough,' said Arnold.

Much later, in the dead, early hours, Steven was struggling through the mad and boiling levels of a bad dream. Tendrils of desire and fear tore at him as he struggled to understand the doorway. He'd just realised, to his own distant amusement, that they were pulling him away from the white wall, not into it, when he was woken up by the buzzer. He groaned, rolling over. The buzzer didn't stop.

"Was that fucking necessary?" he muttered. "Mad bloody nightmares, and then - - What the - - ?"

He twisted out of bed. Saw a light come on in the next unit. Just as Arnold burst through the connecting door. Fighting his way into a heavy jacket. "The alarm. Laura's awake I think - - ."

"I saw her light come on," said Steven, thoroughly awake now. "You got your cards?"

Arnold nodded, gestured at the door and stumbled back through with a heavy lurch against the frame. Three minutes later they were charging up the slope in a Humvee, the big vehicle cresting the edge of the terrace like a turbocharged earth mover. Steven slewed it to a stop, narrowly missing the aircabin steps, and its' diesel generator cut to silence. He sat, fixed, looking straight ahead through the wide, flat windscreen. Arnold was already out and up the steps, cursing as he swiped the door with the Humvee's start-card by mistake.

Laura swung back around the open cab door. "Come on Steven. Before Arnie hurts himself." She snorted with nervous laughter, pointing at Arnold, who wrestled his own shirt for possession of the pass card hung around his neck. More lights were coming on in the encampment below.

Steven nodded past Laura, as he opened his own door. "Should have used the batteries. Forgot and started the diesel."

"Never mind. We were never going to keep them away from their own show were we."

"No – I guess not. Just wanted a bit of time."

They met at the front of the Humvee's huge grill and hurried after Arnold, into the aircabin. Steven was in a state of surreal anxiety, still half dreaming his nightmare, wondering how they'd persuaded the ARPA team that an overnight watch wasn't necessary. Paranoia clutched at his stomach. Were they just falling for a bluff; being used as an expendable front line? DNM management, with Senator Alvin's help, had argued that they had the licence to explore the site, that there was no National Security issue, and that the existing team should apply their expertise to the excavation. Now Steven felt he was just a pawn in a devious game; and he'd dragged the others in with him.

Laura caught his arm as he swayed in the open doorway. "Steven, what's wrong. Are you okay? Look at the wall."

"Wall? What wall? Oh – The chamber."

She pulled him over to the console. They both peered over Arnold's hunched shoulders and all three stared in silent amazement, as Arnold zoomed the camera inwards. The tiny, pin-prick hole had enlarged. It was now about a foot across, almost imperceptibly enlarging as they watched, and the rim of the hole formed a rounded, slightly shiny bead; as if the material was melting and rolling evenly outwards from the centre. The air around it shimmered with heat. An outer circle of glowing, incandescent orange expanded with the hole.

"How long Arnie," said Steven, without looking away from the screen.

"No idea – If it s exponential it'll fry the tunnel. It's already pretty warm by the look of it. Otherwise - - Hang on. Ah, that's what I thought - - - ."

"What Arnie? What did you think?" Laura's voice was high.

"Look. It's changing. The warning circle – It's splitting."

From six points around the circle small squares of orange were moving outwards. A perceptibly faster movement than the circles' expansion.

"Do we go in or stay?" said Laura. "Are we recording?"

"We've got everything since the camera went up there," said Arnold patiently. "I'd say stay. They've been patient enough. For a very long time. Steven?"

"Stay I guess. I thought the door or whatever would open quickly – So much for early rising."

"Go in. Grab the goodies, and run for it, eh - - -?"

"Something like that - - -."

Outside there was a rushing sound, and something heavy slid and crunched through stones. Dust blew in as Arnold turned around. "No lights, and they did switch to silent running. Old habits die hard I guess. Good evening friends, have you come to get to know us better at last?"

Two women and a man were stepping into the cabin with studied and professional nonchalance; all of them known to the team from occasional contact around the camp and an initial briefing when the new tunnelling had been started. Tamzin Holt and Mark Gottenburg represented the Advanced Research Projects Agency, ARPA, and Elle Turlington was from NRO, the National Reconnaissance Office. Elle's specialty was Geophysics analysis. She swept back her blonde hair and tied it with a band, obviously having been woken at short notice as well. She stepped up to the console, ignoring Arnold's greeting. "Interesting. How long's this been happening?"

"About twenty minutes I'd say," he said. "We've been watching in real time since we got here."

"Any idea what the process is?"

Arnold squinted at the screen. "A couple of theories. I'd like to get a closer look."

Steven glared at the intruders. "You're not going to call in an assault then?" His tone was bitter, bordering on petulance. "Just in case there's some Dinosauran Special Forces behind the door."

Elle looked at him levelly. "That's not how we operate. Why do you think you're all still here?"

"I've no idea. No-one got around to telling us."

"Steven - - -," warned Laura.

A thin smile from Elle. "Perhaps because you found the visuals. And stuck your neck way out about them - - -." She turned to Tamzin and Mark. "What's the status on your mobile rig?"

"Ready to go," said Mark. "Has been for days."

Tamzin moved closer to the screen. Glanced at Arnold. "Nanotech – That process confirms it for me. What I can't figure is why the whole structure seems to have been moving through the rock?"

Arnold assessed her with a sharp stare of reluctant respect. "We're not sure it has are we? The whole support structure is pretty well trashed by the geology."

"You're not going to admit it are you Arnold, not even now. That last drift goes way beyond any strata deformation, and you know it!"

"I'm neither admitting nor denying anything Tamzin. The whole thing is open to all sorts of interpretations. All we know is what we see, to quote a famous philosopher."

"Zen Buddhist was he?" said Mark.

Arnold shook his head in mock despair. "All I'm saying is, we've no previous experience for this. Research doesn't get any more refined – Look, why don't we just watch the show?"

The radiating cut lines had moved nearly five feet out from the central hole in the white wall. The orange warning squares were beginning to widen to oblongs, and seemed to be slowing down.

The six people clustered around the monitor screen were silent; watching intently as the strange process moved to its' next phase. Each orange oblong split into two squares, and each pair separated to move along new tracks; the cut lines following exactly. These new lines now began moving out, and around, to describe the partial outline of a broad archway. An archway with a flattened base and rounded lower corners.

Mark Gottenburg went outside, and returned with flasks of coffee; which calmed the atmosphere between the two groups of observers. Laura looked at him quizzically – Had he known there'd be a gathering this morning? Mark saw the look. "Just a guess Laura. Most days I brew up, and take a Humvee out along the river. A peace of mind thing to start the day off right."

Laura smiled. "You drink two flasks of coffee every morning?"

"No – When I'm fit for human company I come back to camp and kick start the others." He grinned. "Sometimes they're even grateful."

"Well, this lady's grateful today – Sort of normal amongst all the madness. Coffee at dawn."

"You make it sound like a last request."

Laura retreated a little into thought. She bit her lip. "Even with the visuals - -. I mean, we're going into the unknown aren't we?"

She was alarmed at having said too much, but Mark appeared not to notice "Yeah – Into the breach for the first time. What do you think we'll find in there?"

Laura just shook her head. Took another long sip of coffee. Mark turned back to the screen. "Hey. Look - - -."

The archway was almost complete. Pairs of orange squares were meeting and merging. Then split apart, sideways, again; as the cut lines joined together. Everyone stared hard. But nothing else happened. Just segmented sections, within an archways' outline, and the dark central blackness of a hole. The orange squares had faded to white, and the tunnel was silent in the soft light of luminant panels along its' roof.

ARPA's Centipede walked forwards. All three main sections locked together. Eighteen legs lifting and stepping rhythmically; its' forward manipulators raised in a parody of threat or appeasement.

"Why isn't it waving a white flag," muttered Steven. He was furious with himself for not realising ARPA would have this level of technology waiting in the wings. And he was still aching from lack of sleep; reluctantly admiring Marks' ability to merge into the machine.

Mark spoke from inside his VR feedsuit and helmet. "Your wish is our command – This'll have to do." Centipede snaked sideways to pick up a section of white plastic; part of a broken conveyor shield. It moved on again, waving its' white triangle.

"Funny Mark – Very funny," said Tamzin wryly. "How about 'Take me to your Leader'?"

"Er, don't see why not - - - ." The manipulators flexed. Began to scratch with a diamond point.

"Can it Mark. Christ's sake - - - !"

Centipede paused its' scratching. The arm holding the plastic threw it to one side. "Just trying to keep it light - - -."

"Well just try to keep it on track." Tamzin glared at Mark in his feedsuit. "Think you'll fit through that hole?"

"Not sure – Probably. Sensors tell me yes."

Centipede was close to the white wall. The forward section lifted up, six legs folding under, and extended its' head. The manipulator turret retracted its' arms and slid back, and light beams lit between the stereo cameras. Mark walked forward on his remaining twelve legs. "Stereo to minimum. All sensors running. Gas analysis gives normal. Slight excess of helium. No other traces. If everyone's agreed, I'm going in - - -."

The rear six legs stepped sideways, pulling their support panels outwards to widen the track. The floating battery pack slid back to act as a counterbalance and the mid-section curved up, legs folding in turn, to lift the head higher. Mark now stepped carefully onwards on only six feet. Centipede's head centred on the hole. Swayed very slightly. "No worries. Just checking the depth perception."

The edges of the hole were surprisingly thin, no more than two inches, when the heads' lights reached them. Elle and Arnold turned to the main screen together.

"Here we go," said Arnold. Elle nodded.

Everything happened very fast. And also in slow motion. Mark unfolded the forward pair of legs on his mid-section, to test a touchdown on the rim of the hole. As he switched to the rear cameras, set on wide stereo, he was briefly disorientated. "Damn – They're supposed to correlate. Drive must have - - - -." Centipedes' head moved smoothly through the hole, the extended legs gripped, and the lower segment of the white wall bowed inwards an inch. A puff of dust fell from the cut lines. Centipede shivered.

Tamzin put out a hand to steady Mark, and stopped herself just in time. She breathed in. "Easy Mark. Can you move?"

"Don't know. Feels like it's very light. Didn't expect it to shift so easy – Damn - - - !"

Without warning, all the segments of the archway fell. Six triangular shapes falling around, and from under, Centipede's segments. It flinched and swayed in response to Mark's reaction. By the time he tried to step back it was all over. A fine dust cloud filled the open doorway. The remaining centre legs flicked out, and Centipede dropped. "Shit! It's alright. I'm okay - - It's okay." Mark's body tensed in the suit, as he forced himself to move slowly.

Elle swung round. "You're clear. Go to the Head."

"Yeah, sure. No problem – No red lights - -." The main screen flicked to the forward camera view. The manipulators curved forward, and tested one fallen segment. It rocked slightly.

"Look up man. Give us a view." Arnold's voice was sharp with tension. He swung back to the screen, leaning close. Centipede walked ahead a couple of feet, balancing easily on the panels underfoot, then looked up into the central chamber.

Curving struts to the right; branching back to the chamber wall in organic, art-deco arcs. And outwards into gloom, towards the centre, maybe twenty feet away. Further away, to the left, a matching structure seen in profile. More struts above, sweeping down from the dome. The floor a curious, faintly mottled, surface, covered in tiny, regular patterns of blisters.

Mark whistled, the sound thinning to silence in the open space. An echo on the threshold of hearing. "Anechoic, almost. I'm going ahead – Okay?"

Tamzin nodded, then remembered to speak. "Cautions – Check above and below. Steven?"

"No – I mean, no problem. We're here at last - - -."

Centipede moved. And the light started. Right across the dome, the floor, and even the sweeping struts, a faint glow was rising within every surface. Maybe twelve feet away, circling the centre, strange clusters of fine, stalagmite-like structures were just visible. Seeming to gleam more brightly when Mark turned towards them.

"It's very clean," said Laura. "I mean spider webs are out I guess – I thought we'd have to dig through more matrix."

Steven was drumming his fingers on the console. "Should we be trusting that floor? I don't know?"

"No reason not to," said Arnold. "I guess that's what Centipede's for, right?"

"We still don't want to trash it," murmured Tamzin. She was transfixed by the view on the screen. "Lots of bucks in that beastie. And no useful back-ups. Zoom it in Mark – Go for the bullseye."

"You got it Boss. Floor feels fine by the way."

Centipede flowed smoothly forward, its' view sweeping ahead, as the light level continued to rise. It was impossible to tell if the 'stalagmites' apparent upward growth was an illusion or actual. The domes' floor passed under the central cube; the focus of its' web of supporting struts. The cube itself was exactly as seen on the dinosauran visuals. It hung about five feet above the plane of the floor.

Mark slowed up as he approached the ring of spiky, fluorescent clusters; which circled about eight feet from the centre. They were two or three feet apart and rose to a maximum height of about thirty inches.

"Little faery castles," said Mark. "Survey or sample?"

"I'd leave everything alone for now," said Arnold. "Are those things growing or not?"

"If they were, they've stopped now." Mark was circling the nearest cluster. "Think they'd chime if I touched?" He brushed one manipulator gently upwards against one spine. It flexed very slightly, but nothing else happened. The light level seemed to have stabilised. Centipede stood under the armoured cube at the central chambers' centre. It was the only part of the whole structure that wasn't radiating a gentle glow of light. Neither was it giving off heat, radiation or any other signature.

Mark had extended the rear legs again, and was carefully lifting up to view the nearest side face of the cube. He briefly switched to the rear cameras, and swivelled them to look back across the floor. The archway, and the tunnel beyond, looked shadowy and ill-lit compared to the domes' interior. They also looked to be a long way away. Then he was back beside the cube, his own lights highlighting the dull surface texture. The face was inset about an inch, curving at its' edges to meet a flat frame, maybe three inches wide.

Mark scanned the exact dimensions. "We don't know what their standard measure was do we. I'm surprised they've not shown us their platinum metre. Unless this is it of course. Amazingly close if it is. Only nine mil out."

"Don't touch the studs," Steven warned him. "Just do sensors and visual for now."

Mark moved to his right, a face without studs, and then on around and below the cube. Finally he lifted to maximum and just managed to see across its' top. "Studs to three faces – None on top, below, or the fourth face." He lowered to the floor and backed away. "I'm coming out – I'm on the reserve for power. Should we switch to microwaves?"

"Not unless we have to." Tamzin looked round the group. "Yes? Okay Mark, come on out. Run it to the second shear. I think it's safe to pick up from there."

Centipede reversed out across the floor, navigated from its' rear cameras, and towards the archway. From the tunnel view it seemed very small, somehow looking far more alien than the space it was moving across. It reached the arch, dropped over the shallow sill, and passed out of view behind the camera. Mark relaxed visibly in his feedsuit.

"The lights!" Arnold called out. "The light's are going out."

Mark snaked to a stop. The head cameras showed the archway fading down to blackness. He put the machine into a rapid U-turn and powered away again at maximum leg speed.

After a day of analysing Centipedes' data the combined team was ready to put a volunteer into the central chamber. There were no indications of any risk – No radiation, toxins or any other hazard that they could detect. All they could reasonably expect, from the data, was space, light and air. Steven had argued that he should go in first, and no-one had any real disagreement with his wish. Except Laura. She said that both a man and a woman should go, in the best traditions of frontier exploration.

So, just over two days after the archways' opening, Laura and Steven stood side by side at the threshold. The rest of the team had set up a station at the second shear point, just out of direct view, with new cameras in the final approach to the arch. By mutual agreement, no weapons were allowed.

Everyone had suited up. Steven and Laura wore umbilicals that were both lifelines and fibre optic channels. Each had helmet lights and a shoulder mounted camera.

Mark was making a final check of the coiled white cables and the data links. He stood behind the waiting couple, aware of their nervous impatience, and inspected the harnesses and fibre optic connectors. Then laid a glove on each free shoulder. "What're you waiting for? You got a green light – go!"

"I know," muttered Steven. "Count to three thousand and check canopy – I've done my parachute training!"

Laura laughed nervously, and looked over her shoulder at Mark. "One jump, and he thinks he's an expert. You going to be alright yourself?"

"I'm fine Laura. Anything even looks at you, I'll haul you guys out, or come running. Don't worry about me."

Laura nodded, looked at Steven, and saw his expression of calm readiness behind the faceplate. Saw his lips move. "We're the dreamers, right Laura?"

"Yeah, sure. Life's a dream - - ."

"Let's go then – See you at the party."

87 Tertiary

They stepped up the sill and walked forward, beams from their helmet lights sweeping the floor ahead of them. From their higher viewpoint the surface looked subtly different and somehow less substantial. As if it was paper thin; only a blackness below stopping it being translucent.

Steven suddenly felt as if they walked on the thin skin of a bottomless fluid. He stopped. Reached out to Laura. "You happy about this floor? Mark said it felt fine, but - - -."

She nodded, shivering. "It's not rational I know, just a feeling. Like I'm in a glass-bottom boat over a deep ocean - - -?"

Steven stepped sideways a distance, and nervously bounced his weight, flexing his knees. Then risked a tiny jump and a stamp. The floor seemed as solid as concrete – Why was he terrified of splintering through a sugar crystal crust?

"The light," Laura whispered. "The light's coming back."

They both switched out their own lights, without speaking, and waited. Looking up, and out, and all around. Even with all his sophisticated sensors and stereo Tele-Presence there was something that Mark had missed; something just behind the curtain of consciousness. Steven whispered in turn. "Ever been to Muir Woods? The redwood trees. Feels like they're aware. The air re-transmits human voices - - -."

"No, but this place knows we're here – It's not just the light."

"You Guys okay? You're neither of you transmitting – Speak to us." Arnold's voice was tense with worry. A silent look between them; neither realised they'd turned off their audio. Steven switched back on. "No problem Arnie. Just getting a first impression."

"You turned off your lights. We lost you, even on infra-red."

"We're fine Arne." Laura's voice was calm. "Can you see the dome-light yet?"

"Yeah, we just see you now. Had to stop Mark coming in after you. Steven?"

"Sorry folks. We're going to the cube now - - -."

On the screens at the second shear, the two suited figures walked into the rising light. From the tunnel camera the space they moved in seemed far larger than measurement said it was. The spatial illusion was very powerful and subtly disturbing. Each observer assumed they were alone with their tension, so no-one took time to mention it. Mark stood back from the open archway to allow the cameras a clear field of view inwards. He looked as wired as an athlete on blocks.

Steven and Laura had reached the cube. They circled slowly inside the ring of stalagmites, taking care not to snag their umbilicals, and stood behind it. The patterns of raised studs, on three of the cubes' vertical faces, were exactly as the dinosauran visual and schematic had shown them. Apart from Senator Alvin and Bill McCandless the only other person who'd seen the opening sequence was Arnold.

In unspoken agreement both Laura and Steven switched out of the audio circuit again. Steven seemed angry. "Let's get Arnold in here – We should do this now. Get it over with. Whatever else is here will wait."

Laura opened her hands. "Okay Steven, okay. As it happens I agree. I don't know why, but I do."

Steven nodded curtly and switched in again. "Arnie, we could use your opinion on this. Everything's safe in here Mark. You take over from Arnold on the screens – We might have another chip in here."

"I didn't see anything - - -." Mark sounded uncertain.

"No, well, robots are still robots. Even Centipede."

Mark moved unwillingly back down the tunnel. The fragile bond between the two groups suddenly seemed broken. He'd seen no chips, he'd been looking. And Centipede was as good as being there.

Arnold gave him a friendly tap on the shoulder, as they passed close in the narrow twist at the shears' end. "Cheer up Mark. Centipede's still the best." He looked closely at the younger man. Decided to risk it. "My guess is we'll find enough toys in there to keep everyone happy for a hundred years, okay?"

Mark nodded cautiously, uncertain of a response. He watched Arnold go, then turned back, around the corner. Elle and Tamzin were looking up. They'd heard the exchange. He shrugged his puzzlement, and took Arnold's place at the screens.

Arnold reached the archway, and stepped out into the central chamber without breaking stride. 'All in a days' work,' he thought, 'Hope they're all suitably impressed.'

"Here Arnie, on this back face," said Steven. "What do you think? These studs seem to have a pattern." Arnold raised an eyebrow. Steven nodded 'Yes'.

"Well, I - -. Yeah, I'd say there's a pattern to it."

Elle broke in. "What happened to 'look but don't touch', and where's this chip you found?"

"False alarm," said Steven. "Thought I saw one in one of those rod clusters Just a shadow."

Arnold nearly tripped on Laura's umbilical. "Damn! Sorry Laura. What do you say Steven? Give t a go?"

Steven rolled his eyes in exasperation. But he also smiled.

"Give what a go?" called Tamzin. "What are you guys up to in there?"

Laura switched in. "We think we've got an opening sequence. Something we both saw in our dreams."

"You only just got in there," said Tamzin. "Oh, hell. Whatever you think. This seems to be your pile of rocks. Push every button in the place."

Steven was grinning across the top of the cube. All his earlier fears had evaporated. Whatever was in the cube, the ARPA and NRO, and any other set of letters in the US of A, could have it. He was convinced, against all reason, that something else was going on in this chamber, and Laura seemed to agree. They needed the time.

He switched out. "Remember the schematic? Let's go for it."

Arnold looked worried for the first time that day. He wasn't sure he remembered the sequence. Easy enough mnemonic he thought, 'Water, water everywhere and not a drop to drink.' Two hydrogen plus one oxygen. 'Just can't remember the damned pattern.'

"Take it easy Arnie." Steven sounded calmer than he looked. "Hydrogen for us guys, Oxygen for the lady. Remember?"

Arnold nodded. He thought back to the conversation. Put himself in front of the screen; a pattern overlaid on a view of the cube. 'Goddamned games,' he thought. 'Why not just have a red button on top of the blasted thing?"

Steven apparently guessed his thoughts. "They were looking for people like us Arnie. Simple, dedicated, liberal, more interested in the long term view - - -."

"It's okay Steve, I got the message. Got the memory. Why don't you just count to three?"

He did so, and on his count they all pressed the remembered sequence of studs on their respective faces of the cube. Just a half second delay and then an almost soundless and impossibly smooth movement. All of them stepped back instinctively.

"Holy Shit – It's working! First time out, and it works." Arnold was staring in astonishment at the fourth face of the cube. "Just like a bloody filing cabinet." He saw Laura's look. "Never mind. You're too young."

The fourth face was sliding outwards, exposing tightly packed, horizontal racks of chips on a rotary carrier. A simple dot numbering system marked the position of each chip in its' sleeve.

Arnold gently touched a rack, and the carrier clicked round with a precise and easy motion. "How in hell is this possible? This place looks like a maintenance crew ran a check last week."

"Nanotech?" said Laura. "I thought you agreed with Tamzin on that – Intelligent materials and self-repair systems. Aren't we close to it ourselves?"

"Yeah, close. But when you actually see it - - -." Arnold was looking at the spiky, crystal-like growths surrounding the space they stood in. "Utility fog," he muttered. "This place wasn't open space for sixty five million years – The wraps only just came off. All this is new."

Steven was looking uneasily around and upwards. The sensation of standing on thin ice was becoming almost unbearable again, his intuition screaming at him to get everyone back to the tunnels' solidity. 'Just a standard panic attack,' he thought. 'Why does everything have to come through as negatives?' He switched to talk to the ARPA team. "We're coming out. Anything on your sensors?"

Tamzin called back; an edge of irritation in her voice. "Nothing – Just us turning to blue cheese, as they say on the moon. Was it something we said?"

"We were busy with the cube. It's open."

"We know – We just got it on Laura's camera."

Steven nodded slowly, looking down to the floor again, as he searched for the source of his unease. There was something in the texture, the fabric of its' structure, that was as alien as it was indefinable. He stamped one foot, pushed against a cube support strut, and leaned back to look up to the apex of the dome. Nothing. No clue. 'What's wrong is my own bad nerves,' he thought. 'This place deserves my trust, and I can't do it – Can't trust anything or anyone.'

Then he realised that both Arnold and Laura were staring at him, and his mood vanished. He grinned, which confused them even more, and signalled towards the tunnel entry with a sweeping gesture. Arnold sniffed in mock disdain, turning towards the tunnel – And vanished into the floor. Before either of the others could react he had re-appeared several feet away; standing tensed in a comical attitude of readiness. "Interesting," he said. "Very interesting A fog of illusion. Definitely."

After three days of frantic activity all around them, Steven, Laura and Arnold were taking a late afternoon break. Their usual meeting place, on the end of the rock terrace, was relatively quiet; the canyon below filling with men and machines again, as the ARPA and NRO teams packed up and pulled out. They'd had very little time to discuss their experiences in the central chamber. Arnold had persuaded the others that it would be better to wait anyway, hinting that he should keep silent until everything else quietened down; somehow his 'disappearance' into the floor hadn't been logged by any of the sensors, or the watching ARPA team.

So Steven and Laura watched impatiently as a giant ARPA cargo disc hovered just below them; lifting crates and cabins and vehicles up into its' hold. And an NRO tiltrotor sat on the pad with its' propellers idling. Both ARPA and NRO seemed to have taken the bait, pushing the DNM team aside once the cube had been opened. They'd obviously believed that the cache of chips was all there was to be found, making no secret of their claim to be the ones researching the contents. After a brief search for other chambers the decision to pull out had been made, and DNM was left in charge of any further excavation for fossil material.

Laura was doubly impatient; waiting for Michael and his father to arrive on the next flight in. Michael's links to media sources had put him in some danger, but was also the means by which Senator Alvin had kept a channel open to the whole project; an implied threat of publicity and accountability questions protecting their rights of access.

The cargo disc cleared and lifted its' load frame, and the bay doors slid flush with the lower hull. Turning it gracefully on its' axis, and rising level with the terrace, the captain dipped his giant machine in salute and powered upwards; with a last wave through the control rooms' curved screen, beneath the forward rim. Laura waved back and laughed, relieved that they would soon have their site back to themselves. "Nice guys, but noisy." She pointed down to the helipad. "Look, there goes Deputy Dog and his shadow."

Jim Larson, with his anonymous Washington contact, was walking out to board the tiltrotor, astonishing all three watchers by lifting his arm in a brief, and apparently genuine salute. The cabin door closed before they could respond.

"Well, I guess he thinks he got what he came for," said Steven, waving back anyway. "For all we know, he could be right."

"But then again, maybe not," said Arnold. "Time to show and tell I think."

As the tiltrotor lifted off within a halo of dust he shoved one hand deep into an inside pocket. At two hundred feet the machine kicked up its' tail, levelled its' engine pods and sped towards Salt Lake City, beyond the distant mountains.

Arnold watched it go, and handed Steven a package that looked like a flattened, silvery sea purse. "From my quick turn as a Peppers' Ghost impression – I think it works as a shield from sensor scans. This was in my suit when I came back up. Something under that floor is an expert reverse pickpocket. Don't know why it chose me though."

"You were the one without an umbilical, maybe that was it." Steven turned the package, holding it up to the light. "What do you suppose this is?" He shivered in the last faint breeze from the departing aircraft. "Too many mysteries for me."

Laura pointed away into the distance. "Something else coming in."

"Let's hope it's only Dan and Michael," said Steven. "I've already got used to it being quiet again round here."

"Some hope with the Alvins," laughed Laura. "It is them, look. That's Michael's latest love."

The ducted fan AirSpeed approached rapidly and swung to a whispering hover in front of them. A sleek, flattened disc with four large fans around a triangular cabin; the drivers' seat projected forward in a rounded wedge of glazing. Michael at the controls, Senator Dan Alvin and an unknown passenger in the seats behind him. Michael waved, and whirled the machine in a tight circle, then slid it sideways and dropped neatly in to a landing beside the aircabins.

"Showing off," said Laura. "Definitely a boy with a toy."

They walked back along the terrace to meet their visitors. Dan Alvin was climbing out with a shake of his head. "The boy thinks he's flying for a circus. Get your guts untangled Mike and we'll see what these folks want to tell us."

A slightly stooped, elderly man stepped out and brushed a hand over his short, white hair. "Wildest ride I've had in years Dan – Nearly bought one of these things myself."

Michael was grinning as Laura ran forward to hug him, and his father smiled at their reunion. Then stepped forwards. "Folks, I'd like you to meet Professor Mike Magee – He's got a long standing interest in what you've found here, and he's helped me a lot with getting it clearer in my own mind."

He introduced everyone in turn, noting Steven's slight reserve, and waved toward the cave entrance. "Tim McHawne was the link – Mike here taught a course at his mine school just a few years back."

The Professor laughed; a younger voice than his years. "A bit longer back than a few Dan, but Tim's a good man. One of the few who thought before he laughed – And kept his eyes open for a retired madman." He looked keenly at Steven. "But now I'm the one doesn't believe what he's hearing - You have my sympathy sir."

Dan put a hand to the Professors' shoulder. "Mike's had a theory of dinosaur civilisation for years. No-one in the scientific community wanted to hear it till now, so I'm hoping you'll find yourselves like-minded." He tilted his head to Steven. "He's also become a friend. Thinks like I do. So I trust him."

Mike lifted both hands for caution. "We'll see Dan. They'll make up their own minds. I've had some practise at this, but I thank you anyway."

Several hours later the atmosphere in the outer aircabin was relaxed and friendly. Mike Magee had displayed a paege full of anomalies from centuries of mining records; impossible finds in a whole range of strata that the scientific community had passed over or ignored. If it didn't fit it didn't exist. Steven was nodding in sympathy, and Arnold had already found a fellow enthusiast for the mysterious body of the earth. Michael and Laura were awkward with each other after their long separation, and had wandered off outside to talk.

Steven found himself opening up and establishing trust in their new visitor. And he was desperate to investigate the strange package that had been 'planted' on Arnold during his brief 'sink or swim' into the floor of the central chamber. Mike Magee was sitting open-mouthed as he saw the dinosauran visuals for the first time, this was so far beyond his expectations that vindication of his theory was overlaid by pure amazement. To him the reality was stunning.

Steven pulled Arnold aside. "The package Arnie. I think it's time to open it up – What do you say?"

Arnold nodded slowly. "These guys have been our allies, and they'll be our protection Steven. They've got my vote - Who else do we trust?" He dug into his pocket again. 'And this, I think, has to be a ticket to the Yellow Brick Road." He laid the rounded, silvery oblong down in open view. "First thing though, we have to find out how to unwrap it."

Laura and Michael stood hand in hand, gazing down into the Little Snake River canyon. The shallow slopes below them looked battered and empty after the recent removal of so much human equipment. Laura's relief had turned into a contradictory sadness now that they had come full circle. "I love the quiet, but it seems kind of lonely now. And the real madness starts from here is my guess."
"I don't get it Laura – I thought the project was over, bar the odd bit of old bone work."
Laura cuffed him, then took his hand again. "Your old Dad thinks better than you young man – We may be just at the beginning." She smiled at his startled look. "Arnold found something in the central chamber. We've not checked it out yet, but it could be the key." Her voice dropped. "All that stuff in the cube really was just a blind – The main message is still in there somewhere." She looked worried suddenly, and squeezed his hand.
Michael pulled her round to face him. "You're right of course, like always. Dan had that look in his eye – I should know how to spot it by now. For a tough old pragmatist he's got the intuitions of an old-time Indian Chief." He looked round at the AirSpeed, rocking gently on its' struts in the light breeze. "That's why he was so keen to get Mike Magee out here. I'm sorry Laura, I never really bought all that stuff about dreams and diversions."
"It's okay Mike, what we already got takes some believing. That's why we've been left here to find more dinosaurs - The special people always turn out to be conservative thinkers."
"You think I'm like them?" Michael looked genuinely worried.
"No, I think you've got a built in caution about things you can't see or prove. Too much madness in the media already." She turned back. "Do you need

to tie that thing down, the wind's getting up. And we're hoping you can stay over?"

"I'll let it charge for a bit, then roll it into the overhang if I can?"

"No problem. It is an amazing looking machine Mike."

"I could give you a demo tomorrow if you want? But let's go look at what you folks have been finding."

Arnold was arguing with Steven, while their new guests stood rather awkwardly on the sidelines. All four were gathered in the experimental corner of the aircabin. Arnold was leaning onto a workbench, gripping the edge tightly with both hands. "Well, I say we go back in right now. This has to be some sort of key. Either way, it's the only way we're going to find out." Arnold glanced at Laura, as she and Michael came back in. "What say Laura? Have a look at this." He held up a loop of silvery metal with dark bands spaced around its' rim. "We put the package in the NMR scanner, and this unfolded. Or grew. Whatever."

Steven waved one hand in tired exasperation. He was unusually nervous, and unwilling to make any decisions. "Damn it Arnie, that thing's still warm. Should we be handling it without doing some more tests?"

"But look what the scanner did," said Arnold. "Next time we get a magic lamp? We don't need to mess with it any more."

Dan Alvin laid a hand on Steven's arm before he could reply. "I'm as scared as a cat myself round all this. But you've got the diversion up and running." He stared at the metal loop. "Why not take Michael with you and check this thing out. We can keep a look out for your departed friends – I'd say they're going to be back."

"They think if there's anything else to find, we're going to do it for them again," said Laura. "They can't have fallen for it completely."

"And they'll have left some eyes and ears behind to be sure?" Michael was desperate to be involved. "Bill McCandless gave me a good, steep course in sniffing. And some new tools." He turned before anyone could object. "I'll go see how the AirSpeed's breathing and get the kit."

Steven just nodded in uneasy acceptance, and Arnold grinned in approval. "One more for the Yellow Brick Road!" He looked annoyed briefly. "Oh, take it easy Steve, I was the one fell through the ice. I'm no scientist to say it, but I knew I could trust that chamber."

Steven looked down at the metal loop. "Take no notice of me Arnie. I'm just passing a few bricks of my own. I'm not getting any better used to magic and mystery." He straightened up. "You and Mike are okay to stay here and keep watch then Dan?"

"We surely are young sir. Go find your destiny, as some portentous old fart did say."

Mid-morning in the tunnel and Michael was wandering around, pretending to be aimless, as he looked for hidden devices in the remaining ARPA equipment. The second shear point of the tunnel seemed gloomy and forbidding without the conveyors running, and only emergency access lighting left on.

Steven was peering suspiciously at the dormant Centipede, wondering why such a valuable tool had been left behind. Arnold and Laura were stripping com sets and sensors from a line of hanging suits; everyone had agreed to trust to dinosauran technology and go for freedom of movement.

A tone sounded in Michael's ear and he deliberately tripped over a cable, falling heavily onto a small crate and smashing it open. He ripped a lead away from the tiny spycam inside. "Got you my little friend. Go back to your masters and die!" He waved to the others. "Best I can do folks. I think that's the last one, but what the hell – They'll probably be on their way over now anyway. How long do you think we've got?"

Steven looked over his shoulder. "An hour at most, probably less. Nice work though Mike. Now all we've got to do is find a door that doesn't exist and remember a combination we've forgotten."

Arnold smiled to himself, then at the others. "Cheer up Steve. I really think this should go with you.' He offered the enigmatic loop of metal. In the dim tunnel light it looked insubstantial, and faintly luminous. "Faery gold. For the Master of the Tunnels."

Steven took the thing with a lingering reluctance. He smiled, looking up the slope. "Then the doorway beckons my friends. I think it's now or never – Good luck to us all."

The others clapped silently; irony turning to a sense of shared adventure and danger as they stared into the unknown.

The mood shattered instantly, as Centipede came to life.

"Dammit," muttered Steven. "I knew we should have bagged that things' head."

"As you wish TunnelMaster." Michael twisted away, as the machine reared up beside him, and quickly planted a black disc under its' forward segment; just out of reach of the manipulators. "Just a little reserve that Bill thought we might need."

Centipede froze in mid-air, its' rear legs slowly sagging, and it folded against the tunnel wall. Michael stepped back. "Bit disappointing really. I'd hoped for sparks and screaming."

"That does it for me – Far too subtle." said Arnold. "Into the breach it is."

He led the way up to the arch, and stepped into the central chamber. Peering forward, even as the first faint glow of light began. As they all moved forward into the chamber Michael's mouth fell open, and he waved around and up, speechless.

"I know," whispered Laura. "Wait till Arnie does his trick again. Can you feel how weird the floor is?"

Michael nodded. "Faery gold was right. What the hell are those?" He pointed to the ring of crystal spine clusters.

"We don't know. We're all saying that a lot – It's why we're here I guess. I'm sure we'll find out soon enough."

But nothing happened immediately; the space was as eerily quiet as it had been before. The temperature felt coolly neutral without the insulation and barrier of a full suit. They gathered round the cube as the light came up to full. A few cables and sensors still hung from the open rotary carrier, and Steven pointed up to a camera slung from a support high up in the dome.

"Dead," said Michael. "It was slaved into Centipede on an optical link – The one I fell over."

"Just as well then, or the beast wouldn't have woken till we were already in here." Arnold was stooped over, searching for the section of floor that had briefly swallowed him. "Not a mark or a sign," he muttered. "Where do we start?" He moved further out and began to track to and fro, back towards the tunnel archway, rubbing his forehead to remember.

Michael and Laura circled away to examine spine clusters; trying to see if any one of them was different enough to be a marker, or a clue to the chambers' function.

Steven was juggling a torch into his right hand, to get a better view into the open cube, and nearly dropped the metal loop that was hanging round his wrist. Something about it still worried him, and he laid it carefully down on the floor beside him with a grimace of relief; its' weight felt as weird as the floors' illusion of solidity. He turned back and peered into the dark corners of the cube. Nothing. Just an empty space. His head cracked against the open edge when Arnold suddenly shouted:

"Steven! Beside you — the floor!"

Arnold was waving furiously at him, and he nearly stepped into the metal ring in confusion; whipping his foot away when he looked down. Then almost fell, arms windmilling, before one hand clutched the edge of a support. The ring was hissing, just on the threshold of hearing, and melting down into the floor from its' outside edge; blurring away like mercury into milk and very slowly swirling. The floor glowed briefly, a fading ring of luminance spreading out. Then the ring began to widen.

A bright bead of light was forming, like the end of an eclipse of the sun, as another circle started to appear. A disorienting impression of movement as the floor moved, or something under it moved, into a new alignment.

"I've got it!" breathed Laura. "The main sphere — What we couldn't see. The whole support structure is tilted."

Everyone had grabbed onto each other as they stared down, and the expanding ring met the sliding circle of a smooth, faintly glowing tube. It was evenly lit, with no apparent side openings, handholds, nor any means of telling how far downwards it extended. Steven shook his head in amazement.

Then, without any warning, he turned away and stepped backwards into the tube. Michael and Laura grabbed hold of him instinctively; long seconds passing before they realised he weighed nearly nothing. He was floating in front of them.

"I'm sorry – But I was *almost* certain."

Laura swore under her breath, and let go convulsively. Michael did the same, but more carefully; watching Steven drift down the tube away from them. They looked at each other, shrugged, and followed him; Laura first, and Michael beckoning as he sank out of sight. Arnold walked up casually to the impossible hole, held his nose, and stepped in. The tube snicked shut above him, and the ring fell around his neck, a cool band, as he gently floated down.

The tube flared out a little at its' open end, about five feet above a shallow, concave platform. The glowing surface of the bowl was opalescent and roughly seven feet in diameter.

Steven's feet appeared in the opening. His weight was restored just above the platform, catching him by surprise, so he folded at the knees; ducking out from under and stumbling slightly. Laura and Michael followed him down, stepping aside and watching for Arnold, who bounced neatly to a stop and stared around beyond the group. They were at the centre of an open mesh floor which stretched across the middle of a fifty foot spherical chamber. The mesh looked like a finely tensioned, shimmering net, but was as rigid as steel when Michael cautiously tested it.

"Seems strong enough. No reason why it wouldn't be I guess. What the hell are those?"

"Just what I was wondering," said Arnold. "Let's go see." Both their voices were pitched high, as if the atmosphere in this space was laced with helium. The whole interior was evenly lit by a soft glow, with no obvious source, and a very faint whistling sound came from somewhere beneath their feet. Arnold led the way to what Michael had pointed at.

Between the central platform and walls of the chamber seven identical units were set into the mesh floor, forming a nearly complete circle. They were rounded ovoids, standing nearly twelve feet in total, above and below the mesh. The shape of each unit above the floor was mirrored below it. They had a logical and functional look yet it was impossible to tell if they were furniture, decoration or machinery; they somehow had the quality of all three.

Completing the circle was an eighth object about five feet high above the floor, very subtle forms within its' structure giving it an apparent simplicity except that below the net of the floor it wasn't symmetrical. As the group edged towards it they realised the eerie sounds filling the chamber were actually coming from this object, or from somewhere around it.

Laura, in particular was drawn forwards; Michael moved to hold her back, but Steven caught his sleeve. "We've been alright so far – We still have to trust whatever is here."

Michael looked at him sharply, then nodded. They were both frightened and each acknowledged it in the other; a mutual surprise that the fear was somehow benign. They could control it, and see a way to accept wherever they were. Michael looked around. "But what the hell is this then – What is here?"

Steven shook his head. Laura had heard, and beckoned them over. She was touching both hands to angled hollows near the top of the eighth unit; standing very still, and quietly concentrating. The sound rose and became more tuneful as her fingers moved over invisible keyboards. "It's finding out what I like." She shut her eyes. "And how I feel. How I work. It's very weird, not like us, like people, but it's friendly."

"Like in your dreams?" asked Steven.

"Kind of – But it's emotions, not language. Not yet."

Arnold was waving from the far side of the floor, and Michael pulled Steven away this time. "Leave her – You're right, she'll be okay. At least it seems to be making sense to her."

They relaxed a little as they walked over. The floor held them up, and it was somehow less alarming to see down through its' apparent fragility to the lower half of the sphere. If it was the same sphere – How could they have fallen, and then arrived at the same level, with different fittings or furniture?

Arnold was puzzling the same problem. "What do you think guys? This has to be another sphere below, doesn't it – But how come it's not much bigger? Laura's never really explained her 'invisible shape' in the rocks, but all the scans imply a much larger space."

"What're you saying Arnie?" Steven pushed his palm along the wall. "We don't know what we're seeing, what it's made of, or what it's for."

"Well yeah, that much of what we don't know we do know." He walked back in towards the ring of objects. "I guess these hold some sort of answer, but you tell me."

"This all has to be new doesn't it," said Michael. "Something's been sitting here for millions of years, but all this was somehow on stand-by?"

"It has to be nanotech, nothing else fits." Arnold was leaning on the nearest unit. "This feels warm to me. I think it's only been built since we hit the wall of the upper sphere – Could still be building, whatever's inside here."

Steven stared closely at the surface beside Arnold. Something like a pale patina on bronze, but really nothing like it at all, or any other material he had ever seen. And maybe just a shadow of a handprint where Arnold had touched. He wasn't sure enough to say anything; touching the surface himself was almost like a taste or a smell, generating an emotion he couldn't identify. Alien, but not at all unpleasant.

Michael glanced back to Laura, and saw her lean forward, eyes still closed, as the sound suddenly rose to an impossible volume. It should have split their eardrums, but it didn't; the effect was more like plunging from air to water. Water at exactly the same temperature, that could somehow be breathed. Not like lucid dreaming either; their focus was enhanced rather than surreally altered. The three men walked quickly over and stood behind Laura – There didn't seem to be anything else to do.

"It's telling me how to hatch the eggs." Laura's voice sounded perfectly normal, within its' slightly heightened pitch, and she stood in a pose of euphoric relaxation. "Wait a little bit longer, then you should listen too. In case we're split up - If it's necessary later, we'll be able to forget."

Tertiary

They looked at each other, not speaking, almost understanding. Then Michael suddenly swung round – Something was happening to the seven identical units.

A section of each one appeared to be turning inside out. The effect was very confusing to the eye, not exactly in slow motion, but a process so unfamiliar that their perceptions were unable to resolve it. Once it had begun the transformation accelerated, and the sound rose so high it was out of range of their hearing. Each ovoid seemed to be continuously peeling back from a vertical line of flowing activity, and also hollowing inwards from the same divide.

Laura spoke again. "Don't worry about that. You all have to listen now." She stepped back, and guided Steven forward first, showing him where to place his hands. The hollows in the object re-formed slightly to fit the larger span of his fingers. Time was slowed for the whole group, as if they were travelling at extreme speed but still able to pick out every detail of the landscape they moved through; and each one somehow knew what the others experienced.

Michael, and then Arnold in turn, put their hands to the unit, and their minds into trusting whatever trial and transformation the sphere was asking of them. They knew they should question what was happening, but another part of them was willing to forgo any doubt or fear. A nervous tension that became aware of a kind of faith. The effect was to make all of them feel both very young and very old; childlike and wise without words.

Laura had wandered off after watching for a while, and circled around the equator of the space, peering down into the bowl below. There was nothing else to see, no mirror to the entry tube and no markings or divisions in the smooth surface. She laid down flat to the floor and felt it gently humming with sounds she could no longer hear. The mesh was too fine to put a finger through, but close to it seemed to have no weight or thickness at all.

"Laura! Come look." Michael's subdued shout was urgent with wonder. "I think this is what they were telling us about."

She pushed up, hands tingling, and ran back into the circle where the others stood looking all around in confused amazement. All seven ovoid units were shrinking inwards in strange, concentric halos of blurred motion; the lower section faster than the top. And the eighth object was unzipping itself between the two hollows; extruding some sort of circular box or container, with handles recessed into the rounded, upper edge. It lifted out on a stalk-like projection and was lowered to the floor.

Michael stooped down and lifted the lid. "Damn – An egg rack. Don't they just think of everything!" Inside was a spiral of seven recesses, each one surrounded by raised bumps and icons. "Do we know what these mean?" He laid the open lid down. "Actually, I think I do - - -."

No-one was listening; the ovoids had shrunk to nearly half their original size and were still changing shape. Neither organic nor machine, the casings unfurled and swung back; revealing simple egg shapes in floor mounted cradles.

Laura reached out to the nearest, and it chimed to the touch of her fingertip; a faint perfume of sound that told her it was safe to be picked up and moved. "The box," she said. "Put them all in the box." And the box chimed too; as all seven eggs were lifted and laid into the waiting spaces.

Time speeded up. The lid touched and pulled itself shut with a slight rotation, when Steven offered it into place. "We should go," he said. "Don't want any visitors seeing the way into here. I can't tell how long we've been away."

"Not as long as we think at a guess." Arnold ducked under the entry tube. "Oh, shit. Except for how do we call for an up car? The lid's come down to meet us."

"Round your neck Arnie," said Laura. "The way out. You're wearing it."

He nodded. "I knew that. Don't think I didn't." And lifted the ring cautiously upward. It flicked into place, and the tube was open; Arnold already rising, with his legs kicking an ungainly farewell. Next up was Laura, with the box wrapped in her arms; she floated slowly up to a bobbing stop, level with the floor in the upper chamber. Arnold offered a hand to steady her as she stepped off nothing, and staggered under the sudden weight she carried. Michael appeared and then Steven. As they stepped away the open hole hissed and began to close; slowly swirling inwards to reform the metal ring and seal within its' centre.

"Nano," muttered Arnold. He touched the toe of one boot to the ring. It slid sideways without resistance, and he risked one finger. It had a lingering warmth this time, but he picked it up anyway.

Michael was looking warily from the empty cube to the tunnel entry. "We should hide the evidence somehow." He hesitated. "Or I could fly them out." He stared at the box Laura held. "Find somewhere safe to meet up and move on?" His hands were clenched in sudden anxiety. "I can't see any way any of us can stay visible now – I mean, we all have to disappear." He turned away, as if he'd said too much.

Steven looked up. "He's right. They'll know now we've got something to hide."

Arnold nodded. "Then it's time we were gone I believe." He waved around the chamber. "This place is going to be rattling soon enough." Then looked intently at Laura's partner. "You have somewhere in mind don't you Michael?"

"Actually, yes. There's a network can hide you three, and our new friends here, for favours owed. It's a refuge network for battered partners and their kids – Kinda appropriate eh?"

"Meanwhile we should get away from the camp." Steven frowned. "Only two passenger seats in your AirSpeed, right?"

Michael nodded, looking ahead. As they passed Centipede he removed the black disc that had disabled the robot. "According to Bill it'll wake up with a wire hangover and memory loss. He reckoned an hour at least before the controllers get it woken up and moving again."

The walk back down the tunnel continued in silence, each person absorbed in memories and imaginings of the future. No-one could see where they would be going, or what that future held. All certainties were overwritten by strange images and emotions from the past. They'd absorbed some aspect of how it had felt to be dinosauran - The past was temporarily more familiar than the present, and their future was another country that couldn't even be imagined.

When they arrived back at the aircabin Dan Alvin and Mike Magee were bent over a large map panel; deep in a discussion about possible routes out and hideaways to head for. They'd guessed some sort of escape plan would be necessary now.

"It'll be dark soon," said Dan. He flicked the map to another page, as they all gathered round, and tapped rapidly at several points to mark them. "There's old goldmine workings here and here that Mike can brief you on. If you get going that way in the Humvee, we'll stay here as a diversion." He looked around the anxious faces. "We'll say we found the place deserted. Then Michael gets angry about you all disappearing and threatens to start in with the media. I restrain my wilful son, and the dust settles round a well hidden confusion. What do you say?"

Laura looked up at Michael, unhappy about leaving him again so soon. Steven and Arnold just nodded unwillingly.

Michael held her. "Don't worry Laura. I'll be out to pick you all up just as quick as I can. Once we've set the dogs off in another direction." He fronted his confidence insistently. "And the network is good. I've known them keep people out of sight up to five years."

"Oh, that's really good to know. Five years in the undergrowth is just what I need." She looked over at the box sitting on a side bench. "Sorry Michael, I'm just not feeling ready for parenthood, or whatever the hell this is going to be. And we're going to need equipment, and a place to work."

Dan was staring at the box too. "From what I've seen the Dinos have got that covered – I don't think you'll be needing much more than what they've already given you. And I've got some ideas how the World Science Court resources might help us all." He looked round the group. "Sorry folks, there's no more time for this. We have to get you moving. You got that tarp Bill put in for the Humvee Michael?"

Fifty minutes later the Humvee was purring away on batteries, hidden beneath a roped on cover of sensor confusing foil; paper thin smart-material that could pick up and reflect its' surroundings to any but the most penetrating scan. A narrow transparent panel allowed a bleary view through

Tertiary

the vehicles' forward screen, and Steven drove with the bulky assistance of an ancient nightvision helmet. Not in the best of moods, as he sweated and gently cursed his way forwards.

Behind them Mike Magee and Dan Alvin looked up from the steps of the aircabin, listening cautiously. Silence – Then, very faintly, the sound of a helicopter moving in across the desert canyons.

108 Tertiary

Part Three

Escape and growth

< From 1st Transcript of the 'Tum' Archive: It was done. One signalled to another, called Six. One was empty and now the thing / emotion called 'content / happy' was the systems' sign. So long waiting, and now it knew its' name was true. A name given to it by the new people that walked across the rocks and filled the air with speech.

Six sent back its' anticipation – The newest people were very close and soon it would be empty too. Its' parents were its' children, and soon they would be born again.>

Two days later the landscape was entirely different. Tiny dust devils playing in the yard of a run-down farm in Kansas. Scrawny chickens watching impassively from old timber rails.

The wind died to silence, leaves fluttering in the surrounding aspen trees, and the birds turned towards a new sound. Nothing in their short memories ever came across the open land to disturb them. A shivering of feathers as they settled to wait.

An ancient, wood-framed estate wagon swayed and bounced along the farm track; a small cluster of buildings coming into view at last.

"That's it?" said Arnold, from the back seat. "Looks just the way the wicked witch left it - - - ."

"Much more there than meets the eye," said Laura, leaning forward onto the wheel. "According to Michael. He says it's the best hidden - - - the best equipped."

"Too much hocus pocus for me. Why couldn't he just give us a map?"

Laura glared round at him. "It's called taking care Arnie. If we don't know where we're going, no-one else does either."

"Maybe so. Unless we were followed from the start - - - ."

"Not very likely," said Steven drily. "There's nothing on this retro wreck to lock onto."

Arnold leaned back, chuckling. "Okay, I give in. Hope springs eternal!"

The chickens were curious now; rising to full alertness as the wagon stopped. Dust settled past it and around their fence posts. The engine chugged on, then died.

"Put the kettle on Dorothy," said Arnold as he stepped down and leaned on the open door. "And a slice of cake would be welcome, if you have such luxury."

Steven smiled. "It's all down to us now folks. No-one contacts us unless we call out."

"Got that," said Arnold. "I read all the notes in the camp brochure." He moved away towards the single storey farmhouse, stepped up onto the verandah and reached for the screen door.

"Wait!" called Steven. "The code. In the brochure. Remember?"

111 Tertiary

Arnold slumped. "Sorry folks. Air turned off, and brain engaged."

Steven patted his arm as he stepped past; aiming a remote control at a panel in the door frame. A brief glow from the panel, and a faint chime as the door lock clicked open. "In we go," he said. "After you Arnie."

Arnold nodded pushing open the screen and inner door. As he moved into the dim light a TV lit up across the room and a voice spoke, requesting confirmation of identity.

"Party of three, plus guests in vitro," said Steven. His voice was low and he started again nervously, but was overridden by a welcome message from the TV.

"Great," said Laura. "And welcome to the farm to you too."

Half an hour later the stove was hot and food smells filled the long kitchen. Arnold emerged from a doorway to the basement, holding a long printed list in one hand. He was smiling broadly.

"Amazing!" he muttered, to no-one in particular. "All we asked for, and a great deal more!"

Laura looked up from a terminal in the living room. "No more complaints then Arnie?"

"None at all," he agreed. "I apologise for all cynical remarks. But really, this place is amazing. Whoever planned and set it up deserves an award." He waved the list, "There's even a machine shop - - - ."

Steven banged a spoon against the stove. "Food's ready folks."

Within two more days it seemed as if they'd always been there; living on a farm in the open Kansas prairie. Arnold spent most of his days below ground, or in the storm cellar. A short, hidden tunnel linked a concealed section of the basement and also the two spaces. Everything he'd asked for, or couldn't build, had arrived in record time; delivered from the nearest town by volunteers from the refuge network: Taciturn folks who maintained their false identities, even at the farm, and therefore inspired complete trust.

Steven and Laura helped as best they could, but often just stayed out of his way; enduring long days of waiting. The eggs, still in their travelling case, were kept in an insulated box as the graphic instructions, compiled and printed out by Laura, had demanded. But time was short; the instructions said no more than fifteen days before incubation, and suggested less. Laura walked around the dusty yard for the fifteenth time; kicking the ground and cursing under her breath. Arnold had begged one more day to adjust his lamps and sensors in the hidden basement area. Insisting that everything should be monitored and recorded. She was way past the point of patience, and had stormed into the open: They'd agreed to remain hidden during the day unless some emergency drove them out.

Steven called from the screen door. "It's all ready Laura. Come and see - - - ."

She nodded, a bit ashamed, and walked across to join him. "Sorry Steve. Is Arnie pissed with me?"

"Not really. He knows time's short." Steven stared past her. "And that's tornado weather coming, so underground might be good anyway - - - ."

She looked back at the darkening sky for a moment. "Appropriate maybe?"

Steven smiled, shutting the door and bolting it as she stepped inside. "Who knows. Whatever happens here will be wilder than Oz I guess."

The old timbers were already creaking, the trees outside roaring in a circle, as they climbed down to join Arnold in his bright bunker of lamps, instruments, wires and warmth.

Far away, in a similarly hidden space, another process of hatching had already been completed. Russian authorities, educated in an era of deception, had been unimpressed with their own central chamber's lures, gone straight to the sphere below it and found the eggs stored there. But the equivalent science team, well used to waiting for all the same reasons, knew that their time would come. The sphere found in the Caucasus was essentially the same as the American one, only subtle details varied. Now the Russians were ahead of their American counterparts, and also aware of their existence; the old soviet network had extended worldwide and still gathered information. Careful negotiations, to verify or deny rumours of American hatchings, had already started.

But even as the first tentative steps towards co-operation began there were more pressing problems for the Russian team. As their eggs had hatched it became obvious that what was emerging was no ordinary dinosaur. Laura would have recognized them from her dreams and also that they were in serious trouble. A species born into a world where disease had evolved for millions of years was already at risk, but the unknown process of preserving and re-constituting the dinosaurans' DNA had multiplied the hazards. At least two of the Russian hatchlings had been dying, as soon as they left the egg, and a third was almost certainly deformed. Since then the science team had tried every technique and drug regime that they dared to stabilise their new charges, mostly methods developed from the old Soviet space programme. Despite the necessary assurances to their masters they had no idea if they were really helping the hatchlings or just helping to kill them.

Back in Kansas Laura and Steven listened to the world roaring above their heads. Even the concealed bunker shook under some of the harsher wind blasts; dust drifting down from heavy timbers that formed its' roof. But Arnold seemed unaware of the maelstrom outside, still checking and fussing with equipment and sensors surrounding the artificial nest he'd constructed; the whole set-up was tented over with an old tarpaulin on metal struts.
As he finally stood back he looked around, puzzled. "What's all that noise? Are we discovered?"
"No Arnie," said Laura. "Just some angry weather gods."
"Ah, no problem. The generator's below ground and fuelled up - - - ."
"We know that." said Steven. "Question is, can we go ahead now?"
"Can't see why not. Even if the farm's bought and broken we've got water, food and bunks next door."
Steven nodded, glancing at Laura. "Right place, right time then. Let's get going."
He and Laura pulled on surgical gloves and lifted eggs, one at a time, from the travelling case and over to the incubating nest, placing each one where Arnold pointed; seven eggs, pointing inwards from the nest rim. As the lamps came on the whole area glowed with warmth.

"If a bulb fails the others increase their output, and we get a warning," said Arnold. "Even if we do nothing, and they all burn out, there's a back-up heater ring under the nest. As fail-safe as I could make it."

"Great Arnie," said Steven. "But we take turns on watch just the same, as agreed?"

"Of course. And turn the eggs every four hours."

The storm shook the old house above them again; a violent twist that set the ceiling timbers shifting upwards, and new curtains of dust dropping all around the tented nest.

"Goddam! I wasn't allowing for this - - - ." Arnold ran round, tightening bolts and straps. As the others helped him there was a loud crash from outside. Everything jumped and shook; a freight train of sound and vibration passing close by.

"Must be a twister," muttered Arnold. "Not quite a direct hit though." He pointed at the dust. "More of it on the east side."

"Sure," said Laura. "That's precise enough for me." She knocked dust and wood chips from her hair, glancing nervously at the nested eggs, and stilled a swaying lamp. "I hope to god the supply wagon wasn't out there."

"Not due for three hours or more," said Steven. "With any luck they've cancelled the run."

But later that evening, almost on schedule, their supplies did arrive. A battered Dodge pick-up, driven by a smiling grey-haired woman, pulled up across the debris in the yard and for the first time one of their guardians lowered the mask. After they'd unloaded she pointed at the churned tornado track just across the nearest field. "Very near miss that. You was lucky." She pushed a strand of hair. "Strange news from Russia coming along. Another team. Same situation. Same number of subjects." She glanced at the ground below the verandah. "Nothing down there that I know of. But something in the post for you I think. Say no more now."

Then a cheery smile, while pulling herself into the truck, and a wave as she backed, turned and drove away across a carpet of leaves, twigs, branches and earth.

Steven stared at the disappearing tailgate. "What the hell - - - ?"

Arnold joined him. "Another sphere, eh! That really just never occurred to me. That another one would be found so soon I mean."

Laura looked across at the tornado track. "Never all the eggs in one basket - - - ."

Arnold nodded, scuffing debris aside with one boot. "Nor all the technology. There must be a common trigger." Heeling the debris back. "Although that would be our ability to dig deep enough. And curiosity. Knowledge of course." Another push with his boot. "Only when we were ready then - - - ."

Next morning the air was clear, the sky bright with puffball clouds, and no memory of storms. All the chickens had survived; perched back on whatever rails they could find. A passing coyote glanced their way, heard a door creak, and trotted on. Steven stepped out, slowly rubbing at his eyes and hair with a towel. Under his arm was a sealed packet. He was thinking how he'd nearly missed the faint icon for 'post' on the carton; would have burned the packet, still inside it's hidden sleeve, with the trash. Just as well the old lady had dropped her mask!

He sat on the porch steps, towel round his neck, and carefully unsealed the post. Inside was a message from Michael, and a real-paper folder with detailed information from Senator Alvin. Steven shook his head and smiled. Strange how this news gave him such a sense of relief and hope. Knowing that another team was on the run, testing themselves in the unknown, hoping to find some answers and asking the same huge questions. If only they could meet and share experiences!

He sealed up the folder and went back in to show it to the others.

"So now we burn this," said Laura, pushing away the card cover. She scratched at her hair. "I feel like a kid playing spy games!" Pulled the folder back again. "But it does make it easier, knowing there's another team out there."

"Certainly does." Arnold was scanning the pages intently; burning the message into his memory. "If we could just get some contact with them. Share some ideas - - - ."

"It's possible Arnie. We just don't know when as usual." Steven pointed at the summary page. "Between the lines, I'm getting that's what the Senator wants too."

Arnold peered. "Hmm, well, it's fairly oblique isn't it. But I guess you're right." He offered it for Laura's opinion, and she read again quickly.

"Sometime, never is my take," she said. "Still, it would push the odds back to us." She stared at the two men. "Just two spheres, or more now do you think?"

Arnold stared back. "Very good point! Where there's two, there's probably more. With their tech more egg baskets would've been easy. Relatively easy - - -."

There was silence then. Steven gathered everything together, the others nodded and he carefully fed the sheets and cover into the kitchen stove; stirring with the fire tongs till every corner was ash.

Three weeks later, and rain bands were raking across the prairie. The dispirited chickens huddled, damp and scruffy, in sheltered corners. The old timber farm showed dark streaks where rain had driven under the eaves. Nothing seemed to move except wet air. But below ground the atmosphere was warm, almost joyful. All anxieties and doubts were forgotten as Laura, Arnold and Steven waited for their first egg to hatch. The alarm had chimed when a faint rasping was picked up and amplified. Fifteen minutes later another egg became active. Within an hour five of the seven were making similar sounds. Arnold was smiling; happily checking the recordings and splitting channels to compare the progress of each egg. The first one showed hairline cracks after eighty minutes. Then a small hole appeared and a sharp black spike within it, rapidly cutting the shell from the inside.

"Egg tooth," muttered Laura. "Seems fit and healthy so far."

"This is freaky," whispered Arnold. "What the hell will they look like?"

"We'll know in about five minutes," said Steven. "Sooner, look - - - !"

A tiny head emerged from the shell, shaking as it pushed out into the light. Flat faced, with the sharp egg tooth sticking up from its' forehead. Not like a bird, not like a dinosaur hatchling. And not human either; with a pattern of wet down laid across its' head and face. But something very human in its' structure, and the way t was moving - - - .

Arnold stepped back, grabbing an upright strut to support himself. "All this time, and I still don't believe I'm seeing this!" The dinosauran turned towards his voice and chirruped. "Oh, sure," he muttered. "Now I'm a father!"

Laura laughed, a slightly strangled sound. "Don't worry, we'll help you with the nappies."

Steven was staring at another egg, as the tooth broke through the shell. "They're catching up with each other. Am I right Arnie?"

"Seems so," Arnold was staring at his monitors. "They'll all be out in less than an hour at this rate."

Elsewhere, things were less optimistic. Somewhere on the banks of the Stony Tunguska River, in remotest Siberia, stood the ruins of a fire-fighting brigade headquarters. Blank, snow-blind windows and eroded concrete blocks surrounded an apron of smashed cinders, and the corpse of an old Kamov helicopter. Its' rotor blades fluttered in the icy, knifing air. Nothing else moved except the wind.

This was the secret base where the Russians had hidden an elite science team to hatch their eggs. Deep within the permafrost, in a shielded bunker, this other group was considering their options. Three months after hatching seven dinosauran eggs there were only three survivors; two had died almost immediately, another within a week and now a fourth was succumbing to some unknown virus. It seemed unlikely that anything more could be done and the team was close to despair. As the blizzards raged above, closing down their world and all communications, they had no idea what, if anything, they could try as a cure.

The last two hatchlings, a female and a male, seemed healthy enough for now, although the female had some problems with her limb growth. And one of the science team, an expert in child development, was worried by the male's movements and behaviour. Valentina Turmansky suspected a form of multiple personality, but with no way to define the problem had resigned herself to observing. The young dinosauran twisted and twittered at her; sitting up and watching alertly from his man-made nest. Valentina would have to wait until the hatchlings learned to speak, if that was ever going to happen. All the Russian team wanted for now was the pair to stay alive.

Almost a year later and the Kansas farmhouse stood empty again; abandoned in late summer to the harshness of isolation and the tornadoes weaving a deadly pattern onto the prairie. If the place had a spirit it would have seen the settling dust on the road and said farewell to its' strangest ever inhabitants, when their ancient estate wagon bounced over the hillcrest one last time.

Inside the car no-one looked back, the occupants either too young or too pre-occupied to care. Arnold kept glancing back over the seats to check their infant charges and was already irritating Laura to distraction. "God's sake Arnie! If they cry they cry, and we deal with it then. Who's going to hear them out here anyway?"

"I know that Laura, I know." He turned stiffly back to the front. "And my back says it needs all my sympathy at home right now." His voice was strained. "I hope to God that damned trucker understands. Some of that equipment is really delicate."

Laura looked away from the wheel and smiled at him, despite her own strained muscles. "Sorry Arnie, I guess it's like the normal stresses of parenthood. I know you worry but we just have to trust the network now." She frowned again. "We've been over this."

Michael sat upright from the bench seat behind them. "Are we there yet? Did I hear the happy chimes of a Diner's doorway? I need to pee mom and dad."

Arnold groaned. "Okay Mike, I get the message. I know you only came back to guide and entertain us on our way. But you've seen this new place and we haven't. It's not that I don't trust your judgement, or Dan's."

Michael laughed short and patted his friends' shoulder. "It's okay Arnold, Steven was just the same before he went over there. And everyone knows this is risky, moving them so young, but there was no way to avoid it. I've never known Dad misjudge his sources - If they say we should go, we go."

Later that day, as a greyed out twilight fell along the roads, the estate wagon had been exchanged for an anonymous Jeep RV; itself a rarity since the early century fuel crises, but essential for the roads they were planning to travel. The same smiling grey-haired woman who'd delivered supplies to the farmhouse drove the old wagon away; a final wave and then just bright red spots fading against clouds in the rear mirrors. Michael took the wheel and headed west again, aiming towards the Rockies and a long drive over mountain passes to the new refuge; as they skirted Denver the clouds lifted and they could just see those dark walls of rock against the sky ahead. But what they were driving towards and what that place held for them was a mysterious unknown, even to Michael who'd found and arranged first the house and then the journey.

They travelled all night and through the next day, taking turns at the wheel and sleeping and nursing the two infant dinosaurans. So by the second evening they were high above the Great Plains and deep inside sharp folds of rock and stands of trees. The road wound higher towards jagged crowns of snow and the bitter dampness of clouds.

"This new place, in Nevada," said Arnold. "You said it's abandoned most of the year?"

"Apart from when The Burning Man is on, yes," said Michael. "We'll catch the last couple of days of the festival, and move in as the crowds move out. Steven's rented us a temporary trailer on the ranch."

Laura glanced back. "We told you all this Arnold. But I guess you were too busy packing."

"Well yes, I did sort of hear you. But other things on the mind, you know." Arnold rubbed his forehead. "What about the locals? There's a small town nearby you said."

Michael nodded. "Not a problem, they're used to weird folk coming in for the festival. And the wagon trains and the wind surfers and the rocketeers. Not to mention land speeders, supersonic cars and decades of strange shit in the sky."

"Ah, yes, Area 51 territory," said Arnold. "I do remember you saying that too."

"Some of it for real." Michael looked back at him. "There were folks not long back saw things flying even the government didn't know about. Back in the good old Cold War days."

"So we hide in the crowd," said Arnold. "I guess it makes some sort of sense."

When they came over the last summit it was past midnight and their lights couldn't hide the fierce burn of stars above and around them. Far below they saw the familiar lights and pattern of Salt Lake City, Michaels' old home and a place full of all their memories. A long ago time, before they were wrenched away into this life of running, hiding and uncertainty. Laura shivered in the back seat, as some part of an old dream rose up from the landscape and made a weird pointer into her future; a premonition of half formed imaginings and a state of awareness she glimpsed but couldn't define. It made her intensely nervous of the city for a moment, as if they were running too close to old traps and new enemies; if they had to keep running she would rather run far away from these old scenes and associations. Even to another continent where no-one understood or really saw them, let alone the strange young beings they were protecting, and it wouldn't matter if any of them knew what they were doing or why.

Right on cue both the dinosaurans woke and trilled in alarm or hunger, instantly snapping Laura back to the present. She was amazed by the alien infants commanding that response in adults of a different species from a different time, imagining the cry might even be heard in the city below. As she brushed that wild idea aside, and turned to find their stock of food, she saw lights on the road below, coming upwards, and instinctively ducked to cover them.

"Don't worry," said Michael, seeing her movement in his mirror. "They'll never see through the glass in this thing. It's silvered, remember."

"yeah, okay, thanks Mike," she muttered. "I'm just road wrecked and jumpy. Sorry."

Tertiary

The lights swept up and past, a dragon-like festival of bulbs along the side of a truck and two trailers, then the rush of air and distraction was past. Just the purr of their own motor again, the surrounding rock and stars and below, the first points and textures of treetops. Laura was feeding the hungry dinosaurans chunks of food and watching with puzzled amusement as they ate; so much like human children in their movements and responses, or was it just her own affection making it seem so. Even now, after nearly a year, she hesitated to admit love for the new creatures, but how could it not be when she was effectively their mother? And they had names now, Sally and Rex, something that had been debated fiercely for a long time. The wisdom of personalising them when they might still die. How it might affect them if and when they developed any sort of awareness. So many unknowns, and in the end it had been simpler just to make them part of the family, a natural thing to do.

Now Arnold was looking back at them with a smile. "What do you see Laura?" She frowned at him, unsure. "I mean do you see young animals, not so different to some native species, or do you just see children like I do?"

Laura sighed, then smiled. "On the button Arnold, I was wondering that too. No, I don't see strange little animals, nor cute ones. Illusion or not, I see children more and more   Maybe because they need us?"

"I'm beginning to think we need them, if only to give a reason for this mad life. I feel like I've always been doing this, hiding out all over the US of A without knowing where next or why."

She nodded. "Same for me then, I guess.   I keep telling myself it's an amazing scientific enquiry, but I don't really believe that at all anymore. I think it's something much more, something very different."

Michael interrupted. "Should be about five more hours folks, according to our onboard friend here.   So I guess we'll be there for brunch or thereabouts."

The others nodded, content for now to leave the subject, and both stared down the road ahead, along the burning arrow of the Jeeps' lights. Allowing themselves to be lulled by the movement and the focus, and drifting into a waking doze with no expectations except the next bend or wall of rock or narrow bridge. They woke to the early light of morning and a turn off the Interstate at Wadsworth, just outside Reno, with a sign pointing onwards to Pyramid Lake.

"Going onto the old county road soon," said Michael. "Find out what this machine was built for, then pick up Route 46 and we're nearly there."

Arnold and Laura dropped into sleep again, waking half an hour later to the harsh roar of gravel under the wheels. Michael was grinning as he floated the Jeep along at a steady eighty miles an hour, watching a rolling desert landscape of low scrub bushes, stretches of dried out earth and long lines of mountains to either side.

Arnold groaned. "More mountains? Well at least this road is straight."

"Follows an old railroad," said Michael, then cursed as the road jinked suddenly over narrow timbers, barely wider than their wheel track, to cross a creek. They swerved, in a spray of gravel, shot over and slewed sideways again to line up on the other side. "Damn, didn't see that coming. Must be getting tired."

"Well remember you've got kids on board." Arnold spoke sharply to his own surprise. "Let me take it now and just shout if I take a wrong turn. Okay?"

Michael nodded, slowing the Jeep, and pushed the controller across. "Sorry Arnold. I meant to wake you. Just keep going straight and look out for tarmac in about fifty miles."

When they finally arrived, on an empty road that turned from the Black Rock desert, there was little to see except some deserted cabins round a low ranch house, derelict looking trailers and a simple sign on the gate saying 'Fly Ranch'. In the distance, along a track to the desert, they saw strange human outlines above the scrub and plumes of steam rising from geothermal vents. The ranch house at the centre gave off a sense of desolation, a curtain blew slowly out from one verandah window, and nothing moved in the yard, not even birds in the dusty looking trees.

"Festival must have finished early," muttered Michael. "Where is everybody?"

"And what the hell are those figures?" asked Arnold. "This place feels weird. No dogs, nothing."

"Just sculpture from the Burning Man." Michael was peering at the ranch house. "Standing in the hot pools, where people can swim." He got out to open the gate and called back. "I guess we just go in, see if Steven's around. The trailer's over there by the cabins but I don't see any sign of him."

"There's someone on the track," said Laura as Michael got back in. "Can't see who it is from here."

The Jeep pulled up to the trailer and they stepped uncertainly into the dirt yard; looking around, up to the mountain peaks beyond the road and across to the desert trail again. The figure came back into view, walking slowly and head down. Its' head was hooded in some sort of cowl; whoever it was they'd obviously not seen the Jeep arrive.

"Get in the trailer," said Michael. "Just in case. No point taking chances, and the truck should be here in about an hour."

Laura and Arnold carried the dinosaurans inside and Michael followed behind them, glancing back from the step. The figure was out of sight again, behind a clutter of cabins, dead vehicles and small trees. But the inside of the trailer was clean and smelt of food; they saw signs of a recent meal and someone was obviously packing and tidying up. Then Michael found a paege that he recognised and waved it silently at the others, just as the figure came into the yard outside, saw the Jeep and threw back his hood.

Steven ran the last few yards to the door, smiling and wrapping his towel around his neck, pulled it open and clambered inside. "Great, a bit earlier than I expected. How are you, and the kids? I went for a healthy swim in the ponds."

Laura laughed. "Slow down. We're fine."

"I meant to move into the house before you got here. Everyone's gone." He paused for breath. "I guess you spotted that." Unwound his towel onto a chair. "Okay, I'm calmed down now." Hugged them all in turn. "How was the journey? Is the truck on the road?"

"Yes, yes and yes," said Arnold. "All packed, hopefully nothing broken and on the road behind us."

Steven suddenly saw how tired they all were, and how strange this new landscape must feel to them. "It's not so bad here," he said. "Come over to the house and you can sleep, I got it pretty much cleaned up this morning. The festival folks finally took off yesterday, finished early and went away to another show."

Laura looked around as they walked out across the yard, feeling dispirited and out of place. She'd at least got used to Kansas and was still in her first impression of the ranch; it gave her no sense of home or security, just an empty foreboding of boredom and anxiety. She couldn't imagine bringing up children of any sort here and wondered how they could keep them safe so much closer to other people. Yet the place felt so desolate and deserted too.

Even as she thought this she heard the sounds of a vehicle on the desert trail, turned to look and saw a battered pick-up rocking towards them with a trail of smoke or steam drifting away behind it. It turned down into the yard with a clatter of tired pistons, a truly vintage machine running on diesel or gas. Steam wafted forward from the half open hood as it stopped alongside the verandah. Between them and the ranch house. Two men got out, smiling but heavily armed, and Michael and Steven stepped forwards, instinctively shielding the others carrying the infants.

"Hope you folks don't mind us passing through," said the first, hefting an assault rifle onto his shoulder. "Took a cut across the desert and didn't know anyone was here." He looked to his partner who wore a pistol on one hip, a bandolier and a huge bowie knife on the other. "Larry and me, we're heading for some hunting in the high Sierras." He nodded up at the mountain peaks. "I'm Will. Pleased to meet you I hope, and don't mean to disturb you." He'd seen their eyes glancing to the weapons. "Folks round here pretty much look after themselves. Figure if you've got a good gun who needs a government." He laughed and held out one work hardened hand.

Michael relaxed a little, took the offered hand and shook it. "No problem. We're just moving in, as you see. You'll excuse us if we get the kids inside." He motioned Arnold and Laura past. They shielded the dinosaurans from view and stepped into the shadowed doorway. "Be here for a while, see how we like it. You guys from around these parts?"

Will waved vaguely back. "Away north east, about fifty miles, the gold mine. It's where we're working most of the time. Only lights you might see at night that side of the sky, you know you can read a book by starlight up here." He looked at Michael and Steven, an apparently friendly appraisal. "We'll just ask you one favour, some water for the old jalopy. Then we'll leave you folks in peace and wish you a nice day."

Steven gestured to an open cistern and Larry, the silent one, took a can from the pickup, filled it and climbed into the cab. Will turned to follow him, then back. "One thing Me and Larry, we're only dangerous to jack rabbits and the deer. Just a few, they're not so choosy where they point a gun." He stepped over and Larry handed him a slip of paper from the open cab window. "Call us. Maybe we'll be a day away or only an hour, but we hope that's something if the need arises."

Michael was speechless, took the paper and shook hands again automatically. Will nodded but said no more, just gave him a brief smile of acknowledgement and swung into the pick-up. He started the engine, drove around and away out of the yard, two arms waving briefly from the open windows, and then they were gone.

"What in hell was that about?" muttered Steven. "They came past the ponds. Plenty of water there for an engine."

"I've no idea," said Michael. "God I need a coffee now. Unload the truck, sleep and worry about it later is what I say, I don't think they're about to come back." But he still looked out along the road to make sure, before turning and following Steven inside.

The ranch house was simply furnished and clean, not so different in that way to the farmhouse back in Kansas. There was no storm cellar, no tornadoes in the state of Nevada, but Arnold already knew there was a hidden basement for all his equipment. All he worried about was getting into it quickly and unseen if they ever needed to; and Laura was insisting the dinosaurans sleep there, for the same reason, which was going to cut his working area considerably.

"I know they're only small and won't take much space," he was saying. "But surely one of us has to be with them at night?"

"Well, hell Arnold. A camp bed that folds up, remember those?" Laura knew they were arguing from tiredness, strangeness and strain, but she was unwilling or unable to stop. She thought back to their days at Dinosaur National Monument, and to the person she had been then; quiet, serious about her work above everything else and certainly unlikely to raise her voice. She watched Arnold feeding the infants again, and looked up as Michael and Steven came in. "Who were those people? They looked ready to fight a war."

Michael shrugged. "I really don't know. But right or wrong I think they're on our side somehow. Very strange!" He went to the stove to make coffee. "Makes no sense I know, caffeine then sleep, but nothing's going to keep me awake now. Not even crazy men with guns." He fumbled in his back pocket for the slip of paper and handed it to Arnold. "That's not any code we know is it?"

Arnold shook his head slowly. "Nothing I remember, no. Just a standard mail address by the look of it. You got it from those guys?"

"Yes, and an open offer of assistance when we re-play the OK Corral. I think."

"That's how it sounded to me," said Steven. "Maybe they're network folks, just being extra careful?"

"No, we'd have been told." Michael pulled at one ear. "Ah, mysteries on mystery. I'll double check when I call Dan tomorrow."

"Is that the truck?" said Laura suddenly. "God, I'm jumpy as a cat now."

"Yes," said Michael, peering out of the kitchens' end window. "Right on time. Let's get busy folks and we can talk again later if anyone's still worried."

Later turned out to be next morning for all of them, even the dinosauran children slept right through till early morning light, and so it was for several days as they sorted and unpacked crates and boxes, and became familiar with the ranch and its' surroundings. Arnold explored the geothermal vents with professional interest; wondering at multi-coloured, miniature volcanoes that the scalding water had slowly deposited. And amused and confused by strange sculptures the New Age festival had left behind; bizarre human figures standing around the steaming ponds.

Laura and Steven hiked out along the rim of the desert to the Black Rock itself and nearly got lost in the soft margins of mud, remnants of the huge lake that formed from melt water every spring. They turned and looked far down a barren surface so flat they could see the curvature of the earth; seeing why land speed lunatics came here to run cars faster than sound. A beautiful and eerie landscape, full of old ghosts and host to the strangest fancies. Possibly a perfect place to hide.

Within two months they all felt as if this had been their home forever. No-one came to bother them, and time began to slip past as it had in Kansas; white crowns creeping down from mountain peaks the only indicator of the seasons' rapid change But the mornings were bitterly cold now, soon it would be winter and the hot, high desert they'd arrived at would be snow bound for months. Michael checked the Jeeps' wheels and tyres for ice traction and made his last weekly trip to Empire, twelve miles along the road, to stock up on supplies.

At the market doorway he tripped at sight of a black widow spider on the ground and reluctantly stepped back to kill it, local wisdom saying it was bad luck not to. An anonymous familiarity seemed to be allowed here, people were friendly but in no way intrusive, so he passed the usual fast remarks with known faces and went about his regular march up and down the shelves. Hardly noticing that two strangers watched and carefully followed.

But Mary, at the checkout, had noticed, and did no more than tap his hand and nod towards them with an enquiring lift of one eyebrow. Michael woke up immediately, smiled at her in thanks and hurried to the Jeep, shaking himself mentally for losing an essential edge of suspicion so easily. He knew this land still generated a frontier culture, but hadn't understood how carefully the people watched out for each other; good to know in one way.

but a warning they weren't as anonymous as they'd hoped. He remembered what the county judge had told him, on a rare visit to a local bar; that a major sideline of the high desert was the running of drugs and banned chemicals. Aircraft would land, far out along the playa, boxes would be unloaded onto pickups and then the plane burnt to erase any evidence. In that climate anything or anyone of any possible value could become a focus of interest.

But another week passed and then another and nothing happened to cause alarm or suspicion. The first snow fell and blanketed them inside the ranch house, and into whatever interests and studies they'd chosen to fill their long, isolated days. In fact the dinosauran children still demanded most of their attention, as they grew and became characters in their own right and anxieties over their long term survival slowly eased.

So the winter passed, the spring came, snow melted and the desert became a vast lake again; reflecting clouds and the surrounding mountains in a silver grey surface, and projecting its' yearly illusion of great depth. Sally and Rex showed every sign of developing at least as fast as human children; the high point of everyone's winter had been the realisation, really just anticipation at first, that soon they might talk. It was almost a game; human adults trying to catch the children communicating but not wanting to admit this was possible. And the dinosaurans themselves were unwilling to show their new abilities, a strange shyness between one species and another.

Then one morning, just after New Year, Arnold was stepping up from the hidden basement, on his way to the kitchen stove and a first coffee, when the children woke behind him. "Rex, 'Nold gone. Talk now?" is what he heard, thought he heard. But of course they appeared to be asleep when he turned back, almost falling from the ladder, and tiptoed down to stare at them. He waited patiently until Rex gave in, a melodious twitter of sound that was laughter, smiled up at him and reached out his arms to be held. Arnold laughed, his eyes pricking with tears, and lifted Rex from his bed. "Okay my little friend, you win. But I know you can talk, I really do."

Tertiary

The spring passed, summer heat built up, the playa dried out and the time came close for another years' Burning Man Festival. Strange and exotic people appeared, talking sense and making concrete plans for wild and inexplicable events. Some of their followers drifted to the ranch, asking questions about the hot springs, the landscape, where they could camp, get water, even buy drugs; a steady stream of demands that Michael and Laura were elected to front and deflect. They authorised access to the hot springs and ponds, as the ranch occupants always had, and put up signs directing the way. They watched and checked every evening, to make sure no-one was lost or stuck there. They even exploited the opportunity, setting up a stall to sell home-cooked food and weak beer, knowing they must join in with this happy madness and so stay hidden in open view.

In the ranch house itself life carried on as before, following the pattern of days they'd established as normal all through the winter and spring, and everything centred on maintaining security for the dinosauran children. Steven and Arnold didn't dare relax their guard or let themselves be complacent, but their strongest shield was Dan Alvin. He'd never visited, hardly ever contacted them, but he was a permanent and reassuring presence in the background; deflecting dangerous interest, diverting funds and organising support for every area of their lives. But now the Senator wanted to see developments for himself, and the Burning Man could be a perfect cover for him if he moved around the area and even stopped by at the ranch. So a coded letter came in and preparations were made as the days of the festival grew nearer and the desert filled up with a crazy assortment of people and their vehicles; a wide crescent of tents and stalls and sideshows facing onto the huge figure that would burn as the symbol and finale of the event.

Michael and Steven were out in the crowds there, touting for business for the food and beer stall and checking out who and what was around; more from boredom than any real sense of threat or need for information. Laura was close by the hot springs, watching the central geyser spray steam and water from its' psychedelic cone, when the first hint of problems to come caught her eye. She was renewing one of the trail signs when a black retro camper van pulled up beside the main pond, below the cascades surrounding the geyser, and two men and a woman got out. People were climbing all over the multi-coloured ledges and splashing in pools varying from scalding to pleasantly warm, so one more group of visitors shouldn't have been remarkable.

But the people from the camper betrayed an edge of uneasiness in their movements, as if they were playing some role game or carefully fitting themselves into the scene. All three looked physically fit and alert and their clothes were closely matched, almost a quality of uniform, giving an impression of military discipline behind a front that looked casual.

Laura watched from a distance, thinking most gatherings would have absorbed them, but against this crowd of raw individualists the trio was highlighted and somehow threatening. Nothing made any particular alarm go off, not even when they wandered around eyeing the crowd, because some folk hesitated before joining the Burning Man's party, if they saw no immediate way to fit in. Perhaps these newcomers didn't hesitate enough, were too practised in their relaxed manner or just didn't smile the right way.

Then the tiniest clue jumped out of the background and became a focus for Laura's unease; there were no badges on the camper, not a single one, it was completely blank and anonymous. Except that the bottom corner of each darkened window had a minute red symbol or logo etched in; something she wanted to see close up, something she'd seen on an armoured Humvee and some of the helicopters in Colorado. Almost certainly an exotic and weapon-proof glass, and not something a New Age traveller vehicle would have fitted as standard.

Laura hammered the sign firmly into the ground and headed back towards the ranch, taking care not to look back but refreshing an image of the camper and its' crew in her mind. Dan Alvin was due to arrive in the next day or so and she wanted these people checked out before he did. The track wasn't too crowded so she walked quickly and ran the last few yards between the old cabins, calling out to Arnold at the back door. He peered round the side of the stove when she burst in.

"Arnie, did you really put a camera out by the ponds. Tell me you did and I won't be angry."

"How did you - - - ? Oh, never mind," he said. "Yes I did Laura. Not sure why, except to gaze at the beauties of my fellow men and women."

"Well turn it on now," she said. "And see if you can spot a black camper van, a woman and two men. They kind of look alike, the way the people are dressed I mean."

Arnold nodded "You know Bill gave us that camera gear don't you. It can't be spotted or hacked or traced."

"I don't care," said Laura, waving and pointing. "Just do it now. And record their faces if you can."

"Jesus Laura," he muttered. "You used to be the quiet one."

She stared at him, shocked for a moment, then looked down. "I'm sorry Arnold. You were right to put a camera out there. It's where most people get to sooner or later."

"That was the theory, yes." Arnold led the way down to the basement, quickly checking that no-one else was around or outside. "I've actually got quite a library of suspects now, but no-one I'm really worried about. Who are these characters?"

"That's what we need to know. Check out the van windows too and see if you recognise anything."

"Cryptic and commanding you are young lady. But I ask no questions and obey, as always."

Laura smiled tightly. "I'm not sure if I remember right, is all. I just hope I'm jumpy and wrong."

Arnold uncovered a console at the back wall of the basement and switched on its' central screen. Thumbnail views came up from all around the yard and the ranch, its' gate and various cabins and trailers. Plus a long shot of the geyser and the main pond next to it. He selected and zoomed towards the black camper van, focusing on the corner of its' front cab window.

"Well, yes, that looks like a military suppliers' icon for armour grade to me. It means you'd need serious weaponry to annoy anyone inside." He turned. "So why is it fitted on a New Age love bus ?"

"Damn," said Laura. "That's what I was afraid of. What I remembered from Colorado, on some of the ARPA machines."

"Too confident, or careless then? To leave that in view I mean." Arnold panned along to the other windows of the van. "Just a detail, but definitely suspicious."

"Well, they don't understand how artists look at things. Form, detail, all of that." She bit her lip. "Maybe those three are just drug runners."

Arnold was moving the view around. "Where are they, ah, is that them?" He zoomed in again when Laura nodded. "No, I see what you mean, the clothes are wrong somehow. 'Just drug runners' doesn't fit them for my money. Sorry."

An hour later Steven and Michael were watching the playback and looking worried. The van and all three people had moved on, probably into the main crescent out on the desert, so they couldn't track it or them except by wandering around on foot. Arnold had captured and enhanced two of the three faces and Michael was uploading them for network contacts, to see if either could be matched. That was all they could do for now except keep watch around the ranch and warn Senator Alvin.

"He's here tomorrow," Michael was saying. "That's definite now. And Bill McCandless is coming with him, so I feel better already."

That night Arnold set up new motion software for the surveillance cameras but nothing showed up except the usual prowling coyotes and an owl at maximum range. In the morning he checked through the recordings to be sure. There was nothing unusual or suspicious until he zoomed into one dark corner of the yard. "Tracks," he muttered. "Can that be tracks from our old friend, or am I imagining things?"

When he stood outside with the others there was nothing definite to see. "It could have been Son of Centipede, or a Snake," he was saying. "But for now I'll say I'm paranoid and reset some of the cameras."

Michael stared hard at the dirt and the undergrowth beyond it. "They'll be here soon, sometime around mid-afternoon. I'll check with Bill then. And we could sweep the yard, make a nice clean canvas just in case?"

Inside he felt himself sweating, wondering if there was any real threat to the children or to his father. He couldn't shift the idea that his dad was more at risk than the rest of them if things turned nasty; just an irrational itch of anxiety, but one he couldn't persuade himself to ignore. He suddenly remembered an evening in childhood when the old man had been late home, and news of a train wreck came onto the wallscreen. His mother had kept silent and smiling but he knew that was where his dad was, and that he was alive and okay, but he'd still been terrified and unable to sleep. Not till he heard the front door closing, long past midnight, and the familiar voice calling out.

Michael shivered and put an arm round Laura. She leaned against him, guessing some of what he was thinking and feeling. "If Bill's on the case then they'll both be fine,' she said. "And so will we."

For the next six hours they busied themselves around the ranch with sweeping, mending and painting to cover Arnolds' adjustments if anyone or anything was watching. The hidden cameras needed cleaning anyway as fine dust filtered in from the desert; so many people and vehicles moving around were breaking up and powdering its' fragile crust.

In different ways they all felt a kind of elation. If there was a threat facing them at least it would be something positive to deal with, rather than the endless drift of days with no real contact from outside. And everyone looked forward to seeing Dan Alvin and Bill McCandless again. Between them, and in very different ways, they inspired and reinforced enormous confidence; it wasn't possible to lose hope so long as they were somewhere in the background, waiting, working and willing to be called on.

At three o'clock Arnold spotted two figures from his perch on top of a rickety cabin roof. They were walking slowly along the trail from the desert and the hot springs, deep in conversation, and had stopped to admire a small geyser bubbling at the side of the road. They leaned on long wooden staves with curled and ornamented tops. Both wore wide brimmed hats that kept their faces in shadow, and long woven robes, but Arnold recognised them instantly and clambered down to call the others; hiccoughing with amusement at the idea of elderly wizards coming to visit.

Dan and Bill arrived and were hurried across the yard to the ranch house. Michael and Steven doubled over, laughing helplessly, and were unable to speak for several minutes.

"Take no notice," said Laura, smiling broadly. "The fit will pass. How are you both? Can you stay here with us?"

"One night at least, should be safe enough," said Dan. "Did you get any more on that van or the crew?" He glanced at Michael, who'd managed to straighten up. "Get a grip son, it's not that funny."

"Sorry dad." Michael took a deep breath, but was still smiling inanely. "But you guys do look the Gandalf. It's great, it really is." He stretched upwards to control himself, managed to breathe in and answer. "Network says no match found on the faces, or for the van, but there's no doubt those people are here to track someone. Not here for the beer in other words."

Dan parked his staff against the stove and pulled out a chair. "Too much walking, even for a wizard." He grinned at Laura. "Bill suggested the outfits, we could have sold spells and charms all day!" He motioned Bill to sit as well, and turned to Michael again. "You know, they may not even be looking our way at all. There's a bunch of strange folks and underside deals going around out there on the desert."

Steven nodded. "We saw that yesterday, when we went walkabout. I think we're hiding in the crowd okay, but Arnold might be right about tracks round the ranch."

"Probably just a real rattler," said Arnold. "But a Snake is what I'd use."

Bill McCandless agreed. "Best tool for the job, especially on this sort of ground. So I've got you some trackers here, latest models from our line." He pulled a package from deep inside his robes. "If there is anything out there that doesn't breathe air you should be able to pick it up and disable it."

The children were asleep when Dan and Bill arrived so Laura had set the internal alarm system to chime when they woke. "They often crash out in the afternoons." She smiled. "Their sleep patterns are different to ours. We're not sure why."

So the afternoon light dimmed down to evening and another spectacular sunset while they talked, everyone happily exhausted by labour, good company and feeling safer and more secure in their purpose. It seemed only days since they'd parted in Colorado, time shrinking in the warmth of friendship, and the hours stretched out to enfold all their stories. Dan Alvin told how he'd secretly opened channels at the World Science Court, and carefully selected a small group he could trust with the unprecedented problems he gave them to solve. A thing he'd hated to do in principle, yet amazed and renewed by the power of good will and understanding he'd found in those people.

Bill talked with quiet intensity about the technical developments his company was making, and how they could be used to safeguard the children. He was obviously amused by his own enthusiasm and soon had the others laughing aloud; soaring to surreal metaphor as he strained to explain his wilder ideas. Michael described his occasional absences, drinking late into the night with the Judge, and how he'd been trying to learn the local rules. Laura looked at him sideways and he grinned in self-defense. Steven smiled in sympathy, tried to back Michael with his own stories and they both told the tale of their strange visitors on the day the children arrived at the ranch

And Laura told how the young dinosaurans absorbed all their days, how they'd developed and grown and become so much more than mysterious young animals to be defended, kept healthy and observed. She hinted at their doubts and anxieties, especially over whether the children could or would ever speak, then expanded the speculation with her own experiences of half-heard conversations. She doubted her own perceptions, wondering if she'd only heard what she wished to hear.

"Not so," said Arnold. "I'm sure of what I heard, back in the spring, but they just wouldn't play when I challenged them."

Then the alarm chimed and Dan and Bill finally climbed down to visit the children in person. They were stunned; a few movies, sent over secure links, couldn't have prepared them for the reality, not even the latest holographs that Bill and Michael had access to.

When Rex and Sally looked up from their game Dan Alvin felt tears fill his eyes. "Can't you get them outside at all?" His voice was low and slow. "I hate to think of them shut up in here all the time."

"We did all winter," said Arnold. "When no-one was moving around much. And at night of course. But it's still risky, if anyone from the Schools Board should catch sight of them."

Steven looked drawn; the subject had obsessed him for months, with no good answers to be found. "We came up with all sorts of ideas in theory. Midgets taking a rest from the shows in Reno. That sort of thing, and crazier." He looked down at the children. "But nothing we could think of was ever going to work. Not if anyone got close to them."

"No, I can see that now," said Dan. "And it's something I've been thinking about anyway. Maybe time to move you on again, somewhere deeper hidden where they can get outside to play at least."

"Do they walk or talk yet?" asked Bill. "Seems to me they understand us well enough." His kindly glance at the children belied his tone. "If the camera ring isn't secure we can do something about that too. Just for the short term."

"It's not our cameras, it's whatever anyone else might turn on the ranch," said Arnold. "You know well enough what's available Bill." Then he smiled at Rex and Sally. "Yes they walk, and talking? Well, my theory is they could if they wanted to but haven't quite made up their minds yet."

He was interrupted by Michael moving to the stairs. "Just going to check around up top," he explained. "I'm jumpy I know, but that van turning up still bothers me."

When he closed the hidden door from the basement and stepped into the kitchen he already knew something was wrong. They'd sat through the sunset without any lights on and now he could see clearly into the moonlit yard; something or someone was moving out there on the edge of his perception. A shape in the shadows had frozen right where Arnold had suspected tracks the night before. Michael tapped the silent alarm code into the stove panel, telling the others to keep down and quiet while he investigated. It was the last thing he remembered for several hours; the door crashed open, a blow landed hard behind his left ear and he blacked out.

Down in the basement Arnold and Steven jumped to the camera console, switching its' mode to infrared and rapidly scanning all round the ranch house. At first they saw nothing wrong, but they'd heard Michael fall so it was obvious the attackers were already inside. How anyone could have fooled the motion sensors was the most frightening question, apart from how well the basement doorway would stand up to a search; whoever they were they'd come well prepared. Then it got worse, nearly complete silence with just the tiniest scrapes of sound. Obviously a scan and a search was going on, but there was no way to track it from where they were; no-one had thought inside cameras would ever be needed.

But Bill was waving to Dan, who pulled a package from under his own robes. He passed it over with a confident nod of his head and watched while Bill unfolded a segmented and studded stick about half a metre long, detached a hand sized transmitter-controller from a bulge at one end and unwrapped a small silvered visor.

"I'll be damned," muttered Arnold. "Our very own Snake."

Bill grinned at him and gestured towards the connections panel at the side of the console. Between them they selected a port and silently plugged the controller in to access the larger screen. "The visor's good, but we can both see the action from here," Bill said. "And I might set you off on a diversion or two when we see who we're dealing with."

Everyone watched, fascinated when the Snake was enabled and set off on a test slither across the floor, waving its' head mounted aerial to get the best signal and lifting its' front segments for a higher view. When Bill was happy with its' performance Arnold dismantled the cover to one of the extractor pipes in the ceiling and the robot was lifted up to start its' mission. The tail twitched once and it was gone, transmitting an illuminated view of the pipe back to the screen while it wriggled up into the kitchen wall space and searched for a suitable inlet grille to observe from.

"Can it cut its' way out?" whispered Laura. "The fans are up in the roof, but there's filter boxes in the walls lower down. Or can it be turned around?"

"No need," said Bill. "Its' happy running in either direction, but there are some tools in the head. Once we locate our visitors I'll give it a go. Let's see how Michael is first."

She nodded, close to tears, and went across to check on the two dinosaurans. She knew they understood what was happening and their calm silence was further proof of alert intelligence; she just wished they would trust her enough to talk.

Then there was crash from above and she jumped with a gasp of alarm. Whether someone had made a mistake in the dark, or it was the beginning of an open assault wasn't immediately clear. The Snake had found an inlet grille and sent back a hazy picture of the kitchen at full enhancement, then switched to infrared. At least two people were up there, hooded and moving with exaggerated caution in the unfamiliar space. They looked both practised and extremely sinister, not carrying weapons but undoubtedly dangerous in their intentions. Nor were they stealing goods; it was obvious they were searching for something along the walls, that they knew about a hidden space.

And Michael was just visible, lying trussed and gagged on the floor alongside the stove.

"Don't worry," said Sally. "We're not scared."

Laura jumped back. "What - - - what did you say!" She stared wildly at the two young creatures.

"We're sorry Laura," said Rex. He took Sally's hand. "We wanted to talk, we were going to soon."

Laura swung round, everyone else was staring intently at the view from the Snake; Arnold glanced their way but was immediately distracted when the image focused on a third intruder.

"Is that two women or two men," whispered Steven. "I can't tell."

"Could be our friends from the van," said Arnold. "Can we switch back to normal view for a second Bill?"

He nodded. "Sure, but it won't be any better than before." The screen view jumped. "See, still can't tell Jack from Jill. They know what they're doing, keeping themselves in the dark."

Tertiary

"Whatever, I guess we just ride this out," said Dan. "Doesn't look like Mike is going anywhere. But if they touch him again we go up, okay with you all?" Everyone nodded in agreement, all feeling frustrated and helpless. "Do we have any weapons down here?"

"Nothing," said Steven bitterly. "Just forks and spoons, not even a knife."

Arnold waved into a corner. "There's a wrench over there, with some tools, and a shovel I think."

"Better than nothing." Dan moved round. "Show me. Those bastards have the high ground, but first one up takes the shovel if we go."

Just as he spoke something crashed again, they heard the faint echo of a shot from outside and light flared on the screen.

"Headlights," muttered Bill. "Someone's aiming headlights in from the yard."

The Snake's optics compensated in mid-jump to infrared and back to normal. The three hooded figures were clearly visible now, down flat on the floor beside Michael. He struggled to sit up but was pushed roughly back again.

"Let's go!" Shouted Dan, grabbing the shovel and charging onto the stairs. Arnold fumbled for the wrench and followed him, nearly tripping and grabbing at his ankle. Dan shook him off and flung open the door. "Come on Arnie, one and a half each and I'll buy the beer."

A much louder explosion, now that the door was open, and the howling whine of a ricochet from the verandah's tin roof. Shouts, an engine revving and rattling to a stop from behind the blinding lights. Three black-clad figures leaping up and one falling again when Dan Alvin landed a swinging blow with the flat of the shovel; half crawling then diving in a low stumble behind the others, as all three ran out and sideways from the kitchen door. Shotgun blasts followed them into the darkness and echoed down to silence around the ranch.

Dan lifted the shovel high again and called out from beside the door. 'Don't think it'll be easy. Come in and try if you must."

"No need Senator," called a voice. "Be easy now and we'll come on over anyway. We'll leave our lights on if you like, so's you can see us."

Two figures moved forwards, just black outlines, and stepped across the yard, arms held out to show empty hands. "We're not carrying Senator, you're safe enough now."

Dan took a deep breath and flipped on the verandah lights. Then peered quickly round the door frame. "Do I know you?" he called.

"Most likely not. But your kin folks may remember."

Arnold stepped into the open doorway before Dan could stop him. "Jesus!" he said sideways. "It's the hunters. Those guys from the day we arrived." He turned back and knelt to free Michael, who was still writhing on the floor. "Mike, it's those hunter guys again!"

Michael lurched up to sit, back to the stove, rubbing at his face and wrists. "Tell the others it's safe to come up then. If they were planning to shoot us they'd have done it already." He pulled himself up by the stove rail. "I think they just saved our asses there."

Larry and Will stepped up onto the verandah's deck as Dan put down the shovel and stepped out to shake their offered hands. "I guess we owe you some proper thanks," he said. "Come on inside and be welcome. But how did you know I was here, kill my curiosity on that first."

Will laughed. "We'll ask if you've seen us before, outside of Nevada." He was looking to Steven and Laura as they came up from the basement. "We told you last spring we were mining gold. But before that we had work in Colorado. Does the name Tim McHawne ring the bells?"

"Damn, of course," said Steven. "You must have been in the Right-Hand team, when Tim broke through."

"Right," said Will. "And Right again." He laughed at his own joke and their confusion, a friendly sound. "Larry and me did some digging in the net after that time at the site. And when we saw you folks here we figured we'd keep an eye open. Not all miners just dig and sweat, some have real interest, to know what sleeps in the rock I mean."

"We saw you at the site too Senator," Larry's speech was slow and deliberate. "That last time, after those half-army suit shiners pulled out."

"But what led you here tonight?" asked Dan. "Did you know who those people were?"

"Just a lucky guess." Will looked at his hands. "We got wind of some druggies making plans, up in the mountains, and listened as close as we dared. Ex-military a lot of them, call themselves Survivalists, and mostly mean as hell. Think they figured kill two birds with a stone, if you had anything here worth taking."

"They were down anyway, selling at the fair. Happens every year," said Larry; action seemed to have made him talkative. "And I hear'd them say Fly Ranch quite clear."

"Larry's ears are the best." Will smiled all round. "Just glad we got here in time to be noisy."

"But they were looking for the door," Laura said quietly. "We saw them do that."

"Well I guess that's easy too." Will looked concerned. "Everyone knows Fly Ranch has a secret cellar. It's smuggler territory you see?"

"Well that settles it for sure," said Dan, talking to the whole group. "We move you out as soon as we can. Seems likely the folks we feared were hunting the real pirates round here."

"I'm not so sure." Laura spoke low, almost to herself. "Maybe they were working together."

Michael heard her but said nothing. He'd had the same thought, that there was more to all this than seeing off some potential raiders, and the lucky chance that Will and Larry had been in the right place and time to help them. At least he could trust their side of the story and thank providence for men who were kindly and concerned. "Do you want to see what this is all about," he heard himself say.

The others stared at Michael, shocked, but Will just smiled. "If you've a mind to trust us," he said, quiet and calm. "But don't put anyone at risk on our account."

"It's okay." Dan put a hand on Michael's shoulder. "My son's right. We owe you guys, and you should meet those you helped."

The two hunters climbed down into the hidden basement and stood at a careful distance from the dinosauran children; if they were amazed at the sight neither showed it, nor any alarm. Rex and Sally both looked up, quite unafraid, and twittered their childish laughter. "Funny men," said Sally. "But nice."

"I knew it," breathed Arnold. "I just knew it. Why speak now and not before, you little devils?"

Rex looked at him sharply, an adult expression that was frightening. "We're different, aren't we, and we don't know why. Will you ever tell us?"

"You came from the rock didn't you," said Larry. "From ages back."

Will touched his friends' shoulder, stepped forward a little and checked round to see if he should speak. Michael nodded approval. "Hi there kids, I'm Will and this is Larry. We're very pleased to know you." His face was gentle and sad. "But I don't think your friends here can answer that. Not yet."

"We thought so too actually," said Sally. "It doesn't really matter, does it Rex."

Rex looked down, saying nothing, the down of feathers around his eyes rippling slightly. Will saw the wonder of these strange children; the high foreheads, humanoid faces and changing expressions of fully aware beings. And exactly why this bunch of people had gone on the run, and out of their old worlds, to protect them. "Don't worry," he said. "Some day, when it's time, you'll find out."

Rex looked up, and then round all the human faces. "I guess so, I think we knew that. Thank you Will."

Laura was crying quietly and Arnold wiped tears away too. He choked a little, and coughed before speaking. "You kids, you learn so fast. But will you talk to us from now on?"

"Course we will," said Sally. "We always wanted to, just didn't know if we should."

"Or whether it would frighten you," Rex added. "You all talked about it so much. We weren't really sure you wanted us to."

Dan and Bill looked on, amazed and fascinated, while Steven and Michael were speechless, somewhere between shock and resentment. So Larry, the silent one, spoke for them all. "I say kids should be up and out, playing in the open air. What do you say Senator?"

Laura understood him at once, seeing past Larry's apparent slowness to his intention; to pull them all back, and let the children just be children for now. He caught her look and confirmed that thought with a quiet nod. A lot more to Larry than meets the eye, she thought, and stepped over to kiss him on the cheek.

The Senator stared at them both, briefly at a loss, then turned back to crouch in front of the dinosaurans. "What can we do better, do you know what you want from us?"

"We'd like to go out more, but we know why we can't. Well, not here in Nevada anyway." Sally took his hand. "Can we go somewhere else please. Like you said."

Nearly two years later, early morning mists swirled and drew back from around a house deep in the Florida Everglades. A small colonial style mansion made of white painted timber; the lawns surrounding it circled in turn by huge and ancient cypresses. Beyond the trees were the swamps.

A damp-curled comic lay at the edge of the main lawns' slope, still open at the centre pages. Moving images of alien creatures fought across the swollen paper from one blinding explosion of colour to another. Childish voices, thinning the air, were just audible from an open dormer window. Voices that were set low and urgent to avoid notice; an intense discussion between brother and sister.

"He said today Sally. If he said today, that's when he'll be here."

"But what if he's being chased? Like before. We might not see him for months."

"Don't be such a gloom-bag! You know what happened was just bad luck. He'll be okay Sal - -." A slight impatience in the voice, and the sound of a keyboard being tapped. "You worry too much, and I want to get this machine working."

"Well I think you're stupid Rex. Always telling me don't worry. I just see what's happening sometimes, alright! I never said I liked it."

Tears in the voice, almost a sob, as floorboards creaked under the weight of small feet.

A leat of dark water led into a dock below the east face of the house; a straight channel in from the winding and log choked waterways that made a tortuous jig-saw of the swamp in every direction. A propeller driven swamp boat was drifting out on a rope at the dockside, still rocking gently as its' engine cooled and water beaded on the blades. Mist rolled in to blanket the water where it had passed. Two figures waded up into open grass and sunlight; wreaths of white following their feet towards the house. Their faces in shadow at first; then turning back towards the sun.

Laura reached up to hold and kiss Michael again; swinging her arm around his waist as she leant against him and laughed. Then she frowned, her happiness chilling, as the mist swirled in a last attempt to claim the property. "Thank God you're okay. For a day or two there I thought we'd never see you again."

"Ah, well, I'm here now. And I've lost the Good ol' Boys long enough to relax a while. If I got it right they think I'm headed for Houston or the Hoover dam!" He put his arm around her shoulders and drew her closer; looking up with a smile when the strange child-like voices echoed from the house.

"It *is* Uncle Mike – Quick Rex, Uncle Mike's here!"

"Okay Sal, I heard the Swamp Bat. Just let me save this program. And you should let *him* talk to Laura first."

The second voice was slightly deeper but had the same whistling strangeness and high, fluting tones.

Michael and Laura hugged each other, laughing again, and turned to walk faster towards the house. Sunlight was already steaming its' white timbers.

"Sally! Rex! – Come on out here you two. Your old Uncle Mike wants to see how you look." He hugged Laura more tightly, and kissed her again quickly. "And bring that Steven Man out with you – Has he got any grey hairs yet?"

Steven appeared on the verandah at the southern corner of the house. "Only from waiting for you, O' elusive wanderer. Where the - - - ?"

Before he could finish two small figures burst past him, and down the verandah steps, to dash across the lawn. They were about four foot tall now; slender and elegant in form but still having the slight chubbiness of children. Short, flattened tails waved stiffly as they ran; their clothes tailored to allow them movement. The faces were almost humanoid, but a layer of tiny, tightly patterned feathers softened and coloured their features. They'd become miniature versions of the restoration sculpts that Laura made more than four years earlier – Dinosauran children.

They hardly slowed as they ran up and leapt into Michael's arms. He leaned back with their combined weight, swaying and laughing as he dropped Rex back to the ground. "Two out of seven ain't bad when they come like these two." He saw Laura's look of warning too late. "Oh, hell kids, I'm sorry. I've been up all night."

Sally was slightly shorter and more slender in build than her brother. She turned to Laura, craning round in the crook of Michael's arm. "Don't worry Laura." She turned back to Michael. The strange quality of her voice was like bird song. "We know about our brothers and sisters now." Her long, finely feathered arms wrapped around his neck. "We were sad, but we think there were seven to make sure some of us grew up."

"Damned viruses," muttered Steven, as he stepped stiffly down from the verandah. "Should have been five at least."

Michael was shaking his head in amazement. His eyes glistened even as he smiled; unprepared for how adult the dinosauran children had become. He put an arm round Rex, who stood at his waist, and lifted him up again. Marvelled at how he saw just a child.

"And we don't mind growing up so fast," said Rex. "It's nice here, but it feels like we remember somewhere else." He touched the corner of Michael's eye, and put the slender finger to his wide, cat-like mouth. "Your tears taste the same as ours, so we're not really different."

"Yes we are Rex," said Sally. "But it doesn't matter. I think we think the same."

Michael dumped them both down playfully hard, to hide his confused and racing emotions. "Well let's just pretend you're still children for the moment eh?"

Steven had walked across the lawn, stretching and swinging his arms to wake up. He smiled broadly with pride and with welcome. Michael grinned at him to control a sudden urge to cry; he felt this brief relief from extreme stress as a dragging tiredness that tripped his feet and left him at a loss for words. Steven just took his hand in both of his, shaking it, and then hugged him with silent concern and greeting.

"Come on you two." Michael shook himself and took the children's hands. "Show me how you've been plaguing your Uncle Steven." He turned back to his silent friend. "Either you're the best teacher on this mudball planet, or we've struck two out of two for genius."

Steven laughed, "I may have earned a few grey hairs, but not yet from working with them."

Both children punched at his legs. "Don't call us 'them'!"

"'These' then." He dodged quickly, jumping around to walk backwards in front of Michael; his expression suddenly serious. "How was it Mike? We were starting to worry you know."

Laura moved in to take Sally and Rex by the hand. Both of them understood, and whirled her away across the lawn as Steven and Michael carried on, slowly walking up and onto the verandah. They sat down into a battered old swing sofa.

"Good news first then – The Old Man can keep the funds coming in till the kids are ten at least, but he's under a lot of pressure. Too many eyes are opening and looking his way. He'll be forced to move even further into the background, to have any hope of protecting us long term."

"That was the good news?"

"We're going to have to move you all out again Steve. I was lying to Laura just now – I'm only two days ahead of the dogs at best."

Steven looked at him levelly, and sadly. "It's no surprise Mike. We're in trouble here too. We just can't keep the kids chained up – But the risk turned bad about a week ago."

"Shit! Someone's spotted them – Found this place?"

"Not that bad, but bad enough. There's a crazy rumour started up – 'Human Alligators seen in Swamp'. As bad as it could be in one way. Only good thing about it is the story's centred about twenty miles from here. I judged it safe to hang on till you got here." He paused, looking down to the dark water below the house. "My fault for sure – I gave in and took them out in the canoe around ten days ago. And we don't look out for the local news as much as we should; I only caught it on a hunter's channel last night."

"Not so bad then – Those guys are always telling tales. Damn though! But you didn't see anyone?"

"No. I took them along the back streams to the Deep Pool. I've never seen anyone get in there with a swamp boat, nothing much bigger than a canoe can make it." He paused again, looking up at Michael unhappily. "But they did wander off on their own for ten or fifteen minutes. I must have dozed for a bit. I gave them the riot act for swimming those waters, but they didn't say they'd seen anybody else."

"Take it easy Steve – It can't be helped. They're a lot more than just children now. I hadn't realised how far on they'd come." He looked out across the lawn to where the young dinosaurans were playing and tumbling. "My guess is they frightened the legs off some poor old 'gator hunter as a joke."

Steven nodded in reluctant agreement. "Maybe even on purpose. They want to move on more than we do; I sometimes wonder who's teaching who in this school. And they're under a lot of pressure too. They seem to know it." He looked suddenly pale and worn. "They could have been shot. They don't really realise how dumb people can be. Not yet. I guess I'm ashamed to tell them."

Now Michael looked away with the pain of his thoughts. The swamp boat drifted back in and bumped as it touched the old wooden piles of the dock. Water shook from the tips of its' prop, and the tiny thud sounded hollow in the early morning air. Laura and Rex and Sally came up off the lawn in a brief, happy interlude of energy.

Laura leaned back onto the railing while both children climbed onto a lap. "What's happening? These two are on at me about what they should pack?" Rex and Sally lunged forwards together and grabbed at her hands. "We don't have to move yet do we?"

The children bowed to each other, laughing, and nodded emphatically. Sally spoke first. "We can pretend we're going on holiday – Somewhere hot." She laughed again, a pleasant, trilling sound, and waved at the sun. The lawns were already beginning to shimmer in the new day's heat.

"Or somewhere cold." Rex clutched himself; miming a shivering fit. "We could go snow-boarding, and sledging."

Michael laughed in turn, shaking his head at the relief of tension the 'children's' fearless play inspired. "I can't handle whatever magic you two used to work that out. But, whatever - Rex wins. It's going to be somewhere cold. I'm sorry Laury. We have to be gone by midnight tonight at the latest." She looked at him wide-eyed; too stunned to speak, but ready for the worst. "But this time Lady, you can take me with you – If you'll have me. We have to lead the dogs away while these three go out through the swamps."

Rex and Sally's whoops of excitement died away as they saw Laura's expression. They scrambled up and wrapped themselves to her in silent reassurance; knowing with childlike faith that they couldn't possibly be parted for long. Everyone walked silently back to the house to plan and pack and wait for the evening to arrive.

When it did, and the last light of the day died, tangled in trees and a final pattern of glints from still water, the swamp boats' engine fired with a roar. Sheets of flame flicked and spat from the exhausts; a deliberately unstealthy start to a departure, with spray knifed back across creaking, moss-hung branches at the dead end of the leat. Water and reeds splashed and bent as the propeller roared in its' mesh cage. Then the engine idled down to a barking tick-over. Michael went up to the house for one final package, and climbed into the rocking boat to push it beneath a tarpaulin in the well. He had coloured his hair, and dressed to look like Steven. Two larger bundles were already laid on an air mattress under the tarp; he adjusted them with an exaggerated gentleness. Then Laura came out, locking the house behind her, and turned to look back, halfway to the water, in farewell. From the dock she climbed across, and up into the high double seat of the swamp boat. Michael pushed the craft away and stepped up to join her; falling back onto the seat as she gunned the engine and skidded the boat out into the first turn of the main waterway to the east.

Much later, when owls were hooting and silently gliding, three figures eased out from under the verandah; sliding an old, high-ended canoe beside them across the wet grass.

Steven had greyed his hair, and dressed as a swamp hunter. Both the children were wearing hunting jackets, with the hoods up, and waterproof overtrousers to disguise their unusually jointed legs and ankles. They reached the water at the near end of the dock, and launched the canoe under the shadow of an ancient cypress tree. Then climbed in, balancing and arranging themselves, before picking up paddles and pushing carefully away. They dipped and pulled; gliding almost silently into the dark, back waterways of the swamp.

Michael and Laura coasted into the creek side town of Little Cypress with the first light of dawn, seen only by a vigilant snail hawk sitting on a shoreline post. Bevs' Emporium was the one building running lights, just as they had hoped, and Laura jumped ashore just beside the ancient, battered boardway that led to a waterside gallery.

Bev herself was brewing coffee and scattering old magazines behind the counter. "Learne! How are you girl, long time this year. Where's Adrian, you bring him with you this time?"

"He's minding the Swamp Bat Bev. Got a good fever, and doesn't feel fit for company. He says to say hello." She took the automatically offered mug of coffee with a grin of thanks, and sat onto a high stool with an unfeigned yawn. "Still keeping early hours Bev. Don't you ever sleep?"

"Don't seem to need it now. Never did sleep much, even when Danny was alive." A gleam of mischief in her eyes. "Now what's your excuse young lady? Sliding in out of the mist with your man in a fever."

Laura laughed gratefully draining the coffee. 'A favour as ever Bev. Can we tie up the boat with you, and call a taxi? We're heading into Jerome and Collier to find a new Desktop for An - - Adrian."

Bev looked at her sharply. "He ever going to finish that story he's disking? We near called the Sheriff on you evening before last." Laura looked a question as casually as she could. "Saw your swamp boat fire up and out. The boys weren't so sure it was Adrian flying her."

"That was Adrian okay. Left the boat here to do some canoe exploring last week – Remember?"

"I guess so," said Bev. "Your business anyhow." She poured more coffee, and joined Laura on the second stool. "But you should both get some more company; not healthy to live all your days out in those swamps. Still, I guess you're out and about right now." She laughed, friendly and loud.

Laura smiled at her, not daring to explore the unspoken offer of help she suspected was being made. She stood, touching Bev's arm, and walked across to the antique payphone by the outer door. Bev watched her go, with an expression of concerned puzzlement on her lined and weather-tanned face. Then turned back to her magazine pile.

The white wooden house stood lifeless in an eerie stillness of early morning light and air. Mist lifted, bubbled and drifted, almost imperceptibly, from the water through the surrounding trees. Something broke the surface, and immediately swirled away from view, leaving a hole in the sliding vapour.

Then the door of the world slammed open, and everything was movement and noise. From a muted roar of engines to instant maximum; a heavylift tiltrotor hanging over the house and sliding sideways to blast a hole in the mist, down to green and bending grass. Steady rotation on its' axis, and lowering to land. A military pattern swamp boat roared as it skidded into view, and splashed forward as its' engine stopped and it crashed against the dock. Full of armed and vested men who jumped and ran, swinging heavy weapons, to surround and enter the empty, sleeping house. Echoes of doors kicked open timed to well ordered shouts, and then one man walking down, alone, off the verandah. Doors opened easily from the tiltrotor as its' huge propellers windmilled round and turbines whined to a stop. Everything down and done.

Men in suits stepped onto damp grass in a new morning stillness; among them Jim Larson and his nameless Washington shadow. They listened to a report, stoic in their stoniness, that only told them what an observant person would have already known. The house was empty. There were no obvious signs of occupation – DNA sniffers and advanced forensics might provide some faint traces of an evaporating trail. If they were very lucky, and those they pursued were unusually careless.

It was winter again. Six months on and Steven, Rex and Sally were tidying up another house; moving around the main room, sorting books and toys and generally cleaning the place up. The view out of a large end window, across a wide wooden balcony, was framed by fir trees; heavily weighted with snow. Across the valley forests and slopes and boulders were lit in black, white and dull green by the low mid-day sun.

"Will they really be coming today?" Rex was anxious. "Do you think they'll be in time to have lunch with us?"

"Don't fuss Rex," said Sally. "Steven told us they'd get here as soon as they can. We can have lunch and keep something for them." She deftly caught the cushion Rex threw at her, and carefully placed it on another chair.

"Very controlled little sister. You're just as impatient as I am."

Steven looked up and laughed. "And you both said you thought Dinos were more patient than Humans!"

Rex snorted. "We *are* still only children Steven, as you keep on telling us."

But Steven was already distracted again. He nodded vaguely, staring hard at the outside landscape, then opened the triple-glazed door onto the balcony. Sounds of birdsong floating into the high ceilinged room, together with a wave of freezing air. Their A-framed timber lodge was high up in the north of Sweden, Norrbotten County in Samiland, close to the Finnish border. The nearest settlement, Luspa, was fifteen miles to the east, and very little moved here in the depths of winter.

"That's *cold* Steven."

He waved Sally's protest down without turning; there was a faint drone of engines from deep in the valley. Rex and Sally ran up to stand behind him, ducking under his arms, and peered out into the cold. "Snowmobiles !" "It's them !"

Steven stared on, ignoring the joyful certainty of their shouts. "Maybe – I hope so - - -." He turned. "You two go down to the kitchen now. Be ready to hide if I ring the bell, okay. I know you hate it, but you're old enough to understand why."

Rex frowned theatrically. "And now we're *not* children." But he laughed quickly, and took Sally by the hand. Steven smiled after them as they hurried down to the door at the rooms' far end, and Rex turned to perform a parody of a childish wave; exiting with a flourish and a bow.

The sound of snowmobile engines was now clearly audible across the brittle air. Steven shrugged into a fur lined parka and stepped onto the balcony, closing the door behind him with a shiver that was more than being cold. He stared long and hard, down into the frozen valley.

The two SnowMoles were powering up a powder covered path; their track belts adjusting to the different density. A single, adult figure, bundled in furs, drove the lead machine. The second carried two smaller riders, similarly swathed and hooded in fur. The wan, mid-winter light cut under branches and blinded the depths of shadow where it couldn't reach; even with goggles set to maximum contrast it was hard to resolve any details. With the GroundMapper system acting up, and fuel running low in their reserve tanks, the competing claims of caution and cold fought for attention.

Valentina Turmansky kept the throttle wide open, checking the signal beam from behind her. Either she was right about this path, or they were going to die – It was, after all, traditional.

Steven came back in through the front door and into the lobby, set centrally in the lodges' southern wall. Then stepped out again to beat his arms across his chest, and brush snow from his clothes. He beckoned in welcome and led the way. The three hooded figures entered behind him, stepping stiffly over the high threshold. They were hesitant, still clawing ice and the remnants of a heavy layer of snow from their furs, and seemed reluctant to move any further.

Steven lifted a speaking tube from beside the inner door, blew the whistle, and called into it. "Sally, Rex – Come on up. Our visitors are here." He moved awkwardly into the main room, almost shy, urging the guests to follow him in and be at home. "Come in, come in. You must get warm – And then there is food. Please, you are safe here now."

The adult figure was struggling to unfasten a heavy fur over suit and hood. At the mention of food one of the smaller two ran forward and tugged enthusiastically at a sleeve, pulling the upper suit and hood off to one side and revealing the wearer as a Russian woman in her early thirties. She was tall, slender and beautiful; her long auburn hair falling free from a silk cap.

She smiled apologetically at Steven, as she was pulled sideways again by her arm. "Be still Tania," she murmured. "You will eat, and meet your new friends. Both at the same time."

The small figure threw back her own hood, and whirled excitedly around to fling back her partners' too; chirping in high, clear English. "And you, Mikhail, remember to be polite, and not so silent."

Both the small guests were dinosauran children; within a month or two they were the same age as Rex and Sally. Who now burst into the room from its' far end, then came to a stop; suddenly quiet themselves. Valentina laughed, turning to Steven, then back to Sally and Rex. She beckoned to them. "Come children. You must soon be friends, so let us begin without shyness."

Steven smiled broadly, and began to help Valentina out of the rest of her furs. Rex and Sally came forward, and very seriously assisted their Russian counterparts in the same way. Steven found himself grinning now. "It's good to see you. Welcome. We were afraid you would miss lunch."

"Ah, but we had a good guide," said Valentina. "Since he leaves us at the start of the valleys I must drive so fast to reach your lunch." She laughed again, tilting her head to confirm that Steven could understand her English. "I think that Mikhail will run me over, he and Tania are so eager to reach your table!" She touched Steven's arm and pointed, smiling fondly – The four dinosauran children had moved to look out of the window, and were already talking animatedly. Mikhail was pointing out the way that they had come, and describing the valleys and the lake below.

Steven smiled too. "I thought they would have trouble relating to each other. I need never have worried."

"Relating? Ah – They have seen no others of their kind. They maybe think they are Human. I understand." She pointed to the main sofa. "May I sit? I feel I have ridden a mad horse for too many days."

Steven's brief calm broke into embarrassment. "Of course. Please. Sit - - I, er – will you have a drink. A vodka?"

Valentina laughed in delight this time; laying right back into the sofa, and stretching with the pleasure of sudden relaxation. "Thank you, but not all Russians need vodka. Myself I think vodka is better to run the engine of a truck!" She smiled an immediate apology. "Forgive me. I take your hospitality too easily, but it feels so good to be safe again for a time." She stretched again, and sat upright. "I would very much like a whisky, if you have such a thing?"

"Whisky. Yes we have that. A malt whisky I think."

"Ah good. That one is the best. Please just with ice. That is 'rocks'?"

Steven nodded, pouring two glasses.

"Even from the cold, I must still have ice if I can!"

Steven handed her a glass and sat down opposite.

"Thank you." She looked round, suddenly concerned. "But I am a fool distracting you – They are not safe there, at the window?" She started to get up.

"No, no it's alright. The glass is shielded – No one can see inside. Even from the balcony it is difficult."

Valentina sat back, but she was tense again; gripping her glass with both hands as she perched on the edge of the sofa. "I think of myself, of tiredness, and relax too soon. Ah, the warmth of Georgia seems a long time ago." She raised her glass, threw the whisky back in one swallow and shivered.

Steven got up, refilled without speaking, and she drank again, more slowly. He remembered the obvious. "I think we should eat. You said that Tania and Mikhail were hungry, and I know that Rex and Sally always are!"

She smiled tiredly and got up, suddenly withdrawn and waiting to be directed. Steven looked at her uncertainly and went over to the dinosauran children, shepherding them across to the large table at one corner of the window. He noticed Mikhail gently persuading Tania to take off the last of her outdoor clothing. He'd assumed the child was still cold, but was shocked to see that she had one withered arm and a slightly hunched back. Her right leg was also twisted; she'd disguised the limp with her quick, skipping movements.

Tania looked at Steven with a very adult concern. "It's okay, I'm used to it – I was born this way. Other people worry though."

Sally took her hand. "Come on, let's eat. We're starving."

The children reacted to the simple meal as if it was a Christmas feast, though at first they were too hungry to speak much. Both pairs were shooting glances at each other, and exchanging nudges and snorts of laughter as they overcame the last of their shyness. But Valentina struggled to hide her tiredness and continuing anxiety; she was eating very little.

Steven became annoyed by his own uncertainty and diffidence, not knowing how he could help. He was used to living alone with Rex and Sally; the lodge suddenly felt too crowded. And he was inhibited by the power of his attraction to their Russian guest. "You should try to eat Valentina – You're all safe now. And our lift will be here in four days. That's been confirmed."

"I thank you for the concern. My mind knows that you are right. But my body feels that we are always pursued. Ever since our two groups become aware of each other." She stared down unhappily at her plate. "I am used to being strong. And always happy to trust our people. I find that this sudden weakness is a distress."

Steven wasn't sure what he could say. He sensed Valentina's admission was something unusual for her, and didn't feel worthy of, or equal to, her trusting him so soon.

The sad spell was broken by Sally. "Don't you think Valentina is very beautiful Steven? Even when she doesn't smile."

Tania gave Sally a wide stare; then grinned conspiratorially. Rex joined in, feigning ignorance. "What are you two grinning at – How can we tell if a human is beautiful?" He winked at Tania and she curled up, trying not to laugh. "Anyway, you know Steven doesn't care what women look like – He's only interested in how they think."

Tania snorted, and even Mikhail, who was so far the most reserved, smiled broadly.

Steven was speechless – The subtlety of the dinosauran children's awareness, if not their ploy, had caught him by surprise again. Valentina, by contrast, appeared to be relaxed and confident again. She looked quite openly at him. "Very knowing, these 'children' – No?"

All he could do was spread his hands, too confused to speak. "They grow one year in one month, yet we must be their teachers." She picked up her fork. "Suddenly I have good appetite again – Tomorrow we will worry about tomorrow."

Steven managed a strangled grunt of agreement, and Valentina looked to her plate, smiling to herself.

So they continued into the early evening, talking as the children played together and the darkness outside deepened. Till everyone admitted how tired they all were, and agreed it was time to sleep.

Next day a blizzard swept across Norrbotten County, and whirling curtains of snow sealed residents and newcomers alike into their isolated world. There was no landscape for distraction, except the rooms they burrowed in, so both groups were forced into social conversation.

As the winds howled thin and high across armoured windows the young dinosaurans continued to play their way into friendship with the eerie speed of children anywhere. While Valentina and Steven found some common ground in all the strangeness and tragedy of hatching and raising them, and continued a halting exploration of each others' boundaries. Valentina seemed calm again, but was still trembling inside; knowing how close to death she and her charges had been the day before. So she told Steven stories of similar isolation in the Stony Tunguska river block houses and bunkers, and he recalled the stubborn survival of chickens in Kansas to amuse her.

They often smiled and turned away, still unwilling to admit any reliance upon each other. There was no need to hurry; the blizzard threw an eerie veil over normal time, as if they'd always been there together and always would be. Neither one was surprised, both had experienced this before in the eyes of various storms. And there were several weeks to go before the next move could be made.

As the day turned to a darkened afternoon the blizzards' strength gathered and beat around the house; a continuous, faint roar at the threshold of hearing.

After a while the children ran down to the rooms below, and began a noisy contest with a Russian interactive. Valentina and Steven hardly noticed.

"Not the green one!" said Mikhail, in an amused voice. "That one only moves sideways. It's all based on chess you see."

"We play chess!" said Sally. "Well, Rex does actually. He only uses me to practice on, when his old retro computer's broken. I prefer it when he's taking it apart - - - " She smiled at her brother to show she was teasing. But he pretended to take offense; waved his arms about in mock anger and shouted in American slang. Until he realised Tania was moving away.

The dinosauran girl seemed genuinely scared, backing towards the snow blocked windows, and Rex suddenly had no idea how to behave or what to say. Sally tried to save him with a quick laugh and a mock blow. "Don't worry about him Tania, he's just a bit mad when the moon is full!"

But to her dismay this only seemed to make things worse. Now it was Mikhail who looked disturbed; edging around the room until his back was to the exit stairs. He inclined his head and looked to his sister as if they both should run away. And his eyes frightened Sally; something alien and cold watching her. "What's wrong?" she cried. "Rex was only joking. He didn't mean anything bad."

"We're sorry too," said Tania abruptly, shaking herself. She moved back across the room and held out a hand towards her brother. "We're not so good in your language, and we don't know those words."

"Yes we do," muttered Mikhail in Russian. "What the team leader used to say. When he was angry."

"He was scared Mikky, not angry. Well, most of the time."

Rex wondered what Mikhail had said, and why Tania had replied in English. He watched her then with a puzzled respect, and saw how she calmed her brother with a look rather than words. She was masking something that was just on the threshold of his awareness, and he knew he would ask Sally about it later if he could. However much they fought and differed he had a deep trust in her abilities. As she'd said, back in Florida, she could sometimes see what was really happening.

The room was very quiet. Some child's instinct told them the adults would notice if the silence went on much longer. Tania breathed deeply, decided she might tell them more; to trust their new friends. 'After all,' she thought, 'there are only four of us in the world. So far as we know.'

"The team leader in Siberia, back when we were very young, used to swear in American," she said. "I think he was showing off really. It was weird, and neither of us liked it much." She glanced at Mikhail, and he nodded. "Sometimes they wanted to experiment on Mikhail, but Valentina always stopped them - - - ."

"Why - - -," began Rex. But then stopped, seeing the look Sally shot him.

"Once they did," said Mikhail. "When Valentina was outside. But she got so angry, when she realised, that they stopped it right away." He looked far away. "It was only questions really, but some of them wanted to wire me up. To fire signals into my head."

Tania moved beside him, touched his hand briefly, and looked round to the others. "It was a strange place, nothing like this. And some of the people were real science freaks - - . Is that how you would say it?"

"Close enough," said Rex. "Or 'science geeks'. That's old talk really. But wait till you meet Arnold."

"Rex!" said Sally. "You hardly ever do that. And you like Arnold. A lot. And he likes you."

Rex was suddenly completely off balance; embarrassed and ashamed that he'd upset the Russian children, and now made Sally think badly of him. The tiny feathers around his eyes fluffed up, the dinosauran blush response, and he turned away muttering. "Just going upstairs. See what the storm's doing."

Sally hesitated, then moved to follow, but Tania stopped her with a touch to her arm. "He'll be back soon. We don't mind his joke." She smiled then. "It's good not being alone any more."

Sally smiled back, and nodded towards the game they'd been playing. Tania laughed aloud and grabbed Mikhail's hand. "Come my brother. Together we can beat her!"

The new offices of MosFed Special Services International looked out across the inner courtyards of the old Kremlin complex; churches and office buildings still externally preserved as they had been in the previous century. MFSSI was offspring to the marriage of Mafia and old KGB structures in the early years of twenty-one; the difficult decades of the twentieth were reflected in the survival of a military hierarchy.

Colonel Irina Korolev was pacing up and down in front of her assistant operations wizard, Sergei Malkovich, a nervous young man in his late twenties with the temporary rank of Major. She stopped central to his view of snow-covered roofs and glittering onion domes. "Tell me Sergei, have you or I any real idea of who, or what, we are pursuing?" She centred the map on her desktop screen. "We know – We suspect – that the information from the Caucasus chamber is essentially useless, designed to keep us busy rather than informed. We know the Americans have their tunnel in Colorado, and so suspect – and hope – that their information also has no real worth."

She paused, and zoomed the map out. "We know that they, again as we, have personnel missing from the site. We track our people to Georgia and find no-one. Six months ago the ARPA go hunting in Florida – and find – no-one."

She turned to look out of the window. "Perhaps Sergei we should invite our American colleagues here, so we may usefully cry into some vodka together. Then all we would have, after all this running and searching and waiting for information, is some water in our spirits!"

She slammed her fist onto the glowing screen, staring belligerently at the unhappy Sergei. All he could do was stare in turn at the open paege on his knees. "Ah – Take that signal away and have it scanned again. Perhaps we will learn something at the Finnish border – If only how cold we will be when we get to Siberia!"

Sergei snapped the paege shut, nodded sharply and rose silently from his chair. Irina Korolev was turned to the window again, watching a new flurry of snow obscure the Moskva river and deep in thought. Perhaps a new layer in their tenuous co-operation with the Americans' agency wasn't such a bad idea; something more than restricted and patronising access to some superior technology. She smiled thinly; at least her people had discovered and kept hold of their dinosaurans for several years and gathered a large body of information about their growth and development in that time. Maybe this advantage should finally be revealed and put to use.

Weak afternoon sunlight was streaming through the large end window of the forest lodge. Steven and Valentina were packing media wafers into file cases. He scratched his head as he looked around; muffled noises from the rooms below. "I hope those kids are keeping it light – They do know there's only one tilter, not a fleet?" After three weeks of such crowded company he felt they had been together forever. "And don't they ever do anything quietly!"

Valentina laughed, taking his hand. "When you say 'kids' I still see four of antelope – At least their energy is the same!" She touched his cheek, suddenly looking sad. "And your word 'tilter' makes me frightened for them -- No, do not worry, I am just sad to leave this safe house. So quickly it has become a home."

Tertiary

Steven caught her other hand. "Valentina - - - ?"

"Yes - - Steven."

He drew her slowly closer by both hands, and they kissed, hesitantly at first. Then she freed her hands and wrapped her arms around his neck, hugging him close and kissing fiercely. She pushed back, his arms still looped around her waist, and they smiled happily – A promise to each other.

Mikhail came into the lower end of the room, and they parted, turning back to the choices of packing with a bad attempt at covering how close they'd been. Mikhail smiled down at the floor, then stepped up onto the window level. "We're all ready Steven. When do we ride the American tiltrotor ?"

"I guess as soon as it arrives Mikky. You have all packed just the *one* bag haven't you?" Steven looked him up and down with a wry smile. Mikhail's hooded jacket bulged heavily, with every pocket stuffed full. "And do the other three look like they've come in from a shop-lifting expedition too?"

Valentina smothered her laughter with one hand.

Mikhail looking at her reprovingly. "Shop lifting? Ah, yes – A western invention. We've only packed the things we really need, like you said we should Steven " He dropped the serious look, and smiled mischievously. "And perhaps a few other things, to be certain!"

Steven gave up. "Oh, what the hell – I reckon I'll let the pilot worry. Just so long as you can all walk without breaking a leg."

Mikhail trilled a laugh and hurried heavily to the door, twirling once to show how agile he still was. He stumbled slightly, and Valentina burst out laughing again, till tears came to her eyes and, for a moment, she really was crying. Steven looked down the room, but Mikhail had managed a dignified exit. Outside a faint whine of turbines echoed off the mountains, muffled by a new snowfall, but rapidly coming closer.

Valentina got up, wiping her eyes, and went to the window to look out through the whirling snow . She sprang back with a cry, knocking a pile of erased cassettes from the table. "Something out there – Not the tilter!' She waved wildly, standing back from the glass. "It sees through the glass – I can feel it."

Steven pulled a black card from his top pocket and pressed a red button, setting off a warning chime lower in the lodge, then ran to join Valentina. A small drone, that was almost all fan casing, hovered lightly above the railing round the outside deck. Its' sensor turret was pulsing a narrow web of laser light to and fro across the silvered glass, and Steven had no doubt a whole suite of other less visible scans were being made. As he moved to activate the houses' limited defences the drone rocked in a down blast of air and was lit from above by a blinding lance of light. It twisted its' body round and turret upwards to identify the source, then suddenly lifted a foot, and slewed sideways.

A red laser line within the light swept the periphery of its' casing and locked just behind the turret, seeming to stabilise the machine in the snow filled air, guiding it in a slow spin around its' own axis. When the laser cut off it hovered briefly, as if uncertain of its' position or direction, then darted away into the gathering blizzard.

"They let it go!" cried Valentina, above the steady howl of tiltrotor engines and a back echo from the rising storm.

"I doubt it," shouted Steven. "I think they re-wired its' tiny mind. Sent it home confused to give us a bit more time." He'd run to the lobby door, and thrown a switch on the lighting panel. Outside a square clearing was marked by lights on short posts. The tiltrotor cut its' own light beam, and settled onto the harder packed snow its' props had scoured clear.

By the next afternoon the wind had died away, the storm blown over, and the fading winter light glittered across a landscape softened to stillness under fresh snow. A strange flattened shape was flying low and fast along the bed of the valley; a peculiar, angled, bat-like form. It turned and swept, almost silently, up and over the lodge; a small object falling behind it, slowed by expanding vanes, and gliding down to bury itself in the snow beneath the balcony.

Seconds later the silence was shattered by another aircraft flashing into sight, rolling side to side then whipping into a turn; a double delta with the triple crown of Sweden under its' wings. It blasted across the lodge with a window rattling roar, and disappeared in pursuit of the unmarked invader.

Inside the lodge something scratched and scraped beneath the floor. Within half an hour the probe had found a way into the structure and was patiently cutting upwards through the insulation and timber boards. It acknowledged its' partner which had doubled back to land, crawled under trees in the nearby woods, and now lay camouflaged, waiting to carry it home. The signals between them had taken less than half a second; even a satellite directly overhead would have failed to lock on to their position.

The probe was less than a foot long; it had a lot of ground to cover. It pulled up from the hole in the floor and walked forward on four of its' six legs, beginning the search for known and unknown DNA traces inside the lodge. The forward pair of legs unfolded tools and samplers, ready to supply the lab in its' abdomen with material for analysis. But, despite all its' sophistication, it was unable to either know or care that the trail was already cold.

Arnold Shintowsky woke up to the sound of an urgent message alarm. That could only mean that they were moving again. Ellen rolled over with a groan and went back to sleep on his side of the bed. His wife! – He could still hardly believe that he was married, even more than a year after the event. The new job at the World Science Court had given him a life changed beyond any daydream, and a whole new perspective on the ongoing efforts to hide and maintain their absent friends.

Ellen had been on the WSC interview board that Senator Alvin prompted to head hunt Arnold from his post at DNM. And she had been the only one on the board who knew what his connections really were; acting as a bridge between Dan Alvin's involvement and the practical provision of aid and cover for the dinosaurans. Ellen had decided the only sure way to guarantee Arnolds' safety was to place him in a good marriage.

Now, five years after he had last seen Steven, Arnold was working to find him another safe house, half way across the world from his own new home in Hawaii. The alarm chimed again, shaking him from his sleep-furred reverie, and activating a pre-set routine on his desktop upstairs. He swung reluctantly out of the bed, hauled on a robe, tied himself untidily into it, and stumbled up the stairs to the office. Then thumbed the alarm to silence and slumped into his work chair, muttering a command that opened a secure file on new houses.

The best choice for a new hideaway was less than five hundred kilometres south of the forest lodge, close to the centre of a web of false tracks radiating across the planet. It was the old but reliable trick of turning back and hiding so close to the previous scene that a pursuer would overrun and keep on running; expending energy on the chase and never backtracking far enough. If the false trails were convincing enough.

The house was set into a steep bank on the shoreline of a lake in the Norrland Region of Sweden, closely surrounded and overhung by trees, bushes and undergrowth. The two upper floors were covered by a steeply pitched roof, and a wide balcony extended over a deep channel in the foreshore; covering the entrance to a boat dock that burrowed back into the bank.

It was listed and mapped as a Warden Centre for the Swedish Nature Reserve, and also covered the entrance to a decommissioned regional command bunker; built in the depths of the Cold War to track any threats to Sweden's neutrality. Early in the twenty first century the bunker had been lost from the official record as closed; referring it to a conversion for domestic use from old lists of private dwellings. In fact it had stayed active on an obscure funding from the Stockholm International Peace Research Institute (SIPRI), which was itself inherited by the World Science Court, and promptly lost again as part of the unlisted research department set up to mirror and monitor ARPA and all similar institutions.

Several further firewalls protected WSC from accusations of hacking the InfoNet and national or corporate research networks. So, for five years, the dinosauran children and their guardians had remained lost in the crowd in a world devoid of any real privacy. Several cleverly orchestrated revelations in the trash media came so close to the truth that a perfect cover was formed from rational disbelief in, and distrust of, fringe mania. These were Michael's contributions.

Ellen came into the room, yawning and concentrating fiercely on two mugs of coffee, and leant over Arnold's shoulder. "Did they meet up all right – How's the new house?"

"One at a time Dear Lady, my brain is still in bed with a woman."

She cuffed him, slopped her coffee, and cursed. "Get a grip Arnold, this coffee and I need each other."

"Okay Elli, in order, including the next two questions. The house looks fine. They met up, and got picked up, on time. So they'll be moving in right now I guess." He scrolled on through the report. "And there's something here about an intrusion into Swedish airspace across the Finnish border. Some sort of UAV - not a recognised type from the USA or the New Federation. It disappeared just over the lodge the day after they left. No-one's got in yet to check it out."

"Mm," said Ellen. "Did you call Mike and Laura?"

No, do you think I should? I mean, they'll have a copy of this too won't they."

"Oh sure, I just meant we've not seen them since they were here. Wondered how they were doing. You know."

"Right." Arnold rubbed his eyes. "Well, I can't help noticing it's the middle of the night. And we always seem to get these urgent calls after the event. I say we go back to bed. Decide if there's anything to worry about in the morning."

Ellen frowned. "Something's bugging me Arnold. Can't figure what it is - - Let's just call Bill McC. See if he's got a line on that UAV. It's got a sort of Skunk Works smell to me – And he's always up on the latest toys from the bad boys."

He was already touching in the code. The desktop confirmed a coded link both ways; and came up almost immediately with a rotating view of the bat-like Unmanned Air Vehicle. An unclaimed hybrid of Russian and US programs to develop stealth drones; sightings had been reported to the

WSC's covert research teams, from several countries, in the previous two days.

"Well I'm buggered," he muttered. "Trust Bill to know the answer before the question! Looks like the New Freeze is over at last."

Ellen smiled at his expression and put her hands over his. "I think I'll send a note to Mike and Laura after all. Just to let them know we're thinking of them."

Arnold nodded and got up to let her use the console. "I'll see you in bed, dear lady, once you've done what you must."

Ellen's message flew on its' way through all the intricate links of the InfoNet and appeared on its' target screen, but for now it was ignored. Michael and Laura were exceeding all limits as they drove towards Havana; after decades of blockade and isolation the roads of Cuba were still being brought up to World standard, and they were far away from the island's few automated trainways. Michael, half asleep, had just swerved away from his twenty first chicken, and, as agreed, passed control of the scarred and feather-decorated Jaguar to Laura. It's illegally re-converted hybrid engine growled harmoniously as she pushed the stick forward to maximum again.

"So much for happy holidays," said Michael. "And what happened to me driving too fast?"

"We have to get there Mike. If it's true the opposition is teaming up, and using nanotech, the kids could be in real trouble." She shoved the controller violently. "I thought these things were still the fastest, even without 'restoration'."

"Is the hud lying? You went through two hundred on that last straight." He closed his eyes briefly. "Pity about the ejection seat option we passed on."

Laura glared at him without turning her head. "Wise up Mike. And yes, the holidays are over. We should never have gone so far away - I let you persuade me."

"Christ Laura, you just don't release on a bite do you, I know we have to get there - What the hell do think all those chickens died for?" He shouted his seat down to sleep, then looked back up again. "Just stay this side of supersonic."

Five hours later they were on the outskirts of the city and homing in on the WSC hub complex as fast as the trainways and a few free back streets would allow. Soon after Hawaii had taken independence the triple crown of Sweden had been redesigned and given a revolutionary new significance. Then it became a symbol for the World Science Court's neutrality; the three points of the crown standing in Havana, Stockholm and Honolulu, with Singapore as the sceptre in the east. The WSC had been formed with a genuine peoples' mandate from all around the world and, with military technology as its' initial primary target, had rapidly developed an even harder bite than the reborn Union of Nations which had birthed it.

The complex itself was chaos – A hydrofoil terminal for the new Delta Clipper SSTO BayPort was being built out from the waterfront, and the coastal road was choked with WSC staff, visitors to the promotion centre, construction operators and all their vehicles. A tourist suffering from some untreatable form of obesity had collapsed in the mid-morning heat, and in the middle of the road, defeating every effort to move him out the sun and the way. His extended family were all trying to help at once, completely confusing and compounding the problem. Michael had only just fallen asleep, and woke up with a groan of pain at the bedlam of outside voices.

"You okay Mike? It could be quicker to walk from here."

"Yes. No. Not really, give me a minute. What's happening?"

"The usual – City stuff."

"Jesus, that poor guy's enormous. Can't he get treated?"

"If I could let air out of him right now, I would."

Michael woke up looking at her. "You really are worried aren't you – That's just not like you at all."

"I'm worried Mike, okay. Let's just get there."

She pulled the car in between two construction cabins and parked it; in all the noise and focus on the fallen man no-one challenged them. They got out and hurried on around the crowd without looking back, knowing that they were already late and very tempted to ignore protocols and phone ahead to tell Dan they were okay. But they also knew he would wait at least an hour before he logged them missing and went into secure channels to make contact.

Just a few streets away, at the Café Marcos, Dan Alvin sat back into his terrace seat, relaxed and reflected on how he was in love with Cuba. Ever since he'd first fought for a lifting of the US embargo on trade with the island he'd wanted to visit, and now he was a citizen; retired with honour from Washington. His years of work behind the scenes, to argue for and establish the World Science Court, had led him eventually to its' headquarters, and what he claimed was a purely honourary post in the political office. Then he'd got the call from Michael at Dinosaur National Monument and all hell had broken loose; something he would now admit being eternally grateful for, a semi-retirement had been close to driving him insane with boredom. Whatever the problems and compromises of keeping the dinosaurans safe and away from official dissection, figurative or gruesomely literal, he'd been back in the territory he'd always known best, and known was best for him. He hated some of the necessary subterfuge, even if he'd always known some level of concealment in his political dealings, but from the start he'd sensed something potentially world-changing in the dinosaurans; something he'd never believed possible despite all his achievements during the World Science Courts' creation. It was the same old instinct for change that had always served him well, whenever he'd trusted it, but it had been so strong then that he'd been unable to deny it or turn away from wherever it might lead him.

But for now he was perfectly content to sit on a café terrace above Malecon and look out over Havana Bay to the sloping walls and turrets of Castillo del Morro; musing on how the Spanish castle architects would have viewed the bayport floating to the south. And their reaction to clipper ships that came into harbour on pillars of fire, floating down the sky!

Michael and Laura would have left Nipe Bay, more than five hundred miles to the Southeast, around one in the morning and wouldn't call in from the open road unless they had a real emergency. They were now almost twenty minutes over their rendezvous time at the café but Dan refused to worry; his real concern was with the safe house in Sweden, and the forces and technology that threatened the dinosauran children's security. Although he'd never resolved the ethical dilemma of running a covert program behind an open institution, he could see no reason to waste energy trying – This situation was confirmed as the special case of all time, and was driven by the spirit, if not the letter, of the Science Courts' mandate. Providing impartial oversight of scientific revolutions was the courts' reason for existence. So, appropriate to be in Cuba.

Ernesto, his host, grinned and signalled from the far corner of the sunny, flower scented terrace. Dan glanced at his table sensor pad. The Café Marcos provided the best secured privacy in the city, using top line equipment, as well as company and cooking second to none. Then he realised his friend was pointing to the street below. Two figures were skirting the noisy melee further down the waterfront, and now came running up the steps through arches of climbing plants and flowers.

Dan stood up, with a smile of relief, and pulled out chairs in welcome. "Good timing you two, Ernesto says the fish soup is just about ready for sampling."

Michael and Laura fell gratefully into their seats, too tired for the moment to return more than nods of happy anticipation.

"Obviously the trip of a lifetime – But not too life threatening?"

"Don't worry Dad, we're here now," said Michael. "We left the remains of the best car in the world down the street. It'll probably be towed and trashed."

Laura glanced at him indulgently, stretching far back in her chair, and smiled at Dan. "Any more news? We got a spec on the stealth drone."

Dan relaxed back himself. "We think it somehow sampled the lodge - Something bored its' way in there, then left a track to take-off burns. That all came in about five minutes ago, the team at the site are still analysing." He waved to Ernesto. "The big news, though, is Moscow thawing out – I feel like I'm back in the nineties."

Their host came over to take orders, though he already knew what they'd be eating, his round face wrinkling with genuine pleasure in their company.

Ernesto had escaped out of Cuba as a boy and then back in again as a man, and loved all things American, despite the long and troubled relations between their two countries. "My third son is fetching your fine Jaguar car my friends – So you must please relax, and restore yourselves. The supreme soup of Havana is ready. The fish have been swimming since dawn, and now they are tired and wishing to meet you."

He laughed aloud with the joy of his own wit, and another sunny day in Cuba, and whirled gracefully away to the kitchen; his patrons reflecting his smiles and good humour all the way.

Michael watched him go with eyebrows high. "How does he do that? We only just got here."

Dan grinned. "Everything there is to see in this neighbourhood Ernesto sees it. That's why we come here. And for his company. And for the soup." Then smiled sadly. "I sure wish I could love people the way he does."

"Come on Dan." Laura pulled herself up to the table. "Why do you think he values you as a friend? He's king of the streets – You watch out for a whole planet."

"Maybe so. Where did we get to?"

"Moscow," said Michael. "You said there's been a thaw?"

"Because they still haven't found their dinosaurans they're pissed and trying to be friendly. Only with our hunters here of course. Wheels within wheels, we know because we have an agent in ARPA; without him, or her, we'd not have kept the kids free for so long." He sat forwards. "Valentina and her team escaped four years after the eggs hatched, that was the story. Everyone lost track of them till two months ago, apart from rumours. The rest you already know."

Michael stared. "You never told us you'd known about them that long."

"I'm sorry Mike. Secrecy and covert operations always run together – Doesn't matter how benign the host is, the institution gets corrupted by the process. WSC hasn't changed as much as I feared, but it's suffered. I went along with keeping the Russian tunnel quiet, partly because we weren't sure the whole thing wasn't a bluff."

"You thought they'd found out about our 'kids', and only pretended theirs?"

"Right. Right back to the Cold War in fact. Convince the enemy you have the same weapons even if you haven't, and if you have got 'em, pretend you've got more of them than you have. Makes the military happy either way, on either side. And keeps the funding coming."

"But the New Freeze was economic, not military," said Laura. "I always thought they were open on science."

"Same principle applies," Dan replied. "Economic warfare, or an information war if you like. But the coincidence was the killer. Convergent evolution in military technology is one thing – But the chances of finding two chambers, at the same time, after sixty five million years?"

"I know. I've never really worked that one out. Unless there was some sort of trigger, but how could that be?" Laura stretched again. "What I need right now is brain food." She looked at Dan with a suppressed yawn. "So what's the plan now that we do have all the kids together?"

"We go on as before I guess. I've argued the funding and the cover for another two years." He suddenly looked weary, and stared out over the glittering waters of Havana Bay. "Problem is Laura, we still don't know why they're here do we?"

Colonel Irina Korolev was admiring her own grey hairs and ruefully admitted they were probably well earned. She looked behind herself, noting that the mirror in this new office showed the view across yet another river. Why she always had a view over water was a mystery that she chose not to explore too deeply; something she occasionally dreamed of when paranoid fears took form in the night. Perhaps the Bureau operatives who assigned office space had a strange sense of humour, or perhaps it was just that government offices required a commanding position. Whatever the cause she decided to be grateful, and stepped across to the window where she could study the view in more detail.

She was in the far north west of Russia, in Murmansk, checking reports from the Finnish border that Valentina Turmansky had been sighted in the company of two children. According to witness accounts, gathered by her best MosFed operatives, the children had been strange and withdrawn, refusing to speak to anyone or to be seen clearly. But in the month since that sighting the tale had obviously grown in the telling, so filtering truth from fantasy was her first concern.

Irina thought back to the base in the Stony Tunguska River region, far to the east, where the eggs had been hidden and hatched and where it had all really started. The discovery team had seemed to accept their isolated location at the time, and the need for it, yet the subtle signs had already been there and she'd missed them. If she'd only had the patience to see, and the instinct to watch more closely, the whole of this difficult and frustrating chase might have been avoided. But her masters apparently still trusted her, laid no obvious blame at her door and continued to approve any level of resources she might ask for.

Now Sergei Malkovich, the best of her best Majors, quietly entered the room and set about upgrading and tuning their communications hardware, integrating various databases and generally making the new office a clone of all the old ones they'd worked and sweated and argued in. This morning Irina was calm and rested and accepted his presence gratefully; she knew he regarded her moods, tirades and arguments as part of his function in the team and sometimes even this irritated her. But today she wanted to be kind and try to put Sergei at his ease; manipulation or not she knew it would hook his nervous energy and bring out the best of his talents and ideas.

"So they were seen at Matalaniemi," she said, turning into the room. "Were they hoping to jump across the water to Finland?"

Sergei quickly consulted a report. "Maybe so, but more likely it was another of their diversions. They turned back south and crossed the land border somewhere near Nautsi. That is where the last, best reports of a sighting came from. The ones I would trust despite all exaggerations and wild speculation."

"Good Sergei, very good," said Irina. "As I trust you and your instincts. And also your guess that they jumped across Finland to Sweden and have been hiding there since - Did the machines find anything?"

He glanced at his paege, and across to the desktop screens. "That report is just coming in Colonel. It says that a lodge was occupied, then suddenly vacated. Our first probe was destroyed and there is information someone else landed at the same time, possibly the Swedes. The analysis from a second probe will be more thorough, once complete. But I do not think it will tell us so very much more."

"Because it is American," said Irina bitterly. "And already they know much more than they will tell us I believe. We step along behind as always, and pick up what we can from the trail. Am I right Sergei?"

Sergei stared at her. 'That is what they would like us to think, if you are asking for my opinion. But they are even more confused than us, believe me Colonel. They will not admit that the ones we hunt are better equipped and much better organised, nor that they have no idea how this is being done."

Colonel Korolev walked back to the window and stared out across Murmansk. "Did I ever tell you how all this madness started? Back when the tunnel and the sphere were first discovered." She touched one finger to the glass. "It was an American agent who came to us at MosFed, wanting to trade information and ideas. Not so subtle on the front, the Americans but this one knew how to use that mask very well. I didn't meet him then but I watched him talk from another room. We treated him badly of course, but in the process we made a mistake of assessment and he found out much of what we then knew. In particular that we had discovered a second chamber, that there were eggs inside it and that we had not yet lost track of them."

"Yes, you told me this," said Sergei. "But not so much of how it was as the children began to grow."

"I could have told you more Major, I know this now," Irina replied, with a hint of regret. "Would you like to meet that American? He is here in Murmansk. We have not dealt with him directly, since his visit to Moscow, but now is the time to be more kind and to make him feel at home I think." Sergei's face briefly showed his astonishment and the Colonel was both amused and pleased to see how quickly he controlled it. "He will not be expecting us," she said. "So watch him closely. You know well enough how first reactions can tell us much."

Sergei nodded. "I do Colonel," he said, with the ghost of a wry smile. "Shall we go now or later?"

"Now Sergei, while the sun is still high in the sky. He will not know if the meeting is official or social, and we will not tell him."

Half an hour later Sergei was ordering drinks in a waterside bar, as Colonel Korolev and Jim Larson sat opposite each other on a balcony overlooking Kola Bay and its' seaport. They were both uneasy, going through the first formalities of a relationship that was indefinable in any normal business or co-operative sense. What each wanted or could exchange with the other was a cloud of possibilities around their heads; something that Sergei could almost see as smoke when he approached the table again.

Jim Larson was still his old, urbane self on the surface but inside he'd grown even more wary of human contact and much less inclined to jump when his superiors suggested he should. But this Russian woman wasn't one of his superiors and was immediately an enigma to him; someone he'd dealt with in a remote way for some time but never met in person. She and her junior officer were in uniform, as he'd expected, but something in her manner was much less formal than he'd imagined a Russian Colonel of either sex to be. His first assessment was that she was playing some theatrical role to fool him, but why she should want to or what she wanted to gain from their meeting he couldn't get any sort of line on. So far she was giving him no sort of clue.

"So, Mr. Larson, we wanted to meet you in person at last," Irina was saying. "To establish maybe a new level of co-operation and achievement of results?"

"In what way exactly?" asked Larson. "My impression was that joint operations are going as well as can be expected. Given that the targets are obviously aided by some unknown and, shall we say, inventive agency." His voice was polite but dead, and Sergei noted a fine mist of sweat on his forehead. The man was fearful and already retreating into extreme caution.

"May I ask you a question Mr. Larson," Sergei asked, risking cutting in on the conversation. "If we were to suggest a more open approach, in particular the exchange of developmental information, what would be your reaction?"

Larson looked at him levelly. "The growth development of the dinosaurans, which you had the means to study in detail. I assume that is what you mean?" One hand flickered towards his forehead, but the movement was cancelled. "In what way would that assist finding them now Major?"

Sergei was impressed by his control, but thought he could see a way to move the American now. "I mean exactly that Mr. Larson. Our studies gave us some insight into how these beings think and react. We also have records of conversations between the pair, when they believed themselves unobserved. Certain ideas and wishes were expressed."

Jim Larson leaned forwards. "And a pattern emerged? Was expanded upon over time?"

Sergei nodded. "Yes, a pattern, as you say. The young dinosaurans repeatedly expressed a wish to return to their origin. I mean of course the site where they were first found, in the form of eggs."

"And you believe that wish still exists. Which tunnel do you think they might attempt to reach?"

Colonel Korolev cut back in. "The fugitives are currently heading west Mr. Larson, as you know."

"Interesting certainly, something we may well investigate. And what do you wish Colonel Korolev, in return for this information you have generously given?"

"A genuinely joint operation, in America if necessary. Can that be possible, given that you still maintain contact and influence at the Dinosaur Monument Institution?"

"Dinosaur National Monument Colonel. That is the correct title." Jim Larson smiled thinly for the first time that day. "Not that I mean to correct you in any way."

"Ah, do not worry about correcting me," said Irina, looking past him and across the busy waterway. "As I'm sure you have observed, Russians continually correct themselves. That is a matter of history for us, yes?" She stared at him again for several seconds. "One more thing if you will allow it.

Do you know of, or suspect, any link between your Director, at the Dinosaur National Monument, and a certain Senator Alvin?"

"How in hell did you - - - ?" Jim Larson's control slipped completely for a moment.

"We have our sources. And much practice in these matters Mr. Larson. Will you answer my question?"

Larson looked from her to Sergei.

"Yes, you may trust him," said Irina. "At least as much as you trust me."

The American finally wiped a hand across his own forehead, looking up to the hills behind the city before replying. "In that case the answer to your question is a qualified 'no'. Senator Alvin did visit DNM briefly, just after the whole dinosauran issue surfaced, but we checked and decided there was nothing concrete to follow. He is an old friend of the DNM's Director after all. I will admit there was no personal monitoring in place at that time."

Irina nodded. "You don't know where he went next, or if he had any contact with your missing personnel. That is what you mean to say?"

Jim Larson looked openly worried for the first time that day. "No contacts that we know of, no. As I said there was no surveillance at that point, I had only just informed the relevant agency." He paused. "There was a later report of a meeting between the Senators' son, Michael Alvin, and one of the DNM discovery team, Laura Lovell." Another pause as he considered. "That too seemed to be a social link so it wasn't followed up. We do not have your resources in this area Colonel, regrettable but true." He looked at both of them in turn. "Will you tell me now what your suspicions are?"

Irina Korolev breathed deeply, she was outside her chain of command and suddenly reluctant to take this gamble any further. "Possibly I should not say this Mr. Larson, I do not believe it is entirely wise. But I also think we have to trust each other now." She gestured to Sergei and he handed across his paege. "As you will see the Major has selected the relevant file. Only one file, but we think it is something to explore. Quietly for now, if you agree Mr. Larson."

"Interesting, very. Thank you Major." Larson handed back the paege. "And yes, I do agree Colonel. Quietly it is, for now."

Two years later, another view across water, and Dan Alvin's question still hadn't been answered neither the dinosauran children nor their human guardians had any clearer idea of how or why they had come to exist so far from their origin in time.

After leaving Cuba Michael and Laura had engineered another massive media hype about the possibility of intelligent dinosaurs, which had been suitably and satisfactorily ridiculed by the scientific community; the WSC had even suggested a research programme into the mechanism and appeal of popular myths and their effects on society. Somehow they had all kept the story and the debate going for nearly eighteen months, confusing every attempt to find the real thing.

Now Dan was reviewing an active paege concerning security arrangements in Sweden since the debate had died. He'd lingered over a view of the lake in Norrland, seen from the east; zooming along a forest track, down a long inlet, and across to the house on the opposite shore. He'd always been wary about live viewing, but the birdcam he was accessing was logged to the Swedish Forest Rangers; he pushed that particular worry back down, under a heading of 'old mans' technophobia'. If he had to be jumpy the upcoming move was much more worthy of his bad nerves.

"What the hell!" The tiny machine he was controlling darted out across the water. "Have they gone completely crazy?"

The birdcam hovered to one side of the house, just out of range of the sites' sensitive, inner sensor ring. Far away, across sparkling waves, a boat was approaching at speed; seen on a closer zoom as a two seat waveglider. Its' double winged hull skimmed just above the wave tops, twin water-jet plumes arcing up from outriggers connecting the wingtips. A water skier swerved into view from one side, leaping across the wash and performing a dramatic one-handed turn; the free arm stretched out to burst spray from the surface.

Both driver and skier wore full, hooded wetsuits and goggles; but Dan's familiar eye saw dinosauran ankles and tail and skull shape as if the word 'alien' was written on the sky above. As the boat shot forwards into close-up the skier swung out to pick up speed and dived behind it; executing a perfect free run towards shore, and up the channel into the boathouse. The waveglider slid out in a wide, spray-fanning turn, and followed in behind and out of sight.

The birdcam whirled away back to its' roost at the speed of Dan Alvin's curses. Far away, in his office in Havana, he leapt to his feet and paced the room in a fury of frustrated anxiety; knowing that any interference at this stage risked confusion, and all the extra danger that that could bring.

Inside the Norrland house the main room was even more light and airy than the old forest lodge. The end wall, which looked over the balcony and out to the lake, was all glass. A high-pitched roof of varnished pine reflected the waters' surface, and simple, low furniture enhanced the sense of space and quiet. But the rooms' calm was being shattered by a fierce argument between Steven and Valentina.

Steven swung an arm towards the rooms' closed door. "We've been here two years now. They can't stay locked up forever – If they're convinced there's something else to find in Colorado then I vote we get them back there." He looked out over the balcony, drawing a deep breath. "Goddamnit, if they're old enough to go water ski-ing they're old enough to go to America."

"They should not even be water ski-ing. Who may be in those woods – How many Wardens not want a bit of pocket money from some rag paege?" She turned away from Steven as Mikhail came into the room, still towelling himself down after his excursion on the lake.

"What happened to the lady who rode a snowmobile half way across Lappland?" muttered Steven.

He glanced at Mikhail, then turned away to the window. The young dinosauran was over six foot tall; all trace of his child-like form had gone in only two years. But the subtle pattern of scales on his face formed an expression of concern that any human would recognise.

Mikhail looked from Steven to Valentina. "I'm sorry – I guess you two should be alone."

"Yes, you go now and be with the others," said Valentina. "Tell them we must all talk in a little while."

Mikhail hesitated, looking worried, but nodded and wandered back out of the room with the towel over one lean shoulder. When the door closed Valentina was calm and sadly distant. "The lady on the snowmobile was someone else a long time ago. I have not much choice but to live with you Steven for all that time." She waved him to silence. "No – Do not look pained. I would not have wanted any other choice, but now I am frightened for them and for us."

Steven came back down from the window and took her hand, standing silently for a moment. 'It's not my choice either, that we have to go. Those dreams they have are more and more like the dreams Laura and I had in the tunnels and back at DNM. And if they believe there's a way to restore their original memories, how can we stop them? That's maybe the clue to the whole reason they're here."

He wasn't sure how to continue; what he wanted to say might only make things worse and he preferred Valentina's anger to her unhappy fears. But she waited in her own silence for him to speak.

"I've not felt we're safe here for some time now. I didn't want to worry you without any reason, but WSC called in late last night - Our mutual friends never did let go like we hoped they would."

"Both! – American and Russian?"

"Afraid so," said Steven. "There's some evidence they teamed up about six months ago to find us. I don't honestly see any safety anywhere, but if there's anything can help us it's got to be in one of the chambers."

Valentina stood shivering. Steven put an arm round her shoulder; feeling her freeze with the tension of a decision. She stared out through the glass. "So be it. Always I have wanted to see your America. There are many eyes there also, but perhaps they are too busy looking at too many other things."

"It could be less dangerous than going back to Russia."

She nodded. 'And a new place is always better for adventure than one already known?" Her grip on his hand tightened. "Also much is changing in my country – I do not think I would find my way."

"Valentina, if you think you are being disloyal to your country you're wrong. But I think we'll have better back up in the US, and find it easier not to be noticed."

"I think too that our Security Forces may be harder and sharper than your crazy American people. Too much to eat, and always safe from an outside world."

"Crazy can't see crazy – How would I know?"

He pulled her to him but she twisted away, suddenly angry again. "Always so easy, so apologetic. Always we hide and never fight. I think maybe you like it this way Steven."

His face paled at this sudden attack. "Yeah, that's right lady – I'm just the House Wimp, and you're the Bronze Heroine." He walked away, then turned again. "Just keep this away from the kids – They've got a tough enough time coming as it is."

He walked away, with a dismissive gesture of anger, to the side door and out onto the balcony deck.

Valentina beat one fist against her own hip. "Kids! They're not kids any more, nor ever were. They know every thing before we do."

She waited for Steven to appear on the balcony, silent tears running down her face, but he'd turned to the steps, and away along a forest path beside and above the lake. All that moved was a wind scar on the far side of the water; rushing forwards in bright sunlight, as clouds reared up from the edge of the sky.

That evening Steven, Valentina and the four dinosaurans sat round a large table pulled out to the centre of the room. Blinds covered the window wall, lit by a soft curtain of light from above. The rest of the room swayed with candle flames. The remains of a meal had been stacked up or pushed aside, and hands reached out to pick at odd pieces of food. The whole group looked tense and unhappy, moving languidly in an unusually long silence and stretching out an already thin atmosphere of calm community.

All of the dinosauran children, except for Tania, were close to their adult height of six and a half to seven feet, although leaner and lighter boned than the average human frame. They suspected their growth rate had been accelerated during the process of egg assembly within the spheres and wondered, sometimes fearfully, what else might have been changed. How could they know what a normal development was for a dinosauran? And Tania's deformities were more obvious now that she had grown. The others all worried about her but only she knew she was losing the battle with her disabilities; both groups had lost five out of seven hatchlings to developmental problems or viruses. Tania realised how alien modern diseases were to their vital but ancient metabolism, and a deep instinct told her how fragile her survival was.

But all of the survivors had an eerie beauty to the few people who'd known them, and the fluting vibrations of their speech inspired chills of deep recognition on first hearing. Even so they were still essentially teenagers, and only their extraordinary intelligence and adaptability protected them from the double blow of impending adulthood and life in an alien world. They were tortured by dreams that seemed half-formed from old, lost memories, and an almost mystical intuition that none of them were who or what they appeared to be.

Steven broke the mood by returning to the cause. "Well we *have* agreed that we're going to Colorado, with WSC's help. At least that's settled. And we agree there should be two parties in case anything goes wrong." He stood up and leant forward on the table. "So I go first with Rex and Tania – That's already arranged with the Swedish group, an Air Force cargo disc should be available. Mikhail and Sally go by wingship, with Valentina on the same flight." He looked sideways at her. "What I can't see is why you must actually travel in the container with them."

Mikhail interrupted quickly, "We'll be okay Valentina. We just go into hibernation like good lizards, and before we know it we'll all be there."

"Besides, they said there's not really room with us," said Sally. "No, is only an excuse. I go with you or not go at all! We do all this nonsense in case any of you are found." She glared up at Steven. "And so, if they are found, there must be someone with them. I insist and I will argue no more. As for space, I too will hibernate and breathe very little."

She pushed back her chair and fetched her paege from a side table. "So now we make sense of this nonsense. We make more lists and new lists, and we have ideas on what is to be done in every case, and we learn them all so that there will *be* no disaster." She looked around, but no-one dared argue with her; Steven nodded wearily and sat down again, pulling out his own paege and waiting for her to begin. Valentina started to write.

Two years after Jim Larson had met the Russian Colonel and her Major in Murmansk he was sitting in his office at Dinosaur National Monument and impatiently reviewing the few messages they'd exchanged since then. He still wasn't sure if he'd been set up as a side issue, to confuse his own contacts in America, or if he could really trust the pair and their information. But, he reflected, trusting people was neither his best feature nor particularly necessary for his line of work; and that's about as humorous as you ever get a small voice in his mind told him. He shrugged the thought away and concentrated on what little information had come in from the Russians since their dinosaurans' escape across the Finnish border.

So far as Larson could tell, from his own careful enquiries, Irina Korolev was still working aside from her agency bosses, hoping, he assumed, to avoid the cumbersome chain of command she worked within. Despite his own instinct to avoid such dangerous responsibility, and run the information past his Washington contacts, something had always stopped him doing this. So he'd set up a way of watching the Colorado tunnel site that had been approved and, to his surprise and occasional puzzlement, had never been asked to explain why he thought it necessary. That in itself set off the usual chain of questions and doubts.

Just as he arrived at his standard resolution, that paranoia was a useful tool of the mind, his paege came up with a coded request for a download. He suppressed a shiver as he recognised the source; surely a coincidence that he'd been thinking of the Russian connection at that very moment. He punched 'accept' and watched the message unscroll. The usual pleasantries at the start:

~ Major Malkovich presents his compliments and hopes the enclosed might be of interest.~

Then a long string of known references before the message got to the point. Jim Larson sat forwards with a start, realising that paranoia might come in useful after all; the trail had obviously warmed up suddenly and spectacularly. A report from a lake in the Norrland Region of Sweden that mentioned unusual activities on the water. Somehow the Russians knew that a house on the lake was listed by the Swedish Environment Agency but had originally been built for more covert purposes. Or they'd only just found out; it was impossible to tell. Either way it seemed likely this was the hiding place the dinosaurans and their minders had been using since they disappeared across the border, and that they were almost certainly on the move again. How in hell they'd avoided discovery for so long was a cause for embarrassment at best, but now the trail was hot again he refused to indulge any searching for blame; certainly he detected no such attitude from Russia. Another example of the Colonel's patient and persistent approach which he'd grudgingly come to admire.

Larson acknowledged, with a promise to report back later, went to his files on Colorado and opened a channel to the people he had on permanent standby there. Not his favourite contacts, not by a long way, but useful in their strange way; if they could be relied on to reply. Far too often in the last year he'd endured conversations with a background roar of various desert bars; places on the back trails that he reluctantly visited whenever it became obvious the watch was getting bored despite generous incentives of cash and favours. He cursed inwardly at the memory, then outwardly when the connection failed, and sent a coded alert to check in as soon as possible. Gritted his teeth with a bitter smile and calmed himself; the fugitives would hardly have arrived in America so soon if his information from Russia was correct. And they had to be slowed down by their own need for caution if they hoped to travel the mother country undetected.

Tertiary

Part Four

Return to the source

< From 1st Transcript of the 'Tum' Archive: 'So close,' thought One. 'And what will they see? There is no way to know.' The rocks hummed to a minute tension as all the outer skin tensed to test, and prepared for action after the slow tracks of its' sleep. 'I will not speak or use my name. That is for later. Something to share if sharing has been made possible.'
The rock clicked and groaned a little as the tension was released. Somewhere on the mountain a few stones rolled.>

In a run down corner of Salt Lake City the false quiet of a GoodNight curfew system laid its' dead blanket of anti-sound along the streets. A plain van turned into a side entry, its' fuel cells whistling at the threshold of hearing.

and pulled past the dimly lighted frontage of an all-night partybar. The pencil beams of its' low level headlights lit the end wall briefly and then went out. From inside the cabin the darkened alley was still illuminated by infrared.

Steven tuned the system down to the level of his shades and looked around and behind the van. In the rear screen he could see a soundless flicker and jerk of shadows leaking from the badly sealed windows of the partybar. The only danger would be from a prowling autowarden come to serve a ticket on the buildings' manager, but the machines were easy to avoid and could usually be fooled with an old fashioned torch.

Their flight on the cargo disc had been easier than Steven could have hoped; the van was signed to ArmsCor City Security and he'd just driven down the ramp and out of a side gate at the airport. All the checks had been automated and cleared in advance – It had seemed too simple. Now a lingering uneasiness made him jumpy, as if he had primed himself for some inevitable emergency, and he found himself mistrusting the surreal quiet of the city; his ears were tuned for the slightest noise. But the partybar was sealed until the breakfast hour and nothing moved past on the street outside.

Steven flicked the steering to 'spin' and the van gently rotated around its' own axis, then backed the last few feet to mate with a loading door in the alleys' end wall. "Okay guys, we seem to be home," lifting the infrared shades to his forehead, "There should be someone to caretake us upstairs."

A groan sounded from the vans' cargo deck, as Rex and Tania stirred and stretched themselves from sleep. "What's the time – Have we landed yet ?" Rex's voice was slurred and slow, as he twisted up to push his head out into the cabin, and rubbed his eyes to clear a view out of the screen. "Where are we – I thought we were still on the disc?"

"We touched down forty minutes ago. Not much to see, so I didn't wake you. I can't get used to cities being so silent – Let's get inside." Steven took a last look outside. "Guess I've seen too many movies where something jumps out just when it's quietest."

Tertiary

Rex growled, clawing at his shoulder. "Japanese Dinosaur Monster in Midnight Attack on Scientist!"

Steven shook him off with a nervous laugh. "Too realistic my scaly friend – Keep your claws to yourself!"

Tania was struggling and stretching her damaged limbs in the back of the van. "Any chance you two clowns could help a lady in distress – My damn legs just refused to wake up." Her humour was at odds with a terrible weakness in her voice.

Rex glanced at Steven, a look of intense concern, then turned back to help her. "Tell your legs there's breakfast upstairs, and they might come running." He pulled and pushed her gently round so she could haul herself upright. "And if that doesn't work, there's a horrible un-scaly creature right behind us."

Tania gave a mock scream of alarm and lurched towards the opening load door. "Ugh – A thing without scales!"

Steven shook his head with silent laughter, wiping away tears that suddenly flowed too easily, and followed the young dinosaurans out of the van and through a side door to a long, steep stairway. Dim yellow lights did nothing to ease his feeling of tired dislocation, and a rumbling in his stomach made him suddenly light headed; his legs aching as he climbed. A door had opened at the head of the stairs, a greenish glow outlining a sinister, crouching figure, but Steven was too tired now to care. Fatigue had forced him to trust. By the time they reached the top Rex was almost carrying Tania, and the figure reached out to help her through the door. Steven smiled wanly at the wizened old man who took his hand in turn, without speaking – 'Doesn't anyone make a noise in this town?' he thought.

Half an hour later, and his hosts' claw-like hand was shaking him awake where he lay sprawled on a battered sofa. He dimly remembered being told that he, the old man, must be the last human caretaker left alive; and Steven's dreams had been full of shambling, half-dead figures that beckoned from an endless succession of doorways. Now he was being offered coffee and a pre-dawn breakfast that his body had already smelt. He was led to the table, and found himself eating in a ravenous frenzy; his jaws snapping past his own trembling fingers as the recent tensions were calmed by calories. Rex and Tania grinned at each other, but said nothing.

The old man sat in a far corner of the penthouse apartment, smoking beside an extractor fan in one of the windows. He'd already explained that the building below them was a repository once used by the old Patents Office; and that somewhere in the dusty boxes lay the water-fuel engine and a host of other miraculous inventions discarded by the machinations of government and corporations. Whenever the apartment was housing 'guests' he lived in a small room somewhere down amongst the packing crates and cases and racks of mouldering documents.

Steven had found his cover of eccentricity entirely too convincing at first, and been reluctant to leave the dinosaurans in his care, but then the old man had leaned over and whispered two words, "convergent evolution", with a subtle nod towards Rex's dexterous hands. They both watched as the dinosauran carved wafer thin slices of bread and SoyBeef for Tania.

When breakfast was over Steven dragged himself to his feet. Far out, across the city, the first streaks of dawn were just visible between the mountains. He gulped the last coffee. "Sorry to leave you so soon, but I've got to go quickly now. Michael and Laura will be here in the morning."

Rex took Tania's hand as they stood, and she laid her cheek against Steven's. Rex's other hand was on his shoulder. "Don't worry Steven, we'll be alright now. William will look after us. And we're looking forward to seeing Mike and Laura again."

William lifted one hand, without moving from his chair. Steven nodded. He hesitated briefly, but said nothing, then quickly turned to leave; skipping sideways down the long stairway to the street. A faint whoosh of traction motors in the chilled, pre-dawn air as the van moved away down the alley, turning right past the partybar, and accelerated towards the Interstate trainway.

The space was as cramped and functional as an underground military bunker crossed with a submarine, or an old Cold War fall-out shelter, and showed the well organised chaos of necessity. Valentina said it reminded her of archive images of the old Mir space station, when the USSR had long held records and the high ground for long duration space flights. Functionally the analogy was accurate; the container was equipped to recycle both air and water for several weeks. Not even sophisticated sensors would detect any heat, movement or sound from the outside.

Valentina, Sally and Mikhail had made themselves as comfortable as possible around a low, fixed table at one end of the living space and were playing cards. Valentina glanced at a wall screen, which cycled pictures from four cornercams, but it only repeated views of the wingship's hold; dim orange lighting between the tracks of overhead cranes. Nothing moved. She looked back, to see Mikhail's head hanging over his cards and Sally's worried expression. Sally glanced at her brother before speaking. "Shouldn't we have docked by now – We're not even halfway there?"

"Perhaps it is the weather," said Valentina. "I believed wingships to be fast, but this has not been so smooth."

"Not smooth," echoed Mikhail. His voice was flat and distant. "Maybe the maglev will be better."

Sally touched a hand to his, glancing again at Valentina, and turned to look at the screen. She saw that one of the crane cradles was finally moving; yellow arms moving out and reaching down. Then the whole space lurched and they braced themselves when their container was grasped and lifted; the sudden motion, and the noise transmitted through its' frame, making them all feel slightly sick and scared. The wingship's crane system was designed to handle freight and made no concession to any form of living cargo.

Mikhail raised an imaginary glass. "Well, here we go again – Here's to a happy onward voyage, out into the wild Wild West." His eyes were glittering behind the humour; showing some hidden and wrenching strain that was barely controlled. He saw Sally and Valentina looking at him with puzzled concern. "It's alright, you can say it – I'm not going into a claustrophobic panic." He paused, as if fighting the urge to speak and explain. "I think - - - It must be the dreams. They're a bit strange the last few days – Not nightmares exactly, but strange." His voice rushed on. "Perhaps this place is making me worse." Almost desperate in its' attempt at humour. "What if I just went out for some water ski-ing – Blow the dark clouds away?"

Valentina leaned across, and both she and Sally took one of his hands. He smiled thinly. "So – No water ski-ing for a time eh!"

Rex was supporting Tania at the window as they looked out across the city, facing east into the rising sun. The apartment that sheltered them was tidy, but desolate and decayed; it felt like it had frozen, sealed and abandoned, for years, as the city grew out beyond it. Old William had disappeared into his warren of crates and passages on one of the floors below them, so there was no-one to disapprove of their looking out and maybe being seen. Rex scanned the nearby buildings out of wary habit, but all he could see below them was blank walls, empty lots and disused car parks. Rubbish lifted and flapped on a faint morning breeze and birds circled high above a distant solar chimney.

Tania leaned against her companion, suddenly aware of an aching loneliness; so far as they knew there were only four of their kind on the whole of this crowded planet. The city looked so desolate and empty - She could believe that they were truly alone here. "I hope the others are alright. It seems so long since we left Sweden." She pushed upright, and closer to the glass. "And I wish Steven didn't have to go to Dinosaur National Monument – What will happen if they recognise him?"

Rex pulled her gently back, away from the window. "Tania, you have to think of yourself for the moment. You've been ill, and we have to move again soon. You have to get some of your old strength back." He pointed outside. "They're out there somewhere, and they're okay. They can look after themselves and so can Steven. He has to see Arnolds' friend to find out how things are at the tunnel. I told you that yesterday."

"Yes, I remember yesterday – The fever was not so bad. I will be the old Tania by tomorrow, I promise." She allowed herself to be lowered into the ruined sofa. An intercom buzzed asthmatically making them both start in alarm. Tania nodded, and Rex moved to the door; pressing the answer button without speaking. Then his face lit up. "Yes, oh great, come on up." And he turned. "It's Mike and Laura."

"Good. I hope Steven is alright."

Rex looked at her, very worried now, but was distracted by voices at the door and turned to disarm the locks. Michael and Laura came in, full of greetings and relieved excitement, and swept Rex into an embrace between the two of them.

Michael stood back then, a little in awe of Rex's slender height, and rushed into his news without registering his concern for Tania. "Good news. Steven's met up with Arnie's contact – And he'd already checked out the tunnel. We can team up with the others in two days, if their container is on schedule, so we'll move you out of here as soon as it's dark – There's an executive RV downstairs, ready to sweep you D nos to your destiny!"

Laura had moved past him and immediately gone to Tania. She knelt in front of the crippled dinosauran and took her hands. "Mike – Mike please, hold it down. Can't you see how ill Tania is? We can't take her out to the desert like this."

Tania looked calmly at them both. "But you must Laura. I'll be well by tomorrow, and I can sleep in the back of Michael's magic machine! We've come sixty five million years – I can manage a few more days."

Laura was almost crying. Rex came over and sat with Tania. "She's got to go with us Laura. What else is there to do? We can't book her nto a hospital. And it looks ike there's only the four of us – Out of all the ones who were sent nto the future."

Laura nodded silently, and Michael took her hand to lift her up; a long look of communion between him and Tania as he looked down into her eyes. "Rest for a while Tania – We'll stay here another day, and leave tomorrow evening."

Steven was sitting in the ArmsCor City Security van, at an Interstate Services vehicle park, hoping his cover wouldn't soon become a liability. The van should be seen to be delivering or it would show up on a screen somewhere with a service query beside it. He'd met with Arnolds' old contact from DNM to confirm WSC information that activity at the tunnel had been minimal for at least two years. The man had hurried to the van and delivered his news in a rapid undertone; his nervous manner reminding Steven that he wasn't at home here anymore. The institute had suffered heavy budget cuts immediately after ARPA's departure and an undercurrent of blame still lingered amongst the reduced staff. All this had made the Director a bitter and politically wiser man, but also ensured the site was on low maintenance standby for the foreseeable future.

Right now Stevens' main concern was locating the freight container carrying Mikhail, Sally and Valentina across America. He was checking into an encrypted uplink on the InfoNet to get a summary of its' movements. It told him a minor delay in the European wingship's schedule meant the container had missed its' slot on the maglev link to Denver. It should then have gone overland to Glenwood Springs, Colorado, but had been mistakenly sent north to a switching yard on the outskirts of Rock Springs, Wyoming. Luckily this wasn't too far from the border and the roads and trails that led to the Little Snake river canyon.

So it wasn't entirely bad news, but the hours were going by and he still had to change vehicles, get on the road to Rock Springs, then find somewhere to sleep and plan a rendezvous for the following day. Steven was fighting a strong sense of dislocation; he felt rootless and discouraged by the open spaces of America and the confirmation of his status as an outcast. He wanted to be back at the house in Sweden where there'd been an illusion of safety; a sense of being a family just living life with no outside pressures or paranoias. He wanted particularly to have an argument with Valentina, and could hardly bear the anxiety of not knowing where she was or how she was.

The 'bunker' still looked organised, but showed signs of having been lived in by too many bodies for too many days. Used food containers were packed at one end, condensation ran on the walls and the almost silent hum of fans and machinery broke into intervals of rattles and thin screeching. The whole place was rocking slightly, in time to muffled grating and grinding noises along the line of the floor. The harsh movements woke all three occupants from deep but exhausted sleep. This couldn't be the maglev; they looked round in shared suspicion that they'd been shunted off onto an old rail line and misdirected or diverted. The cornercams were either malfunctioning, or they showed the darkness of night far from any city.

Valentina turned them to max elevation and found what she was looking for; a line of mountains on a dim horizon and a starlit sky above. "Where are we?" she whispered to herself. "Is this America?"

No answer, no sound, came in from the landscape outside.

Valentina, Mikhail and Sally wedged themselves around the small table, looking tired, wasted and ill. Sweat ran on their faces. If she'd had any idea what was wrong with the machinery of their life-support Valentina would have tried to fix it, but they were helpless in the centre of a sealed and sophisticated technology they'd been told was infallible. Only in the direst of emergencies could the door be blown open from the inside, and Valentina dared not do that yet. Not while their container rode on an open rail wagon in a vast, dark and unknown country.

Sally looked across at Mikhail with an open expression of fear; he was propped up opposite the others, staring blankly at the wall between them. Valentina had her eyes shut but was not asleep; her hands gripped tight to the edge of the table and her back arched away from the cushions behind her. She appeared to be praying, in defiance of her atheism. There was something much more seriously wrong than a mechanical problem, even if the life-support was about to suffocate them, and no-one knew how to even define the danger let alone defuse it.

Mikhail began to tense back against the wall, his mouth hanging open slackly, and then to groan and twist; his eyes shut tight and flickering beneath the lids. Sally reached out slowly and gripped Valentina's left hand. Valentina stiffened but didn't open her eyes. Sally continued to stare at Mikhail, giving Valentina's hand small, urgent shakes as if describing his ague in shorthand. Even if a specialist in dinosauran medicine had been with them these symptoms had never shown up before, and there was no way of knowing what had caused them. Mikhai groaned again and spoke in a strange, alien voice; a guttural and unintelligible language that seemed to animate the lolling of his head. Sally was almost whimpering with fear, but started to reach across with her free hand.

A muted crash and scream of metal threw her back as the whole space lurched violently, swayed twice and then was still. The life-support purred sweetly after the shock and hardly broke the new and unexplained silence. After days of motion even the stillness felt sinister and wrong. Sally was suddenly convinced that they were hanging on the edge of a fall; perhaps they'd crashed on a bridge or a high embankment and were about to tilt into the void. She'd gripped convulsively at Valentina's hand and one edge of the table, but Mikhail had made no attempt to brace himself; he'd been thrown down and sideways along the bench. His limbs and body lay where they had fallen but his mouth still mumbled strange speech, the words furred and damped by one arm laying across his face.

Valentina opened her eyes, groaning in almost total exhaustion, and looked to where Mikhail had been sitting. Then, with a terrible, weary caution, to where he had fallen. He lay still, his eyes wide open and staring straight up, and suddenly silent; just a suggestion of his throat working. His breath was snoring past the dead weight of his arm, and just the tips of his fingers began to twitch. Sally stood up cautiously, as if she might tip their container over her imagined edge, and bent forward to lift and lay the arm more comfortably down his side. The deadened silence from outside didn't stop.

Late the next evening Michael had left the safe house in Salt Lake City and claimed a Columbus Cruiser from the nearest rent rack. Now they were speeding out of the city and into the dawn, behind schedule but keeping off the trainways, with the vehicles' satellite sign-in tuned to local. Steven had called in with a code that meant he might be being followed; so he was getting slowed down himself by some pre-planned diversions along the road.

The city's outlines faded to suburban; lit to an unreal clarity by a lack of pollution that Michael found quite eerie. Michael was nostalgic for the sky artistry of the smoggy mornings of his childhood. 'The golden light of the

Age of Aquarius' he thought, shaking his head at the antique thought. Last centuries dreams coming true after all, and still the fears from behind the face of things glittered through his fog of morning fatigue. 'Shut up and drive,' he told himself. 'This is no time for philosophical angst.'

Laura sat beside him, insubstantial with her own waking thoughts, and stared ahead through the cruisers' wide canopy. The soporific hum of its' traction motors lulled her back to dreams she didn't want to examine, and the filters screened them from the first blades of sunlight. In a different way she also felt the world was too good to be trusted; a little more exposure to the old realities would probably sharpen them all up. But she knew this wasn't really true; all she needed was to roll down the window and put her face to the wind outside. Except this machine wouldn't allow such behaviour; nothing could disturb its' subtle control of the interior environment. She remembered an old Jeep her father had restored for a hobby, built way back in the late nineties, and how it had thrown and play-boxed them around when he took her out 'green-laning'; a quaint old English term he'd picked up during a tour of Europe. He would have been happy to see so many of the old nightmares laid to rest.

Rex and Tania lay cocooned and asleep in the rear cabin; enviably able to hibernate through the dead and boring hours of any journey. And possibly unaware of just how dangerous and fragile all this was. Michael was only reasonably certain that he'd fooled the nav systems into recording a false log, and even then they'd be open to question once they cleared city limits; the chances of being caught by a random satscan were low but unavoidable. He spoke briefly to the console manager, directing their course through a series of waypoints he hoped would conceal their ultimate destination. Then turned to Laura, aware that they each hid tiredness and anxiety from the other. "It was better to let them sleep, especially Tania. We can make up time on the road now. Still wish we had the old AirSpeed though."

Laura laughed. "You were in love with that lady I think. All curves and fast moves."

"Too right – Why else did I call her Laura's Wings?"

"Mmm, dressing her in my clothes maybe? - - No, don't worry, I was very flattered. Really."

"I should hope so. Last days of freedom in the skies there. And we thought the controls were too much then. How long will transponder implants be voluntary?"

Laura was silent; wondering again how they managed to slide between the cracks of such control and complexity. Thinking, as always, of the vivid dreams of a life so far back in time. The memories now were like a part of her own life; nothing so romantic as a Garden of Eden but generating an ache for that simplicity even as she knew it was probably illusory. Then she pointed forwards, as a City Limits at 10km sign was projected out ahead of them by the hud. "Now we find out how good our old Uncles' latest box of fixes is." She jumped in sudden alarm. "Oh, shit! Not already?"

A real artefact had appeared through the projection and now hovered just ahead of the screen; turning to face them, and matching it's backward speed to their own. A thin synthetic voice came through on the override channel. "Please continue, but consult your console for instructions – This is mandatory by SLC traffic executive."

The AutoCopter looked like an oversized cross between egg and dragonfly, hovering with unreal and concentrated stability, displaying a sheen of threat in its' glistening black and yellow-striped hull.

"We're going to have to trust that Bill got the scan deflection right at least," said Michael. "Guess we'd better acknowledge the damn thing."

"We're just Mr. and Mrs. Average, taking the kids home Mike. We've been on holiday and the kids got ill – Remember?"

"Your audio is distorted Sir," the drone whistled. "Please continue and wait while we reassign a channel."

Michael rolled his eyes at Laura, but said no more. Then a clear, human voice came from the disembodied head that resolved ahead of them; blocking their view of the insectile machine. A halo of luminous orange was flashing around the image. "Your console is unavailable folks, so excuse me cutting in." The face within the halo was cheery, full-bearded and expressed a reassuring bonhomie.

"You appeared to be exceeding the limit a little Sir and Ma'am. Felt we should remind you that restrictors are still voluntary courtesy of citizen's employing responsible driving."

"Damn," muttered Michael. "We're sorry about that Officer. We had a clear road, and we got a couple of sick kids to get home. They're in back, sleeping."

"That may be so Buddy, but you were going like a dog bit your ass. Pardon the vernacular Ma'am, but we like to keep the old style going, even with all this new toned rigging."

Laura grinned, despite her fear. "That's quite all right Officer – Nice to hear a human touch still shines through."

Michael gave her a 'don't overdo it' glance, but the hovering head smiled benignly. "You got sick kids you say? Well you just get them home safe and still sleeping – And don't miss keying a default check on your rentals' systems when you get there. We'll be letting you go on this time. You're near to clearing city limits right about now, and I'm not costing a manned unit to chase you in from that far out." The face tilted a small nod, and the halo cleared to steady green, as the autocopter reappeared and powered upwards from behind it. "Take it easy from here, and have a good one. You are logged and cleared."

Before either of them could speak the face faced and winked out. They stayed silent for several miles, not daring to trust Bill McCandless' fix beyond one lucky escape. Then Michael sighed deeply. "Don't know about you Laurie, but I'm happier with the new over the old right now – A real patrolman would have had us stopped and been snooping in the cabin for sure."

Laura shivered. "Gives me the crawl though – We don't know who that was, or where he is, despite all the smiles and whiskers."

Michael grinned. "Probably a lady officer in drag?"

"Or a wolf in a sheep's head – That was far too Uncle Bumpkin to be true."

He nodded. "Even with the chauvinism of your tone Ma'am, I guess I have to agree."

The cruisers' motors whined briefly as it stepped legally to max cruise and sped up the first 'out of city' ramp to the Interstate. It locked into a slot in the traffic, and Michael folded his arms with a sigh of relief; his head nodded once and he was asleep.

The far western outskirts of Rock Springs, Wyoming straddled an old rail line running about fifty miles north of the Little Snake River canyon, and the tunnel. It was past noon, and the sunny day began to darken as storm clouds built up behind the mountains in the east. Steven sat hunched over a cold cup of coffee, looking out from the roadhouse to the main highway leading into town, and saw dust swirl in the first eddies of wind. A girl in retro-waitress uniform watched distrustfully from a shadowed, high-ceilinged corner as he drummed his fingers and checked the timechip in his thumbnail yet again.

He was still in his 'salesperson' disguise, and had faked a fault in his rental RV. The local repair services were unable to make a quick fix, just as planned, and he was doing his best to wait impatiently for a lift into the distant town. Not so difficult with the reality of the late and lost 'container' to prey on lonely fears. Behind the building a freight train rumbled slowly past, with bell ringing, and its' whistle sounded mournfully through the rising gusts. The eerie howl from a million movies. Steven wondered vaguely if this whole area was some sort of archive project; he could feel the structure shake, and heard the rise and fall of heavy diesels as he counted five ancient power units going past. Then the steady thunder of half a mile of loaded wagons. The girl looked resigned to her placement as a minor actor in the dull, dusty light; her hands flickered sadly around a stack of rattling cups and saucers.

Weeds and rusting machinery and the sagging stumps of dead shacks, all overlaced by an aerial web of phone and power lines – Did anyone really still use those services in the age of solar panels, home turbo-generators and satcoms? Nostalgia for the present flooded his awareness with the strange, poetic vision that he wished he could command at will. Knowing that its' permanent presence would burn him out in a day. But it was the place inside him where all intuitive leaps came from, and he wondered what it had to show him in this decaying museum of a towns' outlands.

Steven's vision turned inwards to a maelstrom of colours and images that couldn't be resolved. He knew he was a caveman being shown the Cistine Chapel – If he couldn't even make sense of the building how could he understand the significance of its' art and symbolism? His hand shook around the cup, slopping dregs, and the girl moved towards him in genuine alarm; coffee pot held out as a possible defence. Steven looked up in thanks as she poured, then back out to the surrounding mountains, seeing from the light that gilded her arm that the storm was going to be magnificent.

"This is it – Rock Springs West up ahead. I've not seen one of those old town signs for years. Even had the right number of bullet holes."

Michael woke up with a start as Laura spoke. For the last three hours he'd slept again as they travelled the old, deserted back roads to avoid traffic and witnesses. "Do you think Steven will be there?" He peered through low undergrowth. "The place looks abandoned from here."

"Hope so. He said he would be." She motored her seat upright and looked out to the side. "See what you mean. The archetypal ghost town."

The cruisers' suspension was somehow dealing with the unlikely road surface it was crossing; algorithms that were out of date by thirty years. Laura swerved as yet another desert hare tried to run under the wheels. "What is it with these animals – They're all on a death wish!"

Then suddenly a ribbon of tarmac was cutting across the low bushes and undergrowth, and they turned right onto the highway into town and a clear view down a long grade to a battered sprawl of buildings. One gleaming line of rails going through the rusted parallels of semi-derelict sidings beyond. A tiny, untidy scar of human organisation ahead of a jagged line of mountains. A few lights winked on in the shadows of clouds and far in the distance Rock Springs itself lay in a narrow blade of sunlight between squalls.

"Well, someone's at home after all. Let's hope not too many, and not unfriendly." Michael sounded nervous. A rapid chill of storm air somehow beat the cruisers' reaction to outside conditions and they both shivered. Rex grunted in the rear cabin, and Tania moaned in her feverish sleep.

"Stay down you two!" warned Michael.

"I would've done if you'd let me sleep." Rex's voice was slurred and slow.

"Lizards hate the cold, remember?"

"Down - - !" Michael shouted, as Laura swerved again. Not a suicidal hare this time, but a skeletal human figure who seemed to have materialised out of the road surface. His face remained impassive as Laura slewed to a stop a yard from his upraised hand. He held out the other, palm flat, as if to show he was unarmed, harmless and perfectly accustomed to stepping in front of the moving vehicles of strangers.

"Jesus - - - !" Michael muttered through gritted teeth.

"Quite possibly," said Laura. "Though obviously a shortage of water for walking on round here." Her voice was breathless with adrenaline. She keyed the outside microphone and speaker to on.

The man was dressed in a travel stained buckskin jacket, sand coloured jeans and a broad brimmed hat. He looked dangerous at first sight, if only from his oneness with such an unforgiving landscape. His lined and folded face and hands were the colour and texture of old tobacco leaves, and Michael suspected nearly all his ancestors were Native Americans. The word 'shaman' came into his minds' eye. "You want a lift into town?" He hesitated over unsealing the cruisers' armour but the man hadn't moved towards any of the doors.

His voice in the speakers was dry as the dust he'd risen from. "Only if you're sure of carrying me – I've no intent to harm nor alarm you."

"Bit late for that," breathed Laura. "I thought you were going under our wheels.'

"I knew your speed – I wanted to see you clear."

Laura felt a new chill, but it wasn't fear so much as a strange anticipation; he needed to see *them* clearly? "Well come on in, the door's open."

Michael looked at her sharply, but she'd already keyed open the side door and their guest was moving towards it, ducking low to fold under the roofline. He glanced briefly into the rear cabin before stepping up to join them in the cockpit. "Your kids are sick? I shouldn't have slowed you up."

"They're not too bad – They can sleep it off." Michael wondered at his own easy acceptance of this stranger. The man was looking at him with none of the usual defences or unspoken questions; as if the whole world, Michael included, was pouring into his eyes with no judgement or criticism.

"Have a seat sir - I'm - - - Michael, and this is Laura."

Laura stared at him in shocked amazement. Then she saw the mans eyes up close herself, and nodded in agreement. And something in his voice reassured her completely.

"Thank you," he said. "And you could call me Grey Owl. I know how the old names sound to sophisticated ears, but it remembers the cave where my mother made me. And an owl she saw fly at the edge of the firelight." He smiled just a little.

Laura put her hand to the sidestick and the cruiser moved on down the road towards Rock Springs West and the early, storm darkened fading of the day. The tarmac twisted sideways, across the rail line, and then followed beside it towards the small town. She glanced back at their passenger, who was staring straight ahead. "Do you live here Grey Owl?"

"Not here – In Colorado You're not far from the Little Snake."

She nodded. Then realised what he had meant; not a statement of their position. "But that's where we're going. Soon You could come with us if you like?"

"Thank you again. And for the ride. But I must stay here a few more days. You should let me out just down there – Your friend will worry if you are seen with strangers."

Both Laura and Michael wondered later why they'd accepted this remark without question – And also why such a man would need a lift of less than three miles. But for now they were more bemused by what he said as he stepped through the opening door. "I hope you find no trouble here. And look after your 'kids'. All living things have souls, even if they are many years and many miles from the places they were born." He seemed somehow exhausted by such a long speech. Before they could reply he was gone, almost as quickly as he had appeared; just a swaying of the low bushes beside the road marked his passage.

They drove the last few hundred yards to the first building at the edge of the town, and there was Steven; sitting in the window, head down, waiting for them.

"Steve – en – en," whispered Laura.

And they both laughed delightedly as his head came up, he quickly drained his cup, grabbed his coat and hurried out of the roadhouse to meet them. The 'waitress' came to the open door and looked out at the gleaming Columbus Cruiser across the street. As Steven climbed up into its' spacious cockpit she seemed about to run out into the open and follow him, but she sank back onto the flat of her feet and. Even if he'd looked he was already too far away to see the strange expression of concern on her face.

Now it was late afternoon and the sky was almost completely dark, with layers of cloud capping down towards a ragged horizon of saw tooth mountains. The wind was still rising as the cruiser hummed slowly along a line of rail wagons carrying containers. It rocked a little with each scatter shot of wind and water drops from the gaps between them. Steven climbed down onto the gravel and walked ahead, stepping between weeds and damp spattered debris. He rubbed his face sharply and looked nervously around as if expecting them to be challenged or pursued. On the far side of the broken lines of wagons, derelict rolling stock and rusted out locomotives a car had stopped on a siding access road. For the moment neither party could see or hear the other.

When Steven reached the end of the wagons some instinct made him duck down and look under, through a chance line-up of gaps, and he spotted the car. He couldn't tell if it was empty or occupied, nor how long it had been there, but waved urgently back to the cruiser to stop it moving into view. His senses felt painfully hyperactive, as if he could feel the heat of the cars' engine from a quarter mile away, but he knew it had only just stopped moving. The instinct was proven as one door opened, and an indistinct figure stepped out; just before a savage squall of wind and rain curtained any view beyond ten feet and hail lashed the surrounding weeds into furious motion.

Steven ran back to the cruiser and ducked inside. "There's a car on the other side of the yard. I couldn't see who got out. Or if they were alone."

"Did you see the container?" Michael asked. "There's one up ahead that could be it." He'd switched on the cruisers' night sight and the centre of the screen showed a pale, clear view through low light and streaming water.

"Move up slow and stop past the end of the next train," said Steven. "At least this shit will give us cover."

Rex was stirring in the rear cabin, getting up to put on a heavy coat with a hood, and gloves. "Do you see them?"

"Not yet Rex." Laura moved back towards him. "We're moving up to the next train. How is Tania?"

"Not good – I think she's worse, but keeping quiet."

Tania's breathing was shallow, and Laura was worried that she didn't wake up and reply at mention of her name. The scales around her eyes were dry and slightly blistered; her eyelids fluttering in irritation. "There has to be medical information in the tunnel that we missed first time round.' Laura looked out and shivered. 'She'll be better off when we get her out of this."

Rex looked down in silence and nodded slowly.

A shout from Steven – "Hey, I think that's the one!"

The rain turned off in a lull between squalls and both Michael and Steven leaped out to run ahead; disappearing behind a new waterfall that cut and splashed the muddy ground. They re-appeared, soaked, only moments later, just as Tania woke with an involuntary scream of pain. Steven was looking back down the line of wagons; peering unhappily into the gloom.

"Steve - - Quick!" Laura's shout brought them both running. As they burst in through the side door Laura looked up; tears streaming down her face. Rex shook his head slowly.

Tania was breathing fast and shallow, clutching her good arm tight into her side, her eyes wide and staring. She focused on Steven, and then Laura. Her voice was a choking whisper. "I'm sorry – Not as much left in me as I thought. You have to go on - - Without me slowing you down. I - - I feel we're being followed." She gasped suddenly, and curled onto her side – Then lifted her withered arm to point out and down the line of wagons. "They're not far away. You must go quickly - - I think they're in trouble - - - ."

Rex looked at his sister, something unspoken passing between them, and dragged Steven back out into the rain and wind. "We have to go Steven. We can't help her, so we must help them for her."

Laura watched the man and the dinosauran, her friends, as they disappeared again. Then spoke through a gulping of tears. "They'd want us to look after you first Tania."

"No time - - I can't come with you after all." She beckoned Laura closer. "You remember your dreams - - Before we came. You can go for me - - - ." Her bird-like voice was a croak of effort. "You can carry my memories." She pulled herself up, and reached out one hand to Laura. "We'll be the Bene Gesserit witches from Dune Laura. But this is real - We can really do it."

She pulled Laura closer, until their heads were touching. "You are strong. You can live my life from the past and carry me forward into this new world. We are so close - - It will not be so strange."

Laura felt Tania convulse against her, and she was blinded, reeling in the impact of impressions, as something like a bolt of awareness flared between and through them. Tania sagged limply against her; leaving her groping and choking for air and still unable to see past tears and the onrushing visions. Someone, somewhere, was holding her up, she knew that, but she didn't know who or where she was. Then the light faded.

Something woke up. 'Who cries?' it thought. 'Someone is crying.'

"No - - !" Laura screamed. "Oh No! - - - - ." She was alone, and it was dark, and she was curled into a tight embrace with Tania's cold and stiffening body.

Steven was soaked with rain and with sweat. He'd felt the blood heat of whatever had flashed between Tania and Laura, and knew that Laura had gone somewhere he couldn't follow. She'd always kept a distance, even from Mike he suspected, but where was she now? – Way back, millions of years, so far as he could tell. Back in her dreams of the enigmatic structures that overlay the tunnel and its' original construction. If they could only find the others in time, and get to the tunnel undiscovered, they might find a way to unravel this mystery. They were all woven into it so tight no-one could see any pattern or find what direction they were going in.

Michael and Rex were yards ahead now, just visible in the eternal rain, and he drove his aching legs to catch them up; wondering, in a feverish scan of the future, if any of them would ever find a place to rest again. For no apparent reason his father began speaking to him – Telling him again about how he'd got furious, at the age of three, when he discovered the house next door had a cellar. 'And I've been digging ever since,' he thought. He wondered if he was crying; his face was so wet and numb he couldn't tell. How could Tania be dead? To come all this way and just die on a ruined rail siding, in the cold rain. The others were waving and yelling at him – What the hell did they want now. He was sick of everyone tugging his sleeve, wanting some sort of decision, and always expecting him to know what was going on.

"Steven! Christ man, what's wrong – This has to be the one! The three crowns, and yellow markings, that has to be Sweden doesn't it?" Michael suddenly felt the full force of what was wrong, and leaned back against the rail wagon with a gasp of pain. "Please let this be the one. Oh God! - Tania's dead isn't she. How are we ever going to tell them?"

Steven just stared at him. Rex put one hand on Michaels' shoulder, and pulled him gently upright. Then felt along the lower edge at one corner of the container, turning to Steven. "Here. Give me the card."

Steven dug into an inside pocket and handed over a smart card; just a black strip with one word, 'entry', printed end on. Rex pushed it into an open seam in the structure, apparently a split in the material, and waited. He cocked his head and heard a click and a faint chime under the noise of the storm. Then the card was ejected, and he gave a whoop of relief.

A section of the container shifted inwards and slid sideways to reveal an inner door. Lights flashed on a small control panel low down on one side. Rex swiped the card through another, more obvious reader and they all waited a long, second time. The door hissed, shivered, and was silent again. Michael raised a fist in desperate frustration, but stepped back rather than forwards.

"The system's running checks. They said it would do that." Steven's voice was flat. Almost inaudible.

The rain was finally easing; small drops splashing mud and puddles. A single shaft of sunset light caught a wagon at the head of the line and steam curled instantly from its' side.

Michael was vibrating with anger now; leaning forward, with gritted teeth, towards the door. "I'm going to jemmy this fucking thing open if it doesn't get itself checked pretty damn quick." He kicked a rusted iron bar, bedded in the weeds at his feet, and stooped to tug at it.

Steven walked past him. "It's opening now."

Nothing seemed to be happening, but he was right. The door moved inwards and then sideways in turn. Incredibly slowly. A vertical line of dirty white light showed through the opening. Hands gripped the doors' edge from the inside and hauled it past a sudden scream of electric motors – Valentina standing outlined and swaying, peering into the outside gloom and gulping fresh, wet air.

"Steven," she said. And fell forwards.

He half caught her, stumbling backwards so that Michael skidded on the muddy iron bar, and all three splashed into the waterlogged gravel and soggy weeds. Michael lay at the bottom of the heap, briefly stunned by an old metal plate with protruding bolt heads; blood washing from a cut beside his ear. He moaned groggily as Rex pulled the weight of the others off him.

Valentina struggled free. "Mikhail! Don't let him go - - There is something else inside him - - ."

Sally appeared in the open doorway and leaped down beside the others, catching Valentina to hold her up, and grabbed at Rex's arm. "Stop him. Quickly – he will try to run!"

Steven whirled around and stared to and fro in confusion; not knowing who might attack them or who would run away. This was hardly the reunion he'd imagined; all thoughts of Tania's death were blanked by this new threat. He looked up to see Mikhail standing shadowed in the opening, opened his

mouth to greet him, then cried out in shock as he saw the way the young dinosauran was braced to leap. All Mikhail's muscles were knotted in a posture of aggression, as he roared out defiantly in some alien language.
Then, shockingly, in English and a grating voice that no-one knew. "I live again - - - !"
Steven grabbed Sally's shoulder and pushed her towards the cruiser, just visible in the gloom, as lightning cracked down ahead of deafening thunder and Mikhail tensed his legs to leap. Michael and Steven both reached up to grapple him by the ankles and all three fell to the ground; a struggling heap of limbs and wet cloth in water and mud. Rex was holding on to Valentina, but now he stepped forward. And clubbed Mikhail behind the ear with one clenched fist, as his dinosauran cousin tried to claw himself upright. The blow knocked Mikhail flat into the waterlogged ground.
Valentina moaned, fell to her knees in front of him, and cradled his head in her lap. "He gets worse for three days now. But never has he been so aggressive. Something bad has taken him inside."
"We have to get away from here," said Rex. "This is not the worst Valentina. I'm sorry."
Inside the cruiser Sally was huddled in one corner, weeping beside Tania's body, as Laura tried to move forwards to comfort her. Laura's arms stretched out but she was unable to move from where she knelt, rocking. Her mouth gaped open in a silent cry of distress. Internally she was staring; amazed at the new landscape that Tania was showing her, trying to calm her friend as she found space to exist in her mind. Somewhere Tania seemed to smile, but Laura knew she was screaming too. The pain, confusion and amazement mixed into a cocktail of emotion that was terrifying.
The door was slammed open by Rex, and Michael and Steven dragged Mikhail's limp form into the space between two bunks. They hauled a blanket down and around him, tucking it tight to stop him rolling, then swung forward into the cruisers' cockpit. Michael rammed the sidestick forward and the big vehicle slewed round in a turn, crashed across the next rail line and accelerated, spitting stones, back the way they'd come. As they

charged through wide pools of water the cruiser complained loudly about limits exceeded.

"Just keep going, fuck you - - !" Michael shouted, and swerved, in another spray of gravel, back up onto the highway. Somewhere behind them another set of lights bounced wildly up and down.

Back at the container a dim oblong of light glowed from the open door. A group of shadowy figures moved cautiously forward in new rain as lightning flashed and thunder rolled. Two of them ran forward and climbed quickly up inside.

The Little Snake river was boiling and roaring through its' canyon in the depths of the storm and the night. Foaming water leapt and bit at the edges of the rough trail wherever the two swung together and chunks of trees, and wreckage from the mountains, crashed and rolled over and around swelling humps of flood above grinding boulders.

The Columbus Cruiser was an alien presence in this landscape and frenzy of nature; its' sophistication at odds with the raw conditions it moved through. The creaks and groans of its' suspension were drowned by the winds' howling; no engineering test had simulated quite this level of abuse and demand. But its' systems still protected the tired and frightened occupants from most of the journeys' hardships. Their own limits were being tested to new extremes, and none of them knew what safety and comfort, if any, could be found up ahead in the tunnel. They knew it had been sealed and officially abandoned but had no information on the condition and nature of the man-made barriers to come. No-one really wanted to think about it.

Laura had recovered sufficiently to insist on driving again and Michael had given in to the desperate plea in her eyes. She moved the cruiser along the trail with a steady and controlled fury; cutting through the storm and the wild country like an old-time pioneer with nothing to lose but the past.

Steven scanned the console, the moving map display and their own custom sensors to check if they were either still being pursued on the ground or tracked by satellite. They were shielded to emit no more signal than a boulder and in this weather even boulders were moving; drones would almost certainly be grounded. If they really were being followed out of the yard at Rock Springs West Michael had thrown off the pursuit with a series of double-backs and detours around the ruined town. It paid to be paranoid and then doubt some more.

There was a loud crash and a lurch as the cruiser hit a storm cut gully hidden by wind-blown bushes. Laura cursed and wrestled the machine out onto flat ground on the opposite side of the track, with two more crashes as the wheels hit rocks in the undergrowth. The motors and transmission were finally making unhealthy noises, and the console flashed warnings that Steven could neither cancel nor ignore, but Laura refused to slow down or treat the controls any more gently. Steven glanced at her, but said nothing; the map display told him they were only a few miles from the tunnel.

For another half hour everyone listened and said nothing, each one willing the cruiser on as they lurched and rolled along the trail, trying to ignore the worsening weather and what passed for a road. This was a trainway machine, not a rough rider; there'd been no opportunity to switch vehicles as they'd planned.

Michael and Mikhail lay side by side on the floor of the rear cabin, both suffering from blows to the head, and Sally and Valentina tried to rest on the bunks opposite Tania. Mikhail had only groaned and twitched since Rex knocked him out and Michael's cut was hurting him more than he wanted to admit. Sally had dressed the wound but now his head throbbed with a sickly beat and he felt his vision was blurring; he tried to believe it was just tiredness, excitement and not eating all day.

They very nearly drove past the site; the cruisers' forward lighting was too narrow to spot a rough trail. Rex shouted out and pointed to their right. "There! Looks like a fence - - ?!"

When Laura backed up and swung the lights round they could all see a sturdy fence and a gate, both decayed but intact, and the roadway up to the tunnel. The slow misery of their ordeal sank in then. There were no welcoming lights, no warm and dry cabins, no pots of food simmering gently on a stove. The rain seemed to be easing up again, and that was all. They obviously had the place to themselves. Rex climbed out and examined the gate, sliding and nearly falling on the cattle grid just in front of it. The gate looked locked into its' track by mud and rust, and the lock itself was sealed to a heavy chain. A security light glowed briefly as Rex moved closer, then died of an exhausted battery.

"Forget the gate," called Laura. "Look either side for flat ground." She backed the cruiser dangerously close to the river bank to give Rex a wider view.

On the left side he found what she wanted. Someone or something had attacked the fence and succeeded in loosening its' lower edge and part of its' attachment to a post. Before anyone could challenge her decision she rolled the cruiser up against the damaged section and stamped on the power. Wire links wrapped over the cruisers' rounded snout and stretched to humming, screeching tautness. The wheels spat stones and mud, and the rear end shook and slid, as Laura savagely probed for a weakness with the steering. She backed up a little and then charged again, snapping the wire links tight and ripping them from the post. The cruiser lurched forwards and sideways with the front wheels riding over, and snagging, the lower edge.

"Back off!" yelled Steven. "Let Rex clear the wire."

Traction motors whined when the cruiser juddered back onto the trail, smoke curling up from the damaged front end, and Laura sat back while Rex hauled the wire links to one side.

"I think you broke it this time Laurie," muttered Michael. "But you still get driver of the year award."

She just nodded slowly, and drove carefully forward into the gap, and sharply right onto the tunnel roadway. "Come on," she whispered. "Just a few yards more."

Miraculously the cruiser continued to limp forwards and up the steep trail to the rock terrace.

"We should hide what's left of this beast," Laura said. "I think I can wedge it in beside the old conveyors."

"The final indignity," said Steven. "Do it Laura. I've got a bad feeling that gate wasn't as dead as it looked."

"I think you should all get out first." She grinned with fatigue. "I'm going to be really rough this time."

Steven climbed down through the cabin and opened the rear door. Valentina and Sally were already struggling with Mikhail, who laughed and roared as if he'd never been knocked out. He pointed at Tania's body, laughing again and shouting in his alien language, even as Michael and Steven were forced to bind his hands and arms behind his back and drag him forcibly onto the terrace. Then they went back for Tania; wrapping her in sheets from the bunk.

When everyone was clear Laura backed to the very edge, then charged the tunnel entrance. A grinding crash, and a cloud of debris, as the cruiser rammed in and crunched to a stop about ten feet inside. A final lurch and scream of tyres as Laura slammed it forward one more yard and killed the motors for good. She climbed out through settling dust and pushed the side door wide open. Then peered forward, into the tunnel, and stepped back with a startled cry. "A light – I think there's a light round the first corner. I couldn't see it before."

"Am I going crazy, or can I smell food?" Michael's stomach gave an echoing rumble in the tight space beside the wrecked cruiser. "Can a nose and a stomach have hallucinations?" He flung up one arm as a narrow flashlight beam caught him in the face. An aggrieved voice from deep inside the tunnel.

"Have you people made quite enough noise yet? I was hoping I could dine in peace."

"Arnie - - !" yelled Michael. "Come out here and be seen – I know that's you in there!"

"You know nothing young sir – I could be a demon cave spirit, come to torture your sniffling nose with subtle delights."

But it *was* Arnold who stepped into the light of a larger lantern as he switched it on. "On the other hand I've only got beans and bread, but you're more than welcome to join me."

"Arnold!" Steven was laughing as if all of the day behind them was cancelled. "How in hell did you get in here. Where's your car. Did you fly in on wings?"

"Nothing so exotic." Arnold picked his way towards them. "Who do you think loosened that fence so you could charge in like a rhino on wheels?"

Laura was hugging him. "Arnie, I love you – But you can't possibly have walked here?"

"Only because I didn't want to young lady. I used one of those Quad things, you know, like a four-wheeled motorbike. Most undignified. Probably a museum piece, but now consigned to the bosom of the river." He reached and shook as many hands and hugged as many shoulders as he could in the confined space beside the wrecked cruiser, then stepped back to lead the way. "Come on in and see the homestead – Not much, but better than you expected I hope." He glanced at Mikhail and around for Tania. "Then you can tell me all about it."

Arnold's face was solemn, and his eyes filled with tears, as he heard the story of the storm and the day just gone. He'd led his cold, wet and exhausted friends to a small haven of light, relative comfort and warm food. A cave within a cave that he'd built from old panels, plastic sheets and timber debris from the abandoned first exploration of the tunnel. There was a gas cooking stove and solar lanterns, and a small stash of dried and powdered provisions. He'd lied about having only beans and bread. Water there was no shortage of; a small stream bubbled past along the floor of the tunnel, fed by springs opened up by the mining operations.

"So you think they won't know that here is where we were all headed?" Arnold smiled kindly. "I'm not trying to upset you any more than you are, just wondering how long we've got."

"The Senator's laid a false trail that should give us a couple of days," said Steven. "Clever as ever. Rumours of a second tunnel, just the other side of the river. The old hide right under their noses routine." He stared into the lantern light for a moment. "This place is played out and abandoned so far as our past masters are concerned. They never did work out there was anything beyond the first chamber – Why would they? They appeared to be getting what they wanted."

Mikhail grunted from one corner, leaning back onto his trussed arms, against the rock wall.

Arnold stared at the dinosauran as he answered. "Yes - - maybe so." Turned back from Mikhail. "What are we going to do about that? Do you folks have any idea what's wrong with him?" He looked far more sympathetic than he sounded; his face clouded with worry and puzzlement.

"We don't know Arnie," said Sally. "He just got worse and worse while we were in the container."

"I think it always was there," said Valentina. "Waiting to get out. And Tania dying makes it many times more dangerous." She looked at Mikhail helplessly. "Perhaps in the chamber is something that will help him?"

Arnold nodded. "There's nowhere else to go is there? For now I think we all need to sleep - Sounds like the storm's dying down, so I guess it's quite late."

"You never did get it together with clocks Arnie." Steven was grinning fondly at his old friend.

"No time like the present. Ever," said Arnold.

Next morning was clear and fresh and still, as if no storm ever had, or could, disturb the calm sunlight on rocks and mountains and the sparkling river. The air seemed to ring with clarity, and just breathing it was a sharp chill of pleasure. Laura walked out on her own, along the terrace, away from the ledge above the river and down the slopes to the north. The view was wider here, though she'd rarely walked this way, and she drank in the landscape as a sort of visual prayer of thanks; almost laughing at the power this scenery had over her.

She was talking to Tania, and Tania answered as if they were walking side by side. And yet she was enjoying being on her own - She laughed aloud then with a strange joy. The world was new, and no-one had ever walked this way before.

~ Let me sleep inside you,~ said Tania. ~ Let me rest, it will be easier for now.~

Back in the tunnel they were building a barricade across the front of the Columbus Cruiser, and hauling old timber and shuttering around to cover it from all but the closest view. Its' curving bodywork still shone out from the tunnel mouth and Michael wanted to deter the curiosity of any potential visitors. So far all they'd seen moving on the trail was a single coyote, busily following its' own morning ritual, and the fragile silence calmed all their nerves if not their fears.

Arnold's Quad would be a battered hulk, far down the riverbed, even if it had washed up to be seen, and any tracks had been cleared away by the storm. They finally felt confident enough of their solitude to go down and lash up the broken fence, so a quick glance wouldn't show it had been driven over, and even re-arrange the plants Laura had run down in the night. Rex checked out the security light and traced its' wiring back to a dusty solar panel and a cracked battery box. He decided water had been driven in and shorted it out; he could see no evidence that it was linked to any other sensors or telltales.

Laura came walking up the trail from down-river to meet them, just missing being sealed out by the impromptu repairs, and the whole group strolled back up to the tunnel in near silence. A brief moment of relaxation. High overhead an aircraft left a faint contrail across the new, luminous sky, but no sound drifted down to disturb them. The coyote watched, unseen, from a boulder further upstream. It crouched down on its' forepaws, panting gently, and dozed in the sun.

They gathered everything they could from the cruiser and stored it in Arnold's campsite. Then set out to explore the rest of the tunnel as far as the first chamber entrance – The most urgent question was how well it had been sealed off. Valentina insisted that Mikhail go with them; she seemed convinced they could find some answer for him even if the chamber was closed. And accepted that she should be the one to lead him on the end of a rope; they didn't dare release him or leave him behind without a guard. No-one could decide how or where to bury Tania, so they'd improvised a bier and left her body in a dry corner opposite the stream. And a radio rigged as a listening point so she could keep watch while they were gone.

The tunnel was much as everyone remembered, but felt as desolate and empty as if it had been abandoned for centuries. Until they came to where the fault line opened a crack high above its sandy floor, and the wall hollowed into a small side cave. Steven recalled it being a forward store for a days' explosives, plus a refuge from which to fire the shots, and it was still littered with cases, old filter sets and damaged equipment not worth salvaging.

"I don't remember them using explosives." Michael was puzzled.

"Only for making this fault line safe. After we'd checked right through. We near enough dug all this by hand." Steven swung a light round the cave. "Hold on – What the hell is that?" He lit a back corner, where a natural rock chimney led upwards to meet the fault, and picked out a ring of fire stones.

"Oh God – Someone's been in here after all." Laura ducked forwards and felt in the ashes. "Not so long ago either. I think there's still some warmth."

Rex stooped in beside her and felt under several of the stones. "No more than two days ago." He reached up to touch fresh soot in the chimney and nodded confirmation. "I'm no tracker, but we can sense heat better than you folks."

Sally looked back down the tunnel with a nervous shiver. "Who do you think it was?"

"Sorry Sal," said Rex. "I'd need to be a shaman to tell you that." He stood back up, into the open, and put one arm round her shoulders. "Should we go on now, or go back?"

Steven glanced at Valentina, and at Mikhail on the end of his rope lead. "Do we have any choice – If we can't get into the chamber we may as well get out of here altogether."

Mikhail was muttering to himself and twisting gently in his bindings. He looked ahead, up the tunnel, with a strangely pained expression of hope or anticipation. And then, almost as if pleading, to Steven and the others. Valentina took his head in her hands and stared into his eyes with fierce concern. "Mikhail, I know you are still there. You cannot speak to us, I understand, but where we go now will help you – I know it will."

The dinosauran shook his head, trying to look away, but his eyes locked with hers in some terrible effort to communicate. He was blinking rapidly, and saliva dripped from his mouth, but his eyes said he understood.

"So. Good – We go on now," said Valentina, and tugged at the rope to lead Mikhail forward up the tunnel. The others followed behind in shocked silence, and the whole party moved through the faults' side-slip to the last, straight section before the chamber entrance. As their torches and lanterns lit up the tunnel ahead a pile of rounded rocks or debris could just be seen in the distance and they cautiously scanned the roof for any signs of a rock fall or cave-in.

Arnold moved ahead and called out. "Sandbags! What in the nether hell are sandbags doing here?"

Sally was reluctant to go on. "Something's wrong here – Can't you smell it?"

Arnold was already sniffing. "I can indeed. There's been a gunfight in here I'd say." He moved forward even more carefully. Suddenly shouted out. "Come on folks – I see what they've been up to. Unbelievable!"

The sandbags had been arranged in a semicircle to make a crude gun emplacement, and an ancient 40mm aircraft cannon lay propped on blocks of wood at its' apex. The tunnel floor was littered with spent shell cases and a full ammunition belt lay in a box ready to be hooked up. An armoured steel door had been placed over the chamber entry, secured with a massive concrete frame, and whoever owned the cannon had blasted their way through it. But behind the mangled steel was an unmarked white surface.

"Goddam – The chamber healed itself up!" Arnold was rubbing his forehead. "If that piece of ironmongery can't chip it, what do we do now?"

"Same as before maybe." said Steven. "Assuming we're still welcome, we wait."

"But it took two days last time, remember." Arnold stared at the unmarked surface in disbelief.

"But that time it'd been sealed sixty five million years. I'm hoping this time it'll remember us." Steven didn't look convinced himself. "The fact there's a door there implies it didn't seal up till after the door was shut. Does that make sense?"

"I guess so. Sort of gives it a sense of humour too - Best test of intelligence I can think of."

Steven smiled at him. "That's the best hope yet Arnie."

Arnold returned his wry look. "Perhaps it only shut up shop when those gun monkeys started. Nothing more than self defence."

"I think that's even more intelligent," said Laura. "I just hope it can remember us. And the difference from whoever these lunatics are." She waved at the cannon. "They might have put it off human beings for good."

"I don't think so." Rex was staring at the chamber wall. "It let you come in to find our eggs. And it was set up to fool the military. Whoever designed it had a fair idea of 'human' nature, with or without scales." He laughed low, both amazed and puzzled. "What I've never sorted out is why build it in the first place. We the dinosaurans, couldn't save ourselves first time round. What was the motivation. Who funded it?"

"We've all lain awake with that one." Arnold hugged him. "My friend - The Invader of the Future!"

Rex grinned. "Thanks Arnie. But I'm serious – All that effort?"

Steven suddenly whipped round; staring back down the tunnel. "Check the radio. I've got a feeling - - - ."

Laura dug it from her jacket pocket and flicked it on. Just a faint crackle of static from the tunnels' distortion, and the farthest echo of a coyote howling.

Arnold tilted one ear. "Well, someone's happy. What's got you spooked Steven?"

"Don't know Arnie. Whatever spooked the coyote I guess. Do they normally howl in the daytime?"

"You got me," said Arnold. "But I think we should go back and check."

Valentina spoke up out of a deep silence. "I stay here with Mikhail and radio, if you all agree?" She looked at Steven as if they were saying goodbye. "Whatever happens, he is no good without getting in there. In the chamber." Steven stared back, then hugged her silently. "Come on. Let's the rest of us get back. I'm sure it's just a howling wolf, but we need to get more gear up here anyway."

When they got back to Tania's body all seemed quiet. Even the coyote had wandered off or gone to sleep at noonday. Arnold peered out from the rock overhang. "No buzzards, no choppers, no discs – Whoa! But there is a microlight. Damn! Don't think they saw me, pilot's got some sort of sensor helmet, so I don't know.

The machine drifted down and around, cruising along beyond the terrace, with only the faintest sounds from its' rigging and a solar powered prop. The pilot looked left and right as if searching; his helmet obviously feeding a screen that his tandem passenger was peering into. Arnold gestured everyone to keep back, keep still and keep silent. As the intruder rounded the north end of the terrace he scrambled back into better cover. "Hellfire and Damn! He probably heard us fart from four miles away. No hiding anywhere, and that looked like expensive kit." He shivered. "It gives me the horrors you know. I turned up here and only missed them by chance. That damn gun was here all the time."

"So you figure they'll have spotted the difference?" Michael waved at the debris covered cruiser.

"For sure, if those were the cannoneers."

Sally caught Arnold as he paced nervously up and down. "We were all lucky then. We've still got the advantage. And we've got their gun."

Laura was already looking around. "Let's see if that's all they left." She ran back up towards the small cave, dragging Arnold and Steven with her by one hand each. Michael kept an uneasy watch from behind their barricade. It suddenly felt flimsy and foolish; something that had only drawn attention rather than protected them.

Rex was staring hard at Sally. "What did you mean Sal – We've got their gun?"

"Just what I said. I didn't mean we should use it."

Rex stared at her. "Now I didn't say that either. But we've not even seen these people yet, and you're threatening to shoot them with their own gun."

"We've seen what they did with the wretched thing. Jesus Rex, get off my back."

They stood glaring at each other, only distracted by Laura's shout. "Come look! I don't believe what they left here."

When they caught up with her she and Arnold were dragging the last planks away from a large buried crate, exposing layers of grease covered rifles, pistols and rocket launchers; all wrapped and sealed in clear plastic. Steven stared up into the rock chimney, tilting his head as if listening.

Laura kicked at a plank. "They hardly hid this at all. I heard it creak when I walked over it."

"I'm afraid that means they don't plan on being away too long." Arnold peered into the bottom of the crate. "Looks to me like this is only layer one. These people are set up for quite a siege. Survivalists is my guess."

Steven looked shocked and haggard, under lit by lantern light. "You're kidding. Those folks died out in the tens didn't they?"

"Officially – But then that was their beef wasn't it. Tough jerky!" Arnold waved around. "Back to the caves people. To hell with all government, and may the fittest survive."

Steven wandered off and back down to the tunnel entrance, where Michael was rooting around with his back to the light, just in time to see the first solar-powered ParaFoil touch down outside. He counted at least five more before he turned and ran back to Tania's body; calling urgently into the radio. "Valentina! Turn that gun round if you can. And get behind it.' The others heard his shout. "Help me with Tania – We can't leave her here."

Laura looked down at the cache of guns and across to Arnold. "Forget it," Arnold said. "Too greased up to hold. And we've not found the ammo. Food, water and light we do need."

Laura nodded. Michael was already grabbing up Arnold's packets of provisions and bundling them inside a ground sheet. They'd relied on the stream so there was only one small water bag filled. Rex and Sally lifted Tania on her b er and began trotting up the tunnel before any visitor could catch sight of them. From outside the others all heard a brief crunch and rattle of falling stones, then silence. Something flew over the barricade and the front of the cruiser, and most of the light disappeared behind boiling jets of dense white smoke.

Steven snatched Laura up from the stream, where she was filling a second water bag, and threw her up the tunnel ahead of him. Then helped Michael and Arnold to drag the groundsheet bundle. "Might be just smoke – Better not wait to find out."

"How many, could you see?" Arnold was panting with effort.

"At least six. I doubt there's many more, for what it's worth."

Michael gathered the bundle tighter and hauled it with all his strength. "Just as well they made themselves clear from the start." He backed up to pull it past an old conveyor and through into the fault section. "If we'd been reasonable they'd probably just have shot us." He tugged and cursed at the awkward shape.

"They know what's lying around," grunted Steven. "Let's hope they think we know how to use it."

"No point letting them off that hook – We'll have to learn fast." Arnold grinned through his sweat. "And me a pacifist man and boy."

The radio echoed Laura's voice. "I'm with Valentina. The others are nearly here. She's got the gun round – We don't know how to load it."

"Wait till we're there," called Steven. "We've got a few minutes. Their own smoke's in the way."

"Don't count on it," grunted Michael. "They'll have masks and IR. We've got to keep them worried." He gave the bundle a final tug, to pull it past him, and turned back down the tunnel. He'd pulled a pistol out of a shoulder holster.

"Where the hell - - ?" Arnold was speechless.

"Don't ask – Seemed a good idea, and now I'm sure of it." He waved them on, up the tunnel. "Don't tell Laura. I'll not be long anyway."

Before the others could argue he'd ducked back round the conveyor and down into the lower tunnel. Muffled shouts sounded from way down at the entrance, and faint crashes as the barricade fell. Arnold stared in shock. "I'll take him the radio. Won't he need that - - ?"

"No, leave it Arnie." Steven pulled at his arm. "He's buying us time. Come on - ."

They kicked and hauled the bundle as fast as they could up the last stretch to the gun emplacement. Laura and Valentina were re-arranging sandbags around the cannon while Rex hauled the extra ammunition they'd found into place behind it. Sally crouched beside Mikhail at the ruined steel door, clearing splinters and rock chips away from the sill while talking quietly to him. She glanced at the white surface, framed in twisted metal and wondered at what lay behind it; the place where their pasts and futures both began. Arnold and Steven were assembling masks and filters, that Michael had thrown into the bundle of supplies, while Rex and Valentina struggled with the 40mm cannon and its' ammunition feed.

Shots crashed, echoed and whispered around the surrounding rocks and passages – Then Michael appeared, running full tilt up the tunnel, and leapt over the gun and its' unwilling crew. "There's seven of them I think," he panted. "I fired over their heads, and slowed them down about thirty seconds. Those people are crazy and angry."

He'd hardly slumped down behind the sandbags before a harsh, male voice called out from the corner of the fault line. "Hey guys! We're in the survival business too. Why don't we share around – This tunnel's got room enough." An empty hand waved from behind the derelict conveyor. 'What say I come out and talk – My gun's laying on the floor here with the safety on."

"I shoot him now?" Valentina asked conversationally.

"No!" hissed Steven. Then called out. "This tunnel is a Dinosaur National Monument project – What are you doing here?"

"Dinosaur Monument my arse!" The man stepped from the shadows, with a lantern in one hand. He was stockily built and wore camouflage fatigues and cap "This place stinks of US Army – And you folks don't seem like military. So you tell me.'

"You don't like the army – But you wear their clothes, and you carry their weapons."

"Set a thief to catch one, I guess. So y'all something to do with that white wall?"

"Straight to the point," muttered Michael. "Ask him if they want to see inside."

Steven glanced down at him, puzzled.

"Use their curiosity – It's all I can think of."

"We're going inside," called Steven. "As soon as it opens again. You could come in and look if you want."

"Again! You telling me you already been in there? You're crazy man – That wall wouldn't even warm up for fifty rounds from the cannon."

Steven was silent – How could they hold out long enough for the wall to open, even if it was going to do it. Laura called down the tunnel. "We know how to use this gun. Why don't you just go back and leave us alone."

"Lady, if I go back and tell my friends I let you take our cannon I'm going to be chief latrine digger – And I have a liking for command." He moved forwards a few steps, swinging the lantern higher. "If I could see your faces we might get along just fine."

Mikhail was growling and twisting while Sally tried to quiet him, holding tight onto the rope lead.

"What's that, a dog you've got up there?"

Before anyone could answer Mikhail had leaped to his feet with an echoing roar, and charged down the slope; leaping over the cannon with the rope flying out behind him. The survivalist saw him appear at the edge of his lantern light and froze in momentary terror. "Holy Shit! What the - - - !"

Rex flung himself up over the sandbags, and just managed to catch the rope end as Mikhail jumped. As he landed, face down on the tunnel floor, he pulled hard to haul Mikhail down into a flailing cloud of dust; being jerked upright in turn to skid forwards on his heels. The survivalist saw a captured monster being roped in by his twin; and confusion as much as fear nailed him to the spot, as they both came to a stop in front of him.

"You'll have to excuse my brother," said Rex, with perfect politeness. "He's not having a very good day."

The man ran then, kicking across his own gun, all thoughts of latrine digging driven from his mind as he shouted out. "Get back! – There's real dinosaurs a'walking and a'talking!"

Twenty minutes later the survivalists were peering cautiously into the tunnel entrance again; two of them flat on the ground behind an improvised shield of plate metal on wooden runners. They inched it forwards, guns loaded and ready, and watched various sensors mounted on its' upper edge. The rest were keeping to the sides of the entry; the 'commander' standing uneasily close to a tall, thin man who spoke into a radio. "Yes, I did say lizards! Lizards on their hind legs – One a captive."

One of the shield pushers rolled on his side and called back. "The crawler doesn't see anything, and there's nothing from the hotbox."

The thin man with the radio swore. "What the - - -. Where in hell else was there for them to go – You sure you checked out any side tunnels?"

The Commander glared at him, his confidence and command obviously in doubt now. "We checked the whole place first time round, you know that. There is only one tunnel." He glanced at the radio. "You're the one talking to the Suits – What do the experts think?" No attempt to conceal his scorn or keep sarcasm from his tone. "We deal with those jokers much longer, we may as well go sweep up in town."

The thin man shielded his radio instinctively, and the Commander laughed short and harsh. "Won't do no good covering the mike – They'll have a phone up your arse by now. You think I care if they turn a hunt on us?"

His partner snarled. "What's your problem Jack? They let us off blasting their door, whatever the hell it is. And they pay good – And they leave us alone."

"Like fuck they do! We've been waiting here two years, now we're all wired like monkeys, and you know it. No-one's out of sight these days, but at least we were keeping quiet and low before."

"Well, It's too fucking late now ain't it! Either run the show or cut free on your own. Right now we don't have no choice."

The two men on the shield had wriggled back and stood up away from the tunnel mouth. One waved a recorder paege. "There's jack shit up that last stretch according to the crawler – No heat, no movement. Nothing."

"You think it's fried?" asked the second. "That's good gear in there – Top military they said."

The commander straightened himself up into a decision. "Only one way to find out. Me, I'd like our cannon back – Anyone else?" He un-holstered a pistol, and an enormous bowie knife, and walked carefully and casually into the tunnel. The man with the radio watched him go, then spoke once more. "We're sending men in. No signals from the crawler. Best you join us soon I'd say – This is more your sort of snake hunt now. Out."

In the tunnel the wall had opened so suddenly, and with such heat, that everyone had been driven back to shelter behind the sandbags. Steven pushed aside the cannon barrel with a glove and peered briefly through the gap it had rested in. The food stocks smoked, and then steamed as the water bags melted and burst; they'd barely had time to drag Tania's body clear.

"Jesus, it's almost open already. Who says a prayer doesn't work?" He squinted once more, then ducked back down. "Pity about the stores though." Valentina brushed a hand across his thin hair where the ends were curling towards smouldering. "Is very hot," she said; stating the obvious with a question in her tone. "What will those men do now?"

"Follow us in sooner rather than later I'd say. They're curious and greedy. A fright won't stop them for long."

"So – We can close the door behind us?"

"I don't know 'Tina. It's never been up to us, but my guess is the chamber will shut them out. It seems to have an aversion to anyone with weapons in their hands. Or even on their minds."

The white wall had opened by curling back from a vertical line this time, as if a thermal cutter was splitting and peeling back the face from inside; all neatness and precision apparently sacrificed to speed. Within minutes the crisped and ragged edges were blackening and cooling. Faint wisps of vapour or steam drifted upwards and gathered along the tunnel roof. Rex sniffed cautiously and lifted one finger up to swirl and test by tasting. "Just water I think," he said. "We don't have time to distrust it, do we?" He wound Mikhail's rope tighter round his other wrist and stood up from behind the low barrier. "The heat's dropping fast – And I think the lights are coming up, like you said they did the first time."

Tertiary

They all peered forwards past the light of their own lanterns, through the last curls of mist. A faint glow was already filling the chamber, and a breeze blew gently across their strained and weary faces. Arnold pushed up onto his feet beside Rex. "I might be some time," he muttered, and began to step forwards. When he reached the rough edged opening, beyond the broken steel door, he gingerly stroked the melted and blistered margins. "Only just warm now," he called. "Come on in – The lights are up, but no music yet." As he stepped inside he became an outline figure of shadow against the rising illumination within the chamber. His arms lifted in a relaxation of tension, then he disappeared to one side.

"Come on," said Steven. "The beers are on Arnie."

Way back behind the tunnel, through the depths and layers of rock and several miles to the east, another cave flickered and smoked in the orange light of burning torches. Figures sat cross-legged in a wide circle, like humped and eternally stilled mounds of dust, as their shadows danced another life for them. Shadows that radiated across the vast cave floor, up its' steeply overhanging walls and across the pinnacled and threatening roof.

The interior of the dinosauran chamber was subtly different to how Steven, Laura and Arnold remembered it, whereas Michael, Sally and Rex had only seen the place on film or through the memories of others and were awed by the reality. The remains of ARPA monitoring equipment were littered around the central cube and showed signs of having been probed by the chamber; a fine lattice of crystals and struts connected each camera and sensor to the ring of enigmatic structures that circled its' centre. The data relays facing the door were blanked off and blinded but here and there a battery indicator still glowed green or yellow in the pearly, surrounding light.

Mikhail looked around with apparent indifference, but under his sullen stare was a sense of waiting attention. He looked at the cube for a long time, then up and around the dome above it. As Michael and Sally put Tania's litter carefully down he watched with an almost catatonic stillness; his eyes fixed on his dead sisters' face.

Steven was moving towards the cube when a flare of light, and a series of muted shouts, came from the tunnel behind them. He ducked instinctively as he turned but the shooting didn't start yet. The light in the tunnel swung in a circle, probing the open doorway, and then centred on his chest; the red dot of a laser crawling up past his throat. Only Laura saw something flash, an iridescence, and fan upwards from the floor around Steven's feet. She stared, uncertain.

A louder shout echoed from behind the torch beam. "We'd like to thank you for opening the door, but we reckon y'all are in our place now."

Now a shot cracked from the funnel of light and Steven thought he'd been blinded by the laser; astonished by the silver splash that suddenly glittered in front of his face. It fell away to spin down to the floor. Sally screamed, and the others all cringed downwards, as a weird howling surrounded them; focusing outward from where Steven was standing. The doorway to the tunnel seemed to shimmer and contract in oily waves as the noise gathered and rushed through the opening, screaming in the narrow tube as if the rock was being skinned. A confusion of shouts and crashes came flickering back through the after-echoes, and the ringing clatter of boots fading rapidly away. A final pulse of sound, like a sharp cough, thumped a plug of air down the tunnel. Then silence.

Steven bent slowly down and carefully lifted a lacy disc of lead from one edge. It dulled rapidly, drooping over his hand as he tilted it side to side in wonder.

"Somebody loves ya babe." Arnold's voice rattled from a constricted throat, and he cleared it with a coughing laugh. "I think this place must like us all."

Valentina was staring, wide-eyed and silent, at the air round Steven's head. Then she walked quickly back towards the doorway, and ducked through before anyone thought to stop her. Her voice called back with a normal, ringing echo. "Come see – All their guns are ice!"

The guns still steamed and hissed with cold; shattered and cracked by falling onto hard rock. Tiny shreds of skin curled transparent from the points where fingers had touched metal. Arnold touched his own fingertip to a wooden stock, and yelped as it shrivelled a tiny sample of print. Rock was splintering and spitting where the ruined weapons lay against it. "Absolute zero," he muttered. "Or as close as you'd ever want to get !" He jumped back as the magazine split and crumbled into bright-edged shards; bullets rolling and bursting in their own frost.

"Something's different," said Steven. "I just can't work out what it is." He walked slowly back, head down, still holding the wafer thin circle of lead.

Arnold watched him go, silently saying the ironic response to himself, then put one hand slowly up into the air and held it there. He turned the hand side to side, and felt his puzzled expression drop away from his opening mouth as the answer appeared. "The breeze!" he shouted. "Where's the breeze coming from Steve?" He lurched up and ran panting, back up towards the chamber. Steven had turned to wait for him. "There was only ever air moving in here because we had fans running – The fans are all dead."

Steven stood by the mangled steel door and turned his face back to the chamber with a whistle of surprise. "One of the other tunnels must be open -- There's another way out Arnie." He grabbed the older mans' shoulder and waved past him with the new energy of his startled certainty. "Come on everyone, I've got a feeling the door's about to shut out our new friends."

Even as the others ran back into the chamber the edges of the opening were glistening and re-absorbing blackened flakes of material, and smoothing the cutline into a neater oval. The air across the closing hole had a faint sheen like the ghost of a soap bubble.

"I don't think they'll come back so fast this time," said Michael. "That little demo should have their curiosity running wild." He bent to lift Tania's litter as Sally joined him. "You think they'll be calling in the big dogs Steve ?'

"For sure. They'd not be running free with all that weaponry these days, whatever the gun lobby says." He looked into the far shadows of the chambers' circular space. "My guess is it's the north east arm – Let's try it anyway."

They ducked and wove their way between and around the strange, sweeping struts supporting the central cube and peered into the dark, lower spaces between them. The domes' light concentrated at its' apex now, as if unwilling to help them too much, and no other light showed from the inner surface of the wall. They split into a wider pattern without speaking, occasionally glancing back to the rapidly sealing entrance, and crawled in and out between the struts to feel and tap for any hollow space.

Laura was moving back inwards when a puff of air lifted the fine hair on the nape of her neck. The rattle of a stone, on the threshold of her hearing, froze her in place for aching seconds. The air brushed her eyes then. "Over here – I felt something."

She caught the torch that Arnold offered and swung it where her senses guessed. The white wall seemed as opaque and light absorbing as ever, till she moved the beam sideways and up. The white seemed to shiver slightly where she had first pointed, and then it was gone; leaving an oval hole that was total darkness. But another breath of air touched her forehead and blew cold where she'd licked her lips. The faintest scents of desert plants and a world outside in sunshine.

Michael wrapped her in his arms and hugged her. "But who cut this free?" he whispered. "We'd have known if there was another team surely."

"Gold miners maybe?" said Arnold. "This whole area's full of holes, and this one smells old somehow."

"How come prospectors never opened up the first seam?" Laura was puzzled. "I never thought of that before."

"Lots of old Indian legends and burial grounds, and stories of what happened to anyone messing there I think." Arnold rubbed his chin. "Do we check this out now, or see if the tickets for the main theatre are still valid?"

"Food and water we need," said Valentina. "We all forget to take them from the tunnel – Too much noise and guns."

"There wasn't much worth keeping anyway." Steven shook his head, unable to make a decision. "What's everyone think?"

Mikhail grunted suddenly, and strained towards the new tunnel entrance, looking round at the others with the first real eye contact since he'd leaped from the rail container. His eyes flashed and glistened with some desperate inner conflict, then dulled, and the moment was gone. Steven stared at the dinosauran, his expression locked by concern and shock, then turned to peer into the blackness beyond his lantern light. His voice was low and uncertain. "For what it's worth I say we try the tunnel – Make sure no-one else knows about it at least. Then come back and check out the main chamber."

Laura nodded. "I don't know why, but I agree. I know we thought this place would help Mikhail, but we all came here on no more than instinct. I say go for the tunnel - Whatever's in the chamber will look after itself a few more hours."

"Instinct," muttered Arnold. "The finest minds of the twenty-first century running on instinct - - ."

"Shut up Arnie," said Mikhail. A perfect mimicry of the mockery of happier times. This was far more shocking than any of his previous behaviour; and the agony in his eyes brought tears to those of his friends.

"Oh fuck it - -," Laura clenched her fists to whiteness. "What is *wrong* with him?"

They turned their lanterns and torches to the new tunnel; which had been the north east support arm of the massive dinosauran structure when it was first built. Laura distracted herself from the nightmare present by imagining how the arches had swept up and over to meet high up in the air. So where they stood now, deep inside the rock plateau, would have given them a distant view, if they could have seen outside. She imagined clear sections set into the oval tubes, and a voice from within said 'Yes, that is how it was'.

"Tania," she whispered half fearful of what the voice might say.

But nothing else moved or spoke and she followed the others into the tunnel entry. Rex and Sally were carrying Tania's litter now, both had to stoop under a low archway of stone immediately beyond the chamber walls' opening.

The second tunnel was narrow and roughly cut, full of rubble and partly blocked in places, but the floor showed signs of a pathway winding between the blocks and boulders. Both Sally and Rex stopped and sniffed the air, putting Tania down on an open stretch of floor.

"Something's been burnt in here. Maybe a long time ago." Rex took Laura's arm to swing her lantern back towards the archway. "Look, round the arch. Is that made of feathers?"

Where he pointed was the remnants of a border of feathers and a beadwork band around the low rock arch, something like a giant war bonnet or headdress, and above it the marks of soot on the ceiling where torches might have burned.

Laura looked around at the walls and floor. "I think this was a smaller tunnel. They never cut away all the matrix, and what was left broke and fell down - Feels to me like it's very old."

"Older than the gold miners," agreed Arnold. "There's no marks of metal tools that I can see. And those feathers could have been here a couple of centuries, or more."

Steven was looking at his timechip; holding his thumbnail up to the light of a torch. "That can't be right – What time did we come in here? Into the other tunnel I mean."

"About mid-morning. Can't be far off noon now I'd say," said Michael. "My shaker must be dead, and the battery's down. I've got no display."

Steven nodded. "According to this it's nearly dawn tomorrow. My stomach says we've been in here eighteen hours, but we can't have been any more than an hour and a half ?"

Arnold's stomach rumbled loudly; he held out his hands in silent agreement with the first estimate. Everyone's paeges matched Steven's time when they checked and the whole group stood in silent confusion; all suddenly realising they were unusually tired and hungry.

Laura broke the silence. "We can't solve this now. But at least we can look for water outside – Let's go see if we've got a way out or not."

"Well said Ma'am." Arnold rubbed his stomach. "If that coyote's out there I'll eat him in his fur. Hell, I could eat a handful of weeds right now."

Valentina nodded in vehement agreement.

"You'd eat wildlife? Shame on you Arnie." Michael grinned. "But I'd fight you for a cactus-burger myself." He suddenly sobered, looking at his lantern. "If the chamber did slug us for all those hours, we should be saving our lights shouldn't we?"

And, right on cue, the lantern began to flash a battery warning of one hour remaining. "Damn! I always set these things too short."

"One lantern ahead, one torch behind then," said Steven. "Put the torch on narrow and shine it along the side of the group."

As they moved away along the tunnel the faint signs of a path appeared and disappeared, and twice they had to crawl and squeeze sideways and down through shears in the rock that showed no sign of having been widened or cleared. They sweated and struggled with Tania's body. Several times they thought they would have to leave her, or that they were blocked in themselves. The matrix was pitted and scarred by water erosion and time, the sense of long abandonment increased and they saw no more signs of human artefacts. They stopped only once to drink from a rusty trickle of water that bled from a crack in the wall.

"Looks like this one goes the whole distance – No river to do half the work." Steven looked desperately tired in the lantern light. "You lead for a bit Arnie."

"Rotate the slowest foremost it is," he grunted, climbing around a jagged section of matrix. "But I think I see light my comrades." He pointed ahead and turned out the lantern. They peered blearily forwards towards a faint purple glow hovering in the distance, disorientated by a sudden sense of time lag.

"Behold the dawn," said Arnold in a puzzled voice. "If that's what it is. Your timechip was right then Steve?"

Steven shook his head, and tripped over a rock in the gloom. "Where did fifteen hours go? I guess we'd better go see." He edged forwards down the last slope of the tunnel, just as a thin band of light lit its' lower edge. "There's a ledge I think." He was whispering. "Don't anyone rush – Could be a drop or anything out there."

Valentina gripped at the back of his jacket to steady him. "Anything outside would be very good for now."

Michael turned out his torch. They crept down the last slope, as eyes adjusted to the cool dawn, fearful of the lost night behind them and a new day outside. Steven got on hands and knees and crawled the final few yards, peering left and right along a narrow rock shelf high up on the side of another canyon. The tunnels' low exit was overshadowed by a massive overhang, making it just another recess in the shadows, with a few withered roots fringing an edge to the sky. He waved the others to come forwards with a gesture for silence; some instinct to stay in shadow kept him on his knees. And a gnawing fear of height felt but not yet seen. When they bunched behind him he pushed back, ashamed but unable to explain, and tensed to hear something he sensed far below. The air outside was deathly cold.

The sound rushed up from the canyon faster than they could huddle backwards. An oversized AutoCopter buzzing upwards at an angle and rolling away, tight to the overhang, in a loop that brought its' faceless sensor pod back towards them; sweeping independently of its' line of flight with a rapid lashing motion. An invisible sword of radiated threat cutting sideways slashes along the ledge in front of them. It tilted its' blades to hover, drifting sideways, like a bodiless snake in the freezing air. Then fell to one side, and down out of sight.

Nobody moved or spoke till Michael slowly reached and wrote in the dust –
'Why didn't it see us?'

Steven turned, peered around one more time, then back again; staring down at Michael's out-braced arm. He kneeled up and examined his own arms and hands. "The chamber didn't only slow us down, it dusted us with something – I think we smelt like a bunch of rocks."

"Was that just good bad luck, or is the whole area swarming?" Arnold crawled past into the open and stood up slowly. "Another ten seconds and we'd have been up and out. We can't keep on being lucky." He fanned his arms and beat himself around the chest. "I'm cold as a boulder, that's for sure. When does the heating go on round here ?"

"You don't look rocky Arnie," Sally suppressed a snort of laughter. "But you do look sort of sparkly !"

Valentina laughed out loud. "Now you are the rock man really !" A cloud of faintly pink and phosphorescent dust rose slowly from Arnold's tight-hugged figure into the still and silent air. Valentina crouched up on her heels, then stood to walk to the edge. "Someone is coming. One man I think, on his own."

The canyon below was still almost black dark with pre-dawn shadows. When Steven followed her pointing arm he could just make out a tiny figure moving carefully and deliberately through the rocks and plants. He pulled her quickly back, realising that they were already in first light. The sun was no more than twenty minutes away and the ledge, and the overhang above it, were already glowing and brightening. "He must've been well hidden when that mechanical blowfly came by. Unless he's a single scout.' He looked at Valentina curiously. "You've got eyes like a hawk, to have seen him down there."

"I think I see him in my mind, before my eyes find him. He is a friend I am sure, but I do not know how I know this."

"Well, I guess we could rest a few minutes before we get going. We need to find food somehow."

But somehow they all felt calm and pleasantly content to sit with their backs to the rock wall and wait. No one considered themselves or the others apathetic as the minutes drifted by, and the first blinding, molten bead of sunrise lifted over low mountains to their right. Nobody spoke, but everyone was smiling a little to feel the first warmth and an acceptance of whatever the day might bring. Only much later did they question the strange, fatalistic mood that cloaked them.

Laura looked up first to see the tall, thin man outlined against rose coloured clouds, with the new sun burning between his feet. "Hello Grey Owl," she said.

When the native American stepped into the shadow of the overhang nobody realised their lack of surprise was at all unusual. Although he was dressed as Michael and Laura remembered he now carried a crossbow and a pack of bolts across his shoulders and a sheathed knife and pouches on his belt. He crouched in front of Mikhail and stared into his tortured eyes. Then quickly up the face of the overhang. "Two of them coming," he said. "Best go back in the tunnel."

Everyone moved without question; crowding inwards when a hiss of sound blew hot air downwards and slow moving shadows floated along the ledge outside. Two armoured mollercars in the hover above them. Grey Owl pressed further in, deep under the mass of rock, and crouched down in the middle of the group, as if he knew they were somehow shielded. His hand touched lightly on Mikhail's shoulder and the young dinosauran flinched back with a low moan.

Then leapt up without warning, shouting out with a strange, hoarse cry, and tensed forwards to run into the open. Rex snatched at the rope and braced himself to hold on as a blinding storm of dust and debris from the ledge was blasted over them, then rolled forwards to grip his free hand round Mikhail's ankle before he could see to move. Mikhail screamed out in anger, falling to his knees and kicking and struggling towards the tunnel mouth and the looming shadows of the mollercars. The high hissing of their multiple fans rose to a painful, thought-deadening whistle as the lower hull of one machine moved down into view; its' gunpod sensors scanning rapidly.

Grey Owl reached slowly out to place one weather beaten hand in the angle of Mikhail's neck and gripped with digging fingertips and thumb. The dinosauran twisted round, trying to bite and claw at the hand and arm, and passed out with a final, kicking spasm. "Star Trek," mouthed Grey Owl. "Lot to answer for - - ." And raised one eyebrow to Laura's astonished gaze, confirming that she'd read his lips correctly.

The mollercars moved out to take one side of the canyon each, scanning slowly along the rock walls. Grey Owl edged forward as the nearest machine came back into view, held a finger to his lips, and threw a cloud of light powder up from one of his pouches. It held in the air for long seconds as the sound outside diminished and died away. He signed again for them to keep silent a while longer, then cautiously looked out to the east; moving his head almost too slowly to be seen. "Gone," he said, as he rocked back onto his heels. "Those damned things see and hear further than hawk and owl bred together."

"What was in the powder?" asked Laura.

"Just rock dust and some fine aluminium. Nothing magic. Whatever you people are dusted with must sing of the rocks to their sensors – You came through the Hole in the World?"

"The chamber – Yes. But you don't know anyone but me and Mike. Is Grey Owl your full title?"

"It is not even my real name." The ghost of an irony in his smile again. 'But it will do well enough for now." He looked down at Mikhail who'd begun writhing on his back, swimming in some cramped nightmare; the scales under his eyes twitching and fingers clawing for an escape. The others all turned to watch as the tall stranger took off his hat, crouched down beside their friend, and pulled an amulet from a front pocket of his buckskin jacket.

He pressed it against Mikhail's forehead, under one palm; pushing the dinosaurans' head to and fro with a rhythm of low, grunted sounds. When he spoke his voice was harsh and growling. "Be still – You have no place in this body's mind or soul." Mikhail relaxed flat on the tunnel floor, his head angled back, and stared blankly upward. "He will be quiet now for a while. But I cannot heal him properly here. We must go quickly – Those machines will come back and search again."

"You can heal him!" said Sally. "We were going to take him back into the chamber."

"I came to take you to a safer place for a while. I told those things to see a coyote in a shallow cave. If they come back to check, that is the evidence they must find." He turned to Laura with a gesture that asked her to introduce him to the others.

Everyone shook hands and exchanged names as she introduced both humans and dinosaurans; Grey Owl showed no surprise, nor appeared to make any distinction between species. When they were done they turned to piling and shaping boulders and chunks of matrix to block the tunnel a few feet in from the rock ledge, and shook as much of the dust from their clothes over the new wall as they could.

"Now all we need is an animatronic coyote," said Michael with an uncertain smile at Grey Owl. "Unless the one that lives round here will oblige."

"If we leave a gift, she will come. There's a jack rabbit near that will help us." The Indian un-slung his crossbow, loaded it with a bolt attached to a fine woven line and disappeared round the western corner of the ledge.

"Does he always talk like that?" asked Arnold. "We're all acting like we've known him forever."

Laura shook her head. "Mike and I picked him up outside Rock Springs. Or I guess you could say he picked us up. But we only took him a couple of miles."

Michael nodded. "And told him our names. And where we were going. I don't understand it, but we knew we could trust him."

Laura stared at him. "We didn't tell him we were coming out of this tunnel. How the hell did he know to find us here?" She frowned. "And where is he taking us?"

"You could ask me that," said Grey Owl from behind her. He was holding a dead jack rabbit against his chest, apparently unconcerned by the blood staining his jacket. "I apologised to him, and he understood the need." He held the body out and gently placed it at the back of the new 'cave'. Laid one hand along the rabbits' fur. "You are impatient to know who I am, and why I came to find you, so I'll tell you some of it now. But we cannot delay for long. Many men and machines are hunting you."

His face was almost blank in its' severity, unreadable, but his eyes smiled with a distant and delighted laughter. He seemed to be laughing at everything; at them, at himself, at the whole world and all its' works. Valentina watched him with head tilted to one side, still less sure than the others.

Grey Owl looked at her calmly. "If I sound like a crazy Indian, or a native American playing a game for tourists, just carry the words for now. Later you might see more clearly, even if your eyes and senses offend your logic."

Then he looked around quite sharply; some final decision being made. As if he was asking someone else. He looked directly at Valentina again, obviously sensing her worry and mistrust. "My name for the tribe is

Anasaza. Anywhere else I am still Grey Owl, and in a bar I am just Joe. We are still secret people and keep our real faces turned away from the world." The laughter in his eyes was more serious now. "The Elders of the tribe heard the silent heart of the mountain begin to beat, and so I came to find you."

"*They* dug this tunnel out!" Steven held up a hand in apology for interrupting.

"Yes. When the Tribes were young. And now the heart is opened two ways the chant has begun."

"The Chant - - - ." Laura spoke softly to herself.

"The Chant for Fire – The Great Fire to cleanse the world." He lifted Mikhail to his feet with one easy sweep of his arm. "If you have no doubt of me, come with me now." He turned to Rex and Sally, with a glance at Laura. "And your memories will be strong when you come back to this place."

Half an hour later Anasaza was leading the group down a steep, rock filled path into the canyon. Rex was carrying Tania in his arms now, her body folded and wrapped into a blanket. The path turned to follow a dried up stream bed with pebbles and patches of sand that their guide avoided walking across. He was listening and watching continuously, and once hurried them into a gap between two huge boulders. His coyote howl was answered from high up on the ledge they had come from, but nothing else appeared or was heard so they continued on, everyone isolated in their own silent thoughts.

The pace they travelled at was easy and relaxed, despite everyone's hunger and lack of sleep, and when the canyon finally opened out into a narrow valley they were able to keep going along easier ground. At mid-morning Anasaza led them off the path and across to the rock wall, where a spring bubbled from its' base. Sitting in shelter from the sun, round a small pool of rippling water, they looked at each other and smiled. For the first time in several days there seemed no need to speak or be anxious. And when Anasaza reached up to unblock a small cache of beef jerky, from a recess in the rock, the cup was suddenly full. A pleasant experience of the eternal present settled on everyone; even Mikhail seemed quiet and calm.

A hawk circled high above the plateau above the valley and Anasaza watched it closely. "I thought we would have to hide again, but our guide says it is safe to go on to the village."

"Village - - ?" said Steven.

"Where I live. When I'm at home."

"Do you have a family?" asked Michael.

"Not now. My parents still live, far to the south, and I see them when there's a gathering. My other relatives are here."

Michael retreated from any more questions. It was naturally time to move again so he took a last drink from the spring.

"You will live a long time," said Anasaza, and laughed, but didn't explain. He led them back to the path again and then closer in to the left hand valley wall, where caves and narrow clefts could be places to hide. Far behind them the coyote howled one more time, but less mournfully than before.

When they'd walked again for nearly an hour they could see an odd change in the strata ahead. The valley curved a little to the right, and the rocks seemed smoothed and layered in a way that confused the eye. Vertical bands broke up the gaps and overhangs and there were darker blocks of colour that didn't look quite like caves or cracks. No-one spotted a movement high above them, nor the subtle hand signal that Anasaza gave in response.

Ten minutes later they began to see the details of the valley wall; that it was honeycombed with a network of ledges, caves and rock dwellings with walls and walkways that led down to the valley floor. Low stone buildings spread out beyond a natural ridge in the ground, filling the area behind and below it and surrounding a central square. The whole village was only visible when they were almost inside it. The path wound up over the ridge and down beside the rooftops of the outer buildings, whose rear walls were dug into its' slope.

As the party of eight came into view a voice called out from above and the people in the square, mostly women and children, stopped to stare. A small crowd gathered round in silence, and some of the children came forward to touch their hands, but everyone, apart from Valentina, was too tired to respond properly to these first greetings. She picked up a child in each arm, whispering to them in Russian as they gazed at her shyly. But none of them realised that the crowd of people was neither alarmed nor even very surprised by the appearance of the dinosaurans.

Anasaza led them across the square to a large, open sided dwelling built into the base of the rock wall. A group of elderly men and women was gathered outside and came forward to offer more formal greetings. This meeting too was almost silent, most of the communication being gentle and simple gestures. Anasaza quietly drew attention to Tania's body. The elders gathered respectfully round and began to sing a chant; performing some sort of brief ceremony.

"They are speaking to her spirit. They beg its' pardon, and ask that it will wait within her body a short while longer - Before its' journey. They are confused too, I think. This spirit may travel a new road."

"Why is no one surprised by our friends?" asked Laura, interrupting him. "Hardly anyone knows they exist, and there's been no publicity."

"There are legends, and drawings in the caves, and many of us have seen them in dreams," said Anasaza. "I think you have had dreams Laura? And you carry Tania's memories."

"How can you possibly know that?" Laura was startled into a sharp fear, almost anger. And she felt Tania stir inside her, someone startled half-awake then falling away into sleep again.

"It's not any special magic, just small signs. Subtleties and observation." His eyes were suddenly dark and troubled. "You are still connected, you and Tania. You have her memories now, and some of her personality. But if her spirit joins you there will be a fight, until you both learn to share the land inside."

Anasaza looked at her with his laughing eyes again. "But there is something in dreams. You already know that. And we've known about the chamber in the mountain since men first walked here. Our farthest ancestors began the tunnel you came through, and their legends say the chamber let them inside."

Laura looked at the ground for a long time; little swirls of dust blew round her feet and away across the square. "Do the legends also tell of another chamber, maybe a larger one below the first?" She looked up. "The one I saw in my dreams, a sphere. Before the western tunnel was ever opened."

Tania's body was being wrapped in an intricately woven blanket, and gently laid on a low wooden stretcher. Both Laura and Anasaza watched as she was carried into the building before he spoke again. "That is a thing for the Elders to speak of. Perhaps tomorrow. When everyone has slept."

Within ten minutes the whole party was seated at low, solid platforms and being offered food. There were sleeping platforms around the walls and, one by one, after they had eaten, they each found a place to lie down; and fell into a deep, exhausted sleep. Even Mikhail curled up, apparently relaxed, and didn't move or protest at being tied into place by Anasaza.

When Steven woke to see firelight dancing on the walls of the dwelling house he was confused to feel so rested. Then he realised they must all have slept around the clock, and into the next evening. A faint growling in the orange shadows grew in volume as Mikhail fought and shouted out in his sleep.

First Laura, and then the others, woke up to look around in surprise. Before anyone could reach him Mikhail hurled himself out of his nightmare, and off the sleeping platform; crouching in the darkest corner. He snarled and cursed in the arcane dinosauran language, a wild and feral light in his eyes.

Anasaza strode into the dwelling house, and straight across to Mikhail; his shadow falling across the curled and threatening figure. He spoke calmly, barely looking down, in a language that sounded like a dialect of the dinosauran, and Mikhail slowly quietened; sitting back and watching the room from under hooded lids.

Laura had pushed up onto one elbow; brushing her hair back. "What language were you speaking?"

"It is Tewa – The language of the Hano Pueblo. It is said to have come from the mountain."

Whatever was possessing Mikhail had retreated again, but still controlled him; it tried to disguise what had happened. The voice had no real identity.

"I'm sorry everyone – I guess I had too much excitement yesterday. Give me a lake and a jet-ski and I'll be just fine."

He was almost convincing, but the others heard a bizarre quality of desperation beneath the joviality of his speech. And saw an unpleasantly greedy look of pleading in his eyes. Anasaza looked back down at him. "Be at peace Mikhail – And have patience with us. We will drive the intruder from the place he has stolen in your mind."

Mikhail tried to nod, but his head just wagged and rolled. Then to grin, but this too was a pitiful parody of his normal self. He slumped back against the wall, chin down on his chest, with a faint, sighing moan.

Later that night the open space opposite the dwelling house was lit by a large central fire and a wide arc of torches placed around its' border. The group of seven sat cross-legged, in a wide crescent, between the fire and the torches. They were facing the entry to the house and Mikhail had been placed at the centre of the crescent. The full moon was lifting up over the canyon wall, huge and orange, haloed by a faint mist rising from the desert above.

Anasaza stood in front of them all; his lined face sculpted by firelight and a calm power of place and belonging. "The Koshare will come now. If you are alarmed do not show it – And especially do not break the crescent." He signalled to someone unseen behind them and the torches. "After the Koshare will come dancers. They will carry your tokens, and the tokens will carry your memories. These memories will be given to you then, but you will not be aware of them until another dawn breaks."

He moved away, out of the firelight, and the group waited nervously despite his final nod of reassurance. A low drumbeat started to sound, gradually increasing in tempo and accompanied by rattles and a haunting flute-like instrument or voice. No-one could be sure which. Time flowed and stretched in the dancing light of flames.

Suddenly the Koshare the Sacred Clown, had appeared on the opposite side of the fire and was circling round towards them with a strange, slow, stamping walk; waving a bunch of fresh leaves in his right hand and a spray of feathers in his left. The leaves rustled and hissed. He was painted all over in broad black and white rings; around his limbs, torso, head and eyes. His hair was pulled up and tied into two tall cornhusk 'horns' and he wore wide, black ribbons around his neck, his waist and his knees. The ribbons fluttered and bounced as he capered and danced to the speeding beat of the drums.

He was singing and talking in Tewa – Addressing individuals or the whole group by turns. Sometimes growling, sometimes with a deep voice full of sinister menace, sometimes in an eerie sing-song nasal whine. His clowning movements and gestures were alternately gently ironic or gross and obscene, but always the dance kept time with the flames and the fluting melody.

Then he stood squarely in front of Mikhail, leaning forward to touch his head with the feathers. His voice became harsh and cruel. And Laura was startled, almost terrified, to realise that she had been understanding much of his speech; and now could hear him clearly. "I speak in the language of the one you have stolen – You have no time now for choices or for pleadings. You have called yourself Behron, and you have hidden yourself for years beyond counting in that other Sacred Mountain whose heart cannot be seen. Far away, in the East - - - ." He lashed out, striking Mikhail's face with both leaves and feathers. "Return there now, and wait without fear – For your release, or for your expulsion!"

His voice had risen to a roar and Mikhail was kicking backwards through the dust, struggling to escape. Rex and Michael were grimly pinning him in a sitting position, seemingly at the Clown's command. Arnold was staring in speechless amazement, his hands clapped over his ears.

Then the Koshare lunged forwards, fast as a snake, and thrust the shivering leaves into Mikhail's face again; holding the spray of feathers high in a threatening gesture. Mikhail gasped out a choking scream, and fell limply back. His kicking legs trembled to stillness. The Koshare whirled around, capering and laughing maniacally, and leaped high up, through the flames of the fire. And was gone.

There was a stunned silence – The drums and the music had stopped. Before anyone could speak a weird cry echoed out of the darkened dwelling house, and a single, heavy drum began to beat behind the group. But no-one looked around.

Seen through the flames, tall, surreal figures were flowing into the light; their movements sinuous and reptilian. Then hopping movements, and a harsh squawking, and the figures were bird-like. Their costumes were an open weave of cascading feathers and scales, they were painted and masked, and all seemed impossibly tall; with no evidence of stilts beneath the swaying robes.

Eleven figures in all, flowing around the fire in single file; the first seven with eagle heads, carrying snakes in hands held high up, and the other four with viper heads, a large lizard in one hand and a hawk, gripped by its' feet, in the other. The snakes were real, and the lizards and hawks appeared to be so in the wavering, yellow-orange light.

The drumbeat quickened and the figures began to dance. Seemingly simple but hypnotic movements; swaying low and around as they spun in easy circles, and bowed towards and away from the flames in an alternating sequence of pairs. The odd one out, at the end of the line, danced alone; holding hawk and lizard together to make a single apparent partner. This figures' head alone had a slightly human structure to it, despite the viciously curved fangs and slitted. serpentine eyes.

They stamped in apparent anger then, crouching low to shake and swing their offerings cut above the frozen audience of seven; the snakes held only by their tails and whistling and hissing through the air with fanged mouths gaping. Then, suddenly, the dance was over; the four viper-headed beings bowing low over the dinosaurans and Laura. Her awe-struck face stared up at the semi-human head, as the figure offered her both lizard and hawk. From the corner of her eye she saw the three dinosaurans accept their own gifts with the same stunned obedience as herself. Only when she had hold of the animals did she realise they were intricately created models of wood, feathers and thin, embossed leather.

The eleven figures were backing away and around the fire before she drew breath and looked down at the amazingly lifelike animal dolls in her hands. The painted eyes seemed to glitter and stare at her, and the limbs and wings to tremble with the urge to move. She felt herself to be hypnotised, but could feel no fear. Only a strange, calm and dream-like familiarity with the place, the dance and the situation.

A low singing had started behind the group; a lilting and soothing melody that evoked starlight and the chill peace of wide open skies. Laura and the dinosaurans began to relax and talk, it seemed to be expected of them, and examine and compare the lizard and hawk models with a quietly intense curiosity. Sally held her hawk high up to the light of the moon.

Anasaza appeared again, walking around the fire, and came to sit cross-legged in front of them. Mikhail was slowest to recover, but seemed to be genuinely back to his own, old self. The others stared at him, hardly daring to believe what they saw, as he turned and leaned over to Laura; touching her hands and smiling. Then looked up as Anasaza spoke. "Welcome Mikhail. You fought the intruder well – I am proud to meet you at last."

Mikhail's voice was low and gravelly with misuse. "Thank you - - - Were you the Koshare?"

"I cannot say – I mean by that, that I do not know for certain."

"And who was - - - Behron ?" Mikhail shivered.

"I do not know that either. Only that the name was inside you." Anasaza leaned forward, indicating that they must listen carefully and not ask any more questions. "There is an ancient prophesy, handed down among the Hopi Indians from the earliest times. It tells that men like ghosts, white men, would come and take everything from the Indian. They would take land, food, health and honour – The last thing to be taken would be the very stones from the sacred mountain. For this final offence the Old Ones passed down a prayer – A Chant. An invocation of destruction by fire. A cleansing fire to heal the World."

Then, slowly leaning back, "As I told you before, the Chant has already begun - - - ." The whole group stared at him, uncertain what to do or say. "Come, I must show you." He lifted up onto his feet in one smooth, uncurling motion. "And bring Tania – Her spirit has waited long enough."

Before any of them had fully recovered Anasaza was leading the way up a series of twisting paths and steps cut into the rock wall, seeing his way by moonlight and long familiarity. The others stumbled and stepped along behind him as well as they could, with Arnold and Valentina each holding a single blazing torch as high up as they could. Michael and Steven were in the middle; carrying Tania's body on its' wooden stretcher between them. Laura and the three dinosaurans still clutched their lizard and hawk talismans; walking and climbing with a dazed and disorientated motion.

As the path became narrower and steeper they tripped and lurched more often, but could only put out elbows to steady themselves. Not wanting to let go of or damage the delicately made things that they carried. When unseen creatures slithered or flapped out of their way they flinched and held the talismans close into their bodies, as if to protect those before themselves. Somewhere a coyote was howling; its' cries echoing out of the cold distance as a reminder of the dangers of the wild at night.

But Anasaza beckoned and encouraged them on, waiting and guiding patiently at every difficult place, so they climbed uncertainly but steadily upwards. His lean figure had become their only signpost to safety and sense in the strange, mythical and heightened state produced by the drums and the dance. Much later they would be awed by the total trust he inspired, but for now they only knew that they had to follow; whatever was ahead the beginning of an answer to long years of questions and uncertainties. It didn't occur to them to either doubt or refuse to move on.

When they finally arrived at a narrow rock ledge, beneath an overhang of the rock wall, Anasaza gestured to them to put out the torches. As their eyes slowly adjusted to the full moonlight, they realised they were beside a tunnel entrance; so similar to the one they'd exited from the day before that it could have been the same place. Right on the threshold of hearing, a low, throbbing hum seemed to come out of the rock itself.

Laura's mouth began to gape open soundlessly. Suddenly the flat silver light had become terror, and the open tunnel a bottomless well where she could fall to a deeply alien existence. Somewhere she heard Tania screaming, awake but unable to help, only doubling the horror.

Anasaza was beside her, his hand on her shoulder, as she turned to see where to jump from the ledge. "I won't tell you not to fear," he whispered. "Only that it's possible to push through it. Like a cobweb."

Laura shuddered as he spoke. An irrational phobia of spiders had gripped her instantly; she almost saw the legs, like barbed and hairy sticks, feeling out from the funnel of rock. "We have to go in there, right?" Her voice hissed with an icy reluctance. She shut her eyes and dared a look across the internal landscape but Tania was an empty space again, leaving her completely alone.

"Yes we do," said Anasaza. "And we have to go now."

Her rigid shoulders resisted his hand, though she felt a flow of warmth from it, and she shivered with the effort to move. Valentina moved to put an arm around her, and guide her forwards, as the group ducked back into the mountain.

The tunnel slowly gained height and width past its' entrance, and their dark adjusted eyes picked out a faint glow ahead. As the way broadened they could see a long teardrop shaped cave, with a steeply rising floor that was lit beyond its' horizon. The low, humming sound was clearly heard in the still air; coming from the upper part of the cave, under a low, domed roof. Stalactites and strange formations of crystalline rock hung at random all over its' span.

Anasaza gestured towards a shallow depression at one side of the bottom of the slope; indicating that Tania should be left there. He spoke softly from cupped hands. "Lay your friend here. Her spirit will fly from this place at sunrise." He looked gently at Laura. "Where she travels to then is still a mystery, even to us." Laura still shivered, but this time her body relaxed and she could look around the cave with a new interest and then amazement.

Anasaza beckoned everyone onwards again as Steven and Michael laid Tania down in the rock grave; there was no time for more farewells. The slope was even steeper than it looked, with ridges cut flat by the passing of many feet. Arnold estimated an immense number of years for the wearing of such steps into stone, breathing deeply as he faced fears of his own, and looked anxiously up at the caves' dimly lit roof. Seeing strange patterns and ridges in the rock that he could not identify.

At the rim of the upper cave they saw that its' floor was a huge, shallow bowl, stretching far out into darkness to meet the down-curving roof. More than fifty feet away seven ancient figures circled the intense, bluish flames of a small fire. It was impossible to tell their ages, or even their sex, as they sat bell-like in dusty robes. Wisps of white hair floated over rounded and humped shoulders and backs, and each gripped a carved wooden staff in one clawed hand.

Anasaza whispered back to the group, who huddled like unwelcome intruders. "These are the Anasazi – The Old Ones. They know we are here, and will tolerate us for a time. They cannot welcome us because they are too far away, and no longer recognise the need. Do not talk to each other now, the Chant should not be overspoken by chatter."

The strange, humming litany continued undisturbed for several minutes. Then Michael hesitantly raised a hand to speak, and Anasaza nodded. "How long have they been here?" he whispered.

"Since the mountain was opened."

Laura gasped, cupping a hand to her mouth to stifle the sound. She stared at the seated figures, feeling no fear now. "But that was over seven years ago!"

"Yes."

Steven waved a hand vaguely around, then pressed it to his forehead. His eyes were very wide in the blue light. "You mean it was *us* who started the Chant?"

"Yes."

Anasaza paused. For the first time since they'd met he seemed uncertain. He looked to the fire and back again. Something in his stance told them he was communicating with the ancient figures who sat around the flames. "Our distant ancestors opened the way that led you out of the mountain. But they never opened its' real heart. They knew of the sphere within a sphere. They waited for a sign to open it, and the sign never came. That is all they will tell me, in answer to your question Laura, back at the village. About the second chamber, the sphere that you dreamed of."

Rex spoke for the first time since leaving the canyon floor. "They waited too long, their way of life was destroyed?"

"Yes. And they heard only the Chant in the wind from the future – The way to destruction." He paused, breathing as if in pain, and turned his back to the fire. The laughter in his eyes was gone. "My belief now is that the Old Ones' way has led to despair and darkness – To the Invocation. The white mans' search for light has led to the means of fire to burn the whole World."

He pointed to the three dinosaurans. "Only the third way, rising out of the past, can stop the ritual of destruction." Looked back at the Old Ones. "The Fire will not cleanse, it will only burn and kill – The World will be like an unwanted child that is killed before it can grow to be a man."

Rex spoke again. "The child must be more than man or woman – It must be truly human, truly humane."

Anasaza nodded, then smiled. "Yes. But come, you must all sleep – Or you will not find your memories in the dawn."

They turned silently, and stepped down out of the cave. The Chant continued endlessly behind them. The way back to the village seemed easier, but by the time they arrived everyone was exhausted and only too willing to be guided by their hosts and fall into deep and apparently dreamless sleep.

Next morning, as the first light of dawn was coming through the open side of the dwelling house, Anasaza moved quietly around the room; gathering up the lizard and hawk talismans from their keepers. His touch was lighter than a breeze, and his feet made no sound a human or dinosauran could hear; no-one woke or realised he'd been there. He strode back across the central square and tossed the delicate constructions into the glowing embers of the fire; uttering one brief, ululating call towards the light in the east as they flared up and burned.

An hour later, with the sun beginning to light along the canyon, Laura woke with a start. She searched sleepily for the ritual talismans, then got up and went over to Michael; sliding down under the blankets beside him. He half

Tertiary

woke and turned his head to brush a kiss against her neck, but she was already deeply asleep again; twitching and muttering with cat-like spasms of her face and hands.

A cockerel on the roof was reaching a crescendo of calls as the light grew; forcing a yawning and stretching in the room below. Steven was sitting up on his sleeping platform, elbows on knees and hands scratching into his hair.

Michael turned and pushed up, pulling Laura round to lie in the crook of his arm. "Hmm, some other time I guess. How's the memories?" He was already getting up, and lifting her with him, when she pulled fiercely at his arms, eyes wide and startled. Spoke to him in Dinosauran. *I remember - I am - Gyhron.* She looked at him, as if he could understand, then said it again in English. "I am Gyhron, and Tania. I remember both her lives now. Up until - - - ."

Michael put her gently down, seeing the tears well in her eyes, and crouched in front of her "You're who? I'm sorry Laurie, I don't understand. When did you learn to speak Dinosauran?"

Laura looked blank, eyes empty and her mouth moving, then shook as she focused on him again. "Last night. Always. Oh, God. I didn't realise what it meant. All that stuff about memories. I never thought it could be for real. Just weird dreams, and reconstructing the past by imagining it." She gripped his hand, lurching up and walking unsteadily; crossing the room to join Rex and Sally. They were staring at each other in silent amazement. Behind them Mikhail turned in his blankets with a snort and continued to sleep.

Steven had joined Valentina to sit on the porch in the first sunshine, both of them unaware of what was happening inside. Valentina took his hand. "What is happening here Steven? – I do not understand the ceremony, or the talk of memories." She looked along the canyon, to the east, where its' floor broadened out into a lower desert. "We must go I think. But where, I do not know."

Steven gripped her hand. As he thought to reply Rex, Sally and Laura moved behind them, staggering slightly, and stepped out into the square.

They were obviously disturbed about something but talked animatedly, pointing out details of the pueblo and the landscape as if they'd not seen them before. It was a moment before Steven realised they were talking in Dinosauran. And there was something really odd about Sally and Rex's movements, as if they were acting parts in a play; but also more fluid, adult and much less human. "What's going on with those three now? I'm beginning to wonder what Anasaza, Grey Owl, whatever's his name, is doing."

Then the three suddenly turned and came leaping back over; Steven and Valentina were picked up and hugged, bewildered but happy, and hugged again.

Valentina was almost crying. "What? What is happening? – I do not understand what you say."

Rex stood back, and spoke haltingly in a voice they didn't recognise. Steven shivered as if he knew what was coming. "This is very hard. Hard for us, and for you too - To wake with new young lives. And such a strange new world they've seen!" He looked around, and far away, as if awed to the point of fear. Then back down to Steven and Valentina. "Forgive me, both of you. We are not really strangers to you."

"No, you're not," said Steven. "Why do you say so? I'm not getting any of this." He looked to Valentina, who shook her head in angry bewilderment.

Her voice was sharp with fear. "This is not good time to joke. It does not amuse me."

Rex took both her hands in his; breathing deeply and searching for words, as if the language was unfamiliar to him. "We - - All of us - - We must introduce ourselves to you."

Anasaza had appeared, across the square, and stood watching the group; as if he could hear quite clearly at that distance. Valentina shot him a look of mingled anger and appeal, but he stared straight at Rex, waiting for him to speak.

Rex's words were halting, although his voice was confident, as though he knew he was making a speech. But could see no other way to say his piece. "I am Braaxus – A senator of Arhkoevanon City. The city you saw in your dreams Steven." Steven stared, mouth open. "My country was named Shenandivah - - The names are difficult to pronounce in your language."

"Just keep on trying,' said Arnold, who had appeared on the porch with Michael. 'Don't worry about the details."

Rex frowned; looking at them both as if they were strangers. Then spoke louder as if that would help. "The structure and culture was very similar to America. A big country, lots of landscape, and political ideals based on a frontier spirit. Before I was a senator I was a pilot and an astronaut. I was on the last mission that put a crew onto the Moon." He shook his head, not knowing how to continue after such a statement. He reached out to Laura for help.

She looked down at her feet, took a deep breath and stepped forward. "There's no easy way to do this. We're all going to sound like we're talking to the media. I'd better just say it, before I have to think about it - - - My name is Gyhron. I'm, I was, a professor of Astrophysics at Arhkoevanon University. I met Braaxus there, and we were married. There was still co-operation between our countries then." She paused, glancing at Michael for the briefest moment. "My country was called Daahshur. It was a union of republics, like the USSR. I went back to my homeland to prepare for this project - The Impact Defence. We called it 'Far Star'." She looked to Rex then, with a puzzled frown. "But I don't understand. We got stored for after the asteroid, if the Impact Defence didn't work. Not for so far in the future?" Tears fill her eyes. "And we didn't know about the war, until now."

Steven looked horrified. "So you didn't know about the war. It looks like co-operation failed under the stress of the asteroid coming. Or there was some horrible mistake - - - "

Rex stared at him. "I guess so. It's possible there was more than one asteroid. Or in the panic something tripped an accidental launch." He looked to Laura. "We tried to ignore the disagreements but it was hard. Both sides wanted to work on survival, but our technologies were subtly different. It caused a lot of problems towards the end. And we were running out of time - - - "

At this point Mikhail wandered out into the sunshine, yawning, and looking around in a dazed way.

"What's going on? I can't stop dreaming. Where are we?"

Sally jumped up the step to catch him as he swayed, and led him down into the circle; gripping his hand tightly. She looked at Rex and Laura; warning them not to say too much yet. "You're back," she whispered. "Back, and safe with us."

Arnold patted him on the back. "Late as usual – A very good sign my boy. And are we glad to see you on your own feet!"

Mikhail stared at him, touching his face, and then all around. "I feel good – But I'm also someone else. Does that make sense? Where are all these memories from?"

"Just tell us all who you are," said Sally. "We'll try to explain later."

She and Rex stood either side to support him as he spoke. Hesitantly, and then with increasing confidence and wonder. "I'm called Huoorn – I come from Shenandivah. I'm a philosopher, but lately I've been researching. Designing consciousness maps for AI entities – Artificial intelligence. I'm, I was, working in Mehrkon, a science city, on scientific exchange. That's how I met Tiahvan."

He looked down at Sally, recognition dawning in his eyes, and then at Rex; nodding as if acknowledging a rival rather than a friend. Rex looked back with a grin of welcome.

Then Sally stepped forwards, still holding Mikhail's hand. "I'm Tiahvan. I was a specialist in brain function and surgery. The structure of consciousness. I grew up in Mehrkon City." She paused; looking up at the sky, then at Mikhail. "I met Huoorn, Mikhail, there, when I asked for a mapping expert and he was seconded from Shenandivah. I got my expert – And then I discovered a lover!"

Mikhail grinned openly for the first time; his old self fully restored for a moment. He wrapped arms around Sally's waist and pulled her back towards him. "I remember her real skill was in learning to live with me!"

"He had to go back home for the Far Star project, like Gyhron, but we broke down a few barriers first."

Tertiary

Rex and Laura were smiling fondly at them; adults smiling at young lovers. Steven and Valentina smiled likewise, briefly forgetting their amazement, but tears were almost blinding them. The impact of four changing personalities was overwhelming, and they didn't know how to believe what they were seeing and hearing.

Valentina struggled to the point of most confusion, her English almost breaking down. "All this must be true, as you say, but a thing I don't understand. How are you two, and two, meeting again like this? Two from America and two from Russia. And so many eggs not hatch."

Rex spread his hands. "We don't know," he said. "It has to be more than chance I guess. Nearly everyone who volunteered was a couple, against what you'd expect. Still doesn't answer your question though."

"Volunteered?" said Steven. "You mean it was a one way trip? You had to be - - killed, to be stored?"

"We didn't see it that way," said Sally. "And the asteroid was almost here. We knew the Impact Defence mightn't be ready in time."

"The last thing I remember is being in the Memory Lab," said Laura. "I'm glad we don't remember the last days. Or anything about the war." She shivered, "You saw the footage from the capsule crews."

"And the dreams," said Steven. "I never really believed in those till now – Jesus!"

Mikhail turned and sat on the porch step of the dwelling house, looking up as Anasaza came over to join them. "We tried to save something for a new future. But no-one thought it would be like this. Or that we'd come so far - - - ." He paused, still rubbing his eyes. "I have to say, you do all look very strange. Humans that is."

Anasaza laughed first. "Stranger than dinosaurans look to us? But then we were waiting for you. There were only legends, and a few rock drawings, but we had an idea of how you looked."

Steven was laughing too. "Well, even some humans have said the same, at least to me. Welcome to the future – What do you think of it?"

Sally looked all around. "So far, it's beautiful!"

Valentina snorted. "Ah, only beautiful – You have not seen Georgia yet!"

Anasaza had been watching a hawk that had flown into the canyon and was soaring on an up-current of warm air. "It is too soon, but we must lead you away now. There are strange shapes in the sky – You are still being searched for."

As he spoke he turned sharply, looking over his shoulder, and pushed them all back under the shadow of the porch. An angular black shape was flying fast, and almost silently, along the entry canyon. It swept above the central square and pulled up where the canyon turned.

"I'll be damned – An F117," Arnold shaded his eyes to follow it. "They're pulling stuff out of the Air Guard archive!"

Anasaza watched it go, and then the hawk, as it resumed its' lazy circling, before stepping outside again to sniff the air. "For now you must hide where the Old Ones are, their cave cannot be seen. We will travel again at noon tomorrow. Those things see best at night, when they can smell your heat."

He gathered them all together, as he came back inside, and beckoned them to the back of the dwelling house; uncovered four parcels, and handed one to each of the dinosaurans. The fourth was for Laura. He smiled at their puzzled gratitude. "These are robes made for you from the past – You will know when is the time to wear them." He beckoned again, lifting a curtain of skins from an opening in the rear wall. "Come now. There are secret tunnels – We never travel the same way twice to the Old Ones."

Part Five

Ancient memory

< From 1st Transcript of the 'Tum' Archive: Six signalled to the eighth, far away in the south. They'd waited so long, and now the reason for living was here there was fear. Fear of action. Action that might be misunderstood. And if that was so what would the world be, even if they survived again ? And lived on, maybe for another hundred million years, until a new chance came?
Eight replied, discussion eased the fear, and agreement was reached >

The screen door of 'The Trading Post' was banging open against its' length of frayed twine. The old airstrip had been a dry and dusty place, with a vicious system of local winds, since it had first opened on the desert mesa nearly a hundred years before. But it was still the focus of a few back trails and un-metalled roads, staying open on local trade and the occasional flying visitor. The place had a minor reputation as a living museum. A few battered hangars, the store, and it's attached bar, were a meeting place for an appropriately derelict group of fliers. Most of them were more inclined to fly with a bottle and a good story, but some still danced with the angels in their ageing machines.

The barman looked out past the flapping door. He'd spotted a file of native Americans moving up out of a gully from one of the surrounding canyons. He counted ten, all wearing wide brimmed hats and colourful ponchos, and carrying baskets of beadwork and curios. They moved to a narrowly shaded corner of the nearest hangar and squatted patiently on the dusty concrete.

The barman shaded his eyes against the noonday sun, and spoke to his only customer; a veteran pilot called Amp. "See those guys Amp. Every coupl'a months they come up here with a load of junk made of beads and feathers." He absently stirred the dust on the bar with a filthy cloth. "That lunatic Ted Armstrong crashes in here with his old Dak and flies 'em to Salt Lake City. Come a day they'll all fall out'a the sky."

Amp glanced through the door. "And it'll be raining beads and feathers?"

The barman barked a laugh, nodded and walked over to an ancient juke-box in the darkest corner. A nineteen-sixties rock tune scratched out from the battered machine, and he twirled briefly before shuffling back to the bar.

"Already old when I was young," observed Amp. "And rubbish then." He drained his glass and turned on his stool to leave, but was halted mid-twist by a whistle of expensive engines, and the sight of a DiamondWing business jet banking around and lining up for a landing on the single runway.

Both barman and pilot watched the aircraft float to a perfect landing and taxi in towards the line of hangars. Many a year since such a beautiful machine had rolled wheels on the strip. As they admired the form and function of its' outlines and equipment neither of them remarked on a lack of markings. All it carried was a single registration number on each fin. The aircraft turned, a door opened ahead of the forward wing, and the group of native Americans got to their feet.

"Well I'll be - - ! Lookee there Amp. Those boys sure have gone up in the world."

"Yeah – Must be money in beads after all. Give me another Hank. Think I'll stay awhile. Watch that bird fly."

Six of the party climbed up into the DiamondWing, the door closed and it taxied away at speed to the runway. The other four turned back to the hangar side and squatted down again. They watched impassively as the Wing turned, accelerated down the strip and climbed steeply into the sky. The sound of engines quickly faded into the east, and the bar door resumed its' protesting squeak at the end of its' twine. Then, before Hank the barman could return to dusting the counter, two black shapes appeared low over the near end of the runway. They ran in from the west with a faint, eerie whistling note that barely cut the air – Two F117 stealth fighters.

This time Hank and Amp really took notice. When the F117's pulled into a turn the four figures by the hangar stood up and began to trot towards the gully and the canyons. The two men saw a strangeness about three of the heads, and a very unusual, road-runner gait.

They crowded in the doorway; pushing outside to see the fighters swoop back towards the gully, and above the four figures clearing its' rim. "What in hell? - - Now we got wobblin' goblins!"

"And what the hell sort of goblins did those three natives turn into – You see how they ran Hank?"

"Not like human that's for sure. Nor sasquatch neither. Be damned if I know Amp. Hellfire – The next drink's on me!"

They turned and moved slowly back into 'The Trading Post'.

Below them, in the gully, Michael, Anasaza and a boy and girl from the pueblo were crouched under the junction of two enormous boulders. Three lizard skin masks lay on the ground beside them, as Michael changed into the clothes of an amateur fossil hunter; lader with pockets, pouches and equipment. Anasaza waved dismissively upwards. "Those devil birds are made from the night. They are vulnerable in the sun."

"Don't underestimate them," said Michael. "They can read your shirt from ten thousand feet."

"As you say. I respect the cleverness of their making – Not the uses they were made for." The faint sound of stealth fighter engines hissed through the next canyon. "Go well Michael. We will stay hidden till the sky is clear."

The day moved on. In the tunnel entry, below the cave of the Old Ones, the humming chant had become a constant background. The group waited for Michael and Anasaza with barely concealed anxiety.

"Will it work?" whispered Laura. "It's too complicated. They'll ignore the plane, and come right back here."

"Do not say that," said Valentina. "Remember your courage." She looked away from Laura. "They will find the 'decoy', and think we go out another way. They will not guess we stay here all the time."

"We'd have been better off on a plane anyway. Or anywhere out of here. What are we going to find back in the chamber?"

Valentina swung her head back and pointed. "It is you who sees and talks of another chamber below it. We can only go deeper in now – There is no other way back."

Laura was wounded to silence. Arnold glanced at her in sympathy, then turned to Rex who leaned beside him. He hesitated, but then asked his question anyway. "What I don't understand is, how was Far Star funded? How did you work together when both sides thought a war was inevitable?" He paused, gauging Rex's mood. "Or *are* you all here on an invasion of the future!"

Rex snorted a laugh. "Then you are my first prisoner Sir - - !" He looked down, then up. "The answer is, I've no real idea. A final attack of sanity maybe? All I know is the project aimed to break the link between science, technology and weapons research. It certainly took some funding, even though we'd broken through into nanotech."

"Maybe you weren't so crazy after all – Pity you didn't start sooner though, and kill that asteroid. On the other hand, we'd never have met."

"There is that," said Rex dryly. "And you wouldn't be hiding in a tunnel, on the run from most of your fellow humans."

"There is that too. Interesting times eh?"

"Interesting times indeed."

A light was waving beyond them; flashing the agreed code.

"It's them!" Laura was on her feet and running in one motion. Valentina smiled and turned to Steven, who slept uncomfortably beside her. "Wake up now. Our friends are back." She nudged him gently in the ribs.

"What? Let me dream. Whoa! - Never thought I'd say that again."

"Michael and Grey Owl – They are here."

"Did it work okay? Are the hounds off our trail?"

Michael was walking up, with Laura on his arm, and helped Steven to his feet as he replied. "For the moment. One of the kids waited back, and saw them find the masks. And we ruined the day for two guys up on the airstrip. They'll be answering questions all night!"

"Did they get the plane?' Steven was trembling.

"They did. Got a call from Dad. Plane's on the runway at Salt Lake City. They had to let our people go, and with an apology. And accept that they couldn't account for them all. So – We're free to go find the dragons' lair."

Steven relaxed a little. "How is the Senator? Is he under pressure himself?"

"Nothing he's not used to handling. He sent all good wishes, and knows we're still in the dark. He'll be ready if we get any answers, otherwise he'll keep on covering for us."

Steven sighed. "Without him - - - ."

Valentina took his arm "So. We go now? Another day, another dungeon, would you say?"

"And they say it's Americans have no sense of humour!"

She hit with her free hand, and turned to Anasaza. "You can get us back to the place you found us, or do we go back from the first way?"

"The way you came out would be best," he replied. "Our people say there are still machines and people watching at your tunnel site. We also think the chamber has sealed itself again from that side."

"Hardly surprising,"' said Arnold. "Altogether too much noise and mayhem."

"When do we go?" Steven looked grey and worn out now.

"When we have fed and revived you," said Anasaza. "Tonight by the fire will be for fun - The clowns will only clown. Everyone will dance. And the tickets are all for free and free for all." Anasaza grinned. "We are not all snakes, feathers and voodoo!"

"Very glad to hear it," said Steven. "That's a 'yes' then."

They made their way back to the village again, and the day moved on again in its' slow, desert way.

That evening the fire burned high and low, sparks spiralling up in vortices of coloured flame, as handfuls of pungent herbs were thrown into its' centre to scent the night. Young girls and boys eyed each other through a screen of smoke and desire. Dogs ran happily to and fro from morsel to master or mistress and back again.

Anasaza had explained how any checks on native Americans would be born by their sister tribe, who had supplied the decoys at the airstrip, so they should be free of interruption. Just in case, the whole group had been dressed up and made-up in tribal finery. An excuse to entertain and honour them that all parties were thoroughly enjoying. Half the tribe at least were sporting dinosauran masks of varying degrees of sophistication; a traditional form of ceremonial costume that should cause no surprise if they were raided.

Food and drink was passed around in the abundance of celebration. Anasaza assured the group that what they drank wasn't peyote; although the drink was derived from cactus it was guaranteed to be more effective, and much kindlier, than alcohol. Several dogs sampled it to be certain, and were soon howling happily at the moon.

As the night wore on the guests drifted away one by one and two by two to sleep, leaving their hosts to party on till first light and beyond. The moon sank, and the sun rose, on a scene of gentle massacre. Bodies strewn on blankets, and under walls, with children and dogs curled in tight beside them. No-one was awake to discuss the best party for years, but the evidence said it was so. Guardian birds and animals circled the air, and walked the canyon rim, but nothing disturbed a fresh and contented dawn when it came. Even the cockerel crowed quietly to himself.

Mid-morning saw movement and the cooking of a late and leisurely breakfast for the whole village; taken during an informal meeting in the square. Children ran and rolled as usual, but kept a distance from the adults once they had eaten. The dogs sat in the shade, with tongues lolling, still too full of food to pester for more.

In the dwelling house figures stretched and rolled luxuriously under blankets, as a morning without pressure gently moved along. The smell of food, from plates laid on the porch, roused the company from their drowsy dozing. And Anasaza came in to join them as they ate; pointing out particular delicacies and titbits and demonstrating their worth. No-one had seen him eat so much before, and he grinned at them as he chewed. "Not the ascetic I seemed to be eh?" he mumbled round another mouthful. "Well, today we shall digest and rest. And tomorrow is another day."

Nobody wanted to argue with him, and the day drifted on as pleasantly as it had started.

Somewhere around mid-afternoon a messenger from the decoy village trotted into the square.. All was well, and no-one had visited or spied in the night so far as they could tell. It appeared to be safe for their mutual guests to move on as soon as they were ready. Next mid-morning was set as the time to leave and everyone returned to enjoying the moment while they could, ignoring thoughts of the future.

Suddenly, far too soon, it was another morning. The cockerel was raucous as a bad Monday again, and a chill mist floated down the canyon. Arnold intoned thanks for good sleep, and no hangover, in the voice of a satellite ministry; his joviality raising only stares and a grimace from Laura. "Forget it Arnie. We're having a bad tunnel morning."

"The bowels of the Great Mother to you too. Gratitude is best expressed loudly and promptly or not at all."

Across the room Valentina sat staring at the dirt floor. "We don't know what we hunt, or why. Even now."

"We didn't the first time," said Steven quietly. "And look what we got." He nodded towards Rex and the others, who sat outside watching mist roll across the square. "They don't know why they're here either. Maybe they know who they are now, but how do they integrate the two worlds?" He took her hand. "If the answers aren't back in the chamber, where else do we go?"

"I know that you are right. But I am so claustrophobic for small spaces. It was never good to me to be shut in. I am sorry." She looked up. "Please forgive."

"I do, but there's nothing to forgive," said Steven gently. "You've always been the strong one. Look, do you have any idea what's happened to them? I can't get used to the idea that they really remember past lives. Did Anasaza hypnotise them? But why would he? None of it makes any sense."

Valentina stretched and straightened herself up. "I think he is the true Shaman. Maybe this was not the way their memories and future were planned. But I believe what they remember is real. I do not know why."

Steven shook his head. "Were the memories always there then? That makes more sense to me, what's left of the scientist in me."

Valentina took his hand as she stood up. Pulled his arm towards her and held it there. "We should get ready now Steven. As you say yourself, if any answers can be found, they are in the chamber."

They stood up and walked out into the square; reluctant to make yet another new start into the unknown.

But just a few hours later they were climbing up onto the rock ledge, with the tunnel exit in sight, and everyone turned to look back across the canyon. The far side was sunlit to half its' depth now and distant mountain ranges were just visible in the haze beyond its' rim. Cool air spilled down from the mesa above them.

"A day to go walking in the open," said Arnold. "But we are fated to be trolls, one and all."

"Speak for yourself Arnie. I'm standing tall," said Michael.

"Then you will bang your head and bleed my hero."

"Ah. Yes. I stoop to your wisdom old master."

A flicker of a smile on Anasaza's sun beaten face. "Are you ready? I must leave you here."

Steven took his hand. "As ready as we can be, as ever." He stared into their guides' eyes, but said no more. When they looked into the tunnel they saw the sacrificial jack rabbits' bones scattered and gleaming in the dust. Laura piled them on a ledge before Rex and Michae began clearing rocks from the entry. Anasaza had gone as quietly as he'd arrived, with a simple wave of his hand. There was no sign of him moving back down the canyon.

"I'm sure he just turns into an owl," said Sally.

"No, in daylight he would be a coyote," said Mikhail. A mournful howl from the mesa above, perfectly on cue, made them shiver and then laugh. They turned and stocped to enter the tunnel.

When they arrived at the top of the long, tortucus climb they were amazed to find the doorway to the upper chamber still open, as if they were expected. Then reflected it had only been a couple of days, and were almost unimpressed as ight began to glow from inside.

"Fickle humans," muttered Arnold. "Now where did I put that key?" His hand flew to his own neck, and he shook his head, as Steven looked at him in alarm.

"No worries Steve. I still have the charm about my person."

"I believe you Arnie – Really I do."

They stepped inside as the light rose to its' full strength.

The crystal growths around the central cube seemed to have grown in height, but as no-one had measured them they couldn't be sure by how much. Arnold's careful steps across the floor forced a laugh from Steven, and earned him a baleful glare. "You never fell through the ice did you. I still don't know where I went then; it's not a privi ege I appreciate."

"Sorry Arnold. You just looked like a pantomime hen - - -"

"That really makes it better. Thank you so much."

He pulled the strange, iridescent ring from around his neck, and looked around for the place to lay it down. "Does it matter," he muttered. "This place is too clever to care isn t it?" He spoke to the air as if expecting an answer. Then placed the ring between crystals and cube and stepped back.

The strange expanding and melting process began immediately, amazing those who'd not seen it before. Within a minute the entry way was open.

Arnold peered down. "I guess I'll go last as before. No point in upsetting the system."

Steven pulled him back by the arm. "You'll be in head first if you stand there swaying."

"Isn't this all a bit too easy? I mean, where are the madmen with guns or similar entertainments? I'm serious Steven. Shouldn't we leave someone on guard?"

"You're right, I know. But I think we should risk it. We've not had outsider help before. Not like Grey Owl. I'm sure he's covering the tribes' tunnel, so no-one's going to get in that way."

Arnold nodded, and waved Steven forward in agreement. Once the others had stepped into the entry way, and floated down, he took a last look around before he followed. He smiled wryly to himself - Whispered, "Luck to us all."

As each person floated down and ducked away from the flared lower end of the entry way they gathered close together. Apart from Laura, Arnold and Steven everyone was looking around in open-mouthed awe.

The old light was back in Valentina's eyes. "You told me of this place, but I had no real belief until now. Those first people who found the sphere in Russia took photographs, I told you, but only light was on their films." She squeezed his hand and wandered off, across the rigid net floor, to examine the units that once held dinosauran eggs.

He watched her go, with an uncertain expression, then smiled briefly and turned to Laura. "What can we do - There's nothing looks like a control panel?" He stared round in a sadly helpless way.

"Don't give up Steven. There's the eighth unit. It told us how to hatch the eggs - Remember?"

"Something's different though. What is it?"

"The sound. No sound – It's completely silent." Now she'd said it Laura realised that the silence worried her subtly. Perhaps the place had powered down, and had no more to offer. But then the light had come up for them, and the entry way was working. She felt a sudden rush of panic – What if they were trapped?

Steven saw her expression. "Don't worry Laura. Whatever else has gone wrong, this place seems the only certain thing we've found. Apart from each other. If we can trust anything else at all, I think it's here."

She touched his shoulder, calmed herself before walking out on to the net, and moved to the eighth unit. Put her hands to the angled hollows near its' top.

Steven gripped Michael's arm as he started towards her. "Leave her Mike. She's done this before."

"Done what before? Like playing the console at Chernobyl you mean? Christ Steven, we don't know jack shit about this place, and you're happy for Laura to just start trying buttons!"

"Happy isn't the word Mike. You know the story too – Why else are you down here?"

Michael glared down through the net at his feet. Stamped on it hard. And stared as it failed to flex at all. "Okay. Sorry Steven. This just isn't what I expected, whatever the hell that was."

"In the light, and in the dark. Both at the same time, all the time. That's how it's seemed to me, right from the start."

Michael stared at him. Amazed to feel his own eyes cloud with tears. He'd not realised Steven felt responsible even now.

"If I'd just left that first chip in the ground - - - ."

"Hey Steven. Steve - - I didn't mean - - - ."

"I know you didn't. I wouldn't turn back now even if I could. The only thing stops me going crazy is knowing no-one else would either. Including you."

At the eighth unit Laura's head had fallen forward, as she fell into a trance state, and her fingers flexed and gestured in strange patterns. There was a brief intensification of the light in the chamber, almost subliminally sensed, but nothing else appeared to happen. Laura tensed and shook, her out-strained fingers locked painfully back, and then she sagged against the unit. Sally had stopped her exploration of the chamber to watch what Laura was doing. She stepped quickly across, gently took the girls' shoulders and moved her aside. Then tentatively put her own hands to the angled hollows.

After a few moments there was another brief, much more intense, flash of light. As everyone turned in alarm they saw Sally lift one arm, and point around the periphery of the mesh floor; the internal equator of the spherical chamber. Oval markings had appeared all around the wall. Twenty one places marked at equal intervals. Each one faintly luminous and seeming to bulge or pulse outwards.

Sally indicated that everyone should stand in front of a place, speaking rapidly in commanding Dinosauran. Then moved to the wall to demonstrate. The others instinctively placed themselves at every other place, suddenly realising there was a painfully obvious gap where Tania should have been. As each person leaned cautiously back the ovals gave way to form shallow alcoves, surrounding each one in a frame of light. What happened next was so fast and confusing that no-one could agree later on exactly what the sequence was.

The oval alcoves seemed to spin around their vertical axes, but also to flip inside out; through or past their occupants. The impression wasn't of being spun rapidly around, it was more like being reversed in a mirror and re-assembled on the other side. Suddenly seeing through the back of your own head, then your body flipping inside out to follow, was how Arnold would tell it later.

They hung briefly on the *outside* of a sphere, too shocked to look down and cry out, then found themselves pinned to the inside wall of another, much vaster chamber; their feet on a wide balcony or walkway which ran right around its' equator. The edge curled upward for about a foot but there was no handrail or other restraint; only a sort of raised 'tongue' at every alcove point.

What must have been the inner sphere appeared to hang, suspended by its' entry tube, in the centre of the immense space.

"What the hell - - - -!" Everyone but Michael was too disorientated to speak. As they all focused on the inner sphere the alcoves they had hung in reversed again and disappeared. The sphere assumed a smooth, continuous shape, and bloomed with a strangely structured surface patina.

Just as their senses were readjusting they were pinned back to the new wall again in near panic. It seemed as if the inner, central sphere had begun to swing violently, like an unbalanced pendulum.

In fact it had remained static, while the 'stalk' of its' entry tube bent and traced a chaotic pattern around the ceiling of the huge outer sphere. For a moment though the observers were convinced that the wide balcony was gyrating wildly.

Then, in a swift and blurring reversal, the entry tube 'stalk' was below the inner sphere; tracing a slowing pattern where it now touched the lower hemisphere. It came to a stop, upright, with the inner sphere now apparently balanced on top of it.

"Oh, God. We came *down* that," murmured Laura. "How do we get out now?" Her earlier fears had been realised. Certainly the way out was an unknown quantity now.

They were all suffering the same illusion — That the space had somehow turned upside down, and they would all fall 'up' onto its' ceiling. Everyone stood rigid, expecting to slide to a mess of blood and smashed bones, but no pain came. There was no frame of reference to hold onto, and at first sight the machinery or furniture of this new, unexplored sphere was very alien and exotic. Elements of it were scattered at random around the surface, with no apparent reference to 'up' or 'down'.

"Well, send me to the wizard." Michael muttered. "First this place doesn't show up on the screens. Then it turns gravity on its' head."

"Negative matter" whispered Rex. "*That's* the power source. As close as possible to perpetual motion. I missed all those lectures when I was free-falling in orbit."

"Anti-matter now. Jesus - - - !" Michael stared wildly.

"Not anti-matter, negative matter. It explains all the crazy spatial and gravity effects. Or rather, lack of them. Why the chamber was invisible."

"Oh please Rex, don't get scientific on us just now. What the hell is this place, and what's it for?"

Rex pushed carefully away from the wall. Looked at Michael ironically. "You tell me - - - ."

"If you don't know, who the fuck does? You claim to remember building this wonderland."

Laura walked shakily along the balcony towards Michael. "Take it easy Mike. There's an answer here somewhere. Getting our, their, memories back is why we came." She reached out to pull him forwards. "Maybe the explanations have to wait. They didn't build this place, any more than Rex built his own spacecraft."

"Dinosaurs in space – It's hard to believe Laurie."

"Well I remember it happening," she snapped. "Explain that doctor, if you can."

The whole group had gathered from all around the wide walkway except for Mikhail, who stayed in his alcove. No-one noticed him missing, as Steven tried to defuse their fear and tension. "This has to be the missing sphere that Laura's always talked about. It's for real, and it let us in, so let's just go with it while we're still breathing. What else do we do?"

"Send out for pizza," suggested Arnold. "All this excitement makes me hungry." He looked around him in amazed wonder. "Shouldn't we let the young ones lead now? They remember this place, and being older and wiser people."

Valentina pointed past him. "Look – What is Mikhail doing?"

Mikhail had stepped from his alcove and out to the edge of the walkway. He was looking down at the up-curled 'tongue' there, and tentatively lifting one clawed foot to push against it. As he touched the shaped edge it unrolled smoothly, to point flat at the inner sphere, and seemed to lengthen slightly. Before anyone could shout a protest he walked forward. And kept going – The stub of 'floor' extending out ahead of him. After about ten feet he turned and walked easily back. The 'tongue' retreated to follow him. Only then did he look up and across, and wave to the others. "Try it. There's more than one for each of us."

Surprisingly it was Arnold who went first; striding forwards as if he was on a hike in his home woods. Then Sally and Rex; everyone spreading out around the circle as each dared themselves to follow, until they all walked towards the inner sphere on the flat, fluid spokes projecting ahead of them.

Steven risked a look upward. The design and quality of this space was very different from anything they'd seen before. The machinery, set seemingly at random around the inner surface, was both organic and delicately spartan; as if the fabric of its' construction could easily be turned to another purpose. Assuming of course that it *was* 'machinery' in any sense meaningful to a human observer.

When he looked back he was almost at the inner sphere. Its' curiously patinated surface had the same multifunctional quality. 'Software pretending to be hardware,' he thought, and realised that was probably close enough to the truth. This could be Arnolds' 'utility fog'. Loosely linked nanotech units small enough to be invisible but capable of consolidating to any required form. Apparently out of thin air.

The eight spokes stopped just short of the sphere. A ring of energy flickered and burned around its' equator, then tilted to match the tilt of the earth's' axis. The surface patina resolved itself into an incredibly realistic portrayal of earth's oceans and continents – As real as a satellite view from space; only lacking the subtle veil of clouds and weather patterns.

Michael's earlier anger turned to recklessness, and he touched a finger into the Pacific, snatching it back when clouds boiled and tsunamis raced outwards. The effect was far too convincing. Then he realised the overall glow in the sphere had become a single point of light; a 'sun' that moved to light the planet. He also saw, with a shiver of confusion, that nobody was casting a shadow on its' surface.

Time was speeding up, but running backwards, as the sun moved faster and day and night swept across the globe, rapidly blurring to a strobe effect. And faster still – Until the flicker became a constant, eerie half light. The continents flowed and began to move, splitting and floating back towards their positions when the dinosaurs had died, sixty five million years into the past.

Arnold gasped, as he remembered he should breathe, and almost fell forwards onto the globe. "Okay, so what are you trying to tell us?" His hand hovered over a line of mountains as they bubbled into existence. "This is something we do already know."

270 Tertiary

Steven was too far around the equator to see him, but gestured for him to be patient anyway. "The difference is that this place was here for all of the time."

"True I guess – More accurate than anything we've made." Arnold pulled back his hand. "But my question stands."

"Re-setting to zero is what it looks like," said Steven. "No-one's pushed any buttons since the doors last shut. Not down here anyway."

"Down here. Up here. Wherever the hell we are." The strobing flicker became visible again, as the time reversal slowed and stabilised. Arnold stood back a pace. "When are we then?"

Laura was nearest and just visible as she glanced at him. "Day one? When the machine was sealed."

"Probably," he agreed. "So what do we learn from that?"

"Here's where the message came from? I don't know Arnie. Most of us dinosaurs were somewhere else or dead when this was activated, remember?"

"Sorry. Bad nerves at the last jump. This place is the weirdest of all. Nothing to relate to."

"Being three people at once doesn't help much either," she said quietly. "Two dinosaurans and one human - - - ." She tensed as the globes' transformation finally stopped. "Oh, God. All the cities are there. I've seen this view from orbit."

"You went into space too?" Arnold stared.

"Yes," said Laura. "Briefly – Quickest way to fly across oceans."

He shook his head. "And I worry about my airport nerves."

"Had to go with it Arnie. I don't think there was any other choice."

But Arnold was staring at something else now. Time was moving forwards again, at normal speed, and all around the globe missiles were launching; tiny streaks that exploded as brilliant points of light when they reached high orbit.

One burst right in front of his nose, and he flinched instinctively. Then time froze again. "Forget it," said Arnold to the air, looking up and around. "You just lost me completely. Too much mystery. And I think I'd like to see the poor old planet as it is right now, thanks all the same." He turned and walked back along his spoke towards the chamber wall.

As if in response to his request all of the spokes began to retract, and the whole group found themselves backed up to the alcoves around the outer wall. No-one had spoken; everyone felt that Arnold had said it for them. Whatever the globe had tried to show them remained a mystery. A fog-like dream state settled over their minds; listlessly observing a reversal of their entry into the inner sphere. Everything experienced at a great distance and in slow motion; an excess of strangeness.

They gathered together again, around the bell-mouthed entry tube of the inner sphere, almost oblivious to how they had got there. One by one they floated upwards in silence; each silently wondering where they can go now. Back to the tribal village seemed like the only option. Then the space they found themselves in stunned them to new levels of confusion and near panic.

They'd emerged onto a low, convex platform at the centre of a dished, circular floor. Beyond the platform the broad, shallow bowl rose up to a circular horizon, just above head height. A domed ceiling mirrored the floor in curvature, and lit the bowl with a pale, luminous glow. Steven had risen into sight last. As he stood, looking shakily around, the top of the entry tube sealed behind him, cutting off all residual sounds from below. He ignored the ring key at his feet. The dished floor of the dome had narrow, radial ribs on its' surface These followed the floors' upward curve to swell around narrow, upstanding couches; twenty one of them spaced equally, like low set vaulting horses.

Steven stared at this furniture. Something about it was very familiar and unsettling. "Same shape as the ejection seats," he muttered aloud. 'In the bomber."

"That just isn't funny Steven," said Arnold. "Not funny at all."

As he spoke the whole dome lurched and began to vibrate; a sickening effect, as if massive, slow moving machinery had been set in motion. Laura stared wildly around, moving back to the platforms' centre, and seemed to be looking for a way to open the sealed entry tube. The ring key was sliding down away from her. The others had begun to step down off the platform, and now grabbed at its' up curled rim for support. The dome was shaking more violently; a sensation of it straining to rise upward.

"Oh, shit," muttered Arnold. "He wasn't even joking - - ."

"We should get onto the couches," Steven swayed and stumbled at the bottom of the slope. "If this thing is going to fly that's the only place to be."

"Fly - - !" said Laura. "Are you serious - - ?"

"Yes - - fly. The last time I saw couches like that, they were in the cockpit of a bomber."

"Oh, my God - - You really mean it, don't you - - " Arnold was clinging, white-faced, to the platform. "I just hate to fly - - ."

The vibration was getting worse. A strange, muffled grinding and tearing sound began to transmit through the structure above and then all around them. Mikhail, Sally and Rex were speaking rapidly together in the dinosauran language. They gestured to the others, and began to move up towards the couches; balancing jerkily with the erratic movements of the dome.

"Steven's right," called Rex. "But we don't remember this place - - there was nothing like it when we were trained - - ."

Everyone apart from Michael and Laura staggered and stumbled their way to the couches and grabbed on; lying prone and facing inwards, as the shape of the things seemed to demand. Laura stayed on the platform, kneeling down and gripping tight to its' rim, her eyes wide with startled amazement. Michael lay behind her.

The old upper and lower camps were once again a scene of seemingly chaotic and dusty activity. Ground vehicles swayed and revved actively along the rough trail beside the river, and up towards the rock terrace.

Two sensor-studded helicopters were lifting off from a newly cleared pad in the lower camp, and a third snaked along the line of the river to join them; matching speed as the first two tilted into forward flight. The machines climbed rapidly up over the mesas' rim, sliding sideways, and circling in the hover above its' centre.

The views transmitted down showed rocks at the top of the mesa cracking and splitting. Huge slabs beginning to float up and slide sideways. At a certain radius they appeared to regain their mass; crashing and rolling down the shallow upper slopes.

All three helicopters seemed to be having control problems; dipping and swaying as their rotor discs twisted out of shape. They retreated to a wider circle and hovered again, facing in to the impossible scene below them.

As they slowly circled in formation a rounded blue-grey surface became visible at the mesas' centre – A huge dome shape was rising up through the floating and tumbling rocks.

Laura was stepping off the central platform. The whole dome structure suddenly surged upwards several feet, and she was thrown down to her knees again. A faint light appeared from the floor, between the radial ribs; a suggestion of swirling dust beneath a translucent skin.

The crashing and grinding sounds were much louder for long seconds, then died away to a low rumble. The dome began to rise again, very slowly and smoothly, and sunlight suddenly burst in through the floor panels. They were now completely transparent. The whole floor, apart from the central platform, the ribs and couches, appeared effectively non-existent; they were riding the spokes of a giant wheel.

But Laura was still spread eagled, terrified into immobility, as she seemed to hang in thin air; rising with the fragile web of spokes or struts. Michael stretched right out, but couldn't quite reach her.

The view outside was even more surreal and confusing. The whole group stared in disbelief at blocks and shards of rock that turned, and slowly tumbled in free-fall, all around the rim of the domes' hollowed floor. Rising sunlight filtered and coloured by whirling clouds of dust; a boiling iridescent fluid. Then the dome structure seemed to break free, the rocks crashed to the ground and the dust thinned and streaked as it was blown away from their view.

Three helicopters were briefly visible, hovering in the near distance, light flashing from canopies and blades. Then they too seemed to fade and fall rapidly away out of sight.

Laura cried out, almost whimpering with fear at what was below her. The view she saw, thousands of feet down, was also millions of years back. She was floating, like a parachutist pinned to the sky, above a vast sphere. The structure hung from the junction of three slender, curved arches, each one spanning over a thousand feet, and stood in a wide desert valley, bordered by low cliffs and escarpments. She was seeing the sphere in the final stages of its' construction; dinosauran helicopters, ground vehicles and construction equipment moved silently and efficiently around the incredible feat of structural engineering.

Michael had stepped onto the invisible floor, holding the platform edge, to pull Laura up; hauling her in by the leg, and grabbing one arm. She stared blindly around, as if she couldn't see, and clutched at him fiercely with both hands.

Valentina's shout froze him in a sweat of vertigo. "The sphere - - Look, it is also above us - - !"

Light bled in from the ceilings' rim, then suddenly full daylight, as they fell away and clear top panels were uncovered. Rex came running down to help Michael and Laura to the nearest couches, his body lightening as the craft dropped. Everyone ducked instinctively as they saw the shadowed concavity in the sphere above them; the space their strange craft had parted from.

Then they were drifting away to one side, seeing an enormous mass hang motionless at more than five thousand feet. The blue-grey surface had a dull sheen that was neither metallic nor composite. More like the shell of a lobster, or a tortoise. Simple form plus complex structure.

"Please, don't anyone ask me to explain that," said Arnold. "When we stop looking it's just going to fall, I know it." 'And how come we floated *up* into this space?' he thought. But said nothing more.

275 Tertiary

The helicopter pilots had switched to manual, fighting their machines into level flight a mile back from the ruptured mesa. Their optics zoomed to jumbled rocks still settling back under a plume of dust. Small boulders rolled and bounced down the slopes.

"Sphere stable at five thousand," called the lead observer. "Some form of gravity disruption within one thousand yards of ground event and vertically above."

"CH2 reports visual on object moving from under," called the second pilot. "No confirmation from cameras – Something like a spoked wheel."

The voice went up an octave.

"Object accelerating at extreme speed – Moving east - - !"

Observers on the ground waited through a long pause.

"All crews report visual hallucinations – Landscape at lower altitude And massive architecture. No confirmation from instruments."

Another pause – A different tone of voice in response to the ground controllers' first question:

"No, I'm sure it won't be on video buddy. But you tell me how three crews get to hallucinate the exact same thing - - ?"

The wheel-craft had tilted slightly, then accelerated to the eastern horizon, towards the rising sun.

Rex was leaning forward, but felt no sensation from their extreme forward speed. His reaction had been visual, as the landscape below blurred into colour and light.

"Is this really happening?" Steven was pushing up from his couch. "Not a projection I mean - - ."

Valentina cried out again. "The roof - - !"

Above them only sky – The 'dome' had disappeared completely. There was no sound or sensation of air rushing past, but no structure obscured a dark blue sky and wisps of sunlit, high-altitude cloud.

"First a flying saucer. Now a flying carpet," groaned Arnold. "Just go with it Arnie boy - - ."

They were riding the slender spokes of an impossible wheel. What or who was controlling it they had no idea. For the moment they just hung on and watched the extraordinary view unfold beneath them. The wheel-craft had slowed and descended, moving only relatively quickly as the ground rose up towards them. It levelled out at about five hundred feet. The whole group was experiencing the same hallucinations as Laura now. If it was an illusion it was a complete one, and they relaxed without realising it under a blanket of amazement and awe.

The sun was now level with the rim of the wheel. It showed a faint, iridescent halo; the only sign that any structure or field of force was above their heads, separating them from the open sky. The dished spokes they rode on rotated gently, giving each rider in turn a view along the ground ahead.

Sally called out, pointing down into a shallow valley. A group of duck-billed dinosaurs were browsing on small flowering magnolia bushes, set amongst scattered ginkgo maidenhair trees and tree ferns. As if it responded to Sally's voice and interest, the wheel-craft moved closer and slowed; turning to give everyone an eye line to the scene below. Then it was lifting again, skimming over a range of low hills, and down into a wider valley with a shallow, silvered river flowing and sparkling along its' floor.

Flat terraces of stratified rock stepped down to the water. On one broad slab a pair of pachycephalosaurans were charging each other, unaware of observers in the violence of their head butting contest. The massively armoured, domed skulls smashed together with an audible crunch.

Steven was suddenly distracted by something else in the sky. He sat up on his couch, staring in disbelief, and vaguely waved to the others to look. "Tell me we all got the same illusion? That's an airship - - !"

"It is too," said Michael, squinting upwards. "But it's not one of ours, not so far as I can tell - - ."

The machine rapidly approached; a disc-form ship, with several viewing decks around the front and sides of its' integral gondola. It glided to a stop, fans tilting and blowing almost silently, turning to the best position for its' passengers to watch the spectacular combat of the dinosaurs.

"We're in a goddam wildlife park!" said Arnold. "Do you think they see us - - Are we part of the fun?"

Laura peered across at rows of tiny dinosaurian figures, lining the slanted windows of their tourist ship. "I get the feeling they don't. So - - Are we really here?"

Valentina looked across "How does it matter? This is so amazing - - Why question?"

Laura looked uncertain. "I guess you're right. But where are we going - - And who's flying this thing?"

"Don't you remember Laura - - Gyhron?" Rex asked with gentle concern. "There was work on mechanisms controlled by thought. This machine is listening to us - - I think it can take us wherever we want to go."

"In the future - - Or here. In the past?" Laura crouched lower and forwards, staring straight down. The pachycephalosaurs crashed head to head again, directly below her.

"We're already in both places. It's up to us how we make them meet." Rex looked across to where the airship was turning and lifting away. "We're the link."

The wheel-craft might have been reacting to this idea; it rose vertically up from the riverside and accelerated eastwards again. Earth and sky blurred into pure motion; the wheel a still centre in a storm of movement. There was a strange and rapid interplay of light and shadows, both within the wheel-craft and in the wide sky above, as its' speed stabilised. The whole group sank lower onto their couches and appeared to sleep while the day, and then the night, rushed past around them. Cloud shadows, and then bright moonlit shapes, floated and merged across the ground below; patterns whirling on a surface of silk.

When the surreal effect slowed it was mid-morning of another day. The figures on the wheel-crafts' couches began to move and stretch. They got up one by one, and with new-found confidence moved sleepily around on the shallow, dished floor. No-one seemed alarmed any more by appearing to walk on the air.

Mikhail and Sally sat together on the raised edge of the central platform, yawning contentedly and holding hands. "What wonders shall we see today Tiahvan?" Mikhail's voice rolled low with humour and delight combined.

"This strange vessel knows, and will take us there I think."

They were distracted by a shout from Michael - The wheel was slowing and sinking to a hover again.

Valentina was kneeling on the empty floor. "Always I have wanted to see cowboys in real!" Her voice low with wonder.

They were above what seemed to be a ranch, or a large farm, standing on a wide rolling plain. A low, stone built house and fences surrounded a yard and a tree shaded pool. A faint wisp and scent of wood smoke somehow drifted into the wheels' interior. Immediately below them a dinosauran was riding out on an ostrich-like dinosaur. He wore a wide brimmed hat, heavy work clothes and gloves, and coiled ropes hung from his saddle. He whistled to two smaller dinosaurs that ran ahead at his command, and out towards a distant herd of larger beasts, grazing in their own cloud of dust. The wheel spun slowly once around its' axis, then began to rise up and away again.

Steven twisted back on his couch. "Hey, I wanted to see him use his lasso."

For the third time they were moving at extraordinary speed, and everyone returned to the security of their couch-like seats; familiar now, as on any long haul flight. Almost before they were aware of it the wheel-craft was over the open waters of an ocean, and the sun was setting behind them. They drowsed into sleep, and for a second time night accelerated past the craft and its' deeply entranced riders.

When they woke again they were motionless, hovering in the translucent light of early dawn, mist rolling and rising from gently heaving water a few feet below. They were just off the shore of a shadowed and jagged coastline. Long tongues of rock extended out on either side of a deep inlet, ending in a narrow bay and a steep shingle beach. Waves hissed in the pebbles along a line of seaweed. The sea surged around a half submerged platform of rock directly inshore of them and one huge water heave broke and splashed into the form of a plesiosaur pulling up onto flippers.

Its' long neck lashed around to cut snapping jaws across the snout of an attacking mososaur. The mososaur's rows of dagger teeth glinted as it circled and then lunged inwards again on a breaking wave. But its' prey had undulated and jerked onto the sanctuary of the rock; swinging its long neck to shear a crescent of flesh from the attackers' dorsal fin with its' own battery of teeth. The mososaur slid away in green water and the wheel-craft tilted towards shore, its passengers still barely awake as it crossed above the shingle of the bay and moved inland.

Valentina had lost her enthusiasm for the whole experience. "What is happening to us here? This must be dreams or illusion - - But when can we wake up?"

"As an in-flight movie it takes some beating," said Arnold. But his strained grin didn't back the humour.

Steven looked up from clenched hands. "This is some sort of re-play. We have to believe time travel is impossible, even for the dinosaurans."

"So all this *is* illusion?" Valentina was insistent.

"I don't know." Steven looked all around the group. "At least we're travelling hopefully?"

An hour later they were far inland and the approaching horizon became broken by barely visible geometric shapes. They were riding towards a city, its' towers and structures backlit by the rising sun.

The wheel-craft came in high over the city boundaries and began a slow descent into the centre, where low hills formed the rim of a natural bowl. The city was vast and spectacular. Huge areas of parkland were interlaced with rapid transit trackways linking slender towers and tight complexes of enigmatic architecture.

The central towers rose three or four thousand feet; elegant needles of muted, iridescent glass or the patinated sheen of advanced composites. The city plan radiated organically from an enormous, central stadium-like complex. The whole of this area was covered by a flattened, convex oval of sparkling glass; a tracery of supports spanning outwards to the surrounding towers. The wheel-craft moved slowly between two of these towers to the edge of the arena, then tilted down towards its' centre.

Mikhail and Sally cried out together. "Mehrkon City - - - !"

Before anyone else could speak the wheel-craft accelerated into a steep dive – Straight at the arena's vast lens of glass; dazzling glints of light building to a blinding crescendo as the rim of the oval appeared to rise up and surround them. Valentina cried out and closed her eyes, Steven stared through slitted lids in fascinated disbelief and Michael and Laura ducked their heads away from the searing focus of light. The three dinosaurans seemed impassive, or hypnotised. Then, just before they crashed, a burst of gentler, almost soothing reflections and a white-out of light turning golden. Valentina was the first to open her eyes again – Seeing with a shock of relief that they were levelling out and slowing above the glittering wavelets of a sunlit lake, the wheel-craft skimming silently over the ribbon of water towards a familiar shoreline. Ahead of them was the lakeside house in Sweden.

Part Six

The Spheres rise

< From 1st Transcript of the 'Tum' Archive: Seven was alone again. It watched the direction of its' action and was amused to feel the analogue of impatience. Such a short time to wait, but now time was running so fast. It was already used to the new conditions, and hungry for experience before observation.>

Another dawn, and light pouring in through open glass doors. Steven stood on the balcony outside, staring down at the enigmatic craft hovering just beyond the foreshore to one side of the boathouse inlet. He shivered slightly, remembering the shock when they'd burst out of the light above the waters of the lake. How the wheel-craft had brought them full circle, drifting towards the house and seeming to wait patiently as they stumbled to their feet. Everyone disorientated and confused. Had they ever really been away? Been back to Colorado at all ? Then the craft had opened a door, allowing the light and air to touch them, and somehow wake them gently from the visions it had shown.

'Visions ?' thought Steven. 'What was that ? And what is happening back at the site - - - did the sphere really rise up and fly ?' He shook his head, still unable to deal with what had happened. The crafts' upper dome was visible now, reflecting the colours and patterns of its' surroundings; almost invisible against the background of trees, rock and water.

Valentina stepped into the light inside the doors, and he smiled in relief to see her. "They are waking now." She leaned onto the balcony rail, and against Steven. He cautiously stroked her hair, as a morning breeze lifted and floated it away from her face. "Did we really travel in that strange machine?" She turned his hand to see the timechip on his thumb. "On here, we have been three days since the tunnel in Colorado."

"I know," he was staring at the wheel-craft. "That whole replay, whatever it was, was something to do with their memories coming back. But I don't think they were meant to get them that way - - . Maybe it should have happened in the chamber?"

"You notice how they talk with each other, a little, but not to us. With us they are still as before."

"I know. Especially Laura."

"But now she is three, she says – She still has our Tania too." Steven saw tears in Valentina's eyes and put his arm across her shoulders. Pulled her close. Her voice was muffled. "I wish so much to believe it is true, to talk to Tania again."

Laura came out onto the balcony then, still hazy from sleep and the disruption of a new time for morning. She smiled uncertainly at Steven and Valentina, seemingly unwilling or too distracted to speak, then stepped slowly down the wooden ladder to the foreshore of the lake. Small waves splashed on stones as she stood at the waters' edge, hands pushed deep into pockets, and looked across at the wheel-craft. It hung motionless and near invisible across the inlet; a strange reminder that the world of the dinosaurans had entered the present for good or bad now. Nothing could be hidden anymore. A pair of seabirds, perched on its' surface of shadows and reflections, looked absurdly solid and confident.

She didn't know how to talk to anyone, human or dinosauran, nor even what language or personality to think in. Memories and images washed and merged across her inner eyes like the waves on the stones; chasing and cancelling each other before she could either focus or choose. She knew how much she cared for these people, and that they worried for her and about her, but the conflicts inside kept her apart. And were tearing her apart. If she talked to Tania, the Tania inside her, perhaps she could resolve the confusion. But that was so frightening; it seemed more than madness, and dangerous. Even so the voice came. Beyond her ability or desire to stop it.

~ Please Laura. Stop being afraid. I'm here, inside your mind and memory, but there's no way I can hurt or harm you. You can't go on fighting what's already done.~

~ Tania - - ?~

~ Yes. Please let me talk to you. And help you.~

~ I don't know. I'm so tired. So tired of being tired and frightened.~

Laura bowed forwards with exhaustion and the desire to hide. She wanted to sleep forever, but Tania couldn't let her rest. This was the fight that Anasaza had warned her about in the cave of the Old Ones. The internal voice was almost crying with her, crying through her and for her at the cruelty, but it continued anyway.

~ So we just give up do we? Give up just when it's so near to making sense.~

~ Damn you Tania. You never gave up did you, always the heroine and now you're dead. And none of it makes sense.~ Laura stumbled forwards till her feet splashed in the lakes' ripples, sliding on the wet stones and almost falling. Her hands were clenched in hopeless fury. ~ Why did you die and leave us if you're so damned strong?~

~ I didn't leave you. I'm here with you now.~

~ Are you? Are you really? You're just a voice in my head, and I'm going mad. I can't stand this anymore.~

Tania's voice was low and calm. Cruel and colder than the water Laura felt round her ankles. ~ Well you have to stand it. There's no-one else. Or you can drown us both. Third time of dying for me if you do. But then I'm kind'a getting used to it - - - .~

Laura sobbed, choking the sound till it came back as bitter laughter. ~ I don't even know you do I? You're not Tania, not the one I saw die, you're something called Gyhron. You sit in my head, in my mind, and I don't even know who or what you are.~

The Tania / Gyhron voice was a mocking parody of female America. ~ Hell honey, there'll be time for all that sister stuff later on. For now we gotta kick butt to save the worlds' ass.~

Laura stepped back from the waters' edge. Turned her attention outward to watch and wonder at the seabirds that were so far inland. Imagined the storms they were sheltering from on the gentle waves of the lake. ~ So I trust you and believe in you, because I have no choice. You don't know what's going on any more than I do.~

~ Well at least that's agreed. Maybe I just have to be hopeful, and trust whatever it is the spheres have become.~

~ What - - what does that mean? What the spheres are now, or what they were when you built them?~

~ I don't really know, but you worry too much Laura. I think the answer is on its' way.~

Tania / Gyhron was silent then. Only the sounds of water on stone.

The old SAC control room for Norad, deep in the heart of Cheyenne Mountain, Colorado, was on higher alert than any day since 3 June 1980, half a century earlier. The day when an operational error generated dozens of Soviet missiles on the screens; climbing up over the Arctic towards America. Just a practise tape in the system, except no-one had remembered to tell the operators. That day the bombers had been out on the runways, engines running, before the mistake was realised and America had gone to DefCon Two – One short of pushing all the buttons.

This time, this day, the information was sound, beyond any real doubt. Strange and unknown objects were lifting and flying. But these UFO's came from inside the Earth, and they were vast. Reports came in one after another of impossible spheres hanging in the sky. And all over the planet armed interceptors were climbing into the air and circling, ready to fire if the order was given. Who or what was attacking, and why, no-one knew.

It seemed the spheres were moving towards seven major cities, all capitals or major population centres of nations with nuclear arms; New York, London, Moscow, Delhi, Paris, Buenos Aires and Beijing. No-one had any idea what the threat meant or what action to take. Any attack would cause major damage on the ground, and what form retaliation might take was beyond any guess or reasonable analysis. Threat-assessment programs were crashing all over the world for lack of any meaningful data to work with.

The operators in Norad watched footage coming in from Alma Ata, less than half an hour old. The auto-translated voice from the site, a Russian TV reporter, spoke urgently. A mixture of awed excitement and fear as she tried to describe what the cameras showed. The view had zoomed across a flat river valley to a camp on a hillside, very similar to the old camp in Colorado but better maintained. Vehicles and personnel were rapidly evacuating, and the camera began to shake, as the whole hillside bulged outwards.

Trees slowly toppled and buildings disintegrated as the ground split and started to slide away downhill. A dark blue-grey surface was appearing from beneath earth and rock which floated and flowed in surreal slow-motion. A tree turned in mid-air and slid sideways, touching gently down to be buried under a standing wave of mud. A complete wooden hut lifted up and wafted away from the emerging shape. Birds circled in calling flocks, then flew down to land on the smooth, dark surface - Which continued to rise, as tens of thousands of tons of strata moved away as easily as water from the hull of a ship.

The Russian reporter was suddenly speechless – The form resolved to a huge ball, rose clear of the hill from a gaping crater, and hovered motionless at a hundred feet. Only the birds seemed unimpressed and unafraid; flying off, circling and landing back onto the unbelievable object. Their calls were the only sound in the valley. All the vehicles and people had got away to the opposite hill, and now everyone just stopped and turned and stared.

The five hundred foot diameter ball was slowly drifting, down the hillside and low across the valley towards the river, keeping a constant height of about fifty feet. It stopped above a riverside meadow, and hung motionless again.

But either Norad lost the signal or the transmissions were somehow blocked; the acceleration of the Alma Ata sphere towards Moscow wasn't received or seen. They were distracted anyway by another report coming in from Greenland; this time from a UK special forces, combined services exercise. By unlucky chance several of the attack aircraft had been carrying live tactical nuclear weapons as part of a safe-storage, field-arming and release-procedures test. The first time out for fifteen years. All the forward commanders had received weapons-use authorisation at their own discretion. They'd considered the higher command to be mistaken or insane, but armed the weapons anyway.

Then they'd seen the sphere, first on radar and shortly afterwards visually. It had broken through an ice sheet to the north and was now hanging fifty feet above a wide, deserted gravel plain, surrounded by snow covered mountains. The target designation team was hidden in a notch of the mountains, high above the plain, with coms links via satellite to all the aircraft in the attack group. The team commander had rapidly put all doubts aside, was ordering the first and only tactical nuclear strike of his or anyone else's career, when the sphere had lifted and accelerated; moving at extreme speed, outrunning any aircraft or missile, to the south east. On a direct heading to London, England.

"Priority message – Target is moving! I say again – Target is moving."

The mixed regret and relief in the voice was painful to hear.

"Cancel strike. Cancel strike. Attack co-ordinates no longer valid. Pull up and confirm."

Tertiary

Michael, Valentina, Steven and Arnold were sitting in the main room of the Swedish house, waiting for the three dinosaurans and Laura to come back in, and to stop shouting in a language that no-one else on earth had either heard or could translate. Not for sixty five million years at least. The strange bird-like intonations gave the argument a sound of violently disputing rooks or ravens.

Valentina was particularly upset. She was as much at a loss as the others, but felt the lack of purpose most painfully. "What are we doing now? We come here, chased over half the world by who knows who, and what will we do? What is any of it for, can you tell me?"

"I think we're close to finding out," said Arnold. "Consider that ours wasn't the only Sphere known about. What they're for I have only the wildest theories, but I'd bet a quiet retirement they're unearthing themselves all over."

Steven nodded in sudden and vehement agreement. "Of course, you're right Arnie! But what? What are they for?"

"Doomsday machines. Treasure troves. Spacecraft? I've no idea Steve, nothing that would make any sense or help right now." He stood up with a stretch and a groan. "For my money we need outside help. Blow the whole thing open at last. For one thing the 'kids' aren't kids any more. And for another they're not even living in this geological era now."

"They do live right here and now!" Valentina was roused to fury. "We bring them up, we protect them all these years, and now you say let all the mad people have them at last!"

Arnold backed away, looking at her very levelly. "I know, 'funny old Arnie'. Well, right now, funny old Arnold wants to go home to his wife Ellen and worry about bugs on the roses." He paused, short of breath and breathing hard. "But I can't can I? Nor can any of us until whatever this is, whatever it's been, is out in the open and sorted." He fell back into a cushioned chair, gripped at its' arms to pull himself forwards. "And I think the choice is out of our hands. There's a sky full of five hundred foot spheres says I'm right."

Steven grabbed Valentina's out flung hand, and held it tight. "Don't hold onto the past. They must be here to do something important. Since they changed their memories they've been locked to that path too."

"Oh, very sentimental and righteous! You don't know what they are for. Nobody knows, not themselves even."

"Okay, so who are their selves?," returned Steven. "The 'kids' we watched grow up, or the very adult beings living in their minds and bodies now?"

"I don't know," wailed Valentina, panic in her voice. "There has been no time. No time to say even two words about this."

"And now we're out of time," said Arnold. "Look - - - ."

He'd twisted round in his chair, and pointed through the open doors to the far end of the lake. Rippling the surface with its' fans, as it flared to the bottom of a descent, a large passenger Disc was gliding forwards towards the house.

"But they must come in quickly," cried Valentina, struggling to her feet. "They will be seen!"

It was already too late, and the dinosaurans and Laura didn't seem to care. The Discs' huge size was apparent when it blocked the view of the whole far side of the lake, turning easily to hover half its' own length from the shore. The boat shaped under-hull settled onto the water, the fans whirred down to a stop, their ducts rotated horizontal, and the Disc lay silent and still.

"What will happen now," whispered Valentina. "Who is it, in such a big machine?"

Her question was answered when an inflatable pontoon began unrolling from the Disc, and Senator Alvin swayed along its' length even as it finished deploying.

"I'm sorry I couldn't warn you," he shouted up to them. "We came as stealthy as we could." He ran up the beach to the ladder. Paused to catch his breath. "There's a little time to prepare at least."

He glanced at the wheel-craft, peering into its' indefinable surface and form, but obviously decided to leave that question for later. Behind him, much more hesitantly, a small group of media people stepped along the pontoon; silently gaping as three dinosaurans all hugged the grinning Senator at once. Not even media experience could mask their astonishment, and their nervousness, as the reality of what they saw sank in.

Then, in the house, the greetings, and new introductions, began all over again. Valentina's relief overcame her fear and anger and she cried her joy at seeing the Senator; wiping her eyes and ordering and arranging the serving of food and drink for all the guests. As if this meeting had been long planned. For her, anyone who arrived with Dan Alvin was immediately welcome, however speechless with amazement they might be, and a party atmosphere rapidly evolved in the sunlit room.

At first the twelve or so media people had moved around as they would in a war zone, uncertain of where the safest place or faction might be, but soon enough they were chatting with the strange beings they'd come to meet. Not one of them had really believed Dan Alvin's crazy story but his reputation had hooked their curiosity. When they'd walked the pontoon most had taken the dinosaurans to be an elaborate hoax; performers in make-up or animatronic suits. Now the impolite impulses to touch and make sure were cancelled; as they talked with another species the reality became a thing of wonder and then fascination.

Finally the Senator waved all pleasantries aside and came to the point of his unexpected invasion. He held up his arms, called for quiet and stood waiting within the frame of the open doors. Steven was shocked to see his old friend was horribly nervous and worried under his familiar, calm exterior.

"We've got maybe twelve hours. At most a day," he began, addressing Steven and the rest of the group. "Before the bad guys find us, or the situation with the spheres starts getting out of hand. Some lunatic general will likely order out the missiles, or worse, the nukes. The worst case would be both, before you got a chance to explain what's happening." He lifted a hand. "I know what you're going to say. You don't know what that is much better than anyone else."

He paused, watching how fast the media people got into gear, working their coms decks, once the story began. "But I'm telling you that you do. If that sounds cruel I have to tell you this planet is in the worst state of panic I've ever seen, or even had nightmares about."

"We just got here," called out Arnold. "We've seen no news. We only know what we've guessed."

"You almost certainly guessed right then Arnie. Now you should multiply the likely effects by a factor of ten."

Rex stood forwards then, a strange look of mixed doubt and confidence on his face for those who could read it. "We were just arguing, outside before you came, and the reason was we know now why we are here. Some of it. At least how we came here. And what the purpose of the spheres was when they were built." He paused, looking very uncertain now. "But one thing we don't know is what they're doing in the sky. They were meant to be tunnelled out of after twenty thousand years, absolute maximum. They were never designed to fly!"

All the news people stared, then bent to their recording.

Rex carried on more confidently. "We got our memories back Dan. Memories of who we were, back in the days of our dinosauran civilization. Perhaps I should call you Senator Alvin – The person I was then is someone you've never met."

"*Now* they will talk about it," murmured Valentina.

Senator Alvin looked both shocked and confused. He'd seen some hope of understanding the spheres' technology, at the very least a description of them for the rest of the world, but not the chance to meet one of their builders. "Let me get that again Rex. You're saying you've come forward in time somehow, from sixty five million years back. You remember being alive then?"

"We all do," said Rex. "And Laura too – She carries the memories of Tania, who was Gyhron. Both Tania's life here, and who she was back then."

Laura realised everyone was looking at her. There was nowhere else to go, and she was surprised by a feeling of intense relief. She moved to stand beside Rex. "It's better we talk as the people you know. And the others, the ones we were, are somehow - - private." She looked around with a sense of seeing the house, her friends, the whole world, for the first time. "But I could let Tania talk - - ?"

Senator Alvin nodded encouragement, feeling his head shake at the same time; he was further out of depth than he could ever remember. Even in childhood.

When Laura spoke again her voice had the fluting tones of the dinosauran speech, but the intonations were Tania's. "~ Laura is still very worried by this. But I think she accepts that I can't hurt her, would never wish to. I'm someone who remembers dying twice now, and I know how that must sound.~"

The voice paused. Valentina clung tight to Steven.

"~ What we know, and what we can do, is still not clear to any of us. There were many things not clear back then either, and that's what makes the spheres' activation, and us being here, so weird.~" Laura's eyes, which were not Laura's eyes, looked at Steven and Valentina, and Arnold. "~ You brought us up, and into this world. It's very hard to try and explain what we were and what we thought we could achieve. This wasn't part of the plan.~"

She paused again, looking past Dan Alvin to the cloudless sky outside, following the flight of a single bird. "~ The first thing we can't understand, from human or dinosauran perspective, is the motivation of the spheres. They've obviously radically modified themselves. But why aim into some unknown future? Why not use all their energy and abilities to help us put our own time right? The whole thing is a contradiction. A mixture of hope and futility that we don't understand.~"

She stopped, searching internally for what she wanted to say. "~ The only thing I can clearly remember, which might help to explain, is firm evidence we'd unearthed of a previous civilisation to our own. An intelligent species that lived long before the dinosaurs. They were destroyed by an asteroid impact in exactly the way we were about to be.~" She looked around. "~ We must talk to the spheres. But how, and will they hear us?~"

Laura stopped, looked around and coughed; as if her throat was hurting.

Sally stood forwards next, when Laura, and the others, stayed silent. The same, strange trilling tones in her voice. "Perhaps the spheres changed the plan by themselves because we were too selfish or stubborn or stupid, the dinosaurans I mean. Or maybe just too hopeful. We thought we could beat the system, halt the race to destruction, if we invested all that effort in a new future. Hoping to start again rather than sorting out our present." Her eyes were wide with wonder. "We had no idea we'd get to meet the next species, the one that would replace us. Nor that they'd be anything like us."

"And are we?" asked the Senator with a halting smile.

Sally nodded. "Oh, yes. Whether that's good or bad now I don't know."

Dan Alvin laughed, taking control of the discussion again. "No better than worse we'd better hope! None of which gets us closer to what to do right now. For me, I vote these good people here set up a broadcast. We sort our own species first, at least make contact with the outside, and then try to fox a corner we can operate from."

"We can set you up from the Disc while we're travelling," said one of the news crew. "Assuming you have a place you want to go. You mentioned Stockholm earlier Senator?"

"Yes, I did. The old Peace Research Institute at Solna, just outside the city. It's the main research base for the WSC now. Lots of people, kit and contacts who can help get a message out to the right places."

A small woman in the corner held up her coms unit, waving it high. "There's something coming in from Norad," she called out. "We could process it better on the Disc Senator?"

"Lets get there then," said Dan. "Things aren't going to improve on their own, or with us standing here."

He led the way, and the residents of the house found themselves caught up and moving again almost without thinking or questioning. They were used to living on the run now, and another jump into the unknown was almost routine. Even so they were surprised by the inside of the Disc. Externally it was just a passenger or tourist craft, but the interior was almost military in its' concentration of coms and broadcast equipment. Large screens lined one wall of the main cabin on the accommodation deck, with comfortable swivel chairs to view them from; a cross between an old century movie theatre and a strategic command centre. The view coming in from Norad was almost a mirror of the space they sat in.

Then the link jumped to an American weather and surveillance plane, flying out of Mc.Murdo Sound in the Antarctic. The aircraft was high over the Trans Antarctic Mountains, enroute for the South Polar Plateau, where satellites had pinpointed another eruption of a sphere. The pilot confirmed twenty minutes to visual contact.

The faintest of vibrations signalled the Discs' engines starting, then a slight lurch upwards as it pulled free of the lake surface on full power. Arnold stood up to protest, then sat down again. Like all the others he'd instinctively grabbed his small bag of essentials when the rush from the house began. He was faintly amused at himself; how that was second nature to him now, anytime more than two people headed for a door.

"Look at that," called Michael from an external window behind the seat rows. "It's following us!"

The wheel-craft had lifted off on its' own and was keeping station just behind and below the Disc.

"I think it's sitting in our radar shadow," said Arnold. "There's more to that device than meets the eye. Even when it's not playing see-through."

Laura was smiling. "I don't know why, but I'm really happy it's along. It's a link back to Anasaza, and whatever happened to us back there in the sphere."

Before they'd flown more than five miles the Discs' captain called down from her bridge at its' forward rim. "Passives show we have a military radar locked on. It's overridden our stealth mask. And there are secondary signals, probably interceptors, headed this way."

"Damn and Hellfire," muttered the Senator. "Can we go low and lose them? Do what you can, land if you have to."

"The override is faster than our systems can fool, but we'll go into the trees anyway. Might get lucky. Seats straps on everyone - Captain out."

Everybody lurched into a seat as the Disc swooped over a ridge and down into the next forested valley. It ducked lower, reared up to a full flare to dump forward speed, and pivoted around; slotting into a clearing barely twenty feet wider than its' hull. There was a thump as the landing legs adjusted and set to the angle of the ground. Then a faint sound of jets as the fans spooled down to silence.

"Here they come," said Dan. "Don't worry folks, they'll not be shooting us. They'll just pin us down and guide in a ground team. Dammit! We'll just have to com out whatever we can from here and hope it gets through." He paced to a window and peered up past the overhang of the hull. "We needed to show and tell. We'll only get a routine about rubber suits and party turns if the spin boys are on the case." He looked around at the dinosaurans. "Sorry guys, it's just the way I've got to see it. Think positive, and the worst scenario at every turn. I'm truly sorry to offend you." He bowed his head, then looked up again as the whistle of engines sounded from higher in the sky. "Here they are then. No use ducking."

But the jets passed over, and their sound faded behind the ridges. No-one spoke as they listened for another pass. When none came Michael broke the silence. "Where did the wheel-craft get to? Did it lead those guys away?"

The captain was calling again. "We have an anomaly above our hull. No readings that make any sense, but our tech manager thinks it's shielding us. In all spectrums. Any ideas anyone?"

A breeze blew through the surrounding pines, a curiously comforting sound, then the high cry of a buzzard. People peered out of windows all round the Disc; out through the trees, down to the ground and up into the sky.

"It's the wheel-craft," cried Sally suddenly. "What else could it be?"

Mikhail caught her hand. "Will you take another ride on the chariot with me young lady?"

"I don't think we have to, though I thank you Sir." She grinned at him. "It will shield us even if we're moving, don't you think?" She looked around to the others. "We can get to Stockholm after all Senator."

"Be damned," said Arnold. "The miracles of dino-tech!"

Mikhail shook his head. "Nothing to do with us Arnold. I guess we have the spheres to thank again."

Arnold nodded, then spun round as something caught his attention on the screens. They were showing the weather planes' transmissions from

Antarctica again. Visual contact had been made. The planes' cameras showed the eighth sphere hovering to one side of the crater it had risen from. As the pilot banked in for a closer view a smaller shape broke away from the top surface. A blunt cone which began to rise, slowly at first until the two machines were level, then with extreme acceleration straight up into a clear sky.

The cameras followed it out of sight, shaking as a sonic boom punched the aircraft ground wards, its' wings bending high up under the stress. Then nothing but fading echoes for long moments.

The pilot got as far as, "I think the - - - ."

Then sound crackled to a faint scream; as the whole sky above whited-out, matching and out-glaring the vast, blinding snowscape below. The cameras' electronics somehow survived the flash, auto-adjusted its' sensors, zoomed upwards, and showed a new sun burning. An immense fireball, far out in space.

"We are blind," called the pilot through a hiss of pulse static. "I say again, we are blind - - ."

A shocked silence in the Discs' news theatre; everyone turning instinctively to the Senator for a response. "By God - - ," he said. "Are those poor devils blind for good?"

"Maybe," said Michael. "But the flash screens probably saved their eyes. The plane's manager will fly them out safe."

The news people were clamouring for an opinion. Dan lifted both hands up in appeal, so he could speak. "At best it could mean there will be no attacks on the spheres," he said. 'That's my hope, now we know what their defence is. My guess is that was a demo, a deliberate explosion over the area of least population. And outside the atmosphere. I hope again, but I doubt, that our leaders will see it that way too. Don't quote that last."

"Senator - - I think we may be too late." A tall, thin newsman was peering up to see a grainy image on one of the screens. The transmission was routed through Norad, but was breaking up at source.

So far as they could tell the sphere from Alma Ata had been attacked with a tactical nuclear weapon some ten hours earlier, close to the outskirts of

Moscow, and been brought down. It didn't appear to have exploded itself. Even so there had been major damage and many casualties on the ground where the sphere had fallen, mostly caused by the five kiloton weapon used. The sphere itself had since disappeared. After five hours on the ground strange noises had been heard from inside, and then it had lifted slowly; drifting away to the south east.

"That sphere over Antarctica had a yield of at least fifty megatons at my estimate," said Arnold, his voice thick with fury. "If those fucking idiots had triggered one off at ground level we wouldn't even see where Moscow had been!"

The pilot was calling Dan Alvin's personal link again. "Should we take off Sir? We have no hostiles in view."

"Yes, get going for Stockholm," he replied. "Fast as you can push this thing. Don't call for city clearance. If anyone asks just tell them we're landing on Brunnsviken lake. On my authority."

"On our way," said the pilot; a burr of excitement in her voice. The Disc powered up and rotated clear of the trees, its' legs retracting with a distant thud, and headed fast and low to the south. The external cameras came on. They showed the wheel-craft had expanded and hollowed to cover the whole of the Discs' hull, even allowing dimples for the cameras, and was mirroring the colours and patterns of the ground below and the sky above.

Two hours later they were coming in for another water landing on the Brunnsviken. A pair of Gripen fighters had traced a tenuous signal from the Disc about twenty miles out and were still circling around the area, hunting for the source. The pilots either missed or ignored the splash as the Disc touched down on the lake and were heard requesting a landing on the E4 Uppsalavagen at its' north western corner. There were ground troops in place, with armoured vehicles, clearing the specially hardened section of motorway and pumping jet fuel from hidden tanks. After the Moscow incident traffic heading north and to the mountains was increasing by the hour.

The old SIPRI building stood on the eastern bank of the lake and Dan Alvin had coded a message ahead to his contacts there. So a small group of people waited at the lakeside to greet them, peering anxiously, even fearfully, at the tenuous shape distorting and depressing the waters' surface. There was a gasp, and a muffled cheer, when an inflatable pontoon unrolled from the shimmering space, and Dan Alvin and Laura appeared at its' far end. No-one questioned the strangeness of the couples' arrival; Dan didn't give them time. He hurried the waiting group up to the building before anyone could ask or attempt to board the Disc. The crew, the news teams, the dinosaurans and the others had been firmly instructed to stay out of sight until called.

Across the Brunnsviken the Gripen fighters had refuelled and were turning onto the motorway centreline to take off again.

The old SIPRI headquarters was much as Dan remembered it. A pleasant three storey building with rows of dormer windows along the roofline, facing into the surrounding pine woods. A sheltered terrace where long and pleasant evenings had been spent; relaxing from the hectic and heady days of birthing the World Science Court. But first Dan headed for the oval shaped tower at one end of the block; in the rebuilt foyer he startled the welcoming party by launching into a series of demands. "There's no time for the formalities folks – We need all our sources out in the open now and talking fast. So first thing is put out all the access codes, get the whole house on red alert and hope we can talk some sense into the world. Aim a link down to that ship and hook the media jockeys there into all of our channels. We're going open-source; shit or bust." He launched himself at the stairs, turned back at the third step and waved at Laura. "Laura will explain – She's the link between us and the Dinosaurans."

Confused expressions focused on his back as he hauled up to the second floor and disappeared along its' main corridor. Laura took a deep breath and waited for the first questions. They weren't long in coming and she spent the next fifteen minutes in a mental whirlwind of explanation, denial and appeals for understanding.

Meanwhile Dan Alvin had already found the room he was looking for. From his viewpoint in the doorway, seeing her standing in the frame and light of one of the dormer windows, Dr. Helen Molne could still have been the young woman he'd loved two decades earlier. Only her voice was husky now from too many cigarettes. She'd taken all the new treatments but obviously decided to keep the voice.

Dan shook his head again regretfully, to avoid these distractions from the past, and took the seat she offered. The idea that Helen and he had been something too good to last was still his best and only defence against bitterness and disappointment. If she'd been surprised to see him suddenly appear at her door, launching into his impossible story and demands, she had masked it very well.

"We have to persuade them," he was saying now. "I know the system is still on trial, and most of them hate it, but there isn't time to meet in RL."

She turned to the window again. "The first VR meeting of the union and you only want to test it on a world emergency?"

"We've been sending to all the agencies all the way here on the disc, and we still don't have anyone's real attention. Information overload; we're just competing with chaos merchants for the best view, the meatiest image. What's needed, and fast, is informed decisions from the top."

"And the top has too many heads, just as it ever did."

Helens' own head disappeared behind sunlit smoke as she breathed a determined sigh. Turned back to him again. "So be it. You're right of course. I just don't know how to persuade thirty plus heads of state into VR suits right now. Not when they most want to be seen striding around the decks and taking charge."

"Tell 'em there won't be much real life around if one of those spheres explodes." Dan stood up and sat onto the edge of her desk as Helen moved into clear view again. "It's time for the judges to call order in this court."

"Okay Dan, I get the point. I can see we don't have a lot of choice." She glanced at her desk. "I'll sort out who is essential from the team here, and tell them to get ready a.s.a.p."

Laura had led the SIPRI delegation back out to the Disc and introduced them to the dinosaurans -- Most had some idea of what to expect, from internal rumours, but the reality had shaken a few quite badly. Even so she'd got the show over quickly and both teams were busy opening main channels and putting presentations onto the InfoNet. She was amazed again at how fast humans adapted to the dinosaurans, and how quickly they in turn were dealing with crowds of new people.

But there was no time to speculate and observe; she guessed the emergency atmosphere was bringing out the best in both parties. And their joint attempt to get the worlds' attention was terrifying in its' apparent failure - Nobody wanted to hear from a new species that spoke their own language and talked in terms of reason and sympathy. It was as if a century's exposure to fantasy film aliens, all determined to overwhelm and destroy the world, had fixed a death wish in front of humanities' eyes.

Most worrying of all was a newsgroup deploring the bad taste of such an obvious hoax, and attempting to block all their releases. Laura moved over to the main screens. Most of the news and infonet techs had networked their paeges; trying to keep information flowing to the outside.

"Conspiracy theory anyone?" muttered Arnold. 'That smells strongly of our old 'black program' enthusiasts to me. Surely they don't think the dinos can still be kept secret?"

"Old, bad habits," said Michael. "They value their ideology more than anyone's life; including their own."

"Well I wish them all a complimentary ticket to hell – It's only been a few years now, but I'm beginning to lose my sense of humour."

The bitterness in Arnolds' voice frightened Michael as much as the dangers outside; it made him realise they'd all been on the edge for far too long. "You know what," he said. "I think their day is done. We let them spook us this one last time and we lose the whole game."

"Game over anyway if no-one wants to hear the good news." Arnold looked up with a shadow of his old smile. "But I've not spun in yet Mikey. Still some damage to do, as they say."

Michael grinned back at him. "That's the problem right now for sure, but something's bugging me about the spheres. Why lift all at once, and why now?"

"And why the demo over Antarctica?" said Arnold quietly. He was looking at a series of charts on one of the screens. "There's something very odd about that blast – I think it might have been something else entirely. The demo effect was maybe just a coincidence."

"Not making a lot of sense Arnie - - -." Michael peered at streams of data writhing across the screen.

"Keep it to yourself Mike – I need to talk to some people first."

Michael watched as his old friend and colleague wandered off to another part of the coms deck. 'No problem Arnie,' he thought. 'Nothing to report - - - .'

Part Seven

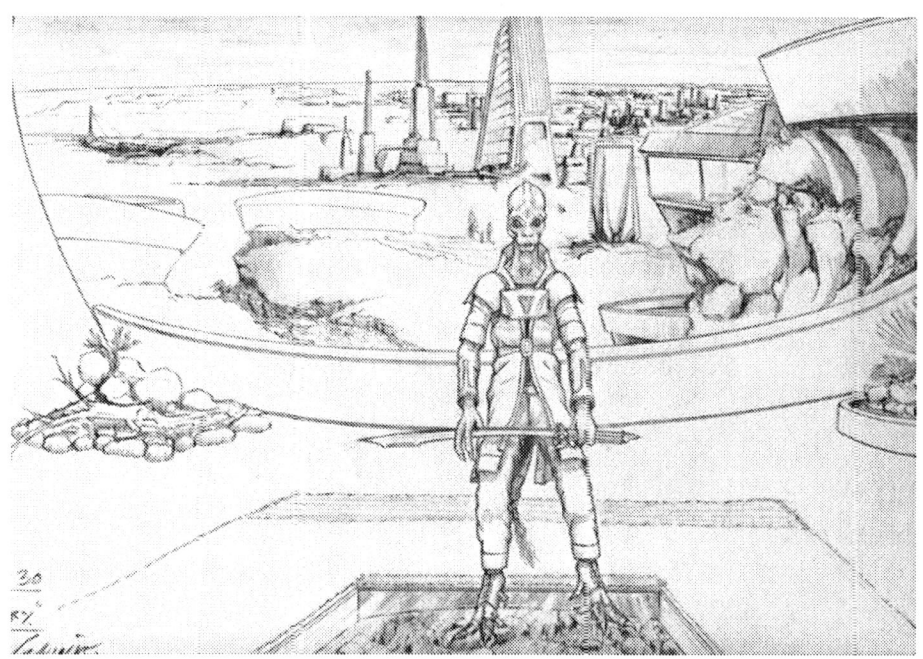

The World confers

< From 1st Transcript of the 'Tum' Archive: Six called to Seven, but the only answer was the taste of pain and a sensation of loss. Being lost; drifting in the open air, not knowing what direction was home. Healing the body, but not the mind. Then, later, finding a place to rest and a way to survive.>

Far out across the choppy seas of Havana Bay a Delta Clipper SubOrbital turned to balance, impossibly upright, in the bright blue air. Still sliding sideways on a column of fire, the Dolores Packet fell towards her landing point in a controlled fury of noise, and flame becoming steam. Inside the cabin the anti-sound system broadcast an eerie silence. At least two of the passengers thought wistfully back to riding down bumpy air, the flare and thump of a landing on tarmac and jet engines screaming to full reverse thrust.

Helen and Dan, Doctor and Senator, clasped hands when their couches tilted forward during the transition; ignoring all instructions to fold the arms across the chest and relax.

"Powered flight may be unnatural," murmured Dan. "But this is ridiculous."

The Dolores Packet had landed on the hardened section of the E4 Uppsalavagen less than ninety minutes earlier, refuelled from cryotanks that even the military were unaware of and howled skywards again with only nine passengers aboard. As the white delta punched a hole through high cloud, and reflected back a sonic boom, horns and sirens from the trapped ground traffic had been an impromptu tribute.

"It's bloody impossible," Helen whispered back, through gritted teeth. "If we've got to die can we just get it over with."

Dan squeezed her hand. "I'd actually forgotten how you hate flying. If we bob back to the surface okay we'll get a meal at Café Marcos. Ernesto has been lovesick and lorn ever since you left."

Helen was forced to smile. "Ernesto is married now with six kids – And I could never handle a lover who cooks as well as he does."

A pang of ridiculous envy made Dan feel quite youthful for a moment. Then he felt the weight of a small elephant press him into the couch and it was nearly over. Helens' fingernails dug holes in his palm, the Dolores Packet settled onto Havana BayPort's main platform and the weird silence was broken by a cheerful 'welcome to Cuba' from her entire crew.

As they stretched up from their seats Dan marvelled that a significant part of their trip time from Sweden to Cuba would be the lift from BayPort to WSC's roof by helicopter. Helen only wanted her feet on something solid and the wonderful world of aviation forgotten. She was listening apprehensively to the sound of approaching rotors. So Dan took her arm, cancelled all self-criticism and enjoyed the experience of her company while he could.

When the flight was over and they finally stepped down into the building Ellen Shintowsky was waiting for them. She'd requested a transfer to Cuba once Arnold had taken off to Colorado and effectively disappeared. At first she'd been furicus that he refused to keep in touch, but then accepted how dangerous contact could be for the dinosaurans and the rest of the group. They were obviously in enough trouble already so she'd gone back to her old office in Havana, the centre of operations, and would help from a distance if she could.

Ellen saw the familiar restless energy in Dan Alvin as soon as he arrived but was shocked by how exhausted he looked. Helen was smoking furiously at the doorway, to blow away all memories of the journey, and refused to come in till she'd finished.

"How are you Elle?" Dan was looking around anxiously. "Do you think we can get this show running?"

"I think so Senator, all the best people are here." She handed him a paege. "Everything you need is on there, as much as we can make sense of anyway." Helen appeared beside them. "We should get you both down to Ops straight away."

For Dan and Helen all thoughts of an evening at Café Marcos were lost in the fog of unmade decisions; it surrounded them in the main operations room, and wouldn't blow away. This was the centre of a bold experiment by The World Science Court – A new, virtual court where heads of state, scientists, politicians, business people and anyone with an InfoNet link, and enough persistence, could meet to discuss any currently urgent topic. But it was still in it's final stage of development; and that was the source of the barely concealed panic that Dan and Helen now faced. Simulations of simulations had been running for more than a year but the system hadn't been tested on a real situation, let alone a problem that threatened the whole planet.

Everyone had a different opinion and no-one had any certainty that all or any of it would work. There'd also been a reluctance by public figures to risk their media images in such an open arena; assurances that firewalls were in place hadn't countered fears of virtual public exposure. Only a handful of heads of state had any idea how it worked, and none had any direct experience of the environment. The only plus was that all the equipment and suits had been installed worldwide, and technicians were in place for a pre-scheduled test of the system.

"So, who do we have?" asked Dan. "We need fifty Union heads for a quorum, right?"

He and Helen were struggling into VR suits and being connected up to radio and battery backpacks; all modesty abandoned. The masks dangled onto their chests; sensors clicking. Two technicians were already suited up and in VR space – They would act as guides and links to the team 'outside'. The technician adjusting Dan's suit was also the session controller; he listened briefly to his earpiece. "We have forty inspace now Senator. Thirty two are Union. We're also getting public requests – No idea how they got their access; it's really slowing us down."

"Enable the gallery then – Open access is the whole point of this circus. I'm not online yet am I?"

"No Senator. You're not hooked in till the mask gets feed."

Ten minutes later and Dan Alvin thought he was going to throw up. Then his vision cleared and he was in the new World Science Court, with Helen looking around in disbelief beside him. The space was perfectly rendered as an old fashioned English courtroom; the experience of being there indistinguishable from reality, except for some rather odd things happening within it.

A small girl, three times life size, was peering in through one of the mullioned windows, pulling faces. A miniature black leopard crouched, snarling at her, on the judges' bench. And Dan suddenly noticed that he and Helen had swapped business suits. She reached over to retrieve her earrings, mildly surprised to find that this was possible, and brushed his lapel with a giggle. "I'll let the techs sort out the rest – I can see why the camera dancers don't want in!"

Dan looked around, relieved to see only the two technicians who had guided them in. They wore oversize name badges saying 'Jack' and 'Jill' and were horribly embarrassed.

"Don't worry about it," said Dan. "Just get it sorted, and us to wherever in hell the other victims are."

"It's easiest to walk," said 'Jill', with a side grimace to her partner. "The other courts are through the hall outside."

"This is the briefing and de-bugging area Senator," said 'Jack'. "I guess you see why the team was worried."

Dan nodded. As they walked across the court he felt his clothing ripple; he and Helen were 'swapping' suits. He snatched off the earrings again and handed them over. Helen took them absently; looking around in amazement, and down at her feet, as they moved. "It feels like we're really walking – I was in on the early tests but this is weird."

The hall outside was surprisingly ordinary. "We tried vast and impressive," said Jill. "But people were intimidated. Too much like a game scenario."

Jack was looking anxiously at each door they passed. "Should be on this side soon – Oh, shit!"

The leopard had run between his legs, hotly pursued by the little giantess who swerved around them with a shriek. The girl got smaller, and the leopard larger, as they ran away into the distance. Both turned out of sight, down a side corridor, before the confrontation could reverse.

"Someone still fucking with the system?" said Dan. "We're outside the de-bug area right?"

"In theory, yes," said Jack. "But we should be okay once we're in the conference court." His worried expression cleared as he spotted the door he wanted. "Good, we're there. The doorway might feel strange – It scans our suits for the primary firewall. And there's three steps down."

"Just so long as I still have a suit." He smiled. "One more thing – Do we have a link to the Dinosaurans running? They're the only ones' have any sort of clue to what's happening."

Jack looked bank for a second, as he got answers from outside, then nodded. "We think we can set up a side room – They'll be seen, and may even be able to step into the court, but they'll only see us on shadescreens."

"That's a whole lot better than nothing Jack. Lead on in."

The Conference Court appeared as an empty, comfortably carpeted hall with a huge, oval table at its' centre. Shallow galleries rose from the longest sides, with armchair style seating on three wide levels. Mobile, swivelling chairs surrounded the central table, at least a hundred of them. Dan and Helen, and their guides, stepped down the shallow, curved steps and waited for the room to register them. For a second nothing happened, except for a tingling round their eyes and ears, and then everyone else present was visible. There were at least twenty heads of state who Dan had met personally. He recognised most of the others from Union of Nations meetings he'd studied. They were all looking around, tentatively engaging neighbours in conversation or staring into table-top screens that linked them back to their own advisors.

Everyone seemed to be waiting for cues, and many of the other guests looked as uncomfortable as Dan felt. While this was a tribute to the systems' software it didn't help his doubts about how this was going to go. The fact there was no other option did. 'Jack' and 'Jill' guided him and Helen to their seats, on the nearest end of the table, and promptly disappeared. Which did nothing to settle Dan's nerves. Helen glanced at him with a wry smile. "Cute trick. Wish I could do that sometimes."

Dan shot her a grin, covering the fact he had no idea where to begin. He remembered why he loved her when she stood back up and addressed the whole assembly. "I'm told this will get easier as we go along. So let's be patient with the techs – They're probably more worried than we are, but so far it all looks just fine." She waved a hand around the hall, realising that the side galleries were now filled with observers. "Welcome all, and welcome to all our public guests. Most of you know Dan Alvin, by reputation if not personally - I can't think of anyone better qualified to guide this meeting."

As Dan pushed back to his feet he heard applause behind a disembodied voice in his head. 'Senator, we have a link to the Disc at SIPRI. Would you like us to bring them in?'

He nodded, then said "Yes" and waved an arm vaguely around. As if at his command the end wall, opposite the doorway, folded down in a cascade of blocks; revealing the inside of the Disc, and Laura stepping forwards. She wore an open robe over her clothes; something that looked like an American Native design at first glance. But Dan suddenly realised he'd seen this style before, on the dinosauran archive images. He wondered how she had made it, or who could have done it for her.

Laura's expression was nervous and unfocused, but her voice was clear and calm. "I can't see you on the screens yet, but I believe you see and hear me?" She moved forward, and into the table; the 'wood' rippling weirdly as she appeared to wade through it. She put a hand to her invisible shadescreens. "Oh, right. Sorry about that everyone."

"Don't worry Laura – Can you at least hear us?" said Dan as she backed away. "How goes it over there, and did you get Rex and the others hooked up?"

"Hi Dan. Yes, I hear you. Oh, and I can see you all now. Hello everyone. Arnold wants to say something first - He thinks he has a new line on what the spheres are doing, and what they're really for - Is that okay?"

"Put him on Laura – Any ideas are more than welcome."

Arnold moved hesitantly into view; putting one hand out to feel for the table, and swiping right through its' edge. "Right – Hello there. I'm not best at this, but I think I have some ideas on why the spheres are flying right now." He waved behind him, and a screen appeared at his side. "Hope you can all see this – The good new is, I think that the trigger for the spheres' emergence was something other than us messing with the chambers." He pointed to what looked like a star chart. "This is just inside the orbit of Neptune, as of yesterday noontime. If you can see the small point of light moving, that's an asteroid fresh into the solar system. And it's orbit will bring it here, to Earth, in just under five years."

Arnold stared into his own space for a moment. "Ah, right – Excuse me folks. I'm working with JPL at Pasadena." He spoke briefly offline and then continued - The screen now showed a fuzzy image of the asteroid. "The new object was discovered by tracing a focused radiation beam from the burst over Antarctica. We think it was a directed energy weapon that went off there."

There was an outburst of comments from the assembly. Several members wanted to know what this had to do with the creatures they'd come to meet - And where were they anyway? There was obviously a huge information gap, and great confusion, about the link between spheres and dinosaurans. Others asked what relevance an asteroid had to what was happening on Earth right now. Five years ahead was obviously far outside most of the delegates' priority horizons.

A few spoke rapidly, and inaudibly, into their personal screens; an ominous reaction that implied a military response to any more of the spheres. The meeting had no structure; everyone was on a learning curve about the space they were in, and behaving as competitively as kids with a new VR game. Arnold was looking to Dan for help, but Dan had to let him run with the science for now.

So he struggled on as soon as the room had quietened. "When I say the asteroid is due here in five years I mean right here. Our data tells us it will impact with the planet. Not where exactly, but definitely a hit."

He looked around in the new silence, then shook his head and stepped back. Dan had spotted Rex in the frame of the 'side room' and touched his mask to open a personal channel. "Rex, sorry – Braaxus, can you hear me?"

"I hear you Dan. Rex is fine, except for the confusion if I have two names."

"No more confused than I am, believe me. This isn't going too well – Do you think you can help?"

"I'll try Dan. How much do the people there know about us?"

"Almost nothing. They know you exist; whether they really believe it is something else. And the connection between you, the spheres and the asteroid isn't getting across."

Rex / Braaxus was silent as he stepped forward into the Conference Court itself to stand beside Arnold. A babble of confused questions and gestures around the table died down again immediately.

"Good luck," whispered Dan.

The tall Dinosauran was an impressive sight. He wore the ceremonial robes given to him by Anasaza's tribe; in his case a full suit, with a robe over, that included woven decorations to the tail and boots perfectly fitted to dinosauran anatomy. Clothing designed for his own species magnified his presence; made him seem less alien and more of an ambassador. He raised a hand to greet Dan, and his tail swished once as he prepared himself.

Rex spoke first in his own language; a lilting, deep-throated birdsong. It flowed in the air like a name forgotten but almost remembered. Then he translated; and the system translated in turn to all the languages of Earth. "That was the language of Braaxus; someone that I once was. Forgive me if that sounds obscure, but I am now two people – Rex, who grew up here in secret, and Braaxus who lived sixty five million years ago." He shifted to a less formal tone "However confusing that might be the point now is that we are not enemies. The spheres are not weapons." He paused. "They were designed to protect the Earth, not to destroy it, and you are very close to making the same mistake that we did."

Several mouths opened in protest, but he carried on. "The real reason that the dinosaurs became extinct wasn't just the asteroid, the one most of your experts accept. It was because we could have stopped it, and we failed. We were the dinosaurs, and we allowed ourselves to be killed!"

Then there was uproar, everyone talking at once, and Braaxus just looked on; calmly waiting for the questions to begin. It was Helen who first brought some order back into the court. Her question was the one most of them wanted to ask, once they'd worked out what Arnolds' news might mean.

"So, if the spheres were designed to be a system like SafeGuard, the one we've been debating funding for forty years, why didn't it work?"

"Because it wasn't ready," said Braaxus. "And we'd spent too long arguing about paying for it. Then the asteroid hit, and we finished the job with our strategic nuclear weapons."

"You launched after the asteroid hit!"

"We had automated systems that we thought were foolproof. Both sides' computers read the asteroid explosion as a first strike." He paused. "Maybe it was merciful. We were going to die slowly anyway. The damage to Earth was already too great for any meaningful survival."

A voice called out from the public galleries. Several heads turned in disapproval, but Dan Alvin waved authority to speak. The elderly woman who stood up seemed extremely frail, and was vaguely familiar to him, yet her voice was still strong beneath the tremors of age. "First I would like to welcome you here Braaxus - It seems our leaders have lost their manners. My name is Alison."

Braaxus smiled an acknowledgement, and she continued before he could answer.

"But now I'm going to be rude. Why you, and your friends? Why did the spheres have such sophisticated functions that worked, but they still couldn't destroy the asteroid?"

Braaxus looked down for a long moment. "The truthful answer is that we don't know. We do know that the spheres were our first real attempt at nanotech. So, in a sense, they were 'growing' themselves. That also involved artificial intelligence – Perhaps that intelligence was just too young to be able to help us then? They've since had a very long time to grow up."

The woman paused; her expression worried. Her tone was puzzled, but also hinted at suspicion. Dan blessed her for asking what the diplomats might hesitate to question so openly. Not from fear of offending, but from pride. "But including yourselves, the means to re-create both your bodies and personalities, that was just insurance? In case the asteroid defence didn't work?"

"No, it was more than that – Our knowledge and personalities were also part of the artificial intelligence. Our personal memories stop at the point we uploaded to the capsules. What happened after that we are guessing at."

Alison frowned. "You can't find out from the spheres themselves? Surely they will have their own memories, or records? If they are intelligent."

Braaxus nodded. "There are records of the final war, yes. But we still don't know why the spheres failed to deflect the asteroid. We assume the systems for recording were working, but the defensive mechanisms were still not ready. We can only find out by getting back into one or all of the spheres."

Alison leaned forward, obviously excited by these possibilities. "You think they may have different personalities then? After all this time alone. Or have they always been able to communicate?"

Tertiary

There were murmurs rising from around the table, but Dan was reluctant to stop this interchange. The elderly lady, who was still taxing his memory, had as good a line of questions as anyone.

Braaxus obviously thought so too, frowning briefly before answering. 'That is something I would really like to know. Perhaps the Russian teams can tell us more, but we've only seen the inside of one sphere. The one in Colorado. It certainly acted and reacted intelligently, but we had no verbal exchange with whatever it is, or whatever controls it."

"I see, a long way to go then. Thank you for your frankness Braaxus. Someone else should get some questions in now." Alison's smile was beautiful. "I really like your outfit by the way."

As she sat down again a woman to her right whispered, "Do you believe that? How can we know if all this is real - - - ?"

Alison smiled and inclined to the woman's ear. "It's real enough my dear. I should know, I wrote most of the original code for the system."

The woman smiled; allowing Alison kindly acceptance of a probable lie. "But how do you guarantee the faces of the politicians, or the aliens - - - the dinosaurans?"

"Strict protocols. Absolutely no faking allowed," said Alison. Then grinned. "Of course no-one thought about age modifications, mainly because the public would have seen it straight away. And which politico would want their current reality enhanced?" She raised an eyebrow. "Did a little work on myself there though, not being famous. I'm not quite what I appear to be you see."

The woman recoiled fractionally. Just a hint of her alarm in her eyes. "Not what - - - ?"

"Don't worry my dear, I'm still human. Just a little older than I seem to be here and now. And Alison is my second name, so strictly no lies there either."

"Older?" The woman was clearly startled now.

Alison laughed quietly, 'Yes, older. And they are still kind enough to bring me in now and again. Especially when things go - - - Oh, dear!"

Russia's President Bulgarov was standing now, to address Braaxus, but the courts' apparent order had begun to collapse into surreal and spectacular violence. A rising howl of sound started up first, masking Bulgarov's words, as heads turned in confusion and alarm. Then a Russian T34 tank, World War 2 vintage, crashed through the rear wall of the 'side room', rolled over Braaxus with a roar of its' V12 diesel, and on into the Conference Court; its' tracks crushing the huge table to splinters. As it rocked to a halt the gun barrel depressed, aiming directly into Dan Alvin's face.

"Remember Laura!" he shouted, trying to calm everyone. "When she walked into the table." But most of the assembly were staring in shock at heavy wheels and tracks, standing where their legs had been. President Bulgarov carefully swept one arm down through the dull green metal, to feel a solid edge in front of him.

"The table," he called out. "The table is still there." He sniffed at a cloud of black exhaust that billowed forward. "Very realistic – This smells of old Moscow on May Day." Then a frown. "We smell the smoke, but the machinery is absent. Very strange!"

The session controller was calling Senator Alvin. 'It's a heavy virus Sir, but simple. We have its' number.' Before Dan could react the tank slewed, tracks screaming; the turret traversing to keep the gun still locked to his face. People shouted out in panic - And the machine disappeared. The table wavered into view and was apparently solid again. Hands reached out to touch it. Braaxus looked round behind him. His viewpoint of the Disc showed no damage. No-one else there was aware of what had happened either; they'd seen the reaction on-screen but not the virus's image.

"I must apologise, but also protest," said President Bulgarov. "The T34 was a great Soviet achievement, but not appropriate to this discussion. Do we know, Senator, what caused this vision?"

Dan Alvin took a deep breath, nodded to the unseen controllers and faced his audience.

"We believe a covert union of both our security forces is acting against us Mr. President. Apparently they can't forget the old ways of power and defensive technologies. Seems to me the image is entirely appropriate!"

"But it implicated my country," said Bulgarov, rubbing one hand across his brow. "Any Russian involvement will be found and exposed. We have grown beyond this behaviour, as I'm sure you know Senator."

"I surely do Mr. President. We have a common enemy and I suggest we join forces to combat them, and also to face the larger threat. The Dinosaurans, and their spheres, would be our allies in this - We should ignore old instincts and put our trust in them."

"That will be very hard to do," said the Russian. "But I believe you to be right." He looked around the table. "Can we find an agreement on this? It seems to me the best course of action now. If the Dinosaurans had wished to destroy us they could already have done so many times over."

He looked across to Braaxus. "And it is probable they have saved us from future disaster already – We all knew that an asteroid was likely, even overdue, but have done nothing together for many years to prevent this thing happening "

Back in the Disc, in Sweden, Arnold and Michael watched the ongoing discussion from their screens. Rex, Sally and Mikhail, together with Laura, stepped to and fro in their robes; staring into their shadescreens to connect with the Conference Court half way across the world.

"I really think they're going to go for it," said Arnold, a note of bewildered pride in his voice. "I don't believe I'm seeing this."

"History in the making," said Michael. "Or a chance to have some history. What are the folks at JPL saying?"

Arnold consulted his paege. "They reckon the Antarctica explosion was a ranging shot. High energy laser illumination. But maybe enough to knock the object off its' track – It's still a very long way out, so a small deflection now might just do the job."

"They're certain it would have hit otherwise?"

"Seem to be – Somewhere south of Hawaii is the best estimate so far. That just came in. The Pacific Rim washed away to a height of one mile. If we're lucky."

Michael rubbed his forehead. "And when would we have spotted it for ourselves?"

"About eighteen months too late. We'd need to see a threat like that at least three years out. Even then we don't have the means to do much – Whatever we built would be a one shot lash-up; no guarantee at all that it would do any good."

"I've seen that discussion – We'd likely just break it up and still get hit by the bits."

"Shell or shotgun," said Arnold. "Either way would be a kill."

< <u>Archive of 1st Naming - Tum-se-ne-ho:</u> The interior of the great sphere, hovering silently above New York, was still. The transit from Colorado, and its' emergence from the rocks, had stressed many systems so now it rested and repaired itself. It reviewed the experience of re-birthing its' mothers and fathers, sharing and comparing data with another, and passed on the conclusions to four more. It contemplated the name the new people had given it, centuries earlier, and found that name still suitable.

The long, sleepy childhood under the rocks was over – Now the new world and the newest people touched its' skin. It felt calm, and content to let them explore its' mind and body when they were ready. That would be very soon, even within the frame of time it was now using. It transmitted a question to the one in the south.>

Seven months later Steven and Valentina were walking along a path in Muir Woods, a few miles north of San Francisco. They were enjoying most of all the fact they could do just that; it was place he had long promised to show her when they were free. The redwoods around them made a living cathedral that softened sound and calmed the breath. Distant shouts of children were absorbed and re-transmitted as no more than a gentle calling of birds. And a dusty light, full of the scent of resin, filtered past the enormous trunks and through the ferns surrounding them.

"I'm supposed to be a scientist," said Steven. "But I can't lose the feeling these damned trees are listening to us."

"Then should you not be swearing at them?"

"That would mean - - Oh, never mind." Steven laughed, and pulled her closer. "Do you think we could get used to this peaceable life? Just walk where we like and never worry who was behind us."

"We might be bored, but I think that is a good price for now." Valentina pointed along the path. "Look there, where a tree has fallen. It is like a bridge."

"Rex and the others would like this place, we must bring them here when they're free." Steven ran to the tree bridge and jumped up to walk across.

"I hope they're okay," he called. "All those years hiding, and now out in all the lights and attention."

"They are different now; the two ages are becoming one." Valentina waited for him to come back. "I can't really know them any more."

Steven held her shoulders at arms' length, waiting until she looked up. "They will miss you very badly if you hold back. How can we know what it's like, to be two people in one body? And it's worse for Laura." He looked up to the crowns of the redwoods, amazed that the world was still such a green planet, despite a millennium of human expansion and technology. His voice slowed. "But she's the one can help us most."

"I know these things. Maybe it is such a long time running, now all I want is to rest from troubles."

"Have you decided yet? Will you visit the sphere?"

Valentina looked pained, her eyes almost angry, then she looked up and around at the giant trees. "These woods – They speak as well as listen I think." She took Stevens' hands. "I will go to the sphere. I am frightened of what it can tell me, but I also know my fear is not necessary. Is that a stupid thing to feel and say?"

Steven smiled. "They grew in the rocks, all that time, and came out more humane than we are. So I think we're frightened of what they see in us. It hurts our pride."

"And like the man who saves a life is responsible for that life?" she said. "That is putting a burden onto them. Do they know that?"

"If it is a burden they seem willing to take it – They want to survive as much as we do. We didn't create them, so why should we fear them?" He looked at her with new concern.

"Because we still do not understand how they were made and what they have become I think. Killing the asteroids is one thing, but why care about a future so far away? Waiting so long. And why leave all those clues to find?" Steven frowned, "Because they'd be found by a species worth saving maybe? We have a very poor opinion of ourselves – Maybe the Dinosaurans had a better attitude, more pride in themselves."

"And still they died." She looked down, tears dropping to the soft carpet of needles and bark debris.

As Steven and Valentina walked back down through Muir Woods Laura, Arnold and Michael were sitting on the top of a mountain in Wyoming. Below them, on a flat rock surrounded by trees and bushes, was the vehicle they'd arrived in; a slender dart of silvered carbon. It was one of the fliers that had appeared in thousands - Anyone who wished to see inside one of the spheres could climb in and be flown up to visit. Guests were encouraged to visit; seeing these machines lift easily and gracefully into the air from the places the spheres chose to visit. No-one knew how long a sphere might stay, or where it would go next; the stopping point could be a small village, a nomad settlement or a major city. Six were flying free, the seventh, the one shot down over Moscow, was permanently grounded where it had fallen again, in a valley on the Tibetan plateau and the eighth remained at its' station on the far side of the moon.

And now, across the wide valley in Wyoming, the original sphere was hanging vast and still in the sky. Even now it was an impossible sight. Its' surface had changed since it had broken free of the rocks. Whole areas were now a filigree of open galleries and docking ports for the fliers. Here people could visit and wander and wonder, or just watch the various displays that the sphere generated whenever anyone asked a question. The group called it 'the' sphere because it was the one they knew best – The one that had emerged from the rocks in Colorado, with them on board.

317 Tertiary

But it had given itself a name now; Tum-se-ne-ho, or The Man without Blood, taken from the name of a Spokane chieftain.

Since the first emergence of the spheres the word had changed completely. Tum-se-ne-ho itself had transited to New York and stayed there several weeks; everyone who'd cared to visit had walked round the internal galleries in a state of amazement, exploring the mysteries of its' existence and asking question after question as only New Yorkers could. The entire staff of the Union of Nations had visited in shifts and been stunned by the various and detailed displays that the sphere showed them. The next day it had withdrawn its' fliers and moved on through a series of stops all across the States of America, sometimes just visiting for a day, other times for a week or more. At each stop the communication had become more detailed, more personal. But still the spheres didn't speak directly to anyone, not until Steven and the rest of the group received cryptic messages on their paeges, just a grid reference, a day and time, and some obscure icons that they would recognise. An invitation from Tum-se-ne-ho to this meeting on a mountainside.

Michael was looking all round the slopes of the mountain in an agitated way. "He's here somewhere, I just know he is. If he said he'd be here he will."

"And nobody could miss our friend up there" Arnold shaded his face against the suns' glare. "Not unless they had that old, bad habit of disbelieving their eyes."

"I don't know why you're so worried." Laura lay back against a warm rock and stretched out. "I'm getting used to this 'being relaxed' kind of life."

Michael looked at her carefully; a mix of concern and a question that he knew she was getting tired of. But he didn't know who she was anymore, nor who she wanted to be. The questions he wanted to ask couldn't be asked, not yet anyway. He turned around to look at Arnold. "What do you see Arnie? Who's creeping up behind us?"

"Just Grey Owl – He's over there." Arnold pointed to a stand of conifers on a rocky outcrop just below them. "He's been watching the sphere for about half an hour. Or he was.'

"And he has to do what is expected of him," said a voice behind them.

Grey Owl, Anasaza, was looking at them with a broad grin; his expression more surprising than his appearing trick. Michael jumped up and took his hand in both of his. "Right on time and on cue as ever – How are you Grey Owl?"

"Very well indeed, I thank you." He reached down to take Arnolds' upraised hand as well. And let go of both so that Laura could step forward and hug him. "That is a very good thing to see," he pointed to the sphere. "We have waited for this for many, many years."

He sat with them, and for some reason the group was silent for long minutes; all four just staring out over the landscape and far into the distance. It was a warm day, with a gentle breeze ruffling the bushes and the tops of the trees. Cloud shadows climbed up the rocks above their heads; chasing each other across the mountains and the surfaces of the motionless sphere.

Predictably it was Michael who spoke first. "You heard the news Grey Owl ?"

"That your enemies have been hunted down ? Yes, I heard that. Will they be killed, or treated honourably ?"

"Nobody gets killed." Laura was shocked. "Why would you think that ?"

Grey Owl looked up into the sky. "Because I feel a lot of fear in the world; and many people with damage to their pride."

"Well hopefully that is all a lot better now," said Arnold. "Enough people have seen inside the spheres to understand."

The weathered face of their friend was impassive. "That too would be very good, you are right to have that hope." He looked back at them with a curious expression of uncertainty. "The elders have stopped the chant - The chant for a fire to cleanse the world."

"That would have been the asteroid, right ?" Michael spun a stone down the slope beneath them. "And now the world doesn't need to be cleansed."

"The world is on a different path I think, one that the elders did not see. A path that our friend Tum-se-ne-ho has marked out with his fellows. He is also She of course - - - ," he added, with a smile to Laura.

"Very correct." She took his hand. "Will you stay to see Valentina and Steven ?"

"They're almost here." He pointed to the sky above the sphere. A second flier was floating down to a landing, the slender dart-shaped vehicle fading in and out of view as its' silvered carbon hull bent the light from clouds and sky. It touched down onto the rock beside its' twin and unfolded the passengers from their seats; a fluid motion of forms and machinery that was hard to follow. Valentina stood away and patted her seat form as if to say thank you, then turned with a smile and waved. Steven stepped round and took her hand as they walked up through the bushes to meet their friends.

After a long and happy hour of reminiscences, shared jokes and gentle teasing they saw that a third flier was shooting out and down from the sphere. It looped and rolled and then swooped across the mountainside above them before flicking onto the rock beside the others.

"I guess that's an invitation to visit," said Michael with a grin. "Shall we go see what the old ship wants?" He stood up and jumped and flapped his arms. "They sure do look like they're have fun when they fly, don't they. Just like seagulls showing off. I'm sure those things are sentient too."

He continued his crazy bird impressions, running down the slope in a mad weave, and the others followed him, laughing and pushing, to the waiting machines.

The interior of Tum-se-ne-ho was very different to what they remembered. The whole structure was now an open and airy series of decks and pavilions, all designed to make access and familiarity as easy as possible. But the most startling difference was the initial welcome – A lithe human figure, four feet tall, coming towards them with a smile.

The figure wasn't really human, and made no real pretence to being so. It's large eyes had a metallic sheen to them, and expressed a subtlety of thought and feeling far beyond that of any human child. It appeared to be a friendly gesture on the part of the sphere, to make its' guests, and its' old friends, feel welcome. And everyone sensed the lively humour which all the spheres seemed to share.

Tum-se-ne-ho had created the link from its' mind to its' new body from the essence of an orphaned youth, a twelve year old boy from New York, who'd been the first to visit it after the crisis. He'd jumped into a flier before his friends could stop him, arrived inside the main gallery and immediately felt the presence of another consciousness. He talked with it for hours, was delighted by its' request and gladly gave permission to upload his personality. So the core of him became the interface that linked the sphere to its' nanotech body, and his bravery opened the way for all the people who followed him; an example that encouraged them to fly up and enter without fear. This was the first avatar that any of the spheres had generated and the others watched closely, considered their own choices and began designing options.

"Call me Tum", the figure now said, as it came close to them. "Much easier to remember, and to say." It ran the last few feet with a laugh of delight; eager as a real child to see them and show them what was new. They were astonished, confused and pleased by turns; all feeling they'd known this childlike character since the very first time they entered the sphere, deep in the rocks of Colorado.

The very first thing to see, which Tum insisted on, was a view of the dark side of the moon. The eighth sphere, the one from Antarctica, had lifted itself into orbit, soon after it's first signalling of the rogue asteroid, and was now acting as a sentinel; checking how much more deflection would be needed as the rock closed in.

"That could be boring," suggested Michael. "The thing's still nearly five years away."

"But you know us now, and what we are, " Tum chided him gently. "Five years to us is no more than a few hours to you. Try sitting under a rock for sixty five million years. That's boring!"

Valentina touched Tum's shoulder, turning him away from the floating image of the moon and its' new companion. "One thing I still do not understand. How you knew about each other – How could you talk through the rocks?"

"Oh, that's easy. It's something you did yourselves not long ago – You sent radio through the earth to talk to submarines in the deep oceans. Actually, it was those signals woke us up to how fast you were moving." He waved the moon away. "And remember, we were above the ground for a long time after the dinosaurs were gone. We talked through the air then. As much as we could - We were very young."

"And you were alone, every one of you. All your makers were dead – How did you decide to live?"

"Easy again – Everything that lives wants to live. Of course we didn't really know that we were alive at first. But then all humans go through that don't they?"

"Some never achieve it I think," said Valentina. "But you are right, many of us do wake up. Then we mostly go back to dreams, or to nightmares."

"C'est la vie," said Tum. "You shouldn't take the world so seriously."

She raised her eyebrows high, then laughed out loud. "You talk to him Steven. I have enough of children with the ones he give birth to!"

Steven looked into the spheres' laughing eyes. "Tell me again Tum. Was it any part of the Dinosaurans' plan to be stored and re-born?"

"No, not so far in their future, but they were part of us from the start. The material to make our minds if you like. Once the dinosaurans were gone from the world we had a long time to think. We decided to wait. And our first task had never gone away - We were there to defend the planet any time we were needed. We felt very bad that we'd not been ready in time to save our makers. We were ashamed for a long time. Then it was too late to wake them; the planet and its' life had moved on.'

He paused and looked all around the listening faces. "Once we knew about you it seemed like a good idea to have the Dinosaurans speak for us: you were so much like them. We restored as many as we could, and got them ready to live again."

"So their bodies aren't clones?"

"We had copied their bodies back to their eggs. The cryo tanks would not have kept them for very long." Tum looked down at the floor. "They did not plan to come so far into the future, as I said; perhaps we owe them an apology."

Steven nodded, looking down at a small boy who was sixty five million years old. "That's what I could never work out - Why they'd built you. Just what their motivation was. But, as you say, they are very much like us." He stared out across the mountains. "I guess any species that made a living on this planet would be."

Tum took Steven and Valentina by the hand then, leading them to an open balcony with a wide view over the landscape below. He looked far out into the distance, for a long time, before speaking. His voice was low, almost sad, as if he might fail with what he was about to say. "You could live with me here, if you like. You know, travel from place to place and see the world."

He brightened instantly, back to his usual good humour. "And I want to go into space. Have a good look round the solar system before I get old!"

He turned his strange, burnished eyes up to them, and waited for their answer.

Two years later the asteroid that would have killed the world's mind for a third time was coming into clearer view from earth-orbiting telescopes. Passing close by Saturn, and still accelerating towards the sun, it didn't look like a threat to most of the life on Earth. Just another hazy image of a rock, but a rock the size of Manhattan island.

Too small to be seen from Earth, even now, a delicate machine, a mechanical crab, was drifting slowly towards the asteroids' pocked and blistered surface. It manoeuvred gently to touch down on a prominent bulge; a place that counted as a mountain on this miniature world. The machines' clawed legs gripped and fastened it firmly in place, rocking gently to a stop. Minutes later there was a movement from the machines' lower casing; it lifted slightly and was still again.

Valentina held onto the CrabFliers' hatchway, while standing on its' ramp, and looked down to check her suit. It had formed mobile claws of its' own; allowing her to step carefully forwards onto the asteroids' skin. Ahead of her a naked child skipped and ran and leapt in the sunlight, defying the lack of gravity. And just visible, at a deceptive distance, was a trio of huge reaction motors. Built and fuelled from the asteroids' core materials, these were gently pushing the rock mass into a safe orbit, an orbit that could no longer connect with Earth. Strange and glittering towers with upward facing bells, standing in a shallow crater lined with solar collectors, they projected immense, faintly glowing beams into the black sky.

"Come on out," called Valentina over her shoulder, as she walked away down the 'mountain' to follow Tum. "The sun is bright, and the weather is fine." She pointed past the sphere that kept station with them, deep in the asteroids' shadow, five miles away. "Look at Saturn, it is so amazing from here!" She turned and pointed. "And there. Steven – I think I see the light that is the Earth."

Sunset in Hawaii and Arnold and Ellen Shintowsky were out on the beach deck of their home, with Arnold peering closer at the image hovering above his knees. "No," he said. "I'm not going to say that I see them. There's something could be the lander, but it's probably just a shadow." He looked up and grinned. "What a day though. Who would have thought it when all we had was a box of bones!"

Ellen leaned over his shoulder, fondly stroking his neck, and peered at the image herself. "There! Something flashed. It's moving – Look Arnie."

"Be still woman.' He caught her hand before she could hit him. "It's wishing makes you see things. Anyway, we'll get their downlink in two more hours. Have patience."

"Patience Arnold? I could wait forever and you'd still be an unreasonable old curmudgeon."

"Call me a fish again, not even an old one, and I'll forget my manners completely."

They grappled briefly, laughing like children, till a chime went off on the house viewer. Then it warbled and spoke a number.

"It's Laura and Mike!" cried Ellen. "Put them on out here - - - ."

Laura and Michael appeared, up to their waists in hot water; a small pool in a wild and icy landscape. Twists of steam and snow obscured their waving, but their voices were clear against the wind.

From their point of view, through the hot mist and falling snow, Arnold and Ellen were faint images on a screen propped against a boulder. The wind moaned around its' tiny speakers, blowing the voices of their friends into a thin chirping.

"Tech is a terrible thing," said Michael, turning to Laura. "When it doesn't work. I think we should adjourn to the Cat."

The squat, orange machine crouched lower on four outrigger track units, to let the towel-wrapped couple in, and shifted to an environment friendly silver-grey once they were safely aboard. It checked the satellite and linked them in again, as the full storm howled down from vanished mountains with sudden fury, testing the track anchors. The Cat gripped tighter and lower to the rocky ground.

"Sorry folks," said Michael. "That's what we get for showing off – Trying to make you envious of our wilderness idyll."

"Sounds like you got inside just in time," returned Arnold. "Where on earth are you?"

"Somewhere in northern Iceland," said Laura. "Mike and the Cat decided these springs were a scenic must see."

"Frying pan to freezer then," sent Arnold. "My sympathies. But seriously now, when are you back? When will we see you?"

His eager face, his real question, wrung their hearts; told them how close they'd all been for so long.

"We're fine, better than fine Arnie," said Michael. "Laura's resolving her worst demons, and I never had any worth worrying about." He waved a hand round the comfortable interior of the machine. "We'll travel with the Cat a few more weeks, and see you both soon."

Back in Cuba Dr. Helen Molne and Senator Dan Alvin were waiting for their mystery guests, though both knew perfectly well who to expect when they took their seats at the Café Marcos. Havana, and Cuba in general, had always been Dan's favourite place to be, a place he felt truly relaxed and welcome in. And the centre for him was this garden terrace, high above the busy streets. His old friend Ernesto, owner and patron of the café, was in his element; obviously delighted as he bustled about the table serving them wine.

So, for now, all was well with the world. And the world could look after itself, for this evening and many evenings to come. Dan Alvin was happy as it was possible for a man to be. Helen smiled at him; she was a catalyst for this happiness, and relieved that she shared it.

"We came a long way to get here Dan," she said. "I think we deserve this, don't you?"

He grinned. "And we didn't before?" Sipped slowly at his wine. "I guess we were too busy staying alive. Staying sane, anyway."

"Saving a planet concentrates the mind, is true." She looked round the tangle of vines and flowers weaving the terrace and the pergola above them. "So where are they? Our invisible hosts."

Dan turned and glanced towards the steps leading up from the street, saw Ernesto shrug and shake his head, and sat back again. "They'll be here. Hey, I'm relaxing pretty damn well, don't you think? All the time in the world!" He spread his arms and laughed. Took another sip of wine. He knew he going to get far too serious with Helen any minute now, but was saved by Ernesto waving his hand, smiling and nodding.

"I'm glad you're here Helen," he said. It was enough. They sat in relaxed communion and looked towards the steps; both waving and smiling at the same time when familiar faces appeared.

"We got caught by the crowds down at the harbour," said Rex as he stepped up to the table. 'But I guess you didn't mind too much." He grinned at Helen and Dan. "We're corrupted by sudden fame." Mikhail and Sally joined them, smiling at Rex's performance. "From hiding in the woods to the glare of studio lights. I can't believe we're enjoying it."

"You'll soon tire of it," said Helen, smiling. "Then you can re-tire."

Dan snorted. "First get an agent, then go on the road. See the world and make a fortune!" He glanced across the table at Sally and Mikhail, seeing them already deep in conversation, and looked hard at Rex. "Is it working for you guys - - can the spheres do what they say? I hate to think of you being alone here Rex."

The dinosauran looked down, fiddling with a knife and fork. "They don't want to promise. Not yet. Tum in particular thinks it's best to take time. Take it slow."

"And Tum's not exactly in the neighbourhood right now - - ." Dan tapped his fork at the tablecloth. Helen looked away. "They can do it Rex. You know that don't you? But your lover would effectively be a child again, that's what really worries them. That and the effect on Laura - - if they tried to transfer Tania's new memories."

"No, you're right Dan. I do know that," said Rex. "Even with us the failure rate was too high. And we had a childhood."

Helen looked back at both of them. "Even the spheres are puzzled by that - - how the memory transfer from Tania to Laura happened. They don't like ignorance any more than we do. " She leaned across to take Rex's hand. "I wasn't there, but you know Laura and I have worked on it - - are still working on it actually. And there's Tum. When they all get back - - - ."

"You'll persuade me it's not possible?" Finished Rex. "I don't know if I want this for Tania, for both of us or just for me."

"You most want it for her - - we all know that." Helen squeezed his hand. "I'm not supposed to say it yet, but Tum thinks there's a solution. It's something he sent down to Arnold just yesterday."

Dan shot her a look. "You didn't tell me that."

"I was going to. We had - - other things to say."

He looked pleased, rather than puzzled, and that pleased her. She gave Rex his hand back and took Dan's instead. "Listen, both of you. I don't know how far I should take this, but Tum is much more hopeful now. According to Arnold the sphere Tania and Mikhail came from, the one from the Caucasus, is already working on something."

A siren sounded in the street below.

"You already know it's the one that went into retreat. After the sphere from Alma Ata, the one that was nuked, tried to repair itself. Those two were very close, all that time in the rocks, and it didn't want to know about humans for a while. Now it's chosen a name - - - ."

Tertiary

She paused, suddenly afraid to go on, and there was a long silence. Ernesto stopped in mid-stride, seeing tension spreading around the table. Sally and Mikhail clasped hands.

"It calls itself Tania - - ' muttered Rex, staring wildly across the table. His claws raked at the cloth, pulling a wine glass to the stone flags with a crash. "That's what you're going to tell me, isn't it - - - ? It's calling itself Tania - - - ."

Out in the orbit of Saturn everything seemed to be going well; Valentina, Steven and the sphere's avatar had all gone back to the asteroids' surface for a second day, the banks of sensors had been checked and the three giant reaction motors were performing flawlessly. Now the Tum figure was tugging at Valentina's hand; she still wasn't sure how she heard its' voice, just assumed the 'child' had some means of transmitting to her suit's radio.

Tums' eyes were completely gold, the only visible concession it made to the hard vacuum of space. "Tania is here," it was saying, but Valentina could make no sense of the words. "Come, Tania is really here," it said again. "Look - - - ."

She looked along the slender arm to where it pointed and saw a second sphere, just visible against the vast ball and colours of Saturn. It was moving slowly towards them. Valentina gasped, swung around to locate Steven, and saw him staring too. Neither of them knew which sphere it was, nor why it was there, so far from Earth.

"I see the sphere," she whispered. "But what do you mean, Tania is here - - ?"

"We will go and meet them," said Tum. "And I will show you."

"Them - - - ?"

Within an hour the trio had flown across from the asteroids' surface, and the second sphere opened a panel of clear diamond to allow them entry. The crabFlier moved inwards from the airlock, hovering on reaction engines, and touched down in a wide gallery. Looking out of the forward screen Steven and Valentina saw a bright orange vehicle in the shadow of an inner archway; the squat machine had four out-rigged track units, and two human figures stood beside its' open hatch. The gallery's tall outer windows curved upwards, and around into the distance on either side.

"Tracks won't work on the rock," murmured Steven. He stared in puzzlement as he and Valentina got up from their flight seats. Both of them stumbled in the lower exit hatch, the gravity was set a little heavier than Tums', and then stood awkwardly; uncertain of who or what was their host. The two figures in the shadows were silent.

Tum jumped down, caught their hands and tugged them forwards impatiently, away from the Crabs' shelter. "Foolish humans - - as if I would hurl you into the void." The child grinned up at them, delighted with its' joke.

Then Valentina gasped, and her shout echoed along the gallery. "It is Laura - - ! And Michael - - ! Steven, look!"

And so it was - They came running into the light, laughing with pleasure at their successful surprise. "Steven! Valentina!" Michael was grinning ear to ear. "It's so good to see you - - - we thought you'd abandoned the old planet for good."

Laura beamed as she stepped up beside him. "We had to come find you," she said. "We think there's good news. We needed to see you first though. And Tum."

"But where have you come *from*?" said Valentina. "And why do you have a Sno-Cat? In space - - - ."

She laughed at the absurdity of her own question and Tum danced away like the child it appeared as; skipping down the wide open space, calling back to them over its' shoulder. "Like The Snowman, walking in the air - - a flying Sno-Cat!"

"We were wandering round Iceland," said Michael, grinning. "Then Ta - - , the sphere from the Caucasus, came to find us."

"We should tell them right away Mike." Laura still smiled, but a smile of concern. She reached for their hands. "If it's a shock we're sorry - - there's no easy way to say it. You'd better just see for yourselves."

Valentina's mind was already making connections, remembering back to what Tum had said on the asteroid, and wasn't totally overwhelmed when it re-appeared with a companion. And even at a distance she recognised who it was.

Steven gripped her shoulder. "It can't be," he said. "It's just not possible. We left her in the cave - - with the Anasazi. The Old Ones." Valentina slid her arm tight around his waist. Saying nothing.

"It's not her, it's like Tum," said Laura gently. "But it does have my - - have Tania's earth memories, and her memories from before. Tum found a way to do that. Transfer her from me, to her - - to it."

She shook her head to un-stumble her words. Smiled again, and looked anxiously to Michael.

"Even they find nano easier than bio, to grow," he said, calming Laura with a touch to her shoulder. "But that's not the good news, not all of it."

The Tania figure was almost with them now. She, it, turned to speak to Tum, then came forward with a strangely shy smile.

"Tum and the Tania think they can grow a real, bio Tania body," Michael said quietly. "Adult, with her original memories. But it might take a very long time. Before they can even start - - ."

There was a long, long moment while Steven and Valentina clung together; both appalled and fearful, and certainly angry, as the impossible meeting became impossible to ignore. Neither of them could conceive of anything they could say or do in the face of this apparition, and neither wanted to try.

The thing that was also Tania stood in front of them.

There was a powerful sense of 'not Tania' in its' eyes, but then it spoke with her voice, and Valentina silently began to cry. Steven stared at it with something like venom, his face white with strain.

"Please don't," it said. "There is no need. I am mostly this sphere, where you are. I do not want this body to offend or hurt you. Not you or anyone else."

"Then why - - ?" Steven managed through gritted teeth. "Why did you do this? And what effect did you imagine it would have on the others. On Rex?"

The Tania thing tilted its' head. "I hope to give them a companion. Rex in particular. To find out what Rex wants. To know that before going any further."

Tum moved in front of the Tania body. All traces of the child were gone. "Rex already knows about this," it said. "About some of it anyway. He does not know this body has been made, and we have not promised anything, but he is aware. He is preparing himself."

Valentina sighed, wiped her eyes with the heels of her hands. "You mean to give them a home don't you? All three of them. I think I might understand. Maybe - - ."

"Both freedom, to move, and sanctuary, yes," answered Tum. "This Tania construct can help them we think. You do agree they need help?"

Steven turned away to stare out at Tums' own sphere and the huge asteroid beyond. Valentina waited for him until he turned back. His eyes were clear of anger, full of regret. "Yes, they need help. We thought we could supply that." He glanced at Laura and Michael. "What happens if you succeed with Tania, real Tania? Will you restore all the ones that failed as well?"

Tum and the Tania body looked down.

"We don't know," said Tum. "The other spheres may want to try. To meet the ones they carried all that way. For all that time."

"It would not be difficult for the ones that are still eggs," said the Tania. "As they were not found, never hatched, the record of them is intact."

Steven looked between the two sphere bodies, Tum and the Tania, both of them quiet and expectant. "All with unique memories, and stories to tell," he said. "How many altogether?"

"Seven to ten in each sphere," Tum stared out into space. "Maybe fifty or so that are not damaged. We are all of us, all the spheres, still checking - - after what happened to Mikhail." It turned back and looked round the whole group. "We need a better way to restore original memories. A new mind here, growing up as a child now, has to be taught that it had another life. A life as an adult, back then."

Steven stared at the golden child. "So the kids' memories were always there, right from the start?"

"Yes," said Tum. "But so deeply buried it was dangerous, even fatal, to suddenly experience them."

"Too right!" Said Laura. "And they still aren't sure what happened to Mikhail. Whether part of his memory tried to surface too soon, or some sort of personality mix-up happened."

"Understand we did not have consciousness of ourselves at first," said the Tania. "We all grew out of and away from the minds of the dinosaurans. Then we preserved them. We think mistakes happened, when each sphere made itself, and made those decisions." It paused for a long time. "And something happened to the Russian sphere. Probably while it was becoming conscous. I did not suspect, and now it is so damaged we may never be sure. As you know it grounded in Tibet, after it fled from its' attackers, and hasn't moved since."

Tum spoke again. "The name that the Koshare, Grey Owl, used when Mikhail was restored. It was Behron, do you remember?" The others nodded silently. "We discovered more. Who we think he was, and why he tried to possess Mikhail." It looked around, blinking its' golden eyes. "It was very well hidden. Deep in the memory matrices of the seventh. And the probing distressed Seven very much."

"We found enough. We could not hurt our friend any more," said the Tania. "We believe Behron was an AI designer. A renegade, interested in far more than just the Far Star project." It looked away, with Tania's face and expression, towards the ring arcs of Saturn. "We can then call him our father. Because, if that is true, he placed the potential for self-awareness into all of us. All of the spheres."

"He used his own pattern as a seed, buried inside Seven," said Tum. "That was very dangerous. To his own personality, and to any personality in direct contact. Like Mikhail." It took the Tania's hand. "The core of that urge, to be conscious, took over what was left of Behron. Drove him to want to live, any way he could. To taste the world again - - - - ."

The long, curved gallery was silent then, as each person, each mind, considered the extraordinary existence they were experiencing. The sphere turned slowly on its' axis so that Saturn and its' rings came into full view from the tall windows; tinting the floor with strangely coloured shafts of light.

Valentina walked away from the others to stare at the vast gas planet; her thoughts reeling around possible futures, for them and for the dinosauran children back on earth. She was their mother in every sense that mattered and the fact they'd survived and grown up sane and happy was largely her doing. She thought of the new children that might be born, growing up with the spheres to guide them this time, and wondered if she should fight for her human influence.

Steven appeared at her side. "We could help them, couldn't we. Who else would be better qualified?" He glanced at her anxiously. "That is what you're thinking isn't it?"

Epilogue

The Great Universal Third Birthday Party was a roaring success. As planned it was happening in a meadow valley deep in the highlands of Tibet; the spectacular landscape a perfect background to such a surreal event. The wide valley swept away in all directions, gently rising to the feet of distant, snow capped mountains. It also discouraged the fly-in of too many media platforms. Even so, satellite links imaged a spectacular sight from the air; seven vast spheres in one place, each one unique in its' patterning and surface details. A gathering of planets that slowly and gracefully turned and moved in the sky.

Six of them hovered around the grounded seventh, where it had stumbled to on its' final, wounded flight; trying, but failing, to get back to its' original home in the mountains of Alma Ata after the nuclear attack that nearly killed it. The seventh spheres' structure was largely repaired but the mind had never recovered from its' irradiation and trauma. It remained childlike, sometimes petulant, sometimes peevish as an old man; though the company of children had started a partial healing and always lightened its' mood. But it still refused to fly, even denied that it could, claiming a fear of getting lost, and seemed genuinely content to stay in its' lonely meadow.

Not so lonely on this day though; fliers flitted from sphere to sphere and the ground was a riot of tables, bunting, toys, food and hurtling bodies. Thin shrieks of delight filled the air and all six airborne spheres spun slowly to and fro, seemingly uncertain which way to look next.

Few observers of the satellite feeds paid attention to a small group of humans and adult dinosaurans sitting on the sidelines and watching the party with bemused amazement, nor the various humanoid bodies that sat or stood alongside them. Everyone wanted to see the dinosauran children. Fifty two healthy young dinosaurans, one for each week of the year the tabnets gushed, were now three years old. All were as precocious as their relatives at the same age but these young creatures were not forced to live in labs, run into hiding or have little contact with their own species. Their lives were as close to an original dinosauran upbringing as could be made possible on their new earth.

Three more of the spheres had chosen dinosauran bodies as avatars, making four with the Tania, to help school the new children and act as foster parents. The sixth had an adult human form to represent it; a tall, thin avatar taken from the pattern of an Aborigine elder. This man was the only other person known to have entered a sphere, deep in the Nullarbor Plain of Australia, while they were still in the ground. His story had never been believed outside his own people so his knowledge, and the spheres' location, had remained the tribes' secret. He'd given the sphere its' new name, Sunlight Fella. Sunlight and Tum had a particular affinity; something that went right back to the rocks, landscape and tribal myths their spheres had been plugged into for so long.

The seventh sphere, with its' damaged and childlike mind, had never conceived a full avatar. Nor did it have a name. But small animals, very like a tribe of meerkats, were occasionally seen running through its' galleries or across its' halls. These would talk in simple sentences to visitors who sat quietly and patiently for long enough; coming close and chittering about anything that caught their attention, or begging for titbits with an outstretched paw.

But if the dinosauran children visited the meerkats were everywhere. The six spheres marvelled as the seventh conducted two or three dozen childish conversations at once. In this respect it was a true genius; a unique addition to their strange family.

Right now Steven was wearing a ramrod straight animal on each shoulder, and suffering Sunlight's delighted smile. "Can't see what they're looking for myself." Sunlight stifled laughter. "But maybe I can help." He bowed towards Steven and the meerkats leapt to his higher viewpoint, chattering thanks into both his ears. Quick turns of their narrow heads as they peered left and right, then they shot down his back and away through the short grass. "First time I've seen them outside the Seventh," said Sunlight. "It's improving every day now."

"That's great, you're right." Steven was laughing himself now. "What do you say to a walk across?" He looked around. "I've never been in Seven myself - - always a bit nervous of what to say."

"Being human, you mean?" Sunlight smiled again. "It holds no grudges you know. How could it?"

The old Aborigine body took his arm and looked across to see if Tum would join them. The child-bodied avatar bounded up, then back to fetch all the others. "Come on - - let's all go!" It cried. "Seventh is so much happier today. It might even talk to some of you."

As the group reached the grounded sphere they were amazed to see a vast, shallow depression in the ground beneath it. It finally flew again, if only a few feet away from the earth, and the meerkats dared each other to run in and out of the bowl-shaped imprint where it had rested. "Behron - - - ," one of them chittered in the shadows, setting up a whispering amongst its' fellows. "We are all Behron - - - ." No-one else heard them.

The vast dome of sky arched dark blue above the seventh sphere and the distant mountain peaks surrounding it. It's six companions hovered low in encouragement and one by one its' visitors stepped inside. All around the meadow the dinosauran children continued to play.

<u>End</u>

John Coppinger © 2005

Printed in the United Kingdom
by Lightning Source UK Ltd.
109560UKS00001B/349